Help Me REMEMBER

Help Me REMEMBER

- Special Edition

NEW YORK TIMES BESTSELLING AUTHOR

CORINNE MICHAELS

Help Me Remember

ISBN print: 978-1-957309-10-1

Cover Design: Sommer Stein, Perfect Pear Creative
Editing: Ashley Williams, AW Editing
Proofreading: Julia Giffis, Michele Ficht & ReGina Kay

Foreword

When coming up with the special edition cover, so much went into the thought process.

First, I value cover art as an expression of the book. I believe that the saying of: never judge a book by its cover, should be true, but it's not.

I know I do it.

So I take a lot of time curating the perfect cover art, then the design part takes center stage. My cover designer is fantastic. She always finds ways to understand what I want without even saying a word. This cover was no different. We found the art we liked and went from there.

I wanted this to represent the town a little, which is why we wanted roses.

However, this story is really about feeling lost in the darkness. Our heroine wakes up without any memory of her life in the last three years. Everything feels as though she's floating. The very foundation of her life is gone. Which is why this cover also speaks to me. Fragments of things, the darkness, the emotions of dark to light and only understanding parts of things.

As much as the original cover is truly perfect, I feel equally as attached to this cover. While the story inside may be the same, the outside each speaks to me in a different way.

In this edition, not only is the cover different, but I included a deleted scene from someone else's POV. Thank you for reading an I hope you enjoy.

Love,

Corinne

Dedication

To Sommer Stein … thank you for not firing me—yet.

CHAPTER *One*

BRIELLE

My eyes flutter open and then slam closed as the blinding light is too much. The ache in my head is so intense it steals my breath. What the hell happened?

There's a slight pressure on my arm, and then my mother's soft voice fills the silence. "Brielle, honey. It's okay. Open your eyes, my sweet girl."

I inhale a few times before attempting it again. This time, I'm prepared for the brightness and the sterile white walls that reflect the sunlight. I hear someone rushing around a second before the blinds go down, casting shadows and making it a little easier for me to lift my lids.

"Where—" I try to speak, but my throat is raw. It's as though I swallowed a thousand knives and haven't had so much as a sip of water in years.

Mom is beside me, and my sister-in-law, Addison, is next to her. I turn my head to see who is on the other side, which is a big mistake as a new wave of pain shoots through my skull. I lift my hands to my head, trying to push the pressure down, but it doesn't ebb that easily.

Who I assume is the doctor barks an order for medication before he lowers his voice to a whisper. "Brielle, it's Holden. We're going to get you some pain medication for your head."

Holden? My brother's best friend is here? I don't understand. He left Rose Canyon years ago and only comes back once a year.

He speaks again. "Do you know where you are?"

I'm assuming I'm in the hospital, considering the monitors and bed I'm in, so I nod. "W-what h-ha-happened?" I choke on the words.

There are no sounds other than the beeping behind me. I will my eyelids to open and stay that way as if it will help me find the answer as to why I'm here. When they finally listen, I find myself looking directly at all three of my brother's best friends. Holden, who is wearing his white coat, is in the middle. Next to him is Spencer Cross, the tall, dark, and sinful man I have dreamed of since I was thirteen but will never have. Behind him is Emmett Maxwell, who . . . is in the military on deployment . . . what the hell?

Why is he in a police uniform? Why is he even here? The emails he sends each week are all Isaac ever talks about because, of course, Emmett had to join the Special Forces. He couldn't just do his time and come back—he needed to be heroic, which isn't the least bit surprising.

"Do you know why you're in the hospital?" Holden asks.

I shake my head, regretting it immediately.

He gives me a soft smile before asking, "What is your full name?"

"Brielle Angelina Davis."

"What is your date of birth?"

"October seventh."

"Where did you go to high school?"

I huff. "The same one we all went to. Rose Canyon High."

Emmett steps forward, he is bigger than I remember, his chest is wide and arms filling out his uniform as though it's ready to split the seams. He gives me his winning smile and rests his hand on Holden's shoulder. "Brielle, do you think you're up for answering a few questions for me? I know you're probably in pain and exhausted, but it's important."

Questions? Wasn't I already answering questions?

The pressure on my hand increases, reminding me that my mother is here, and I slowly turn to her. There are dark circles under her brown eyes and tears running down her cheek. Addy is next to her, and she also looks as if she hasn't slept in a week. I glance around again, wondering where the hell my brother is. Isaac will tell me what's wrong. He's always honest with me.

"Isaac?" I call out, thinking maybe he's in the hallway or something.

Addison's hand flies to her mouth, and she looks away. My mother grips my hand tighter and then reaches for Addy.

"What about Isaac?" Holden asks, drawing my attention back to him.

"Where is he?"

Emmett speaks next. "What do you remember about the last time you were with Isaac?"

"I don't . . . I don't . . ." I look around, not understanding why I am in a hospital or what the hell is going on. "Help. I don't . . ."

"Easy, Brie," Holden says quickly. "You're safe. Just tell us what happened."

I shake my head because I don't understand why he's asking me that, which sends a shooting pain through my head. I squeeze my eyes shut until it passes enough to speak. "No, I don't know. Why am I here? What's happening? Where is Isaac? Why are you all crying? What's wrong with me?"

Holden moves closer, holding my gaze. "Nothing is wrong with you, but I do need you to try to take a few calm breaths, okay?" He exaggerates the gesture, breathing in deeply, holding it for a second, and then slowly breathing out. After a few tries, I manage to mimic him, but the panic is still there, still clawing at my insides. He turns to Emmett. "She isn't ready for this. Why don't you guys give us a few minutes while I assess her and let her get her bearings. She needs a few moments."

My mother stands but doesn't relinquish her hold on my hand. "I'm not leaving her."

"Mrs. Davis, I need to examine her, and it would be best if we can do it with no distractions."

If it'll give me some answers, I'll do anything. Knowing my mother, she'll never go without a fight. "Mom, it's okay. I just . . . I need a minute." My smile is brittle, but she nods and lets my hand slip from hers.

As Spencer, Emmett, Addison, and my mother leave, a nurse enters, and she and Holden flank the bed.

Holden moves in, flicking a light in my eyes before sitting on the side of the bed. "I know that waking up like this can be confusing and overwhelming. I'd like to check your vitals and talk, okay?"

I point to my throat, and the nurse hands me a cup with a straw. "Start with small sips. You have an empty stomach, and we want to go slow."

I swallow the ice-cold liquid, letting it soothe some of the ache. I want to keep going so the sensation never stops, but she pulls the cup away much too fast.

Then he shows me photos of three objects. "In a few minutes, I'm going to ask you about those objects and you need to remember them and answer the questions I ask. Do you need to see them again?"

It's a cup, a key, and a bird. It's not rocket science. "I'm good."

"All right. Can you lift your hands and push against mine?" I do as he asks, and when he seems satisfied, he moves on to a few other minor tests. Then he listens to my pulse and rattles off numbers. As he does that, my mind races, but I'm too tired to try to chase the thoughts around.

Holden speaks to the nurse. "Patient has started to present bruising around her face so we'll need to take updated photos prior to discharge. I'd also like to order another MRI just to verify the swelling from both injuries is abating."

"How bad are the bruises?" I ask.

"Nothing too bad. They should be healed in a week or two."

I nod. "Okay. What about the head injury?"

"We'll know more after the tests and the second MRI. We can go over the results after, okay?"

"Can you tell me why I'm here or what's going on?"

"As I said, we'll go over all our findings once we finish the exam part."

We go through a ton of questions, all the while my mind is swimming. I keep waiting for my brother to come through the door and tell Holden where to shove his medical assessments.

Once I'm done answering those, he puts down his tablet. "What was the first image I showed you?"

I take a deep breath, and then my mind blanks. "I . . . it was a . . ." I lean my head back and try to think. I know it. "A cup!" I say triumphantly.

"Good. Do you remember the second image?"

"Yes, it was keys."

He smiles, and the nurse nods.

"Excellent, Brielle. Now, do you remember the last image?"

I do. I . . . know it. I try to recall him showing me the pictures, but my thoughts are slow and muddled. "I do, but I'm so tired."

His hand moves to my arm. "You're doing great."

I don't feel so great.

"Why don't you tell me about the last thing you remember?"

I stare down at my hands, twisting the ring my father gave me as I try to think. I start with my childhood, remembering holidays, birthdays, and vacations. My brother and I were always causing mischief, but poor Isaac was always the one who got in trouble. My father could never punish me, and I took full advantage of that.

I recall my high school graduation, the lavender dress I wore under my gown, and how my father died two days later.

The funeral is a haze of tears and sadness, but I clearly remember Isaac being the rock that held my mother up as she fell apart.

Then I remember meeting Henry. I was a sophomore in college, and he was in my math class. God, he was so cute and funny. At the end of our first date, he kissed me outside my dorm, and I swore my lips tingled for an hour after.

It was magical.

More dates. More memories of us falling in love and us graduating with our undergrads. We'd been so excited as we opened our acceptance letters to the same grad school in Oregon. I recall the apartment we moved into, ready to start our lives as we pursued our career paths. Two years and another graduation later, we were no longer so excited because we were no longer kids in school and were forced to make adult choices.

Like when I chose to move back to Rose Canyon while Henry stayed in Portland, working for his family to take over the business. That was a few months ago.

When I pull my eyes away from my ring, I find Holden watching me, waiting for my answer.

"I graduated grad school about six months ago. I have been living with Addison and Isaac while I was interviewing for a job."

Holden writes something down. "Good. Anything else?"

"I . . . I know that Isaac and Addy got married. I came home for it. Henry and I were—" I pause as I struggle to think about what we were. I don't know that's right, but I think it is. "We fought. It was so stupid because he kept asking me to move to Portland when he knew I didn't want to. Oh! I got the job I was interviewing for, and I am going to be moving out of my brother's house." My eyes widen as I remember that I just got a job here. In Rose Canyon.

"What do you do?"

"I'm a social worker, but I'm working at a new youth center. I started there a few weeks ago." I smile, feeling like I can breathe a little. I remembered.

Holden doesn't share my enthusiasm though. "You seem excited about it."

"Yeah, I really am. It's a great place, and . . . Jenna was there . . ."

He writes that down. "Can you tell me anything else? Maybe about your coworkers or some of the kids you've met?"

I frown. "Not really. I mean, it's still really new, and I'm getting to know people." Even as I say it, the words don't seem wholly truthful.

"Being new is hard." Holden smiles. "What about why you're in the hospital? Do you recall anything or anyone who should be here with your family?"

I go over the people who were here when I woke up. It's clear he isn't looking for me to say my brother's name since he's probably at the school anyway. So, I run my hand over my face before asking, "Henry?"

"What about Henry?"

My heart starts to race, and I lean forward, confused as to why every muscle in my body aches when Holden only mentioned a head injury. "He should be here but he isn't. Is he okay? Has anyone called him?"

"As far as I know, he's fine, and I'm sure your mother has called him."

Thank God he's okay and isn't in a room next to me. "He should be here soon. I'm sure he'll be here. Maybe he just got tied up at work."

"What do you mean?"

I sigh. "Henry . . . if he isn't here, he will be. That's all. We're working on things." At least, we're trying to work on them. Things have been difficult the last few months for us. He doesn't want to move to Rose Canyon, and I don't want to live in the city. I love this town, and I want to be close to my brother and sister-in-law. Addy wants kids, and I am going to be the best aunt who ever existed.

"Brielle, why are you in the hospital?"

I close my eyes, pushing through the blackness in my mind. I can't see anything.

There's nothing but a heavy fog, preventing me from remembering anything.

I'm lost. I can't see.

My heart is racing, and I try so hard to see anything around me, but everything is dark and something is squeezing my chest.

The panic threatens to overwhelm me.

Immediately, my lids open, and I turn frantic eyes to my brother's best friend as I struggle to draw in air.

Oh God. Something is wrong with me.

"Take a deep breath, in your nose and out your mouth," he says, the calm voice trying to soothe me, but I can't.

"Wh-what don't I know? Why am I here?"

Holden's jaw clenches as though he's trying to keep from saying something. The sound of the beeping behind me quickens. "Was I in an accident?"

"Not an accident, but something did happen. I need you to calm down, Brielle. Focus on my voice and breathing."

A new anxiety swirls in my stomach. If it wasn't an accident, then what? I can't calm down. I can't stop this intense panic that is building with each second. "What happened?"

"Brie, stop," Holden tries to say again. "You have to relax or I am going to have to give you something."

"No, no, because . . . I don't remember why I am." That leaves me with more questions and possibilities. If it wasn't an accident, then someone did this to me. Someone hurt me. I just want to know who and why. I start to shake, knowing that the tears I saw on my mother and sister-in-law's faces are an answer to a question I don't want to ask. Addy loves me, I know she does, but her reaction when I . . . when I said my brother's name—

The machines monitoring me start to beep even faster. I know Holden is talking to me, but his words are swept away by the sound of my ragged breathing and the thunder of my pulse in my ears.

Isaac.

I said his name, and Addy shattered.

Something is really wrong.

Oh, God.

I can't. I need to know. I look to Holden again, my heart pounding in my chest as I force out the single word. "Isaac?"

"Brielle"—Holden grips both arms, staring at me—"try to focus on me and take a slow breath. It's okay."

It's not okay. I can't remember why I'm here. I don't know what happened, and the harder I try to remember, the more frantic that beeping gets. My vision starts to fade a little, and Holden barks something at the nurse.

I'm too caught up in the spiral of thoughts and desperate need to fill lungs that refuse to work to pay attention to what he's shouting.

Then, after a minute, calmness floods my veins and I close my eyes, drifting off to sleep.

I'm in some sort of weird twilight. I can hear voices close to me, as though they're right next to me, but no matter how hard I try, I can't drag myself into consciousness.

"What do we tell her?" Addison asks.

"Nothing," my mother offers. "They were very clear that we aren't to influence any of her memories. We need to be patient and allow things to restore on their own."

"She's going to be devastated."

"Yes, she will, but we'll be here for her."

"I'm not sure how we do this."

Someone pushes hair off my face, and then my mother says, "I don't either. It's as if this is a nightmare that just keeps getting worse. I just keep hoping that when she opens her eyes, she recovers everything, and then at the same time, I almost hope she never does."

A deep sigh from one of them.

"And if she doesn't?" Addison asks. "Then we just lie to her? We have to keep everything from her?"

Mom sniffs, and I imagine she's crying. "It's horrible, but there's no other way. The prosecutor was adamant we have to do it this way or there will be no chance at a case. Right now, they have nothing."

Case for what? What is going on?

"What did Holden say about her waking up?"

"He pulled her off the sedation medication a few hours ago, so now it's up to her body to decide when she's ready," Mom replies. "I'm hoping it'll be soon."

"Me too. I have to get home to Elodie. Jenna has been there all day, and I promised her I'd be home before dinner."

"Of course, sweetheart. Can you wait a few more minutes?"

Who is Elodie?

I push against the bonds trapping me in this state of in-between, wanting to ask them what they're discussing.

"Maybe another ten," Addison says with a heavy sigh. "I also have to meet with the funeral home."

Funeral? Who died?

I push harder, demanding my eyelids do what I tell them to do because I have to wake up. There is no concept of time as I work at it, but finally, I get my body to cooperate enough that my fingers twitch.

"Brie?" my mother calls my name.

Someone, probably my mom, is clutching my hands, and I squeeze, hoping she understands that I'm trying.

More time passes before I get my eyes to open and find my mom watching me with tears in her eyes. Addison is still here, and she gives me a soft smile.

"Hey," Addy says.

"W-where is Isaac?" I get the words out, unsure of how long I can keep myself awake.

Her lip trembles and then a tear falls down her cheek. Addison shakes her head. "Do you not remember?"

I shake my head, keeping my eyes open by sheer will. "I want to. But I can't. I need to . . . see him. Please . . . just tell me."

Even before she says anything, I feel the loss of my brother. Something is keeping him from me and nothing would if I needed him.

"He's gone." Her voice cracks around the words. "He died, and . . . I —" A sob breaks from her. "I didn't want to tell you."

No. That's not possible. My brother is the strongest man I know. He can survive anything. I shake my head, refusing to believe it.

"No. He's not! Stop. Just go get him."

My mother's hand rests on my cheek, and I turn to her. "It's true, baby. Your brother was with you, and he was killed."

"No!" I yell and try to pull my other hand free of her hold. No, this can't be. Not him. Not Isaac. He's . . . he's my best friend.

They're lying. They have to be because there's no way my brother died. "Please," I beg.

"I'm so sorry," Addison cries, her head falling to the bed. "I know you love him, and he loved you so much, Brielle."

My heart aches so much that I wish I hadn't woken up at all. I wish I could stay in the nothingness where I felt free and peaceful and there wasn't this crushing sadness pressing on my chest so hard it felt as if my ribs were about to splinter.

"I know this is a lot for you to process," Mom says quickly. "We almost lost you too, Brielle, and . . ." Her brown eyes turn to Addison.

Addy clears her throat. "You have been unconscious since it happened."

"How long have I been like this?" I ask quickly. I'm so confused.

Addy brushes a tear off my cheek before whispering, "It's been almost four days."

"Tell me what happened. Please. I can't . . ."

"Shh," my mother coos. "Easy, Brielle. I wish we could tell you what happened, but we can't. I'm so, so sorry."

"Why can't you tell me? Just tell me!" I shout, choosing to be angry because it's better than folding into the grief.

Addison flinches before she steels herself and explains, "The doctors and the lawyers think it's better if we allow your memory to return on its own. And, honestly, we don't even know what happened." She looks away.

Mom steps in. "They only told us that you were with him. They want your memory to come back on its own because you're the only witness. You're the *only* one who knows who did this, and the police and district attorney are worried that a defense attorney could use your memory loss against your testimony."

"You mean the memory I don't have? The testimony I can't even give for the person who did this that no one can find?" Emotions swell in my throat and suffocate my voice until it's nothing but a whisper. "Just tell me what happened."

Tears fall down my cheeks like rain as I try to accept my brother is dead, no one can tell me what is going on, and an unknown amount of time has been stolen from my memory.

CHAPTER *Two*

BRIELLE

I fell asleep for about an hour, worn out from crying and still brokenhearted. When I woke up, Holden and Mom spent two hours trying to jog my memory, all to no avail. After another round of tears, I told my mother I wanted to speak to the lawyer and find out exactly what the hell is going on.

I was informed she's here and will be in any minute.

Nerves hit me, but I hold them back.

There's a knock on the door, but instead of the district attorney, Cora, entering, it's Emmett and Spencer. I want to rail at them and demand they tell me what they know. Only, I'm already aware that they won't, and I can't handle another session of try-to-make-Brielle-remember-something.

"I don't know anything, and I won't do this again," I say in a detached voice.

"We're not here for that," Emmett says.

"No?"

"No."

"Then why are you here?" I ask.

Spencer shrugs. "Because we like you, and your brother would want us here."

I turn my head away at the statement. Growing up, Isaac let me tag along with them, and I was the annoying sister they all tortured but also protected. I cross my arms, hating that these guys, who have always been like brothers, are here without the one person I want to see most—my brother.

"The attorney will be here soon so you should just go."

Emmett pulls his chair closer to the side of the bed. "We are staying because you could use some friends."

"I could use my brother."

I miss him so much. If he were here, he'd tell me everything. He wouldn't care about some stupid plan to help me regain my memory. He would never let me suffer like this.

Emmett releases a breath through his nose. "We all could. Isaac was the best of us."

I wipe away the errant tear. "He was."

"He wouldn't like this," Emmett says. "Watching you suffer."

No, he wouldn't. Isaac would fix it. He always did.

"Brie," Spencer says, "all of us care about you. You matter, okay? We want to be here for you the way Isaac would be because we love you."

His green eyes are on mine, causing my heart to sputter.

God, the stupid girl in me wants to make that into something more. I have longed to hear something like that from Spencer Cross's lips since I was thirteen years old, but my head knows better than to let that run wild.

But even now, looking like a ghost of the boy I fell in love with, he's stunning. His jaw is covered in a beard, masking the strong jawline I know is beneath. As much as he looks the same, there is a very big difference in his body. He is broad, strong, and the way his shirt clings to him tells me there is a lot of muscle underneath. But his eyes, those are the same, still that emerald green that I could paint in my sleep.

I push that silly part of myself aside because I have a boyfriend who loves me.

I can't do this again. I can't go down the rabbit hole that's impossible to get out of.

Then another knock comes and Cora and Holden walk in.

"Hello, Brielle," Jenna's sister, Cora, says with a smile on her lips.

Cora is the district attorney and three years older than me. We played on the same softball team in high school, and she has always scared the shit out of me.

Not that she's done anything. She's just one of those women who exudes power, and it makes her come across as intimidating.

However, the way she's looking at me right now doesn't scare me so much as it makes me sad. Gone is the warrior who would tell me to do my job as catcher while she pitched, now there's pity and empathy—I don't like it.

My mother and Addison are the next to walk in. After they both give me brief hugs, they take up spots by the windows.

"Hi, Cora."

She smiles. "You look well, I'm glad to see that."

Holden comes closer. "Have you had any changes in the last hour?"

"No, nothing since the last time you stopped in."

Holden looks around. "I wanted to give you time and hoped the visit you had would help jog your memory before we really settled on the gap. Are the last memories you described still the same?"

"Yes, I need to understand how bad this is."

"Of course. Would you like me to clear the room?"

I look at Emmett and Spencer and shake my head. "No, they're fine."

"I know this is incredibly frustrating for you, Brielle," Cora says. "I want to explain why we are handling things the way we are. At this time, we have no information on the person responsible for your brother's death and the attempt on your life. There was a call about a gunshot, and when the responding officer got to the scene, he found you unconscious. Of course, our hope was that once you woke, you would be able to identify the assailant, but your memory issue poses a new complication."

I nod, listening to the first person to give me any freaking information. "Okay, and how does that lead to where we are now?"

"It is my job as the prosecutor to argue, beyond a reasonable doubt, that the case I have proves guilt. Now, we"—her gaze moves to Emmett—"are all working diligently to establish a case where we may not need your testimony. At that point, it's in the best interest of whatever case we build if we withhold information from you."

"How does it matter now?"

She sighs heavily. "My thought process is more in line of what, if I were a defense attorney, I would be able to use to sew doubt during a trial. Having a key eyewitness who experienced a large memory gap would be easy to spin as a key eyewitness also having unreliable testimony or testimony that has been influenced. What I'm suggesting, Brielle, is that we keep you in the dark about your current life and see if your memories return on their own without the influence of others recounting your life."

My heart pounds as my eyes burn with tears. "So, you want everyone to lie to me?"

"Not lie. I know what I'm asking is incredibly difficult, and believe me, I don't do this lightly. We need to maintain the integrity of your memories. So, if it's okay with you, I would like to put you in touch with a therapist who specializes in cases like yours and also acts as an expert witness when we need him. It's a lot to process and I understand your reluctance, but again, my position is to protect the case, which is also protecting you."

Spencer moves toward the bed. "How long do we all have to do this?"

Cora shrugs. "Until she recovers her memory or we have enough to arrest and prosecute without her testimony."

"And if she doesn't want to testify?" he counters.

My eyes widen at that.

Cora turns to me. "Of course it's your choice. You don't have to, but your account of the incident would be our strongest chance of a conviction."

I lean my head back, turning to Spencer, who is watching me with eyes full of empathy and sadness. He was the closest with Isaac. The two of them more like brothers than friends. He must be aching just as much as I am. "I would do anything to bring justice for my brother's death."

"Okay then."

Spencer's soft smile plays across his face. He lets his smile fade as he turns to Cora. "Keeping her safe is all that we have now."

Emmett speaks up. "If the killer believes Brielle can't remember, it may work to our benefit as well."

"He could be long gone," Spencer adds, eyes still on mine.

"What does it matter? He killed Isaac, and we have no idea who it is," I say, feeling desolate. I turn to Cora, breaking the moment. "Fine. We don't tell me anything. I want whoever did this to me and Isaac to pay for it."

She taps my shoulder. "If you remember anything, please let us know. In the meantime, the police are doing everything they can." Then Cora walks out.

I turn my attention to the group.

"When is the funeral?" I ask.

"In two days," Holden answers. "I think you'll be ready to be released by then. Other than your memory loss, you're healing well."

"Right. We've established that."

Emmett grabs my hand. "This will pass, Brie. I really believe that."

"Nothing in my life makes sense right now. Do you get that? You're the sheriff of Rose Canyon, and yet, the last thing I remember is saying goodbye to you at the airport before you deployed." I look up at the ceiling, hating this. "Can you at least tell me today's date?"

Spencer is who answers.

I close my eyes, focusing on that date. I know the date I graduated from grad school and . . . oh my God, it's almost three years later.

My breath quickens, and I look at them. "But . . ."

"I know," Holden says understandingly. "I know it's a lot of time."

"My heart is broken," I confess. "I feel like I'm broken."

"You're not," Spencer says quickly.

I wish I could believe that. "Well, when I see my brother's body in a casket, I'll be broken then, especially knowing that I can't remember a damn thing. That I could save him! That I can't fix this!"

My tears fall, and Emmett squeezes my hand. "Your brother would never blame you."

"I blame me!"

It doesn't matter what Isaac would've done. He's dead, and I was there when it happened. Locked inside my brain is every answer. I saw this person. I was there, and I can't remember. I might even know why it happened. This person could be anyone in my life, and no matter how deep I dig into the black hole of my brain, it's empty. I have a million questions. Why was I spared? Why didn't that person kill me too? None of it makes sense. I turn to Holden. "How long will this last? When will my memory return?"

"I wish there were a definitive answer to that. With the type of brain injury you suffered, the best thing we can do is give it time. I do believe that your memory will return, you have to allow everything to heal."

"How do you know?" I ask.

"I don't know for sure, but none of your tests are indicative of long-term neurological damage. Your speech isn't affected. You can walk, you aren't showing any signs of trouble with your fine motor skills, and your long-term memory doesn't seem to be hindered. It's why I have the *belief* that it will come back. It just may take some time."

"And everyone thinks this plan to keep me in the dark is the best course of action?"

I ask the question to everyone in the room, but I am looking directly at my mother, who nods even as tears gather on her lashes.

Emmett is the first to break the silence. "I can't imagine how frustrating this all must be for you, but Cora is right. If we influence one memory, then what?"

My blood pressure is through the roof as I grapple with all of this. It's too much. It's all too goddamn much.

Holden comes to my side. "I want you to close your eyes, Brielle, and take a slow, deep breath. Remember what I said about healing, we need to do whatever we can to stay calm."

There is no remaining calm. Nothing about this entire situation is calm. I'm losing my mind. I look to them, not at all in control of my emotions. "I don't know if I'm married or have kids. Am I still working at the youth center? Am I still with Henry? I have to be, right? We were . . . last I—" My mind whirls the questions around like a tornado as I look directly into Spencer's eyes and ask, "Who am I now?"

"You're the same girl you've always been. You're funny, kind, loving, and smart. You are brave, and while we all know you're scared, you will find your way back."

I want to weep because that is the nicest thing he's ever said to me. I wait for the joke about being annoying, but it doesn't come.

Emmett clears his throat. "Is there anything you can remember past getting the job?"

I shake my head. "All I get are tiny flashes, but nothing sticks or makes sense."

"Nothing is tiny." Holden's voice is soothing as he speaks. "Tell us what you see. Maybe if you put it into words, it will help you remember."

I sigh, hating this, but he's a doctor and knows best. "I remember the smell of smoke, but not from a campfire so much as a cigar or pipe or something. It's almost as if I can taste it. I can't explain it, but it was on my tongue. I don't smoke, right? Like, I didn't suddenly take up smoking cigars?"

Emmett laughs. "Not that I know of."

Spencer shakes his head. "As if you smoked it or ate something with that flavor?"

I ponder that for a second. "No, it was more like a remnant of it, but it wasn't . . . I don't know. I'm not making sense."

Holden rests his hand on my shoulder. "This is good, Brie. It means it's not all lost."

"Yes, I'm really relieved that I have some random taste of a cigar from sometime in the last three years."

"It's a relief that it's a memory that you can't attach to anything before three years ago," he counters.

I guess. I wish I could remember why I tasted it. I move my tongue around the top of my mouth and lean forward. "Wait!"

"What?" Emmett asks.

"It wasn't on my tongue. It was on someone else." I close my eyes, trying to bring back that spark of remembrance, and I can sense something else. Warmth and desire. "I was kissing someone who had smoked one."

Emmett leans forward. "Who?"

I wait, anxiety and excitement filling my veins. If I can remember who, then that's a memory that came back. I search through the instance, but it's odd. I close my eyes, trying to focus. No face, no sounds, nothing other than heat and the taste. I lift my gaze, meeting Holden's, and my heart falls. "I don't know. I am assuming, Henry."

Spencer's voice fills my ears. "Close your eyes again, Brielle. I want you to go back to that kiss. I want you to embrace it. The desire, the warmth, the way you felt. Think about the taste on your tongue. Now, think about your body. Was he tall?"

"I can't see him."

"Did you have to crane your neck?" Spencer asks.

I try to remember the kiss. "Yes. I had to lift up . . ."

"Good. What about the kiss itself?"

I remember the way they felt against mine, pushing and teasing. "No, he was playful." And then the memory is gone. My eyes fly open, and I want to scream. "It's gone. I can't . . ."

"It's okay," Emmett assures me. "I know you want your memories back, but trying to force them is just going to frustrate you. You have to allow your mind to go at its own pace."

That is so much easier said than done. "That's easy for you to think, Em. I'm terrified of what happened. I have no idea if it was a robbery gone wrong. If someone came after me, or was Isaac the target? What if the guy or girl who killed him comes to finish the job? I need to remember. I need my life back so I can feel safe and know this person is behind bars."

Spencer says, "No one is going to hurt you. We have officers outside the door now until your new security team arrives to protect you when you're released. We would never allow you to be hurt."

"A security team?"

Emmett nods. "Yes. We'd hire the entire US Army if we could, but these guys are all former SEALs or special ops guys. I trust them with my life, and they will protect yours."

I swear that I'm living in an alternate reality. Maybe this is the dream. Maybe I'm in my room, just waiting to wake up from this nightmare, but this isn't a dream. There is no waking up from this hell. I lie back against the pillow, feeling useless. "If I could just retrace my life . . ."

Holden smiles. "It might help, but it might not." His phone goes off, and he answers, giving one-word responses before turning to Emmett. "The other patient you wanted to talk to is awake."

"Okay."

"I'll be back to check on you in a bit," Holden explains.

I nod. "I'll still be here."

They leave, including Addison and my mother, and Spencer settles into the chair Emmett had been sitting in. He looks exhausted, and the scruff on his face is almost a full beard. "What?" he asks.

I wonder what happened to make him look so broken. Spencer has always been larger than life, but today, he appears a little lost.

"You just look . . . like you came back from a very exciting story." That could be true. Usually, after a big assignment, he isn't exactly dashing. He's been living God knows where, doing God knows what, and . . . well, it's when I always found him a little sexier than usual.

"I wish it were that."

"So, you're not off conquering some unknown horror story?"

He grins. "If I were, I would be much better than I am now."

"I know you can't tell me anything about my life, but can you tell me about yours?"

He smiles softly. "There's not much to say."

"I doubt that."

Spencer was always seeing amazing things and meeting people who had incredible lives. He interviewed spies and diplomats. I think he was working on uncovering a terrorist ring at one point too.

I used to love listening to him recount his trips. Well, about everything but the girls he met. That part I always wanted to skip.

Spencer sighs. "It's true, it's been a while since I worked on anything."

"Why?"

He shrugs. "Writer's block, and I wanted to stick around here."

At that, my brows rise. "You wanted to stay in Rose Canyon?"

"Who doesn't love this idyllic town and all its quirks."

I bark out a laugh. "You and I both know that's a lie."

"I stuck around once Emmett got back from his tour. Addy and Isaac were married, which you remember."

"I do. You were so drunk at the wedding."

"I had to give that fucking speech."

I roll my eyes. "You are a writer! You like words."

"On paper," he says with a smirk. "I hate speaking. I was nervous."

"You did great."

He looks down at his shoes before meeting my eyes. "He was my best friend."

Spencer and Isaac were the closest of the group. Spencer grew up with the worst parents in the world and was always at our house. The two of them did everything together, and more often than not if you could find one, you found the other.

"I know." My voice is low.

"I don't know what the hell I'm going to do without him. Addison and El—I just . . ."

I catch the slip and look him dead in the eyes. "Who is Elodie?"

Spencer shifts and then rests his elbows on his knees. "What has you asking that?"

Other than the fact that he so clearly doesn't want me to ask?

"I heard Addison mention the name, but I don't know who she is."

"Who do you think it is?"

"I don't know. I have a million possibilities. A new friend. A coworker. The girl who cuts my hair. But it was how she said it. The way she was concerned and Jenna was with her . . . I don't know."

"I'm not sure how much to tell you," Spencer says honestly.

"Is she any of those things I just named?" I ask.

"No."

Okay. "Is she my brother's mistress?"

Spencer snorts. "As if Isaac could ever look at another woman. No, but she is a part of his life. Or was . . ."

"Considering the time gap I have, I can't help but wonder if maybe she's my daughter? Am I married and have a kid?"

Spencer shakes his head. "She's not your daughter."

I release a heavy sigh. "Oh, thank God. Then . . . is she Isaac and Addy's?"

I can see the confliction in his eyes. "She is."

"Thank you," I say quickly. "Thank you for not lying to me."

"I will never lie to you, Brielle. Never."

I wish then he would tell me everything. "But you won't tell me anything else, will you?"

"If I could—"

"Yeah," I finish.

My only hope is that something will trigger my memory to return. I'll see someone or hear a voice that will cause the floodgates to open. Who knows, maybe it will happen when I see Isaac.

Of course, no details from anyone.

"Spencer?"

"Yeah?"

"If you couldn't remember the last three years of your life, what would you do?"

He looks at me with sympathy. "I would go back to the beginning and work to find the end."

I rest my head on my pillow, gazing out of the window. "I wish I could have a different ending than losing Isaac."

"But what if that single moment changed your entire story?"

"Maybe it should because my brain doesn't want to remember the plot anyway . . ."

CHAPTER *Three*

BRIELLE

My mother enters the room, but her smile doesn't quite meet her eyes. "Hi, Brie."

"Hi."

"Oh, those flowers are beautiful." She walks over to the counter where a massive bouquet of pink roses is sitting.

"They are."

"Who are they from?"

I smile. "You can look at the card," I grant her permission.

She reads it with her back to me and then places it back. "That was sweet, I guess."

I resist the urge to groan. "Yes, it was. It's the only thing I've heard from him since I woke up."

Mom smiles. "Yes, well, I spoke with Holden just a few minutes ago. He said you're doing well and that you'll get to go home tomorrow?"

Okay, I see that conversation is done.

I always hate how she phrases statements like questions when she already knows the answer. "That's what he said."

"And you both think it's okay to return back to your apartment? I'm just not sure how I feel about it."

If I show an ounce of worry, she'll move back here and that would be the worst possible outcome. My mother is wonderful—when she's four hundred miles away. We are too much of the same person to live close.

"I think that being in my space with my things will really help. It could be the jolt that I need to remember my life."

She sighs heavily. "I don't know."

"It's not up to you, Mom. I know you mean well, but I can handle this."

"Can you? Can you really manage this, Brielle? Your brother is dead, and you . . . I almost—"

The crack in her voice causes my heart to do the same. "I'm sorry."

She turns her head and wipes her eyes before forcing another smile. "No, no. I'm fine. It's just been difficult. That's all. A mother is supposed to be able to help her children, and I can't fix anything that's happened. I can't help you, and now Addison wants to go away . . ."

"Leave?" I ask quickly. "What do you mean, go away?"

Mom's eyes meet mine. "I shouldn't have said it that way. She doesn't want to leave and not come back so much as get out of here for a bit."

"I don't understand, she loves this town."

"And she loved Isaac in this town. She can't handle being here, and everyone is mourning him. Everything she sees reminds her of him, and she thinks it would be best for her to have some space—at least until we find out what happened."

Because this town was them.

Isaac and Addison fell in love here when they were sixteen. They both went to college not far from here, stayed together through it all, got married, and returned to Rose Canyon to start their lives.

Isaac got the teaching and coaching job he always wanted, and Addison worked as a librarian.

Everyone knows them. Everyone loves them. Their lives are here, and I can't imagine Addison leaving.

"Where will she go?"

Mom shakes her head. "East. She's still close with Emmett's cousin, Devney, who lives in Pennsylvania. I guess she has a property that Addison can stay at for a while."

"But she'll be out there on her own."

"It's what has me so upset."

I sigh, feeling the weight of the situation growing. My heart aches for my sister-in-law. She must be so devastated that the future she and Isaac were building was just ripped away. The home, happiness, and family that she dreamed of is gone. I don't have to remember the last three years to know they were happy.

Addy and Isaac were the epitome of love.

Now that's gone, and I would do anything to take that away from her. "Did she say for how long?"

"No, she didn't, but I doubt she'll stay away long. Rose Canyon is her home."

"I'm sorry. If I could just . . . remember what happened then I could fix this a little, that maybe she'd be okay staying."

Mom rushes over. "No, baby. Even if you could tell her every detail, it wouldn't erase the pain she's in. I've never seen two people more perfect for each other than they were, and she just needs some space to mourn. I know that all too well."

Yes, she does. She loved my father beyond reason. "I wish neither of you knew that pain."

"I wish the same, but the time I had with your father was worth whatever pain I have had since losing him."

I think about Henry as she says that, hating that the last memory I have of him is us fighting about living in different cities. His family owns an accounting firm in Portland, and he was being groomed to take it over. We couldn't agree on what our future would look like.

I like the small-town life, which is why I took the job here.

I wonder if we are back to the happy couple, or are we still at each other's throats?

"What's that face for?" Mom asks.

"Nothing. I just hate that my life feels like a puzzle where none of the pieces fit."

"It will, Brie."

I wish I had her confidence.

"Did you talk to Henry?" I ask.

"I did."

"And?"

Mom reaches for her purse, suddenly very focused on digging for something in it. "He was very concerned when we spoke."

"So, we're still together?"

The bag drops to the ground. "Damn it." She takes a while gathering all the crap she keeps in there. "Sorry, so, yes, we spoke. He was very upset and said he'd come as soon as he can."

That didn't answer my question, but I guess this is the new normal for me.

"It's almost time for me to do a few laps, would you walk with me?" I drop the topic because it's too hard for me.

"Of course."

Mom helps me up, steadying me as I sway a little. No matter how slowly I stand, I'm always hit with a wave of dizziness. Holden says it'll fade, and I look forward to that day.

"I'm good now."

She rolls the IV pole over to me, and we head out of the room. We make our way around the floor, and I move a little easier as my muscles get used to the exertion. After spending four days unconscious and another two days being limited to these short walks, it's nice to be up and moving. I do this a few times each day, gaining strength a little at a time.

"Hey there, Mrs. Davis." Holden smiles as he puts a file on the nurses' desk.

"Hello, Holden. I don't know how we would've managed without you overseeing things. I always knew you were special," Mom replies.

"I don't know about that, but I am glad to see Brielle recovering nicely." He looks to me. "You're going slow?"

"Yes."

"Good. Slow and steady is what we want to see."

I roll my eyes. "You have always been the annoying one."

Holden grins. "Well, at least that's a memory you still have."

"Yes, lucky me." Then I stop. "When did you get back into town anyway?" He watches as something starts to form in my head. "You moved to California, so does your being here now mean you moved back?"

His gaze doesn't move from mine. "No, I'm not here permanently."

"Okay, and what about the case you were working on in Seattle?"

Holden and my mom share a look. "What do you mean Seattle?"

"You were consulting on some big case, right?"

He nods. "I did. I was there a few weeks ago, actually."

"Weeks? Were you there before that too?"

He shakes his head. "I wasn't. This is the first consult I did for a case in Seattle. It was a big deal as it was for a research trial."

"I remembered something recent," I say, more to myself.

"Have you had any other glimpses or memories?"

I squint, trying to think, and Mom and Holden watch me. "I have this . . . thing. A key. I don't know what it is. I can't figure out why or what it means."

"Is it like the key of the photo?"

I shake my head. "No, it's an actual key. Like an antique one with the fancy scrolls up top."

"Anything else interesting on it?" Holden asks with encouragement.

I work hard not to get frustrated because, again, I don't know much. Just this key keeps coming into my head. "It has a red ribbon on it. I have no idea what it is for."

"That's great, Brie," he encourages. "Anything else?"

I shake my head. "What's the key to?"

My mother and Holden look back and forth at each other. "I have no idea."

"It's the key I gave you when I asked you to move to Portland with me."

I would know that voice anywhere.

"Henry!" I turn, relieved that he's here.

He smiles, apprehension in his eyes, but then he approaches. "Hey, Brie."

My breathing slows, and he leans down to kiss my cheek. Warmth floods me and a sense of normalcy returns. "I'm so glad you're here."

His hand moves to my cheek. "I didn't know until this morning. I am so glad you're okay." He turns to the audience behind us. "Mrs. Davis, Holden," he says.

Mom moves toward him and pats his chest as she says, "I'm glad you're here, Henry."

Holden takes a step forward, extending his hand. "Good to see you, Henry. It's nice to see Brielle relax a little."

"Yes, she seemed to just now," my mother muses.

I link my fingers with his and tug him closer. "I was wondering why you weren't here when I woke up, but I'm glad you're here now."

His lips flatten into a thin line. "I didn't find out until a few hours ago. I came as soon as I heard."

I turn to my mother. "You waited almost six days to call him?"

"No, no," Henry cuts in. "She did. I was actually away on business and as soon as I got the message, I came."

My mother nods with a strange smile. "You're here now and that's what matters."

"I am so sorry about Isaac," Henry says, and when his strong arms wrap around me, I close my eyes.

"I loved him so much."

"I know."

This feels safe and right. I may be missing the last three years of my life, but this is familiar. The way we fit together makes sense. I look up to him, tears in my eyes. "I am so glad you're here. I needed you."

He smiles down at me and then glances at my mother, who is watching us with wary eyes.

"Mom?"

She smiles much too quickly. "Sorry, I'll give you two time to visit. I have some things I need to do before you're released tomorrow, and I also have to help Addison before the funeral."

"You don't have to leave." Clearly, whatever rift had formed between them years ago hadn't mended. When he and I first started dating, she loved him, but right before graduation, she'd encouraged me to end things. She didn't like how controlling he was and that we never seemed happy when we were together.

"I wasn't going to stay long. I wanted to check in on you. Now that Henry is here, you both could use some time to talk without me sitting here."

I turn to him. "Will you stay for a while, please?" I ask.

Henry dips his chin. "Of course. I was planning on being here for the day, if that's what you wanted."

"I would. You're one of the last things I really remember, and it would mean a lot if we could talk a bit."

"Well, then," Mom says quickly. "I'll visit Addy. If you need anything, just have them call me."

Henry and I walk back to my room, and I hold on to his outstretched arm. We've walked like this hundreds of times, just not in a hospital, and I settle into the familiarity of it. I look up at him, trying to see the differences that may trigger a memory.

"Do you smoke cigars?" I ask.

His head jerks back. "No, they're disgusting. Why?"

"I just . . . I had a memory."

"You did?"

"Yeah, but it was the taste of cigars, and I can't place it. I thought maybe it was you."

Henry shakes his head. "Definitely not."

"So, what are we?"

I sit on the edge of the bed, and he takes the chair. "When your mom called, she explained that I'm not supposed to give you answers due to the memory lapse."

Of course they got to him too.

"No, you're not, but there's this block of time that's just gone," I explain. "It's really frustrating, and people not telling me anything is making it harder. I am not asking for all the details, just something about us now?"

He leans in and gathers my hands in his. "I can tell you that I love you."

I smile and release a breath through my nose. "I know that. You've always loved me."

"Since the day I met you."

While it's nice to be reassured, it doesn't really answer my question. "Do we live together?"

He shakes his head. "No. I live in Portland, and you're here."

"Have you taken over your parents' firm completely?"

"Not completely. Dad should retire in the next year. Right now, I'm managing a team and all high-priority accounts."

Maybe it's a memory because I think I already knew that.

"I really thought we were living together. It would make sense, especially since I remember the key so vividly."

Henry laces our fingers together, lifting them between us. "It was a big night for us."

"Did we get engaged?" I ask, already knowing I'm not wearing a ring. Even if they'd taken it off when I'd been admitted to the hospital, I would have a tan line from it, right?

He smiles, releasing my hand before brushing his knuckle against my cheek. "We'll get to it all, but for now, you just have to allow yourself to heal and see how things turn out. Maybe you'll find that you want things to go differently, and I don't want to change your mind either way."

There's a hesitation in his voice, and I move back. "But what if things were perfect? What if I was happy and I choose the wrong path this time? What if we break up because this new version of me, who can't remember anything, is really selfish and hates being away from you?"

"I'm not going anywhere, Brielle. I can take some time off in the next few weeks if you want. We can maybe spend time together and revisit the places we loved to go. Maybe it will help you remember."

I breathe a little easier because I know that taking time off work is a huge issue in his life. His father is demanding and expects perfection, especially from him. If Henry is close to taking over, I can only imagine that suggesting that wasn't easy.

Hope fills me that we found a way to make our relationship work. It was something that was a source of contention before, I never felt like I mattered when it came to his job. "Really? You'll take time off?"

His smile is wide. "Yes, love."

"Thank you."

"There's nothing in the world I wouldn't do for you," he says before giving me a soft kiss.

Someone clears their throat, and I look over to see Spencer enter the room. "Sorry to interrupt." He looks to Henry and then to me. "I wanted to check on you."

My heart sputters a little at the sight of him. Spencer has always been the one that could wear the most hideous pattern or color and still be incredibly sexy. In slacks, though, Spencer is a freaking God. His broad chest looks as if it's ready to split open the seams of his shirt.

Each muscle is defined, and I force myself to focus on his face. It may be safer.

Nope. It's not.

He trimmed his beard, and his dark green eyes are intense as he watches me.

Dear Lord.

I force myself to smile. "You're not at all."

"Henry," Spencer says cordially, but there is an undertone of something brittle in his voice.

"Spencer, it's nice seeing you under better circumstances."

Spencer's brow raises. "Brielle's brother being killed and her having memory loss is a better circumstance?"

"I didn't mean it that way." Henry's voice is light. "I meant that the last time—"

Spencer turns to me. "How are you feeling?"

"I'm better now." I'd be much better if they'd explain the tension between them, which they won't. "Did you hear about Addy?" I ask.

"Yes, I just left there. She said to tell you she'll be here to see you a bit later today."

Addison hasn't come by since the day I woke up. She's been so busy with getting things in order and handling the funeral arrangements.

"She's really going to leave?"

"I think she just needs to breathe, and we all know the impossibility of that in this town."

"I'll miss her," I say honestly.

"And she'll miss you. She's trying to understand a world where Isaac doesn't exist."

I look to Henry, trying to imagine what that would be for me. We have been dating for a long time, but there were a few times I'd considered breaking this off with him. Clearly, I didn't go through with it.

"I wish I could do something to give her peace."

"I'm sure you living and getting a second chance is all she needs," Henry says.

Spencer's eyes narrow. "A second chance for what?"

"Life," Henry answers. "She's alive and can . . ."

"Can what?" I ask.

"You get to decide if what you want now is what you had in your past. What if things can be different, Brie? What if *we* can be different?"

I look at him as my stomach slowly sinks. "What was wrong with us?"

"Nothing. Everything. I'm just wondering if maybe your memory blocked out a part of your life for a reason. Maybe whatever happened three years ago was painful and you regret it so much you wanted to forget it."

Spencer scoffs. "That's not how it works. She's not blocking out an event. She has a TBI, and her brain is dealing with a trauma."

"But what if he's right?" I ask. "What if I'm remembering up until that part of my life because that's where it all went wrong?" While the medical reasons may not be that, what if it is? What if I fucked up when I took a job here, and this is the chance to fix it?

I look to Spencer. "You told me to go back to the beginning. What if that's what I'm doing?"

He shrugs. "I don't know. If it is the beginning, you have to ask yourself what is the catalyst to it?"

Exactly. I remembered college. I remembered moving here. I remembered fighting with Henry about taking this job and not being with him. I remembered being excited to start something new. So, is it because I should've left him, or that I should've moved to Portland, and that's what this is?

This is so frustrating.

"Well, I need to know. I need to go back to whatever that painful part is and push through so that I can help find my brother's killer and whoever wanted to kill me."

Henry presses his hand to my cheek. "You have to be patient and allow yourself to recover."

I shake my head. "That's not what I need. I am going to figure all this out. I'm already starting to remember things."

"You have always been so stubborn." He smiles, and his eyes fill with warmth.

"And you have always fought to protect me."

"Always, Brie."

"Then know that the only protection I need right now is from being protected." I reach up, brushing the scruff on his cheek.

"Okay."

"Thank you."

Henry rests his forehead to mine. "I was so afraid I'd lost you forever."

"I'm here."

"Just don't ever leave me."

I smile. "I'll try."

"Good." He presses his lips to mine, stopping the conversation.

I remember that we have someone in the room, but when I turn to look toward Spencer, he's already gone. For some reason, the thought of him leaving makes my chest hurt.

CHAPTER *Four*

BRIELLE

I can't do this. I can't.

I can't walk into this funeral home and see Isaac like this.

Addison comes to stand beside me, staring at the oak door to the funeral home. "We have to go inside, Brie."

"How?" I ask my sister-in-law, who is stronger than I ever imagined.

"I don't know, but we do. Isaac would need us to be strong."

I reach out, taking her hand in mine. "I don't feel strong."

Without having to look, I know my brother's best friends are standing behind us. Emmett, Spencer, and Holden are here, lending their support as the two of us take this second together.

They've been here, pillars of strength for both Addison and I. Emmett drove me home from the hospital to my mother's hotel, ensuring I was safe as I had a panic attack before I left, worried that the person who did this was still out there.

Holden came by after he left the hospital to check on me and then went to stay with Addison to help her with anything she needed.

This morning, Spencer showed up with a black dress, shoes, and various other things he grabbed from my apartment, since I was not ready to return there, especially after Henry left for Portland on a work emergency. His father demanded he return and so he went.

Addy sighs. "The last time we were here was for your dad."

It's not fair that I'm returning now for my brother. "I don't know how to walk in there," I admit. "I don't know how we do this."

Addison looks to me. "I know we don't have the details of what happened, but in my head and in my heart, I have to believe that Isaac was doing whatever he could to stop anyone from being hurt. He loved you and this town and everyone. He would've sacrificed himself for all of us because that was who he was, but especially for his family. So, I know we don't have the answers, but if any one of the scenarios I've imagined is true, then he was brave, and we have to be too."

The anguish in Addison's voice is too much to take. Both of us have silent tears streaming down our faces. "He was brave. He was so strong and always did the right thing. If that's what happened . . . if I'm alive because Isaac did something to protect me, then you're right. I owe it to him to be just as brave."

She squeezes my hand and nods. "Let's go inside."

I release a heavy sigh and let her lead me forward. The three men flank us and we walk up the steps, and Spencer reaches forward to pull open the heavy wood door.

This place could be someone's house from the outside. It is a beautiful white exterior with a large wraparound porch. The trim work is ornate and everything about it is inviting, only it holds the final goodbye inside. One I don't want to make.

We enter the home, where the upstairs is actually where people live and I'm taken back in time. The foyer is the same as I remember. Cream painted walls adorned with Oregon-themed paintings. The brown carpet helps to quiet the sounds of our heels as we enter. There are three viewing rooms, all varying in size, and on the plaque outside of the largest room is his name. Isaac Davis.

My mother exits the funeral director's office. She hugs us both before Mr. Moody steps forward, his kind eyes somber as he shakes first my hand and then Addy's. "I am so sorry for your loss. We all loved Isaac."

"Thank you," Addison says softly.

"We will keep everyone else out for the next twenty minutes to allow you privacy," he explains.

I look to Addison first. "You should go."

She shakes her head. "I'm not ready to go in quite yet. I think you should go in first. Maybe it'll . . ."

"Right," I say, knowing what everyone is hoping.

That I'll remember.

That I'll see Isaac, and like a flash bang, the last three years will come back to me.

God, I hope that's the case.

A hand rests on my shoulder, and I turn to see Spencer. "Are you okay?" His deep voice rumbles through the space.

"No. I can't do this alone."

Spencer looks around. "Is Henry here?"

This morning, I didn't answer him when he asked where Henry was. I just said he'd be here. I couldn't admit that he wasn't going to attend. I think that I hoped he would somehow prove me wrong and come anyway. I close my eyes, feeling shame at admitting this. "He had to go back to Portland. He'll be here in a bit if he can leave work."

He doesn't say anything, but I know he's judging Henry for not being here. "Well, you're not alone. We're all here."

Emmett and Holden are a few steps behind him.

They're always here for me. Always have been. Instead of one older brother, I had four. Each one more of a pain in the ass than the other. Each one thinking they knew what I needed, deserved, or wanted no matter what I said. When some boy broke my heart, those four were there. When I was in ninth grade and Mikey Jones got a little handsy after I said no, it was Emmett who broke his nose and Spencer who threatened his life if he ever came near me again.

It didn't matter that Spencer was already out of college, someone dared to mess with me and that boy was terrified after that.

As much as it annoyed me, there was always a thrill when it came to Spencer.

"You've always had my back."

"I always will."

"I know." I look back at the entrance, stalling for as long as I can because I don't want to do this. I am so afraid. "Will you . . . go in with me?"

I don't know why, but I can't be alone and there's no one else I trust more than him. Spencer won't let me fall apart, and Isaac would want him to stand with me.

"Of course."

I nod, inhaling deeply as my body trembles. We walk toward the entrance of the room, and I have the most intense urge to turn and run. I don't want to do this—to see him this way. I'm also so afraid of not remembering anything as well as remembering something so horrific that I'll wish the information were still lost.

We cross the threshold, and I hold my breath, willing my anxiety to ebb.

The panic bubbles up, and then it starts to dissipate when Spencer grabs my hand.

"Don't be afraid, Brielle. I am . . . we are all here for you. You aren't alone and you never will be."

My throat is tight as I force myself to take a breath. "Okay."

He lets me set the pace as I force my feet forward, and by the time

I'm standing next to my brother's casket, I can barely breathe around the crushing loss filling my lungs. When I sink to my knees, Spencer is behind me, his hand on my shoulder as I look at Isaac.

I wait for something—anything—but there's nothing but the tears and overwhelming grief as I stare at my brother.

I don't remember how or who. I don't recall what took him from us all. I only see the truth that my brother is gone. He's dead, and I am the only person who knows and yet doesn't know anything.

My head falls forward as I sob, feeling the guilt and weight crush me.

Then Spencer is pulling me into his arms, and I sink into his hold. "I can't remember *anything*. How can I see him this way and not remember? How can I be so weak and do this?"

"Brie . . . you are not weak!"

"No, I'm failing him. *Him*," I yell. "Isaac, who has never let me down. He is probably why I'm alive and yet, I don't know anything. I don't know what happened to him. I'm the only one who can make this right and I can't!"

"You can't blame yourself."

I push back, no longer feeling worthy of his comfort. "Who then? Who do I blame?"

"The person responsible. That's who."

"If I could remember who that was, then I'd do that, but I can't! For all we know, I did that! What if I hurt Isaac?"

Spencer sighs. "We both know that's not true."

"Do we? How? Because I don't know anything about the last three years. Not who I am. What I do. Where I live. For all we know, I'm a serial killer or I hired someone. I could've staged it. I feel like I'm going crazy, Spencer!"

His hands take my face. "I know exactly who you are, Brielle Davis. You are smart and sweet. You are a horrific dancer who thinks she's the next big star. You sing in the car because you can't stop yourself. You love kids and want to keep all of them from ever being in a bad situation. There is no chance in hell you hurt Isaac. None."

When he pulls me back against him, I don't fight it. I'm far too busy sobbing and trying not to drown in my emotions. My heart breaks as I let it out. The anger and frustration. The rage that someone took my brother, and the crippling fear that I could have died right along with him. Addison is without her husband and they have a baby with blonde hair and—

I lift my head, and tears blur the view into Spencer's green eyes.

"What?" he asks quickly. "What's wrong?"

"Elodie," I whisper. "She has blonde hair?"

Spencer wipes the tear off my cheek. "She does."

"She has blonde hair. I know this. I just knew it. Like, it wasn't a question. I remembered her hair, and . . . she was a chubby baby. I remember holding her, but . . ."

"But what?"

"That's all. I just knew that."

Spencer's eyes grow intense. "That's another thing, which is one more than you had five minutes ago, Brie. I know it doesn't seem like a lot, but these little pieces will start to make sense."

Time isn't something I'm willing to spend on this, but maybe there's another option. Maybe Spencer can help me move time. I have to help find who killed my brother. I have to get justice for Isaac and find answers for all of us. "Are you working right now?"

"What?"

"On a story. Are you currently writing or investigating something?" Sad part is that I don't know if it's even what he does anymore.

"Not right now. I haven't taken an assignment in a few . . . in a while."

Perfect. I shift forward, my hands resting on his chest as my own heart beats rapidly. "I need you to help me."

"Help you?"

I nod. "What would you do if you wanted to know something?"

"What do you mean?"

"I mean that I need help. I can't drive, I would have to get a taxi, but that would leave me wandering around aimlessly while I tried to figure out how to remember my life."

"No, that's not an option."

"Then you have to help me. You're one of the country's top investigative reporters, right? You can probably catch this person before I even need my memory back. Please, you have to. I don't want to do this alone, but you know I will. I'll go back in time, and . . . I don't know where to start, but I'll pick somewhere because I can't just sit around and do nothing."

His face scrunches, eyes narrowing a little in thought. "You can't be roaming around Oregon either."

"Then you do it with me. Treat me like a news story. Where do we even begin?"

"This is crazy."

Maybe it is, but it's what I need.

After a small stretch of silence, Spencer sighs. "I would go back to the beginning, back to the very last thing I could remember, and work my way forward from there."

"The beginning for me is a few months after graduating grad school. If I want to start to make sense of all of this, I need to start there."

"Brie . . ." Spencer's voice is strong with warning.

"If you don't help me, I'll do it on my own. You know I will."

His deep sigh leaves his lungs, and he refuses to meet my eyes. "Holden was clear that you need to let this happen naturally."

"I am, but that doesn't mean I should sit around and hope that maybe the memory will come back. You are the best investigative reporter in the world. You have been involved with unearthing the truth on mysteries that no one else could. This isn't that grand, but it's that important."

His gaze drops. "I want you to remember your life, Brielle."

I move my hand to his cheek, resting it softly there. "Then help me."

CHAPTER *Five*

BRIELLE

"Are you sure you want to head home?" my mother asks as she helps me fold the clothes on the bed.

"I can't stay here."

"It's only been four days. It can't be that bad."

Oh, but it is. My mother is trying and is in pain, but she's driving me nuts. I can't move without her fussing over me.

Not to mention, Addy is leaving and my mother has her life in California. I haven't had any flashes or memories since the funeral, and I'm getting more anxious as the time slips by. I need to go to the beginning and work my way to the present, not that I know what that is. I guess it would be the last solid part of my life that I fully remember. My mother would flip her shit if she knew I was planning this.

"It's not bad, Mom. You just have things to do and I need to sort my life out," I explain.

"Yes, but you'll be alone," Mom says with concern. "I can't just leave you like this."

"I'm not alone."

"You won't have me or your broth—" She stops herself. "You will be here without any family."

"I have Spencer, Emmett, and Holden. They're good substitutes for the time being."

Mom walks over, taking the shirt from my hand. "I noticed you didn't say Henry."

No, I didn't. In fact, I am livid at him. "Did he call back?"

She shakes her head. "Not since yesterday."

"Right."

Henry left the day I got out of the hospital and still hasn't returned to Rose Canyon. He called my mother last night to apologize and let her know he would be here today.

I really can't believe he wasn't here for my brother's funeral. That his job is more important to him than being here for me. And, yet, there's a part of me that isn't surprised.

My mom takes my hand in hers. "Never mind that. Things have a way of working out."

"Does that mean we will be okay? Does that mean we're even together? Nothing makes sense, Mom."

"Well, while I can't tell you those answers, I can ask you to look inside of your heart. Is this okay for you? Is this what you want?"

I don't know. I want to say yes because I am assuming we found our way and that this is something I've come to deal with. However, this is not okay. I don't want to be with someone who doesn't care about me enough to help while I'm clearly in a crisis.

"I can only handle so much thinking," I answer, which really isn't an answer. "Can we get the replacement phone on our way to where I live?"

Mom gives me a sad smile. "Yes."

That's at least one thing, even if it still came with restrictions. They ordered me a new phone with a new number and nothing but my contacts transferred from my old line. Whatever.

I finish packing my bag, and my mom and I head out. We drive through the streets of my hometown. Nothing has changed, and yet, everything is different. There are pictures of Isaac on the windows of the storefronts. We pass the high school where he taught, and there is a large sign with his face. Tears prick my eyes because this world was so much brighter with him in it.

I would give anything to talk to him right now. Isaac was nine years older than me, and while so many big brothers may have thought it was annoying to suddenly have a sister, he didn't. He protected me, loved me, always made sure that I had his support, even when he didn't agree.

We turn down Mountain Rd and pass the coffee shop. At the corner, there is a makeshift display of flowers, candles, and papers that I can't look away from. "Mom?"

"Yes?"

"Why are there flowers and things outside of RosieBeans?"

The last memory I have of the cafe was when it opened, but that was right before I left for college. It was a big deal to get a coffee shop in our tiny town.

Mom fidgets and then makes another turn onto a side street. "Why do you think, Brie?"

Because that must be where the incident happened. It must be where my brother died. "I don't remember."

Mom takes my hand, squeezing it gently. "It's okay."

Everyone keeps saying that, but it's not. I rip my hand away, turning to face the window. Mom stops at the store and grabs my replacement phone, handing it over. As we take another turn, we pull up to the old brick mill. Only, it doesn't look run-down.

It looks like people live here.

"I live here?"

"Yes."

I heave a sigh and try not to be lost.

We exit the car, and when I turn, I see Spencer leaning against his car. He came. He came, and he's going to help.

I start toward him, but someone comes flying out of the building.

"Brielle! Oh my God, you're home! Thank the Lord above. I have prayed every single day for you. How are you feeling? We took in your mail for you, and I have it all in a box," a woman who I don't know says.

I open my lips, but I'm too shocked to actually say anything. Then the woman is talking again, so I give up trying to form words.

"I am so sorry about Isaac. I was devastated—the entire town was. The football team hasn't been able to play since he died. You know how much those boys love him. I ran into Jenna and she was saying how the kids are lost without you too! Gosh. It's just so much."

I turn to my mother, my body trembling a little. I hate this. I hate this more than I can ever say. I don't know who she is, and it's utterly surreal and unsettling for her to be talking to me as if we're friends. I am lost in this world that doesn't make sense. How can I not know who people are? People who clearly care about me. This woman collected my mail, so I must have some sort of friendship with her.

"Thank you so much for doing that, Tessa. I don't know what you heard about Brielle's injury, but she has a gap in her memory. If she . . ."

"Oh, yes, I heard. I just thought with her coming home . . ." Tessa looks to me. "I live in the apartment next to you. My husband, Nick, is the building supervisor. If you need anything, please don't hesitate to ask."

Tears prick at my eyes, but I hold them back as I nod and offer her a small smile. "Thank you. I'm sorry I don't . . ."

"Don't apologize, Brie. Just know that you have people here who care and are looking out for you." The sincerity in her voice eases my anxiety a bit.

"I appreciate that."

"Of course, that's what neighbors are for. Hey is—" She pauses and waves at Spencer. "Hey, Spencer!"

"Tessa, good to see you."

I glance over at him. "You know her?"

"I have been to your apartment." He chuckles.

"Of course. I just don't . . . you know, remember."

Tessa sighs heavily. "I'm sorry I accosted you in the parking lot. I'm sure you have a lot to do. I just wanted to let you know how glad we all are that you're home and doing okay. Well, minus the not remembering thing."

"Thank you," I say. I may not have memories of her or this place, but at least there is someone nice here.

I look toward the building where I live—or, where everyone says I live—and wait for something, anything, to happen.

The bricks are no longer scattered around and I remember climbing to the fourth floor, when there were no windows because they'd been broken, and staring out at the mountains in the distance. And many other nefarious things my mother has no clue about. "How many people live here?"

My mother rubs my back. "There are eight apartments, two on each floor."

"And I live in one?"

"Yes, do you remember anything about it?" Spencer asks.

"Not anything recent, just something old."

He laughs, probably knowing exactly what I'm talking about. I was a senior in high school, and the boys were all home for some event. They decided to have some secret party, but I heard them planning, so I grabbed a few friends, crashed it, got incredibly drunk, and fell asleep on Spencer. Much to his chagrin.

"It was a good party."

My mother huffs. "You boys were always getting into trouble back then, and somehow, Brielle found a way to tag along."

"I was always protected," I tell her. They couldn't stop me from doing half the dumb things, but they always made sure I had a safety net—them.

Spencer nods. "That she was."

"Well, what are you doing here, Spencer?" Mom turns with one brow raised.

"I am helping Brie—reluctantly."

"Helping?" I can hear the concern in her voice.

"Brielle needs answers—we all do, and the only way to get them is for her memory to return. I talked to Holden and Cora, and they agreed that my helping her retrace her life isn't the same as us just dumping the info. So, I'm going to help her do that."

Now that surprises me. "You asked Holden?"

"I mentioned what we were doing and asked him to please step in if he thought it was a bad idea," he says as though it should be obvious. "He is a doctor."

"Yes, but shouldn't I have been the one to ask him?"

He raises one brow. "Did you have plans to?"

No, but . . . I could've.

"I'm not going to put you in harm's way, blow the case, or fuck up your recovery."

Oh. I guess that makes sense.

"I *am* worried," my mother offers. "I have to get back to California soon, and I feel as though I'm abandoning you. I just . . . I have to get back to the store and other things."

I've been so wrapped up in everything else that I never thought to ask about her life over the last three years.

"You aren't abandoning me, Mom. I promise," I tell her. "Besides, I need to remember, which means taking a walk through the last three years of my life. I should be able to handle that, right? Unless, of course, you two would just like to tell me what I've been up to?"

Spencer speaks before my mother can. "It sucks, but it's the only way. We'll work through it and get you to remember when we can."

"And if it's too late?" I ask.

I understand that whatever is in my locked memory will allow the police to find a killer and that tampering with my memory would hinder that, but I don't understand how telling me where I bank would affect that.

"Too late for what?" my mother questions.

"Everything. What if I never remember? What if Spencer isn't Sherlock Holmes and can't help me retrace anything? What if I never find Isaac's killer and they come back to finish the job?"

Her eyes widen, but Spencer steps forward, points to the corner, and asks, "Do you see that car?"

"Yes."

"That's a friend of Emmett's. He was a Green Beret who did four tours in Iraq and Afghanistan. He can probably kill us with a pencil from his vehicle."

I gasp. "That's not reassuring."

"It is to me."

I shake my head. "Someone isn't going to be able to watch over me at all times."

He raises one brow. "Want to make a bet? Emmett and I hired Cole Security Forces to maintain full security on both you and Addy until Isaac's killer is caught and we know you're not at risk. We have no idea if the person who attacked you and killed Isaac is a woman or a man, who they were actually after, or why they did it. Yeah, we are being a little overprotective, but we promised you that you'd be safe, and I don't feel bad about it. In fact, I'm rather happy, and I think your brother would be too."

The fierce protectiveness in his voice causes me to step back a little. I can see the stress in his eyes, and I would be lying if I said I don't feel a little more comfortable.

My mother's fingers settle around my forearm. "Knowing that does make me feel a lot better about leaving."

He nods once. "No one is willing to lose you too, Brielle."

"I know."

He forces a smile and glances toward the building. "How about we go inside and get started?"

I exhale, nerves hitting me again. "Okay."

I really hope I find out that I like the person behind the door.

CHAPTER *Six*

BRIELLE

Standing here, looking at my things, my life, the desolation is overwhelming.

The apartment is all exposed brick and ductwork, and my furniture is almost industrial, but I have never really considered myself a modern type girl. It's all clean lines, and nothing about the space feels personal. I enter the kitchen, my fingers sliding along the cool cement countertop as I take in the dark wood cabinets.

It's beautiful. Even in its lack of warmth.

"Anything?" My mother's voice is full of hope.

I close my eyes for a second, waiting for something to happen, but there's nothing. I don't remember moving in or picking out the couch, or the painting on the wall over the entryway table that adorns my loft. I wander toward where my bedroom must be, hoping that might help. Maybe a memory of Henry and me or, hell, anything.

I take in the space as I pass the bathroom before finding the bedroom. There is a plush rug under the very large poster bed that has two nightstands. Off to the right is what I assume is a closet, and there's a dresser opposite. I walk there first.

I lift a glass frame with a photo of me holding a tiny baby, and I glance to where Spencer and my mom linger in the doorway. "Is this Elodie?"

Mom smiles. "It is."

I don't remember her or this photo, but she's blonde, and on the lines of her nose, I see my brother. "She's going to be beautiful," I mutter almost to myself.

"She's the best parts of Isaac and Addy."

"How old is she now?" I ask, praying someone answers.

"She's eight months old," Spencer says without hesitation.

I place the photo back down and grab the next. It's me and my dad a few weeks before he died. Then behind that is one of me at graduation with my brother and the three idiots. All of us are laughing at something, Emmett is holding my cap above me, Isaac is smiling so wide as he reaches for it, and Holden has his hands on my honor's sash. And then there's Spencer. His arm is wrapped around my waist, holding me as I am almost falling back, reaching for my stolen items.

I look up to find him watching me. "What?"

"I remember this anyway, but it feels like the first time I've seen this picture," I say with a nervous laugh.

It's strange because I can hear Isaac instructing Emmett to toss it, Holden's deep laugh as I started to fall a little, and then the feeling of Spencer grabbing me. As much as there was the feel of him touching me, I remember the safety. The fact that I never once believed I would ever hit the ground because he wouldn't drop me.

Strange.

On the other side is Isaac and Addison's wedding photo, but nothing else. No Henry, which if we are together, why don't I have pictures?

A phone rings, and Mom reaches into her bag. "It's the store," she says before going into the other room.

Spencer walks toward me. "What do you feel?"

I sigh, placing the photo down. "Confused. I don't know this place or the things in it. I don't understand why, if I'm still with Henry, he doesn't seem to exist in here. He made it seem like he loves me and that I love him."

"Maybe he does love you."

"Then why isn't he here? Why is it that you're helping me when he isn't? Better yet, why didn't I think to ask him?" I pause. "I don't think that I'm with Henry anymore and everyone was too afraid to tell me. I mean, he didn't even show up to my brother's funeral. You're like the last guy in the world who would be in a serious relationship, and you wouldn't do that."

Spencer laughs. "How do you know I'm not married?"

My breath catches. "I don't. Oh, God. Are you married?"

"No."

I slap his arm. "Jerk."

"Look around, see if anything sparks a memory. I'll go wait for your mother to get off the phone so you aren't bombarded. Just come out when you're ready."

I might never be ready. He squeezes my shoulder in reassurance before walking out, leaving me to my thoughts.

There must be something here to help me figure things out. A box of things I kept in a closet or clothing of his to tell me if we are together still.

I head there first and see nothing that would indicate that Henry spends any time here. I do find an old shirt, boxers, and a pair of jeans, but they're not the brand he wore. They could be his, but the pants are a little slimmer than he is now. I keep searching, finally finding a black box on the bottom.

Heading to the bed with it, I open it, hopeful but also cautious. The box contains photos of the old days, so there shouldn't be anything in it that I don't already remember. My high school prom, which I went to with Jim Trevino. More of the four guys before a camping trip and another when we all went hiking. Lots of memories, things that I know already.

Then there's one of me standing outside this apartment with my arms up in the air, a huge smile on my face as Isaac carries a box inside. That's so him, he would be helping while I goofed off with Addy taking photos. I flip the picture over, finding it dated two and a half years ago.

I dig deeper and see something round on the bottom of the box. When I pull it out, I see a cigar band. Why the hell would I have a cigar band? Seriously, I'm starting to wonder if I don't smoke them.

When I lift it to my nose, inhaling deep, I'm transported again. I close my eyes and that smell—oak, leather, pepper, coffee, and underlying nutty flavors—fills my senses. No longer is it just the taste, I can smell it on his skin. I can feel the heat of his mouth as our tongues moved. The memory grows stronger, and I sink into it, remembering my fingers pressed against the scruff on his cheeks. That taste, though, I wanted it so much. I was drunk on it.

It's a good kiss—no, it's more than that. It's a kiss that I clearly can't forget.

A part of me is clinging to it, willing the Brielle in the memory to open her eyes. I want to know the face of the man who kissed me as if he couldn't breathe without my lips on his. I try to focus on something, anything else . . .

"Brielle?"

I leap off the bed and turn to face the doorway.

"Mom." My heart is racing, and my breathing is just a little louder.

"Are you okay?"

I clear my throat. "I am. Are you?"

She lifts the phone. "Yes, but I need to get back to the hotel and handle this. There was an issue at the store, and I need some information off my laptop. Spencer said he can stay for a while and then bring you to Addy's for dinner, is that okay?"

"Yeah, of course."

"Okay, we are planning to order food around six."

"Sounds good."

She pulls me in for a hug. "You're doing so much better than you give yourself credit for." Mom leans back, her lips in a tight line. "I would be on the floor and here you are, standing tall, all to try to help catch your brother's killer."

"Isaac would've done it for me," I explain.

"Yes, he would've, but it doesn't make it easy."

That's the understatement of the year. I nod, and she kisses my cheek and leaves. Spencer's large frame fills the doorway. God, he looks so hot. I am totally digging the beard, which is starting to grow back again. He leans against the frame with his arms crossed and lifts his chin. "What's that?"

"What?"

I look down at the cigar band wrapped around my finger. "I don't know what it's from or why I kept it, but it was in a box of photos and little things I've kept over the years. I remembered that kiss again," I confess.

"What did you remember?"

I tell him most of it, leaving out the part that whoever is on the other end is a really freaking good kisser, and he nods.

"May I?" His hand is outstretched, and I gently lay it in his palm.

"Do you know the cigar?" I ask.

He shakes his head. "I'm not much of a cigar guy."

"Isaac was."

"I forgot about that until you just said it. He was always trying to get us to smoke them. As though it made us distinguished or some shit."

I laugh. "Which none of you are."

"Holden is a doctor."

"Yes, but he's also the guy who shaved Emmett's eyebrows before he left for a deployment."

Spencer's deep chuckle fills the space. "God, he was so mad."

"No shit he was! He went out with his unit—browless."

"He shouldn't have fallen asleep first."

I roll my eyes. "You guys are a mess."

"That we are—or, we were. Now we're a different kind of mess."

"A mess is a mess is a mess. *You* are at least a hot mess."

"You think I'm hot?" he asks with a grin.

"You know you are." No point in denying it. I move back to the bed, sitting on the edge.

Spencer's eyes twinkle with mischief. "You are a hot mess as well."

I'm going to hold on to that comment forever.

Now I need to move onto safer ground. "It doesn't feel real to me," I tell him. "Even after the funeral, I can't really believe he's gone. Maybe it's because I don't know anything right now, but it's surreal and not in a good way."

Spencer sits beside me. "It doesn't feel real to me either."

"I loved him so much, you know?"

"I do, and he really did love you. I don't feel like I'm telling you anything you don't already know, but he would've done anything for you."

No, he's not telling me anything I don't know. Isaac was the best brother that ever existed. Sure, we bickered here and there, but mostly, we were best friends. "If Addy leaves, I really don't know how I'm going to get through this."

"I think she has to. Since losing him, she's lost herself. If she can get a break, get herself together, it may be the best thing for her and Elodie."

"Selfishly, I want her to stay, but I'm sure it's what she needs to do."

He links his fingers through mine. "Selfishly, we all want things, but doing what is best for the other person is what love is."

I smile a little, looking up at him. "Like helping your best friend's sister try to remember her life?"

Spencer forces his lips into a grin and then stands. "Like that. Come on, I think we should head over to Addison's and then make our plan for part one of this."

"Oh, there are parts?"

"Yeah, and I'm not sure you're going to like them."

I groan and mutter as I follow him out. "Boy, that seems to be the reoccurring theme in my life."

[illegible]

[illegible] through life.

I think we need to [illegible] together. It may be the best thing for [illegible]

[illegible]

CHAPTER Seven

BRIELLE

Elodie is asleep in my arms as Addison walks around her room, packing a bag. "You're sure this is what you want?" I ask, staring down at the baby.

Spencer ended up dropping me off here and heading to the hotel to help my mother pack her car. There was a fire at the store, and she needs to get on the road. She was going to leave soon anyway, but it still sucks.

"No. I'm not sure, but I know that I can't stay here right now," Addy says, pulling a shirt from the drawer.

"I understand. It's all happening so fast."

Addy gives me a sad smile. "I know. I thought Mom would stay for at least a few more days, but she needs to deal with the insurance."

"You really don't think the fact that her store had a fire is related to Isaac and me?" I ask.

"The investigator down there didn't seem to think so. He said it appears to be the coffee maker that was plugged in, not arson."

"Just weird," I say, staring at Elodie. She's so damn perfect. I may not remember much, but I know I love her already. "It's going to be really hard losing you, Addy. There's nothing I could say to make you change your mind?" What was starting off as a week or two is now open-ended.

It feels so selfish to ask, but Addison is not only my sister-in-law but also my friend. I am a little light on friends lately.

"I haven't slept in almost two weeks. I can't eat. I cry all the damn time. I went to take Elodie for a walk, just to get out of the house, and I was stopped eight times by people who wanted to tell me a story about Isaac and how sad they were. And don't even get me started on the letters and the calls."

Her tears cause my own to form. "I'm so sorry, Addy. I understand, and I shouldn't have asked you to stay."

She comes to me, hands framing my face. "Don't cry. Please. I'm just telling you why I think a few weeks or maybe a month out of here will do me good. I'll visit with Devney, and it will give me a change of pace and a chance to grieve without the whole town watching me."

All of that makes sense, but I wish it weren't necessary. "I love you, you know that, right?"

"And I love you. I think it'll be good for you too, Brie."

"For my sister and niece to leave?"

She nods. "You are dealing with so much, and I don't want to add pressure on you."

"You're not. Trust me. I have enough of it on my own."

Addison looks to Elodie and sighs. "Do you know how hard it is not to tell you everything that I know so that you'll remember *something*? All I want is for you to give us answers, and that's not possible. It's not fair either. My going will allow all of us some time to breathe a little and hopefully heal."

"I know what you're saying, and I understand. Really, I do. I'm just being selfish, I guess. I lost my brother, the belief I was with the right guy, my memories, the life I was living, and now you're leaving. The only thing I have right now is this insane plan to re-walk my life."

Addy brushes her fingers against Elodie's cheek. "The one thing I've always been so envious of is your ability to make a choice and live by it. I know you feel lost, but trust your instinct because I've never seen it lead you astray."

I look up in Addy's blue eyes, which are swimming with unshed tears. "I'm going to miss you."

A tear falls. "I'm going to miss you too, but I won't be gone long. I don't think I can stay away from Rose Canyon. As hard as it is to be here, it'll be just as bad being away. Isaac has been my life since I was seventeen. I . . . don't know that I can ever really stay away."

On one level, I knew she would be back and this wasn't permanent, but I still feel marginally better. However, like Spencer said, this isn't about what I want, it's about what she needs.

"I hope that, when you do come back, you'll feel better."

"And all I want is for you to get better—and not just so we'll know what happened. I want you to remember because before everything went sideways, you were happy. I want you to find that again, so if something or someone doesn't feel right to you, try to remember what I said about your instinct, okay?"

"So, I take it you're not a fan of Henry?"

"I never was."

"No, but . . . you didn't really voice it."

Addison laughs without humor. "You got enough of that from your mother. I didn't need to add fuel to that fire."

"I have this feeling that we're not together. I keep wondering, why would I still put up with this? Why was there no trace of him in my apartment? If we were still dating, there'd be something of his, right?"

Addison gives me a face that basically answers the questions before she shrugs. "Did you want to find something of his there?"

"After he didn't come to the funeral . . . no."

Addy raises a brow. "Whether you are or aren't still a thing, and I'm not saying you are . . . or are not. I was kind of shocked he wasn't there."

"He did call," I tell her.

"Oh, how nice of him. I take it he didn't show up at all?"

"I got my new phone number, and I sent him a text so he'd have it. He called right away, but I was too emotional to answer. He left a voice mail saying he was sorry and was going to come as soon as he could. Then texted me saying how sorry he was and gave me some bullshit about a client that he was required to handle and to please understand it won't be like this again. He wants me to come to Portland and spend some time with him. It's so . . . I don't know. For now, I don't feel much like responding."

I can see on her face that she's not buying any of it. "You should do what you think is right. Not to mention, you're not stupid or a doormat."

"How do I decide what's right when I'm missing all the tools to weigh my options?"

Addison sits beside me, stretching her legs out. "I think you have to follow your gut. Right now, it seems as if it's telling you what you should do, so it's up to you to be brave enough to listen. But, do me a favor, okay?"

"Of course."

"Don't do anything unless it's something *you* want to do. The last two weeks have been a nightmare for both of us, and sometimes it's important to take a minute and just breathe and heal. Also, before you make any decisions about Henry, know that whatever you're experiencing now is likely how your life is or would be with him. We both know you won't put up with it."

There is a beat of time that passes as we take in her words, really letting them settle around us before I look to her. "Thank you. Also, thank you for not hating me," I say. It's been a worry of mine, that Addison would look at me like a failure as well.

"What the hell could I hate you for?"

"I don't know . . . the entire situation."

"I would never hate you. You didn't do this, Brielle. There's no one else in the world who loved Isaac as much as you. He was your hero too."

"I'm going to get to the bottom of it," I tell her with every ounce of sincerity I have. "For you. For Elodie. For him."

"I don't doubt you."

And hopefully, I find myself somewhere along the way.

Spencer walks me to the door of my apartment, and my hands are shaking the entire time.

I am strong. I can do this. I just have to get through the first night, and then it'll be easy.

That's the new load of crap I'm feeding myself.

"I was thinking we should go skydiving," Spencer says, stunning me.

"What?"

"We should do something stupid."

"And skydiving is your top suggestion?"

He tilts his head. "Maybe cliff diving."

I huff. "Yeah, that went over super well the last time."

Spencer grins. "Yeah, you totally didn't listen when we said to jump to the left."

I glare at him. "I was, like, a thousand feet up! I couldn't hear shit. The wind was blowing, it was fucking freezing, and you idiots were waving your hands in different directions. I had to guess."

"You guessed wrong."

Oh, I hate him. "You can say this flippantly now, but if I remember, you were losing your mind when I came up for air."

He was a maniac, actually. Spencer was screaming at Holden, who was up at the top with me. I thought he was going to kill him. Ironically, my brother is who calmed him down after it was very clear I was fine.

A little bruised, mostly embarrassed. I hated looking stupid and young in front of the guys.

"Fuck yeah I was. You could've been hurt."

"Hence the thrill."

"Doing better?" he asks, changing topics.

"What?"

"You were scared. Is it better now?"

I glance up at him. "I was . . . you were handling me."

He chuckles. "I've spent a good portion of my life perfecting the ability. I'm pretty good at it."

"Whatever."

Spencer tosses his arm around my shoulders. "What has you the most concerned?"

"I'm going to be alone and what if someone wants me dead?"

"You're safe, Brielle. I promise that much."

Easy for him to say. I don't know anyone in this building or what the hell I'm supposed to do all alone. It's like the first night I spent at college. I sat in that room and cried for two hours. I was terrified of being alone and in a strange place. Now, I'm dealing with a version of homesickness but because I don't remember any of this.

"How do I know that?" I ask him.

"Because there is a security guy in his car out front, another one in back, and Emmett will be here in about an hour."

"He's coming here?"

"Emmett is staying in the apartment directly across from yours."

My eyes widen. "What? He lives here too?"

"He does now."

I don't know what to say, so I end up gaping at him. "When did he move in?"

"Yesterday."

"Because?"

"Because we have no idea who killed your brother and tried to kill you. So, the apartment is now sublet to your security team. So, if you're scared or you need something, you have people here. They're one of the top security teams in the country. I've made friends during my career and none of us are taking chances."

"I don't know if that makes me feel worse or better."

"Either way, they're only here to keep you safe. You probably wouldn't even notice them if I hadn't told you."

Now he's insulting my intelligence. "Please. I would definitely notice a bunch of hulking military-looking guys walking around Rose Canyon. It's not like we're brimming with new people in this town."

He smirks. "Except that you don't know who lives here anymore. You have no memories of the last three years."

"Ass."

Spencer shrugs. "I told you this to ease your worries about staying here tonight."

"I'm not worried." It's a total lie.

"Sure you're not."

I really hate him sometimes. Feeling as though I need to prove myself, I cross my arms over my chest and huff. "I'm going inside now. I'll see you tomorrow?"

He nods with a smile. "Yes. Also, if you need anything or you just want some company, call."

The last thing in the world I plan to do is call one of them. "Thanks. I'll see you around eight."

"Sleep well, Brie."

"Thanks."

There's very little chance of that.

I head inside, and as soon as the door clicks, loneliness and fear flood me. I am alone for the first time since I woke up in the hospital. In my home, that doesn't much feel like a home. I think back to what Addison and my mother say about my strength. While I don't feel very strong, they all seem to think this is a quality I possess, so I may as well act like it.

I head into the master bathroom and go through the drawers. I have everything perfectly organized, which doesn't surprise me. Again, I search for a sign or a clue about my life. No men's cologne or soap. Nothing that says another person stays here.

Just when I'm about to give up, I find a box of condoms under the sink. The box is open and only two are in there. So, I'm clearly having sex or handing out condoms, which, as a social worker, could be true.

The one thing that strikes me as odd is that the brand isn't one Henry and I used. Not that it means much because I'm not using the same deodorant I used to either. Still, it's one more thing to think about.

I'm overwhelmed and exhausted. No longer feeling like being a spy in my house, I give up my search, head back into my bedroom, and grab an oversized shirt from my drawer. Then head into the kitchen to grab a glass of water. I wish it were wine, but I'm not allowed any alcohol for a few weeks. There's a stack of mail on the counter, and I make a mental note to go through it tomorrow. I'm rounding the island counter in the kitchen when there is a loud bang on my door. I drop the glass, screaming loudly as glass shatters around me.

In the span of what seems like two seconds, my door is thrown open and Emmett, Spencer, and Henry storm into my apartment.

I don't know when I crouched into a tight ball with my arms around my knees, or when I started shaking, but when I look up, all three guys are watching me with concern in their eyes.

Spencer reaches his hand out first. "It's okay, Brie. You're safe."

My body is tight, and I can't move as fear is still in control. The sound was so loud and so sudden that I thought . . . God, I don't know, that it was a gun.

He lowers until he's looking straight into my wide, unblinking eyes. "Can you stand so I can lift you away from the glass?"

"I can . . ." Henry speaks, but Spencer turns to him, and whatever he was going to say he doesn't.

Spencer hangs his head for a second before returning to me. "I'll get you over to the couch so you don't get hurt, okay?"

I want to speak, to tell him I'm fine, but I can't. Tears pool, but he waits for me to nod before he lifts me into his arms as though I weigh nothing. I wrap mine around his neck, allowing him to cradle me to his chest as he takes me to the sofa.

Emmett starts to pick up the glass all over the floor.

Spencer settles me on the couch and then turns to Henry. "You banged on the door?"

"She didn't answer the first time."

"So, you thought you should fucking knock louder? Knowing all the hell she's going through?" Spencer's rage is palpable.

"I was worried because of that! She didn't answer my texts, calls, or respond to my voice mails. And then I get here and she doesn't answer the door. Yeah, I knocked louder and was ready to kick it in if it meant getting to her."

Spencer steps closer to him. "You're an idiot. We've already done everything to make sure Brielle is safe. Her family and friends have handled things while you did, what? Oh, that's right. Nothing."

Henry's hands clench into tight fists.

"Easy, man," Emmett says as he steps between them. "None of this is what Brie needs. Calm down and breathe. Everything is fine."

I want to calm down, but I feel like I may throw up. Spencer runs his hands through his hair. "I need a minute."

Emmett nods. "Go, she's safe."

He walks out, and my anxiety spikes again. With an intensity I don't understand, I want him to stay. It's enough to start to drag me out of the fog of panic. Why do I want Spencer to be here when Emmett and my imposter boyfriend are?

Before I can think too much, Henry sits beside me. "I'm sorry I scared you."

I force the air out of my lungs. "It's fine. I'm tired and overwhelmed. It's been a rough few days, which you'd know if you'd been here."

Henry flinches slightly, and I don't really care. "That's why I came."

"To do what?"

"Apologize."

Emmett clears his throat. "On that note, I'll give you guys a few minutes alone. I'm going back across the hall. If you need anything, just yell."

"Thank you, Em," I say, and he winks.

"Why is he across the hall?"

I sigh heavily, not wanting to explain any of this to him. "It doesn't matter. Why did you come tonight? I didn't answer your messages because I was upset. You could've waited for me to text."

"Because I needed to see you. I got worried when you weren't answering your phone."

"I really didn't want to talk. You weren't here when my brother was buried, Henry. That was when I needed someone to talk to, someone to offer me their support."

He at least looks embarrassed. "Yes, and I know I failed you."

"That's the thing, though. I don't know that you actually did."

"What does that mean?"

Jesus. I really don't want to get into this now, I don't want to talk to him about all the things my gut is screaming at me, but letting this go on any longer is unacceptable. If he and I are still together, well, he needs to know it isn't what I want. So, if this is what it took for me to finally leave him, being knocked—literally in the head, then so be it. I am smart enough to walk away before I spend any more time with him.

This type of a relationship is not okay, and I deserve more.

"I know you're not supposed to tell me anything about the last few years, but I keep feeling like this isn't real. Us. I don't think that we're together, but if we are, I'm not sure we should be."

Henry's lips part. "What makes you say that? Because I had to work?"

"No, not because you had to work. Because there aren't any photos of us anywhere, none of your clothing is here, and I can't find a single thing that would make me think you're still part of my life. The last thing I remember about us is that I was unhappy and wanted to end things."

He rises and starts to pace. Something he always did when he was trying to come up with something to change my mind. "We did end things."

Finally. *Finally*, the truth.

"That's why my mom didn't call you immediately?"

He nods. "Yes, I would've been at the hospital immediately. I never stopped loving you, Brie. Not for a single moment. So, when she told me what happened, I hoped, God, I hoped that maybe this would be our second chance. That I could prove to you that I am the guy you want to be with."

I'm not sure how he thought using this to manipulate me was a good idea.

"So, you lied?"

"Yes, but I didn't like the idea of it. Your mom told me I needed to keep things from you, so I did. I lied because it was what you remembered and I hoped that it was because it was what you wanted."

A part of me understands it. Here was a chance to rewrite our history, but the issue is that we were going to end here anyway.

"I don't know how things went before, but I know that I want so much more than this. I want someone who will be by my side, especially in the hard times."

"My job demands that I handle certain clients. When things come up, I can't just walk out."

"I understand. I do, but I'm not things and my brother's death wasn't minimal, especially not to me. I need to be able to rely on the man I love, and if you wanted this to be our second chance, you failed me already."

"I can do better."

"Yes, I think we both can." But not in that way.

I can find someone else. I can love someone who will be at my side. Henry's not that man, and not acknowledging that because I'm desperate to have a piece of my old life isn't something I'm willing to do.

Henry looks away. "You were always the one for me, Brie. I wish I was yours."

I take his hand in mine. "When I first saw you at the hospital, I was so relieved. Mostly because you were something I remembered and you being there gave me a constant. Only, even then, I knew that wasn't true. Yes, you and I were happy in the beginning, but somewhere along the way, we lost that. Our goals changed, and I think we grew up and apart at the same time. You were the dream, Henry. I think our realities are just too different. You deserve a woman who's willing to move to Portland with you, and I deserve someone who puts me first. I really hope that you find someone, though. I hope she makes you happy and that you can do the same for her. I want you to have the most amazing life, and I really hope that we can be friends."

He lets out a soft laugh. "You may not remember the way we broke up, but it's incredibly similar."

"Is it?"

He nods. "You wished me love and happiness and then handed me back that key with the red ribbon."

I blink a few times. "I told you that there was another's heart that it would open."

I remember. I remember saying it with tears streaming down my face because it was truly the end. I loved him and didn't want to hurt him, but I couldn't do it anymore.

"You did."

"I was sad."

"So was I."

It's funny that I feel the same thing again. "It was the right thing for us, wasn't it?"

He shrugs. "I don't know. Maybe it was because here we are again, and even with a faulty memory, you knew I wasn't the one for you."

My lips form into a sad smile. "I wish things could've been different."

"I think I'm meant to be alone," he says with a laugh. "I'm married to my job, and if I were being honest, it would be unfair to ask any woman to put up with it."

"I think the right woman will make you willing to give up anything for her. I'm just not that girl. Do you think we can see each other, as friends? I am working with Spencer on retracing my life, and I'm sure I could use your help."

He smiles softly. "Of course. No matter what, I still want the best for you. Plus, I've missed you."

"I'm sure I've missed you too. I know when I saw you in the hospital, I was so happy to see your face."

"We'll always have amnesia?"

We both chuckle.

"We'll always have at least that. Come on, I'll walk you out."

At the door, we hug, and a part of me relaxes a little, as though a piece of the puzzle clicked into place. When I open it, Emmett and Spencer are there, and Henry gives them both a dip of the chin before he heads down the hall.

"What happened?" Emmett asks first.

"I told him that I didn't want to be with him, and in doing so, I remembered that we broke up."

"You did?" Spencer asks.

I lean my shoulder against the frame and nod. "Yeah, it was also when I gave him back his key with the ribbon on it." I let out a heavy sigh. "I'm going to bed. Today wore me out and I am on the verge of losing my shit. Good night."

With that, I walk into my apartment, close the door, and prepare myself to unlock all my secrets.

CHAPTER *Eight*

BRIELLE

For the first time since my entire world collapsed, I sleep dreamlessly. Nothing haunts me, and I kind of like it. At least, I needed it more than anything because today starts the work.

I take a shower, loving the scent of the new brand of shampoo I apparently use, which isn't a brand I could buy from the drugstore. After I get dressed, I sit at my desk, rummaging through drawers for a notebook or something that might give me a hint about the last three years. All I find are the typical bills and a few birthday cards.

I smile when I see the one from Holden, Emmett, and Spencer. Since I was a little girl, they've always made a big deal of my birthday. Mostly because I was the most annoying person in the world as we approached it, but I still thought it was sweet.

My phone rings, and I glance at the screen before answering.

"Hello, Mother."

"Hello, Brielle. How are you this morning?"

I walk into the kitchen and grab a bottle of water. I fill her in about the key memory, Henry, and all the other mundane things. I start to ask her about the store, but she cuts in before I can.

"What are your plans for the day?"

"Spencer is picking me up so we can head to Portland."

"You sure you're up for that?"

I can feel the censure through the phone. "Yes, and even if I wasn't, I'd be going anyway. How are things at the store? Anything from the insurance company?"

My mother has only three great loves in her life: her children, my father, and her art store. She's lost my brother and almost lost me, my father, and I don't know if she can endure another.

"I spoke with the insurance adjuster, and he is putting the claim in today so I know what will be covered. In the meantime, I have the water mitigation people here, and Bruno is trying to salvage what he can. I just can't afford to lose everything."

"I'm sure you'll be able to rebuild it," I try to reassure her.

"I hope so. I put so much into it over the last five years. Selling repurposed wine bottles isn't easy, but we've done so much to make each piece unique. I can't replicate what we've lost."

I know that feeling. "Maybe you can't replace it, but you can make something even better."

Mom sighs. "Yes, but I also hate having to deal with this when I should be there with you."

She forgets she would have left in four days, so it isn't as if she'd planned to stay much longer anyway. "It's okay, really. Besides, I have Addy here until the end of the week, and Spencer and I will be working through my past. If I needed you here, I would tell you."

"Yeah right." Mom laughs.

"Okay, I normally wouldn't, but this time, I would."

There's a knock on my door, and I jump up. "I have to go, Mom. Spencer is here."

"Be careful, Brie. I love you very much."

"I love you too."

"Call me tonight and let me know how things went."

"I will. I love you."

We hang up, and I rush to the door, ready to see Spencer.

"Hey."

He smiles. "Hey, you look happy."

"I slept really well."

"Good."

He extends a breakfast sandwich, which I take gleefully. "You are a lifesaver."

"It's just breakfast."

"Yes, but . . . I don't have anything I don't have to cook, and I am starving."

"Well, we all know that you and the kitchen are not a match."

I roll my eyes. "You set the stove on fire one time and you get labeled a hazard."

One brow lifts. "One time? Try four."

"I have no memory of that," I say with a grin. I definitely remember them all, but this memory thing could play in my favor at least once.

Spencer laughs. "Are you ready, or do you want to eat first?"

"I was thinking . . ."

"Never a good sign."

I ignore him and continue. "I think you should go through the apartment with me. There are clues here, we all know that, but I am too emotional to look at things like you do."

"And how is that?"

"Like everything is a puzzle you need to put together to see the whole picture. I need you to help me find the pieces, and I'll see if I can assemble them. You're like the Yoda of reporters, and the things you uncovered were so out of left field no one else saw them. Maybe there's something here that points to what happened that I'd overlook but you wouldn't."

Spencer nods. "And if there's nothing here?"

"Well . . ." I fidget, considering my next comment carefully before I say, "Then maybe you can help me figure out who I was seeing before . . ." I gesture to my head and glance away.

"What makes you think you were seeing someone?" he asks.

"Because the cigar thing and then, under my bathroom sink, I found a box of . . ." I am hoping he won't make me say it because that would be mortifying.

"A box of? Tampons? Pads? What?"

I hate him sometimes. I groan. "Condoms. And it is open and some are missing."

He laughs and then turns his head.

"You ass! You knew what I was trying not to say!" I scold him.

"I had a guess, but it was really fun watching you try not to turn beet red. Valiant effort on your part."

Seriously, why do I like this man at all? It makes no sense. Okay, it does. He is insanely attractive, confident, and commands any room he walks into. Spencer can look at you, see more than anyone else, and never judge.

"Anyway, it's just a few things here and there that make me wonder if there is someone, even if just casually."

Spencer grabs his pocket notebook and writes something down.

"What are you writing?" I ask.

"I'm making notes of things you mention or do, which I'll likely be doing often. I think you should do the same. Even if you think something is irrelevant, you should write it down because it might actually be important. Then, when we agree it's time, we'll compare notes and see what we find, okay?"

"You want me to write notes about a box of condoms?" I ask with a brow raised.

"Ha. Ha. No, I want you to write down things you see, remember, think about. The more information we have to go over, the better."

"You're the expert."

He grins. "Yes, I am."

"Okay, but you should know that I seem to be developing trust issues. Everyone is withholding information from me. Before you do something annoying and point out that I also agreed to this course of action, I would like to say that I hate it and it's overwhelming."

He steps closer. "I understand that. I am a naturally distrusting person. In my job, I have to assume everything is a lie. But if we want this to work, we have to trust each other. I promise I won't lie to you, Brielle. I never have."

My heart races a little at his nearness. "I know, which is why I asked for your help."

He pulls me into his strong arms, and I close my eyes, listening to his heartbeat. "I'm honored you did. Even if it means I'm trailing you around for a few weeks."

I look up into those green eyes I know so well. "You think it'll take that long?"

"It could."

I feel awful. He has much more important things to do than retrace my life. "I'm sorry."

"For what?"

I shrug. "Being a pain in your ass again."

"Again? You never stopped." Spencer winks. "Come on, let's head out to Portland before we lose daylight and go back to the beginning." He leans down, kissing the top of my head.

I step back, turning to cover the blush on my face that always comes whenever he does anything even remotely affectionate. "Let's go . . . the truth awaits."

"Let's look at the facts." Spencer and I are sitting under one of the trees on my college campus. It was the first place I wanted to go because I can remember sitting in this very spot on the day of my graduation, talking to Isaac and Addy about what I wanted.

Even that day, I was sure that I didn't want to go to Portland with Henry and that Rose Canyon was where I belonged.

I tilt my face toward the sun, letting the warmth of the mid-morning rays soak into my skin. "Can we stop talking about everything for just a minute?" I ask.

My frustration over my lack of memory is making my head throb. Nothing new. Nothing exciting. Just memories from college, which I didn't lose.

"No. We are working."

My hair brushes my arms as I turn to him. "You have zero fun."

"I have fun."

"No, you don't—or, at least, you didn't."

"Since you don't really know my current level of fun, you're not one to talk."

I open my eyes and stick my tongue out. "See, no fun."

He sighs. "Would you like me to illuminate you on my many levels of fun?"

"The fact that you just offered to illuminate me about your levels of fun tells me everything. You have none."

He shifts forward. "I have many levels."

He has many levels of something right now. I tone that back, because he has zero levels of desire when it comes to me. "Do tell."

"I . . ." He stops, looking out at the quad. "Shit. I guess I have none."

I laugh and lie back. "See, funless Spencer Cross. Always serious and always breaking hearts."

"You can put that on my bio."

I turn my head, squinting to see his face. "It would at least be true."

"The truth is also here."

I guess he's right. I just am feeling defeated. Not that I really thought we would roll into Portland and suddenly my entire life would flash back, but I hoped it would. I wanted to come back to the familiar and find comfort in the unknown.

"Here's the truth . . . I remember nothing new. There. That's everything."

"Then we don't have time to sit around. We need to move on and keep working, not lie in the grass."

I sit up, my defensiveness flaring. "What would you like me to do? Tell you some bullshit that I suddenly remember? Oh, now I have it. After going to get coffee, I was walking down the road, and I met someone. He was tall, but funny thing, I can't remember his name, or what he looks like. Maybe you'd rather hear the story about when I came to see Henry to break up with him. Again, no details because I have none other than what I told you."

"Brie."

"No, you want a memory, I'll make one up for you."

Spencer cuts me off. "Stop. I'm not asking you to do that. I just want to help you remember."

"I want that too," I confess. "I want it way more than anyone could imagine, trying not to be resentful of everyone who refuses to tell me anything."

"And if we told you everything, would you believe it? Would that make it any easier or would you just end up more confused and frustrated? If I said you quit your job two days before the incident and decided to join the circus as a balloon artist. What would you say?"

My jaw drops but then I scoff. "That you're crazy."

"But why? We told you it's true."

I shake my head. "I would never."

"Would you? How do you know? You have no recollection of the person you were in the last three years. That's why it's imperative we don't tell you who you were. You will either remember or you'll create a new life." Spencer puts his notebook down. "Brielle, I know more than anyone how fleeting things are. I know what it's like to lose everything. I know what it's like to be left behind and forgotten about."

And he does. When he was a kid, his mother would drop him off at our house, promise him she'd come back the next morning, and then neglect to show up. Spencer would hear my mother on the phone, pleading with her not to do it, but nothing she said mattered. Even though he tried to hide it, I still saw how sad it would make him, and I always wanted to cheer him up. His mother was in and out of his life, only showing up when it was convenient for her. When being a mother wasn't something that interested her anymore, she would leave Spencer in my mother and father's care.

"You were never forgotten."

"It was a long time ago," he says dismissively. "I was making a point."

That may be the case, but I'm not letting it go so easily. "Spencer." I wait until he looks at me. "You were never forgotten. Not by the people who loved you."

"I know that."

"Not by me," I say softly.

His eyes find mine, and the way he's staring at me has my throat going dry. I would swear he wants to kiss me, which is crazy because Spencer doesn't look at me that way and we have never kissed . . . well, not like that.

He clears his throat, breaking the spell. "Your family saved me, and I will do anything for you guys."

I tuck my hair behind my ear. "We appreciate it."

Spencer rises and extends his hand to me. "Come on, let's go to the apartments you lived in on the other side of town. We never know what we may find."

CHAPTER *Nine*

BRIELLE

A whole lot of nothing. That was what we found today. I am worn out and over it all. Since my protective detail was in the middle of swapping out when I got back, I told Emmett to hang out, which then led to calling Holden. Now, the gang is here, minus my brother.

"Did you see Addy?" Holden asks Emmett.

"Yes, I was there loading the trailer for her."

Holden sighs. "I asked her today when she'd be back, and she said she didn't know. I really thought she'd change her mind and stay."

"And we wish you'd stay," Spencer counters.

Holden is a prominent doctor in Los Angeles. He moved there right after college and only comes to Rose Canyon once in a while to visit his aunt, who is the only member of his family left. He owns the clinic in town that handles most of our medical care, but he hired a staff to run it. When they told him about what happened to Isaac and me, he came home that night and has been overseeing my case since.

"I have to return to my cases."

"And you have to avoid your ex-wife," Emmett says with a smirk.

He and Jenna were *the* couple. They rivaled Addison and Isaac in every way. Jenna is stunning and ridiculously smart. She started a non-profit that helps thousands of at-risk children in Oregon. She and Holden got married their sophomore year of college and filed for divorce before Holden started med school.

"Jenna and I don't have any issues being in the same room."

Spencer snorts. "Yes, because it happens so often."

"And what about you?" Holden turns the tables. "How is your love life? Is model number forty still around, or did you move on to someone else?"

"My love life is just fine," Spencer says, lifting his beer in mock salute. "Why don't you ask Brielle about her day, Dr. Dumbass."

Holden rolls his eyes and turns to me. "I apologize, Brie. We should've asked. How was your day?"

"It was a waste," I complain as I lay my head back on the couch. "I should've stayed here and went through mail."

Emmett grabs a slice of pizza and flops into the chair. "Couldn't have been that bad."

"Oh, it was. We walked around Portland for what felt like hours and I didn't remember a thing. Nothing."

Holden brings each of us a soda and sits beside me. "It's not a science, Brie. We can't predict how the mind will work."

"Isn't that like, your entire job though?"

Spencer and Emmett both laugh.

"It would be if I were a neurologist," he says under his breath. "I'm managing your case because the medical staff here are a bunch of idiots."

"You hired them!" Emmett points out.

"I did, but I'm better. I can't wait to return to Los Angeles."

"Yes, back to LA, where everything is better, blah, blah." Spencer leans back, resting one ankle over his knee. "You could come home and help the people in this town, who could use your knowledge. And your aunt needs you."

This banter and conversation feels like home. Growing up, these guys were always at my house, laughing and talking over each other or finishing each other's sentences. They are family, and I hadn't realized how much I needed this until right now. Everything inside me is calm despite the grief of losing my brother that still weighs heavily on me.

The tenseness in Holden's spine says that Spencer struck a nerve, and Emmett steps in, eyes on Spencer. "Do you think today's investigation with Brie was a waste?"

"No. I think we got more clues than our pessimistic friend there does," Spencer says with a shrug.

"What clues?" I ask quickly.

"The ones you weren't paying attention to."

"Such as . . ."

Spencer puts the plate down. "Your body language. Things you did almost as if they were muscle memory. You remembered the password to the rewards program for a restaurant that hasn't been open more than a year. You stopped in front of the building where Henry works without knowing he works there."

My eyes widen. "Why didn't you tell me?"

"I just did," he says as if it's the most logical answer in the world.

I recall a building now. It was a brick-front that looked more like a store than an office building. I just stood there for a second, not really sure what it was that had stopped me. I had this feeling that I had been inside, but for the life of me, I couldn't figure out why I would have been.

I'd wanted to go inside.

Emmett speaks. "Careful, Spencer, we're veering a bit too close to giving her information."

"He didn't tell her which building," Holden replies. "The fact that she stopped in front of it is a good indication that the memory is there and not destroyed."

"I promise," I add, looking at Emmett, "no one has told me a damn thing." Much to my dismay.

"Brie, can you describe the building so we can see if it's the one Spencer thinks it is?"

I do that, talking about the large window in front and how there was a windchime on the left side of the awning. Even if it isn't the building where Henry works, there was something familiar about it that could mean something.

Spencer smiles. "That's the same one. It was the way your head tilted or your hand moved."

Holden nods. "You mentioned a place she had a password?"

"Yeah, we got lunch and there was a loyalty program." He turns to me. "You had no idea that restaurant was semi-new. You just put your password in."

As much as I'd love to call that a victory, I think he's wrong. "It's the same password I use for everything. I've been using it for years."

He shrugs. "I still think it matters."

Maybe, but I am going to say that last one was luck. There are still things I don't know, and I am hoping they'll come back sooner rather than later.

"So, we know that Spencer lives here now and isn't currently working. I know that Holden is still in Los Angeles. You are the big mystery to me, Em. You're the sheriff, which is comical since I seem to remember you were the one who heckled Sheriff Barley when he tried to break up a party."

Emmett smirks. "I can neither confirm or deny such a story."

"I can!" Spencer says. "He did it. And then he also let the air out of the tires so we could get away."

Emmett snorts. "That was you, asshat."

"Anyway"—Spencer rolls his eyes—"his misguided youth prepared him for this."

"And," Emmett draws the word out, "I am good at it."

"How long have you been back?" I ask.

He rubs his forehead, looking to Holden and then to me. "It's within your gap."

I groan. "How is being honest with me tampering with my memory? I didn't ask you to tell me the story, I just asked how long!"

I'm on my feet, anger pulsing through me. This sucks. I am so tired of this feeling as though I'm on the fringe of my whole life.

The three of them share a look and then Spencer is reaching for my arm. "We are all trying to give you what we can and also making sure no one missteps. Emmett especially since he will be called to testify once we find whoever did this."

Emmett puts his beer down. "Which is why I shouldn't be here. I should be more careful."

"Em," I say quickly, "I won't ask again. Please don't go. I'm sorry."

He gives me a warm smile. "I know, but Spencer is right. We will be called in, and we don't want to give the defense any reason to claim our testimony is tainted." Emmett pulls me in for a hug and kisses my cheek. "I'll see you soon."

My heart sinks, and a new type of sadness wraps around me. I want my life back.

Emmett leaves, and I stare at the door with tears falling down my cheeks.

"Brielle," Holden says softly as his hand rests on my shoulder. "Don't cry."

I turn with a laugh. "Why not? How much more do I need to lose? Isaac wasn't enough? Addison and Elodie have to go too? You're going to LA soon. Emmett can't be with me in case he's called to testify." I look at Spencer. "You'll get a job or a girlfriend. Don't you see? I have nothing! I have lost everything and don't even know why."

Holden doesn't offer me empty platitudes or assurances that it will be okay. He just pulls me in for a hug. After a minute, he grips my shoulders and pushes me back. "You have so much more than you're letting yourself admit, you just need to have a little faith, okay? It isn't going to be easy, and yes, you're going to get frustrated, but you aren't alone. You never have been." He wipes away the moisture on my cheeks and offers me a kind smile.

I hate that he's right. I'm being ridiculous and need to stop because my getting worked up isn't helping anything.

"You're probably right."

"I usually am."

"You're also an arrogant ass," I say with a smile.

"That is also true. However, in this case, I know what I'm talking about. You have to take care of yourself too, Brie."

I nod. "I will."

He lets out a long breath and steps back. "On that note. I am exhausted and still need to check on my aunt. I'll see you at your follow-up tomorrow. Spence, you want to walk out with me?"

Spencer looks to me and then shakes his head. "I'm going to stay and help Brie clean up."

"All right." Holden grabs his coat off the back of the chair and then shakes Spencer's hand. "Give me a call tomorrow."

After one last quick hug, Holden heads out. "And then there were two," I say, feeling shy.

"Just as it started."

Just as I always wanted it to be.

I shake my head, clearing the thought, and smile. "I am really exhausted, thanks for offering to help me clean this mess up."

"Of course." He clears his throat, and then we make quick work of tossing the paper plates, bottles, and empty pizza boxes into a trash bag.

There is a part of me that wants to work slower or make an excuse to get him to stay longer, but I tell myself it's just because I don't want to be alone with my thoughts.

Spencer stands in the doorway with the bag of trash in one hand and his notepad in the other. "I can pick you up tomorrow for your appointment, if you want."

I am not allowed to drive for a few more days, pending my next evaluation. I was going to ask Emmett to drive me, but I would much rather be with Spencer. "Are you sure?"

"I wouldn't offer if I wasn't."

"That would be awesome. Maybe after we're done, we can do a little more digging. We need to go through the apartment too."

"Why don't we take tomorrow off?" Spencer suggests.

"What? Why?"

"Because you may need time after your appointment. Who knows what tests they may run or whatever?" He runs his hand down his face. "It might be better if we plan for tomorrow to be a chill day."

I cross my arms over my chest and raise one brow. "Is that what you'd do in this situation?"

We both know it's not. Spencer is balls to the walls with everything he does. There is no slowing down or half speed. It's why he's so damn good at what he does.

"No, but I have more to worry about than myself."

"I promise, I will tell you if it's too much."

"Like you did just now?" he counters.

"Okay, you got me. I promise to do it going forward. I honestly was fine though. It's just all the talk of people leaving. It sometimes feels as though the world is going forward and I'm in reverse."

"I felt like that when the guys all went to college and I took the first semester off so I could go look for my mother. Everyone was a step ahead. They were talking about dorm rooms and classes while I was going through shelters and looking for her in the morgue."

"I'm sorry you never found her."

Spencer looks away. "I did, but it was about a year ago."

Oh no. "Spencer . . . I'm so . . ."

"Don't be sorry. Trust me, based on what I saw, it was better that way."

"How did you handle it?" I ask and then hate myself. How do I think he handled it? Regardless of the fact that she was a horrible mother, he still loved her. "That was insensitive and stupid. I'm sorry for your loss, Spencer. Truly. I hated when people said that to me, but I get it now."

"What?"

"That saying. I'm sorry because I can't heal your heart. I'm sorry that you're hurting and I can't make it go away. People said it after my dad died, and it took until I lost Isaac to really get what they were saying. So, I'm sorry for your loss, and I am sorry that it hurt."

"It did hurt for a bit, but then I remembered that we all have the same ending. No matter what roads we take, there is only one outcome. Our journey is what makes life worth a damn. My mother made her choices and I did as well. Her death really caused me to reevaluate my life. I stopped caring about the things I wasn't doing and put my energy into what I was doing." The muscles in my chest grow tighter as his voice drops lower. "I made the choice to give everything to what matters, no more half-measures. It's all or nothing. That's how we go forward."

I look down at my feet and see a puddle on the ground. "Shit!"

"What?" Spencer's gaze drops to the leaking garbage bag before he shifts it out into the hallway instead of the doorway.

I rush into the kitchen, looking for paper towels or a rag, but don't see anything. I start opening cabinets and drawers until I finally find a few dish towels. When I grab a handful of them, something falls out onto the floor, but I ignore it and rush back to Spencer.

"I need to wash my hands," he says once the mess is mopped up.

We go back in the kitchen and take turns doing that. Then I remember the object that flew out. I look around and see a black box in the corner. I grab it, wondering why the hell a jewelry box was in my kitchen drawer.

Spencer looks over. "What is that?"

"I don't know. It was in my drawer, and when I grabbed the rags, it flew out." I slowly lift the lid, and when I see what is inside, my heart drops. My eyes lock on his, and a million questions swirl, but only one comes out. "Why do I have an engagement ring in my kitchen and who gave it to me?"

CHAPTER *Ten*

SPENCER

She found it.

Shit.

She found the ring.

I hid it there in a panic, knowing she doesn't typically go into the kitchen for anything. I could've taken it home. I could've placed it in the drawer next to my bed, but I needed for it to be in her possession, even if she didn't know it existed.

I wait for a beat, praying she remembers, but from the panic in her eyes, I know she doesn't. Once again, I have to pretend that I'm just as clueless as she is and pray that something will remind her of all we are and what we've shared.

"I don't know," I say, willing her to look at me and see. To recall the tears that flowed from those blue eyes as she smiled and nodded, unable to form words.

But Brielle has forgotten everything, and I'm here, praying that even if she doesn't ever remember our past, she'll fall in love with me again.

"I am . . . engaged?"

"Well, you have a ring, but I don't know if you're engaged."

She places the box down without closing it and stares at the three-carat oval diamond nestled inside as it mocks me.

"I have a ring. A very, very beautiful ring."

"It seems you do. Maybe you stole it and that's why you were almost killed." I attempt a joke, needing some levity to keep myself together.

"Yes, I'm sure I'm a jewelry thief."

"Emmett's right across that hall if you want me to go get him so you can confess your crimes."

"Shut up," Brie says, finally laughing a little. "Spencer, I think I'm actually engaged." She pauses and then grabs the ring. "The condoms. The cigar. Now the ring. It's clear there's someone in my life, and now I'm really wondering who he is and why he hasn't shown up yet. If I were engaged to someone who went radio silent for this long, the worry would break me."

He's more than breaking, he's shattered.

"Maybe he is doing what he knows is best for you."

"But how? How can he survive not coming to me and saying that we're engaged?"

He is wondering the same thing. Our entire relationship has remained a secret the last nine months. None of our friends know, and so, no one but me has to pretend otherwise.

"I can't answer that," I tell her the only truth I can. I can't tell her anything, and forcing myself to hold back the words is torture.

"I know you can't. I mean, even if you do know the guy, which I doubt you do, you can't tell me."

"Well, it's one more mystery we can add to our list. Is there anything that you can remember when you look at the ring?"

She pulls it from the box, staring at it while I wait.

When she slips it back on her finger, I almost lose it.

I want to scream at her, tell her it's me and I'm fucking dying here. That night was the best of our entire life.

I wait. All the while, willing her to remember it. To remember her tears and happiness the first time it was placed there.

But when she looks at me, I see the sadness. "No."

As much as Brielle hates this, I would argue it's worse for me. When I see that ring, I remember the pink dress she wore the night I asked her and how we drove out to the beach for dinner. I had a picnic packed, and I held her in my arms as we watched the sunset, feeling like the world finally made sense. For so many years, I searched for something real, and once I found it, it was snatched away from me.

When this started between us, it wasn't supposed to turn serious. I should've known, though, that Brielle would be a force that would conquer my heart.

When I returned from my last assignment, two years ago, I was fucked in the head. The things I saw, the things that I went through, tore me apart, but she healed me. Day by day, she found a way to get through to me, love me, even when I didn't think I deserved it.

Isaac and Addy were trying to get pregnant. Being the best friend and self-appointed uncle, I figured it was as good a time as any to head home for a bit. I missed my friends, and if I'm being honest, I missed Brielle. Not that I even understood why I did, since Isaac was my best friends, but I wanted to see her.

We started off as nothing and she became everything.

Now, it's all gone. Every kiss. Every touch. Every fucking memory was erased.

She pulls the ring off her finger and places it in the box. "I don't want to wear this."

I don't want any of this.

"Okay."

I walk over and close the box. We're so close that I can feel the heat of her body. Sometimes, I think she can sense what I feel, and I want her to right now. I want her to feel the longing I have to pull her in my arms and kiss her senseless, for her to know how desperately I wanted to hold her while she was in that hospital bed.

When she asked for Henry, I died inside. The way she smiled at him broke me. She remembered them, but she forgot us.

"I have a headache."

I would give anything for that to be the only ache I have.

"You should take your medication and rest," I suggest, not knowing what else to say.

"How do I rest knowing this? Also, where the fuck is he? How does he not realize that I'm missing from his life? How can he be okay not talking to me in weeks?"

He isn't okay. He's in absolute fucking agony.

"You have no idea, Brie. He could be dealing with something and not know."

She chews on her thumb. "Maybe he doesn't live here. Maybe . . . maybe we have to keep this a secret so he can't come." Panic flares in her eyes. "What if he's married? Please, God, tell me I'm not engaged to a married man. Or worse, what if he is who killed my brother?"

"Relax. If either of those are true, we'll figure out how to handle it."

She grips my forearms. "I can't be that girl. I can't steal someone else's husband. And if my fiancé is who killed my brother, then I will never forgive myself."

"Easy, Brie. You will do the right thing."

"Every time we get a clue and get the tiniest bit excited, I end up with a thousand more unanswered questions. It's like the hits just keep coming."

"Then pick up the bat and swing back. You can continue to be the victim in this, or you can choose to fight back." Her blue eyes widen as she stares at me. "The girl I know was never willing to back down. She would push her way through any obstacle and kick down doors until she was satisfied."

Brielle drops her hands. "And how do I do that? How do I fight when I am blindfolded, Spencer? How do I claw my way through the thick haze that makes it impossible to know if I'm going in the right direction?"

The crack in her voice at the end almost has me telling her everything, but I know I can't. So, I give her the only thing I'm allowed to at this point. "You take my hand," I say, lacing our fingers together, relishing in her touch. "And you don't do it alone."

"You look like a bag of dog shit," Holden says as I enter my apartment.

I flip him off and head into the kitchen for a glass and ice. I need whiskey tonight. "How much longer are you staying?" I ask as I unscrew the top to the bottle.

"A few more days. I really hoped that Brielle would be in a better place before I left, but I can't stay too much longer."

"Lucky me."

"Yes, I think you are," Holden agrees.

"That was sarcasm."

"I'm aware, but sarcasm can also hold the truth."

I roll my eyes. He goes back to reading while I try to drink my pain away, which actually isn't working. Not whiskey or anything else will take away the ache in my chest, and I can't even talk about it to anyone.

One of the agreements Brielle and I had was that no one would know about our relationship. At first, it was just sex. We had no intention to start a serious relationship, but we were stupid to think that was even possible. Brielle could never be a casual hookup. She's everything.

Then we didn't want to say anything because it was new and we didn't want it to cause problems if we didn't work out.

Then it was too perfect, too right, and we didn't want the real world to come in and ruin it. I wanted her all to myself for a little longer. We laughed at the way no one figured it out. We enjoyed the solace that came from living in this bubble.

Like all bubbles, ours was bound to pop, and we wanted to control when that happened. We wanted to be the ones to tell everyone before it exploded. I wanted everyone to know how much I loved her. I proposed, and we agreed that the time to hide was over and it didn't matter about my past relationships, Isaac's approval or disapproval, our age difference, or the fact that everyone thought Brielle and I were more like siblings than anything else. We planned to tell Isaac and Addison everything.

Now, we'll never get that chance, and I may have lost her as well.

Holden grabs the bottle and pours himself two fingers. "Are you all right?"

"I'm fine."

"You don't look fine."

"I am."

"Did something happen with Brielle when we left?"

Yes, but I can't tell him. I want to, but how can I tell him when she doesn't remember any of it? It wouldn't be right. I also don't want to hear a single one of his opinions on it.

I have no disillusions that they'll handle us hiding our relationship for almost a year very well.

However, I have to tell them about the ring and then lie about it.

"Brielle is fine. She was a little shaken up. She found an engagement ring in a drawer."

Holden's eyes widen. "What?"

"Yeah."

"And she didn't remember anything?"

"Nope."

He leans back, swirling the amber liquid for a minute. "I would've thought something that big would have triggered a memory."

"It didn't."

"Wow." He pauses. "And you don't know the guy?"

"What guy?"

He huffs. "The guy who gave her the ring she wasn't wearing. Maybe she didn't say yes."

No, she said yes. She said yes so many times her throat hurt. She wasn't wearing it because no one was supposed to know for a few more days.

"Maybe."

"Dude, you're like the most observant asshole I know, and you have no clue who the hell Brie was with?"

"It's not like I stalk her."

"No, but—"

"It doesn't seem like Addison or her mother know either, why is that?"

Holden rubs his temple. "I don't know. I guess none of us ever really know what people are hiding, but it's crazy." He shakes his head and then his eyes flash to me. "Do you think it's whoever killed Isaac? Maybe Isaac found out about it, confronted the guy, and that is what got him killed?"

"It's possible," I lie to my best friend. "But I have no idea who killed Isaac."

The more likely scenario is that Isaac would have killed me when I told him. No one in the world was more protective of Brielle than he was. He hated her boyfriend in high school and wanted to rip Henry's throat out whenever he saw him.

"No, but if she said yes to the guy, you have to admit that it is completely possible that Isaac didn't handle the news well, especially if she'd been hiding it from him."

I smile. "No man would ever be good enough for Brie—definitely not to him."

Holden chuckles. "I felt bad for her when we were kids. Can you imagine what Elodie would've endured? It's sad she won't get to know that."

"She still has us, and we're much older and more cynical now."

"No shit. I don't know, being old and cynical has its drawbacks too."

"How so?"

"Life. Family. The idea of having nothing but a job to cling to. You get that," Holden says with a shrug. "You have taken time off to figure your life out."

And look where I am. "It wasn't exactly like that. I basically had no choice. I can't write, Holden. I have tried to write, what? Forty different stories? I sit there, stare at the screen, waiting for the words that refuse to come. I've tried every trick in the book and nothing. I'm not taking time off, I'm fucking blocked."

Holden sighs through his nose. "I'm sorry. I know it's not the same, and I know how it feels not to see progress. I'm struggling with the idea of leaving because I hoped Brielle would be a bit further along. The longer this goes, the more I fear it won't return or it'll be fragments. Then what, you know?"

"No, I don't know."

A long sigh comes from him, and he puts the glass on the coffee table. "If she does remember what happened, the defense is still going to use her memory loss against her. And that's only if they get a chance to argue a case at all."

"I think that's what makes this so much harder to see her go through. Are they still trying to find a link between her office being trashed and the attack?"

"They are, but Emmett is being tight-lipped about it."

Brielle's office was ransacked, according to the information I got this morning. Papers were thrown around, her files completely ransacked, and the hard drive from her computer was missing. Her coworkers are trying to figure out what's missing, but it's a mess.

"It's all really fucked up. I'm worried about Brie, Addison, you, Emmett, and everyone here."

That one part causes me to jerk back. "Why the hell are you worried about me?"

"Besides the fact that you were close with Isaac and came back here mostly for him. Then there's the whole thing with you and Brielle. You guys need to be careful."

My palms start to sweat. "About?"

"That you don't get too close. She's always had that crush on you and it would be easy for her to form an attachment while she's vulnerable."

The fact that he's even concerned about it gives me hope. I want that. I want her to look at me that way again, and if I can't have the last year, I want the next one. "What makes you think that?"

"Just something Emmett said."

I really wish he'd stop having me fish for info. I know Holden well enough that part of him is enjoying this, but it's making me unduly paranoid that he and Emmett know something they shouldn't. Asking him what Emmett said would be like throwing myself right into whatever trap he thinks he's baiting me with, so I let it go. "You and Emmett are always worried about dumb shit."

"And you are always taking risks."

I decide to move off the topic of Brielle and point out the obvious. "To be good at my job, it's kind of a requirement."

"Oh, and are you planning to work ever again?"

I run my hand over my face. "I'm trying."

"Be honest for a second, Spencer, you have always wanted what you think you can't have. Then, once you get it, because you always do, you tire of it. It's why you go for these models and actresses. They are a quest. You've now peaked in your professional career and it scares you."

Everything he said is true. I'm fucking terrified. I want to write. I miss the hunt of the story and the thrill of winning a Pulitzer. That's gone.

And as for the models, he was right, it was why I dated them and also because they were in it for the same thing. When Brielle and I took that step, it was different. She didn't care about my success. She just loved me.

"You shouldn't talk. You and Emmett aren't any better. You both run, I'm just faster."

"How do I run?"

"When the fuck were you back here last? What about your marriage? What about all the damn things you avoid dealing with, Holden?" I'm livid. I am so out of line, but I don't give a shit anymore. "You act like I want any of this but I don't! I was moving in the right direction, doing everything right, and I lost it."

Holden's nose flares for a second and then he shakes his head. "I don't come back here because I see my parents' deaths when I do. I lost Jenna because I wasn't man enough to fight for her, I let her go without even thinking twice. I am not saying I'm better, but I also want more for the people in my life."

"As do I."

"I look at the life that Isaac had, and I don't even understand it. He was married, had Elodie, was doing what he loved. He had no extra money and was the happiest of all of us and look at what happened. He didn't take risks and none of us spent hours worried over what would happen to him. He had what he needed," Holden says, reaching for his glass.

We both fall silent and drain our glasses. "Maybe we should've worried about him more then," I note.

"Maybe, but he would've told us to shut up and that he had everything he needed."

"Because he was stubborn."

Holden laughs. "He was." There is a beat of silence before he sighs and adds, "I honestly don't know how to feel anymore. I deal with death on a daily basis, but I never thought it would be one of us. Not him and not like that. He was the only one of us who was truly happy."

I was happy. No, I was more than happy. I was elated, overjoyed, thrilled, jubilant, and every other synonym there is for happy. I was so in love with where I was that I couldn't even see the ground until I slammed into it.

One name. One fucking name of someone else and I thought my heart had been ripped from my chest. Henry.

She forgot everything we shared. Every plan we had, but she remembered Henry.

As much as I understand that it's not her fault, it killed me. I was fifteen again, waiting for my mother to pick me . . . just one damn time, only to have to watch her pick someone else. Someone who she loved more than she loved her son.

Brielle was never that way. She always chose me.

I don't speak to Holden, choosing to stare at my empty glass instead. He rises and slaps his hand on my shoulder. "I'm going to sleep. It's late and being around you is depressing."

"Thanks."

"You're welcome." He gets to the doorway to the guest room and turns to me. "Hey, I meant what I said earlier. What you're doing with Brie? It's good. Just be careful and pull away if you see her growing too close. Last thing we all need is her falling in love with you. Not that we worry you'll ever reciprocate because, Lord knows you'll never be serious with a woman, but she has enough to deal with right now."

Holden closes the door, and I pour myself another glass of whiskey. "Yeah, you should worry because I love her more than my own life."

CHAPTER *Eleven*

BRIELLE

I can't stop crying as overwhelming grief crushes me. I went to call my brother an hour ago to talk about this ring sitting on my counter. I dialed the phone as though he were alive, and when his voice mail picked up, the truth slammed into me with the force of a truck. He's gone.

I will never hear his voice again. I'll never get to share anything with him again. All I have is the past, and part of that has been erased.

So today, I'm choosing to wallow in my grief.

There is a knock on my door, but I don't care. I am drowning in my self-pity and plan to stay here.

"Brie?" Addison's voice is on the other side. "I know you're home. Your security team sold you out, so open the door."

I wipe my face and make my way to the door. When I open it, Addison immediately pulls me into her arms. "I thought you might need this," she says, clutching me tighter.

I lose it harder, crying and clinging to probably the last person I should be, but Addy is family. She's my sister in every way, and I need her right now.

Her hands rub my back as we stand in my entryway, holding on to one another as we sob.

After a few minutes, we break apart, red-eyed and snotty-nosed. I grab a few tissues before handing her the box, and we take a minute to collect ourselves.

Then we start to laugh.

It's not funny. Nothing is really funny, but yet, it's as though there was no other choice.

The door across the hall flies open, and Emmett steps into the hallway. "Are you okay?"

We giggle even harder. "We're fine."

He raises a brow. "What's funny?"

I try to calm down enough to speak, but the emotions are uncontrollable as they wreak havoc on my body. "Isaac is dead . . . and I called him . . ." I have to stop between the fits of laughter. "And Addy is leaving tomorrow."

Addison snorts as her head falls back. "Oh, and Brie can't remember!"

I drop to the floor, laughing and rolling back and forth. "I have no memories!" I continue as though this is the best joke I've ever heard. "And I might be engaged!"

Emmett steps back, looking a little afraid as he glances to where Spencer stands in the doorway, saying, "I think they've lost their minds."

"What are they laughing at?" Spencer asks as he moves closer.

Addy laughs so loudly Emmett cringes. "Our lives are horrible, that's what!"

Spencer sighs heavily, dropping his notebook on the counter next to the ring. "Your lives are not horrible. Here, get up." He grasps my hand and pulls me to my feet before helping Addy up.

She wipes at her face again and huffs. "You have no idea what we're going through. Either of you. So, yeah, we might be losing our minds because our hearts are already gone."

"Exactly," I back her up.

Emmett shakes his head. "I am not pretending to know what you feel, but we miss Isaac too. He was a brother to us. It might not be the same, but it isn't any easier to deal with."

Addison's head drops, and she nods. "I know. Some days are just harder, and when I heard Isaac's phone ring, I lost it. I had a feeling she might be as well." Then she looks to me. "Did you say you might be engaged? What the hell are you talking about?"

I look to Spencer and then Emmett. While Addison didn't tell me anything, she did at the same time. She doesn't know I am engaged, so either I am a jewelry thief or I never told her. Neither of those options seem likely though.

I walk to the counter and hand it to her. "I found it last night."

Her eyes widen. "Where?"

"In my kitchen drawer, of all places."

Addison shakes her head. "Why . . . who gave this to you?"

Spencer speaks before I can. "Do you know what that ring is?"

"No, I honest to God have no idea. I am truly confused."

"So, this isn't a memory that no one is telling me?" I ask.

"I am just as lost as you are."

I don't know whether I should be happy or sad about that. "If I were engaged to someone, I would've told Addy," I explain. "So, whatever this ring is, it's not mine."

Emmett starts to pace. "Then why would you have it?"

"Maybe Isaac bought it for Addy and I was holding it?" I suggest.

Addison laughs. "You're insane. There's not a chance in hell that my husband could've afforded this. We live on a teacher's salary and my income. We weren't in the poor house, but we weren't able to get a rock like this. Not to mention, the ring I wear was my grandmother's."

I knew that. "Maybe it's a friend's?"

The three of them look to each other. "It doesn't seem likely," Emmett counters.

"It's more likely that it is yours and you put it there for a reason," Spencer explains. "If you were keeping it safe, you'd probably have it somewhere like a closet or your jewelry box."

The phone on my desk rings as I am sitting there, admiring the beautiful ring on my finger. Isaac's name shows on the screen.

"Hey," I answer the call.

"You ready?"

I pull the ring off, place it gently back in the box, and slip it into the bottom drawer.

I lift my gaze to Emmett. "The ring was in my office."

"What?"

Addison clears her throat. "No, it was in the kitchen."

I shake my head. "I remembered it. I had it on at work. It's a blip of a memory, but I put it in my desk. The bottom right drawer."

"When was that?" Spencer asks.

"I have no idea. I just . . . I remembered it."

Emmett looks to Spencer. "Maybe she kept it there, and that's what someone was looking for?"

"Why would she leave it at work overnight?" Spencer asks. "It's more likely she kept it at home."

"Or someone knew that," Emmett says pointedly. "It could be connected to another event."

"What other event?" I ask.

Emmett groans before answering. "Your office was ransacked. We are trying to get a list of what is missing, but since you didn't have an assistant or anything, it is hard to tell."

I gasp. My office was ransacked, and no one told me. I turn to Spencer. "You knew this?"

"Yes."

"And you didn't tell me?"

"I'm not supposed to talk to you about anything that's happened in or related to anything that's happened in the last three years. Also, I didn't want to upset you or get you worried."

I scoff. "Yes, and finding out like this is so much better."

Emmett places his hand on my arm. "We are looking into it, but it could be what they were initially looking for. Spencer, you were there the day before that, did anything seem out of the ordinary?"

He shakes his head. "Nope."

Great. Nothing to worry about other than my office being trashed, a ring that they may have wanted, and a mystery fiancé I may or may not have. All of this is making me sick to my stomach. If the person who gave me the ring wanted it back so badly, who is to say they didn't check my apartment too.

"If someone was in my office, do you think they were in here too? What if they went through my things? Who had access?"

"We were all in here, Brie," Spencer finishes. "We had to come in before you got home to put the security stuff in place."

"Do you think whoever tossed my office was too?"

"It's possible, but if anyone else found that ring, they'd probably take it, not put it in your kitchen," Spencer says before turning to Emmett. "What do you think?"

Emmett shrugs. "It's definitely not *impossible*. Considering nothing was destroyed here, I doubt it. If she's with some guy, he may have a key and was here before we showed up. He couldn't have gotten in after because we changed the locks and there's been surveillance. But why go through all the trouble of coming over here and getting the ring, only to hide it in a drawer? Why wouldn't the person take it when they left? If the ring was in her office, then he wouldn't come here. Honestly, it would help if we knew when her memory was."

"Considering we have no idea who she's engaged to or when he proposed, it's impossible to nail down," Spencer adds.

They continue to volley different scenarios, and I tune them out.

My head is spinning. Why would my would-be fiancé hide the ring? Did he not want me to know about him? It would make sense because no one can tell me anything. So, if he heard about my condition, then he knows I don't remember him. Since I wasn't wearing it, that suggests either I didn't say yes or maybe we decided to wait to tell people. Both options make sense.

God, all of this is so confusing.

"Brie?"

"Yeah?" I turn to Addy.

"Did you hear us?"

"I stopped listening," I confess.

Emmett chuckles. "You're the same as ever. A brat."

I stick my tongue out.

"Anyway," Addison says, "I don't know anything, but Spencer, maybe you can track down where the ring was purchased. You'll have to keep Brielle out of it if you do find it. Sorry, Brie."

I shrug. At this point, I didn't have any hopes they would tell me anyway. "I mean, it's great that you might have some connection to a guy I may or may not be engaged to who might also know what happened to my brother and me. What girl doesn't want to think she was engaged to someone who killed her brother and tried to kill her. It's like, the best fantasy ever."

Spencer nudges me. "Relax, it could be nothing, but we're going to make sure. Right now, there isn't any reason to think the two events are related."

"Yup."

There is a long, almost uncomfortable stretch of time before he asks, "Are you still up for today? If so, I figured we'd take a ride."

"I had plans to wallow, but sure. We'll go, and I'll continue to remember nothing. It'll be fun."

Spencer doesn't give me the reaction I was pushing for. Instead, his smile is bright. "Good."

I sigh and walk over to Addy. "I'll be there in the morning to say goodbye."

"I'll make sure I don't leave until then."

We give each other a hug, and Emmett and Addison leave. I grab my purse and walk toward the door. "You ready?"

"To spend the day with you? Absolutely."

Glad someone is.

We ride out to the beach, which is strange because I don't remember this being significant in my life. Instead of walking down onto the sand, we move to stand in front of his car and watch the waves. "Why are we here?"

He shrugs. "You liked the beach when we were kids."

I laugh. "I liked when you, Emmett, and Holden would take your shirts off. That's what I liked."

Spencer's hands move to the hem of his shirt, and before I can say anything, it's off and tossed through his open window. "There. What about now?"

Focusing on his face is a lost cause. There's no way I can stand here and not take in the man before me. He's tall, blocking out the sun behind him, and my eyes travel from his beautiful face to his magnificent chest. The deep lines etched across his perfect skin provide a map down to his stomach where six boxes of hardness lie. Spencer has aged so freaking well. My fingertips itch to touch him and outline every rise and fall on his lean, hard body.

Oh, how much I want that. I always have.

I may have told him it was all of them, but I only ever saw him.

I would sit on the blanket, my lower lip between my teeth as I stared.

I clear my throat, pushing away the desire pooling in my core. "Just like old times," I say, hoping I sounded indifferent.

From the grin that forms, I failed. "Good. So, let's head down there and talk."

Spencer reaches back into the window, and I silently mutter a prayer.

Please put your shirt back on.

He doesn't. Instead, he grabs his stupid notebook and a bag.

"What's in there?"

"Food," he responds and starts to walk down toward the water.

I can do this. I can spend time with Spencer—half naked—and not ogle him. It will be a piece of cake.

With my spine straight and my mindset, I head to where he's spreading out a blanket. He motions for me to sit, and I do, tucking my legs under me.

"Go ahead," he says.

"And do what?" I ask, bewildered.

"You wanted to sit at the college with the sun on your face. Do it now. Enjoy your moment, Brie."

As much as I wanted to wallow and feel sorry for myself, his suggestion is far too tempting to pass up. And sitting here, in the warmth of the beginning of summer, I realize it's exactly what I need—to feel the breeze and soak in the heat that isn't so stifling I can't breathe.

The warmth of the sun is a reminder that I'm alive and okay. The salt air fills my nose, and the seagulls crow in the back, giving us the beach soundtrack that I know so well. I lean back on my elbows, looking around at the landscape that has been a constant in my life. I can remember those cliffs, the mountains in the back with caps that will be covered in snow very soon. For a few minutes, I allow myself to pretend that everything in my life will find its place. There are absolutes like the sun will rise and the moon will follow, so I cling to that even though nothing feels like it's where it belongs.

"Thank you," I say with my eyes closed.

"For?"

I look toward him. "For being you."

"That's the first time a woman has ever thanked me for that."

"Then you are clearly with the wrong women."

His lips turn up. "Is that so?"

I tilt my face back up to the light. "If they don't know how great you are, then yes."

"Maybe I don't want them to know I'm great or maybe you're a headcase who doesn't know how terrible I am."

A soft giggle escapes, and I sit up. "You have never been terrible."

"I think that you have a very skewed perception of me," Spencer says with deprecation.

Nothing bothers me more about him than this. He is always telling everyone how unworthy he is. Compliments are like barbs to him, and I wish that his mother were still alive so I could rip her apart. The things she convinced him of are deplorable.

"I know that you think that, but you're wrong. You've always been special. Your mother was wrong, and I hate that you still carry that around," I tell him, staring into his eyes, wanting him to really hear me.

Spencer shifts. "I don't know what you're talking about."

"Yes you do. You said you'd never lie to me, didn't you?"

"I meant that about your memory."

"Should have been more specific, but it's too late now. It's officially on the record as a blanket promise," I counter.

"And what about you?" he asks. "Are you going to tell me all your secrets if I ask?"

I sigh. "Isn't that the entire point of this? I have to trust you with everything if we plan to figure out my missing life."

"Yes, I guess it is."

"So, I want the same, and I want more than anything for you to tell me the truth. Do you really think you're a bad guy or unworthy?"

Spencer's eyes turn to the waves, watching as they crash upon the sand, and he considers my question. I start to doubt that he is going to answer me, but then he says, "Every woman I've ever loved has forgotten about me. I don't know where there's value there."

My hand moves before I have time to steady myself. I rest my palm on his cheek, waiting for him to look at me. "Spencer, your mother didn't forget, she just wasn't strong enough to do the right thing. And as for any woman you've loved who has forgotten about you, well, she's an idiot and unworthy of you. There is no one like you, and that makes you unforgettable. And I would know, I have memory loss."

He snorts. "I appreciate that."

"Who did you love?" I ask and wish I hadn't. "Forget that I asked, it's none of my business."

"Consider it forgotten. Not to mention, we're here to talk about you." He nudges me.

"Yes, that's always fun."

"So, you and Henry . . ."

I blink, confused as to why he would ask me about that. "What about Henry?"

"You don't think he's who gave you the ring?"

"You do?"

He shakes his head. "No, but that's who you remembered and wanted."

"Only because I woke up as the me from three years ago. But, to answer your question, no, I don't think he proposed. If he did, and that was the ring he gave me, there's not a chance in hell he wouldn't have asked for it back. Plus, what you and Emmett said makes sense."

"Emmett made sense?"

I smile. "It has been known to happen on occasion. Really, the only two options that make sense are that I put it there or the guy who gave it to me did."

Spencer leans back on his elbows. "You're right."

"So, world-class-investigator Cross, how do we solve the riddle?"

"Lie down next to me," he instructs.

"Umm, why?"

"Just do it, Brie." Spencer's voice is part annoyance, part amusement.

I grumble as I do as he asks.

"Now, I want you to keep your eyes closed."

I turn my face to him, eyes flying open. "Why?"

"Jesus, you're exasperating."

"You're cryptic."

"I have been all around the world, dealt with mob bosses, politicians, royalty, and terrorist leaders who are less suspicious than you."

"I doubt that," I reply.

He glares at me, but there's humor underneath. "I swear, Brie, I am not going to hurt you. When I was in Algeria, I interviewed this woman, Yamina, who was known to be an incredible healer. People from all around the country came to her to heal their ailments. The story was that she could touch someone who was suffering, and within days, they'd start to recover. Miraculously. Of course, I thought it was all complete bullshit."

"Of course, because you're the most pessimistic person I know." I laugh.

"Realistic. There's a difference," Spencer corrects me. "I had a point."

I extend my hand, insinuating he should get to it then.

There is a low huff of annoyance before he goes on. I love irritating him. "Anyway, I stayed there for weeks, ready to document every trick she did. I was so sure I could debunk the claims that I extended my stay for a month. Sometimes she could help with an herb. Other times, it was an elixir that she once said was nothing more than water with ginger and some other natural ingredients. Most of the people she touched weren't physically healed, though. What she did was open their minds to understanding what was broken. She would spend hours with them, calming them, allowing them all of her attention. Yamina made them feel seen and she gave them hope, healing them on a spiritual level. She was patient beyond anything I've ever seen. I can't explain it because there are parts of it that I still don't know how they are possible."

"So, you want to heal my spirit?" I ask, mocking him a little.

"I wish I could. Hell, I thought about flying you somewhere to find someone like her."

"Is she not still healing people?"

Spencer's eyes fall to the pattern on the blanket. "She passed away about a year ago."

"You sound sad about that."

"I am. She was a remarkable woman. Far more intuitive than anyone I've ever met. She never judged anyone who came to her. She had the most incredible capacity to love everyone. The more broken someone was, the more her heart grew for them."

I can't help but wonder . . . "Did she heal you?"

Now his eyes meet mine. "She helped me see what I was missing. So, in a way, yes."

"What were you missing?"

"Love."

CHAPTER *Twelve*

SPENCER

I'm teetering on a very precarious line. One step and I'll fuck everything up, which I can't do.

It's just that, being with her here, in the same place that I proposed, is too much. The way her hair catches in the breeze. How the sunlight dances across her skin makes me want to haul her in my arms and never let go.

Brie seems to be taken aback, and she looks away. "So, you have someone?" Her voice is hesitant.

"There's someone I love, yes."

Not a lie.

Her smile is forced. "Good, but I hope she's not the girl you were complaining about."

There are these times, like now, when I swear she feels it too. The pull to each other and the fact that we have history, even if she doesn't remember it. The tone of her voice that sounds almost hurt that I love someone or how her eyes aren't quite meeting mine because she's trying to hide the emotions.

It's there, under the fog, it just needs to lift.

I choose my words carefully. "And if she was?"

"Then you need to get over her and find someone else."

Never. I will never get over you.

"That's like me telling you to just remember."

Brie turns onto her back and closes her eyes. "Well, I'll let you do your mind trick so we can see if it works. Who knows, the next time I open my eyes, I may remember everything."

"Let's not put that much trust in me," I say under my breath.

Yamina worked with a man in the village who had been injured and still struggled with his past. He could remember, but that was the issue. He needed to forget because the pain was too much. The accident that took his family from him was so painful, he was literally dying from it.

I am going to have Brielle try that same meditation Yamina had me do and pray I have even an ounce of her powers.

"Keep your eyes closed the entire time. I want you to relax, keep your breathing steady, and try not to focus on anything until I tell you to."

"You know that I'm going to see Holden's friend that Cora suggested who does this too, right?"

"Holden's friend isn't into holistic medicine, he's a therapist. But let's pretend this is practice. Now, close your eyes and relax."

"So, what do I think about?"

"Let the thoughts come and go. Whatever they are. Just let it go in and out, not lingering on anything."

Brielle lets out a deep breath, her clenched hands relax, and she nestles deeper into the makeshift pillow of sand under her.

I take a second and just watch her, staring at her long blonde hair fanning out around her. I would do anything to kiss her or feel her body against mine, but I need to be patient.

This isn't exactly something I'm good at.

"Deep breath," I coax her. "In and out. Relax and listen to my voice." She does as I ask, giving me her trust. I move closer, lying on my side, and brush my finger down her face. "Easy, just breathe."

Yamina always kept a hand on her patient. She was always soothing them, so I'm allowing myself this small bit.

Minutes go by, and I continue to speak softly and caress her. Brielle is relaxed enough that I want to try to push her memory.

"Tell me what's in your thoughts."

"They keep moving," she whispers.

"What do you see right now?"

"I see a car, a red one."

I use every ounce of restraint I have not to push her harder and just allow her to speak.

"It has two doors and no backseat."

"So, it's small?"

"Yes, it's little. It's really beautiful, and I want to drive it."

"Okay, anything else?"

"Isaac is outside of it."

Isaac purchased a car that Addison hated. She said it was impractical and stupid, but he was so excited about it. He had always wanted a little red sports car, so it was like he was living the dream. Three days later, Addy found out she was pregnant, and he sold it a week later—to me.

That car sits in my garage and is only driven on special occasions.

"Do you drive it, Brie?"

"No, not then, at least. He won't even let me in it."

And he hadn't. She'd been mad at him for a week.

"What does he say?"

"He claims I'm not a good enough driver." There's laughter in her voice. "Addison is really pissed, too. She keeps saying he needs to take it back."

I come into the memory at about this point. I wait, holding my breath.

When she doesn't, I urge her further. "Does he?"

"I don't . . . know."

"You're doing great," I say, close enough that I can feel her heat. I move my hand to her cheek, resting it there lightly. She tilts into my touch, and I am desperate for her. I want to feel her lips so badly it's fucking killing me. "What's happening, Brie?" I ask, forcing myself to speak so I don't do what I want.

But then she moves her face closer to mine. I inhale her breath as we both share the same air. She's so close, and I want her so much. I move my thumb across her cheek.

"Addy is upset," she repeats.

I close my eyes, letting myself drift a fraction closer as my heart thunders against my ribs. I can't do this. I can't kiss her. Not now and not like this. I shift back, hating myself for wanting it so much.

As soon as I do, the warmth is gone and a cool breeze kisses my skin.

Immediately, Brielle's eyes fly open and she's pushing upright. "It's gone! No! It's gone."

"What's gone?"

"Everything!" she cries out and throws her arms around me. I clutch her tight, feeling the panic radiating through her. Brielle starts to cry, her body shaking with each sob. "It's gone. I can't remember anything more."

"It's okay. This is going to happen."

She pulls back, scrambling to her feet with her arms around her middle. "It's not okay. I was seeing it. I think it was real, but I don't know."

"It was real. Isaac did get a red car, he didn't let you drive it, and Addy wasn't happy."

A mix of relief and then pain flashes in her blue eyes. "I remembered, and then . . . it just stopped. I wanted to remember what happened next, but whatever it was, it just disappeared. I could see something in my periphery, and then it was just . . . gone. Why? Why did it go away? What was there that my mind won't allow me to see?"

Me. That's what she isn't remembering. The memories that include me. There have been small glimmers and all of them fade as soon as I step into the picture.

I stand, pushing down my own frustrations, and go to her. "I'm sorry, Brie."

She shakes her head. "No, you don't get it. Henry said something to me, and I can't stop thinking about it."

Again with fucking Henry. Henry, the douchebag who always put her last. The guy who had a second chance with the most beautiful and incredible woman but threw it away because work was more of a priority. I don't give a flying fuck about anything that piece of shit has to say.

Anger boils, and I step back.

Brie continues. "He said that whatever I'm forgetting is something my mind is protecting me from. As though my head knows that I need to forget it. It's why he thought that maybe it was our breakup, which turned out to be completely incorrect."

The air is pushed from my lungs as though I've been punched. "You really think this person that you forgot is bad?"

"How can I not when he's nowhere to be found? I mean, I can't dismiss it as a possibility. I mean, I don't even have any idea how long he and I were together."

Nine months.

"I have no idea if we started dating after Henry and I broke up or if I ended things with Henry because of this new guy."

No. You didn't.

"I . . . can't stop wondering if maybe that's who did this to me? That when he came into my life, he ruined it."

I would never hurt you.

I can't tell her that. I can't tell her anything. We weren't together at that time, and I can't even correct her.

"Maybe that's true." It wouldn't be the first time a woman said that to me. My mother said it daily. I came around and ruined everything.

"I know you're angry at all of this. You have every reason to be worried, but take a second to realize what just happened."

Her blue eyes stare up into mine. "What?"

"You remembered something. You could see things, remember them, and feel what was going on. This wasn't the taste of a cigar or finding a ring. It was an *actual* memory."

I have to hold on to that. No matter what, she did remember something. It may not be what I wanted, but this is about her.

A tear falls down her cheek, leaving a black track behind it. "I just wish it was the right one."

CHAPTER *Thirteen*

BRIELLE

"I'm going to miss you so much," I tell Addy as I hug her again.

"I'll be back before you know it."

"It won't be soon enough." I kiss Elodie's forehead one last time and hand her over.

So far today, I've done nothing but watch movies. If there's one perk to memory loss, it's this. I have no idea what I've seen before, so I get to watch everything that's streaming for the first time all over again.

Addison leans in and kisses my cheek. "Be kind to yourself. You will get there. I have faith."

"I am trying."

"You have an appointment today?"

I nod. "Yeah. Holden's friend from Seattle specializes in this type of trauma. He seems to have success with memory recovery, so I'm hopeful."

"Is Spencer driving you?"

"No, Emmett is."

Addison smiles and then turns.

"What?" I ask.

"Nothing."

"That wasn't nothing."

"It's funny that you asked Emmett instead of Spencer."

I'm not understanding what makes it funny. "I have other friends."

"Yes, but not other guys you lust after."

I glare at my sister-in-law. "You should probably get on the road. You have a long drive ahead of you."

Addy barks out a laugh. "I'm saying that you have always had feelings for him."

"Maybe, but he has never had feelings for me. I'm that annoying girl who followed him around with puppy-dog eyes. I have no disillusions about how he sees me."

"I get it. I'm not arguing with you, but you have to admit that it's funny."

I roll my eyes. "It's called self-preservation."

Addison settles Elodie in her car seat and then stands outside the driver's side door. "Isaac used to joke about how you would never find anyone because you were so in love with the idea of Spencer."

"He never said that to me."

"I threatened to chop his balls off if he did. It was better for him to feign ignorance about your crush since no one would've been good enough for you."

"He was such a worrier."

"He loved with his whole heart."

I was really lucky to have him as a brother. "He did, and you took up the most real estate."

Her smile is soft. "I miss him so much. All the dreams we had are gone, and being here is so hard."

"Going to Pennsylvania isn't going to make them go away or change, Addy. You'll miss him there too."

"I know, but I won't have to see him everywhere I look. There isn't a single place in this town that doesn't hold a memory of him. I swore I heard him in the shower two days ago, humming to whatever song was popular with the kids. I was so happy because, for a split second, I was sure that my bad dream was over and he was here. When I realized I was hearing things, it broke me. I can't do it. I have to give myself some time to settle my grief."

"I really hope you can."

"Me too. And if I don't, I'll be back here sooner than you think."

"And if you do find that peace there, you'll still come home?" I ask, only slightly joking.

Addison grins. "This is my home. You're my sister, and . . ." Addison looks at Elodie in the backseat. "Isaac would've wanted us to be here."

Isaac would've wanted her to be happy, regardless of the zip code she resides in. "Promise you'll call?"

"I promise. Promise you'll go to all your doctor appointments?"

I laugh. "Yes. I promise."

"Good." Addison pulls me in for a tight hug, and when she releases, we both have tears. "Love you."

"Always."

It's what Isaac would say. He never replied with love you too or anything else.

I watch her drive away and my heart sinks. I know it's what she needs, but I'll miss her terribly.

"I'm Dr. Girardo," says a tall, slender man as he extends his hand.

"Brielle, nice to meet you."

"You as well. I've known Dr. James for a very long time, and he told me a lot about your case."

"I've known Holden since I was eight," I say with a smile. "I'm hoping you can help me."

Dr. Girardo extends his hand, indicating I should sit. "Well, I can certainly try. There is a lot we don't know about the brain, which makes head injuries especially frustrating."

"Tell me about it."

He laughs and crosses one leg over his knee. "I could bore you for hours, but that's not what we need to focus on. I know you've been through recounting this several times, but why don't you walk me through the last thing you remember."

I really hate this. But Holden was emphatic that if there was anyone who could help, it would be him. So, here it goes.

After what feels like hours of talking, I release a heavy breath and sit back.

Dr. Girardo continues to write notes and then places his notepad down. "I want to be honest with you, Brielle, you went a little further than what I know was your last stopping point."

I perk up at that. "Really?"

"According to your records, your last memory was of moving back to Rose Canyon roughly six months after graduation. In our discussion, you recalled the interview for the job at the youth center that Jenna owns and you also mentioned having lunch with your brother after."

My jaw falls slack. "I did?" I start to sift through what I said, I was so lost in the memories I didn't notice where I stopped.

But there it is.

I went on the interview at the youth center in town. I remember Jenna being there with a woman named Rachelle. She was wearing a bright orange shirt with gray pants. She was warm and kind, reminding me of a sunny day, which was why I thought her top was so appropriate. She exuded light. Jenna had told me that she was an amazing supervisor and we would hit it off.

"I remembered that interview," I say more to myself.

"You did."

"And I met Isaac at the school after," I tell him again, as though he didn't already know this.

Dr. Girardo grins. "Did you recall this event before today?"

I shake my head. "The only other thing I've remembered is that my brother got a car he wouldn't let me drive. It would have happened right around the same time," I muse.

"Why is that?"

I glance up at him, a smile slowly forming on my lips. "We took that car to lunch. He said he wanted to drive it one more time before it was gone."

"Tell me about that memory."

I launch into the beach trip and how Spencer helped me relax enough to let my mind drift. "It just stopped, though. Like water slipping through my fingers, once the last drop fell, so did the memory."

He rubs his chin. "What were you feeling during that memory?"

"I don't know."

"Take a second to think about it. Try to go back to that beach with Spencer. Think about the heat of the sun and the sound of the waves. What were you feeling in the moment and not in the memory?"

I push the memory part out and do as he says, remembering the other things around me. "I was warm. I remember feeling this heat, not just from the sun, but from everything around me."

"What about smells?"

"The salty air, for sure, and Spencer."

"What does he smell like?" Dr. Girardo asks.

I smile. "Like sunshine and fresh air with a hint of leather. He smells like safety."

"What does safety feel like?"

"Hope and happiness."

"So, when you're with Spencer, you feel safe and hopeful?"

I look at him quickly. "No. I mean, yes, but not like that."

"Okay, I understand. He's more like a trusted friend who you can count on to listen and never judge. Does that sound accurate?"

"Everything we say here is in confidence, right?" I ask, not wanting to be worried that Holden will know of my ridiculous crush.

Dr. Girardo shifts forward. "By law, I can't disclose what we talk about unless you give me permission to consult with Dr. James."

The groan falls from my lips.

"No, I know that you and Holden are working for the same goal, but if you could maybe leave this part out of your official notes, that would be great."

"You have feelings for Spencer," he guesses.

"Since I was thirteen."

"Are they reciprocated?"

"God no!" I explode. "He doesn't even know. Well, I'm sure he knows. I think everyone knows, but they all let me have the illusion of my secret."

He smiles. "But even though your feelings are deeper than friendship, you feel comfortable enough to ask for his help and trust him to dig into your past?"

"There is no one else I trust more."

"Okay, so let's go back to the beach for a moment. You said you were lying down, feeling the warmth of the sun and heat from Spencer. You smelled the salt air and him. Talk me through what happened right before you were jolted from the memory."

I close my eyes and put myself there again. I can hear the waves crashing on the shore and the sound of two birds overhead. I was there, laughing as Addison informed Isaac that the car was not staying, and then, it was as if the heat was ripped away.

"I don't know what it was, but it was gone. I felt cold and alone and . . . it all left."

"Did you ask Spencer?"

"No, I was too upset. I wanted that memory to stay so badly. I was happy and felt like I was going to be okay, and then I was terrified."

We talk a bit more as he asks questions about the memory and the beach. I answer everything I can as thoroughly as I can, hoping he'll be able to tell me how to remember more of my past.

Dr. Girardo's alarm rings, and he sighs. "I would love to keep talking, but it seems our time is up for the day. We've covered a lot, and it's important to rest as much as it is to work. I'd like you to keep a journal of memories or dreams you have. We can go over them each time. Also, you should try to meditate each morning. One of the keys to your recovery is nurturing yourself. It's like the saying about putting on the air mask for yourself before your child, you can't save someone else if you don't save yourself."

I am going to kill Holden for this. "I don't need saving. I need to do the saving."

"And that's the goal we took our first step toward today, whether you realize it or not."

He's right. I don't think we accomplished anything today. I didn't get any answers, I just went back over all the crap we already knew. "I don't think you're right. I'm no different from when I walked in."

"That's not true."

"I still have no memories of who killed my brother and tried to kill me."

He nods. "That much is the same, but we did learn a lot."

"What did we learn?" I ask with frustration.

"What I look for is a pattern or something to indicate what the brain might be triggered by. For you, it's fear and comfort." When I don't say anything, he continues. "What would you think if I told you that we've met several times before?"

My heart rate accelerates, and my breaths come quicker. What? Did we? Why does this keep happening? How could I sit here and talk to him and he not mention this if we have before?

"Brielle?" he prompts. "Tell me exactly what you're feeling. Describe it all."

"I'm angry. I'm so angry because everyone keeps things from me. We've met? When?"

"Those are questions and not the answer to what I asked. Tell me what you're thinking and your emotions."

My eyes well with tears of frustration, and I spew it all. "I would be hurt and sad. Right now, I am cold, and my heart is racing. The shaking in my hands makes it all worse. Because if we've met before and I don't remember it, then who's to say I don't walk by a dozen other people I've met and have no recollection of? It's terrifying."

He leans forward so he catches my eyes. "I can assure you that we haven't met before today, and I'm sorry for causing you distress, but let me ask you something else." After a second, I nod my permission. "Earlier, when I asked you to recount the memory about your brother's car, what went through your head?"

I look up, wiping the stupid tear that fell. "I don't know."

"I think you do. It's the same thing you felt at the beach."

My lips tremble as the truth crashes around me. "I felt safe."

"Yes, you felt comfortable and safe. You weren't drowning in fear. What I would like to focus on is helping you establish control of it, which will hopefully be a big step in helping you regain your memories."

"How do I control it? How do I get rid of it?"

He smiles. "Start keeping a list of anything you know is real. Concrete and absolute. We will go over it during our next session."

CHAPTER *Fourteen*

SPENCER

"Hit me," Emmett says as he taps the green felt.

"You're going to bust," Holden warns.

"I'm going to bust your lip if you don't shut up."

Tonight is Holden's last night in town. He decided to head back home after his call with Dr. Girardo, which he's been tight-lipped about.

"Let him lose, it's his money," I say, dealing the card he asked for.

Emmett curses. "Damn it. I needed a three."

"You need to learn how to play," Holden notes. "You don't hit when you need a three. It's like you can't count."

"I can count the number of times you've irritated me."

I snort. "You can count that high?"

Emmett flips us both off.

I look over to the screen, which shows a live stream of Brielle's door, wondering if she's okay. She came home about three hours ago and hasn't left since.

My mind has been a mess all day. I keep seeing her on that beach, blonde hair flowing down her back and the sun on her beautiful face. My mind burned the images of those shorts and the tank top that showed every curve on her perfect body. I wanted to haul her in my arms and kiss her until she could do nothing but remember us, but I can't do that.

No, instead I have to stare at a photo in my dresser, tracing her face with my finger through the glass.

"What about you, Spence?" Emmett asks.

"What?"

Holden laughs. "He tunes us out like my ex-wife did."

"Speaking of ex," I take the opening. "Did you see Jenna today?"

We all know he did. Jenna's office is next to the only place in town that serves lunch. She is there every day at the same time, which happens to be the same time he was meeting with Dr. Girardo.

"I don't remember if I did."

Emmett chuckles. "Sure, you don't."

"She looks great."

He rolls his eyes. "She always has. That was never an issue."

"What was the issue?"

"I don't know, maybe it was that we were twenty, stupid, and thought we knew what we were getting into and then realized we didn't. Besides, she's not the only person I ever dated. I'm not a monk."

No, but he doesn't talk about them. Well, other than that one chick he hooked up with when he was visiting his aunt. That was a fun night.

He has only ever talked about what happened with Jenna once, and he was drunk as hell. He said it was the week before he left for med school, and he came home after studying until three a.m. in the library to find her with her bags packed. The way he tells it, she claimed she was miserable, and he loved her too much to be the reason for her unhappiness.

So, they got divorced and have been civil since.

Although we all know he has struggled with not being enough for her.

"You're almost forty and still stupid," I helpfully contribute.

Emmett raises his glass. "That's the truth. Anyway, I wanted to ask if you're going to the dinner next week?"

"The one where they name you Man of the Year?"

It's the stupidest freaking thing this town does. I swear, we have awards for everything. Usually, the winner is the mayor or a town selectman because they make up the committee. This is the first time that they've picked someone outside their brotherhood.

Emmett Maxwell was named MOTY, as they call it, and we are all supposed to go. Not because he was the best choice, but because Isaac had pitched a king-sized fit a few years ago about how the same people are always nominated and win. After that fit, he got a nomination, didn't win, and went crazy over it all over again. So, they nominated Emmett this time. We never thought he'd win, but here we are.

"If I must," I reply.

"Can you bring Brielle with you?"

I turn to him. "What?"

"Brielle, the girl across the hallway that you spend most of your time with. Ring a bell?"

"I know who she is, jackass. I am asking why I'd bring her."

Emmett grumbles. "She needs a ride, and I thought I could take her, but I have to be there hours in advance to go over the ceremony."

Holden laughs. "Don't you just walk up on stage and take the award?"

"Apparently," Emmett draws out the word, "there is more than that. I need to also have my speech approved." He turns to me. "Which you need to write."

"I'm not writing it," I say quickly.

I am broken. I am a prize-winning writer who can't write.

"What do you mean? Who the hell else would write it?"

"Here's an idea . . . you."

He rolls his eyes. "I catch bad guys and protect old women crossing the street. I don't write speeches."

"There you go." Holden slaps Emmett on the back. "You just wrote it. Although, you really aren't doing a great job with the catching of bad guys since there's a killer running around. Maybe omit that part."

I snort a laugh and look down at my phone as it vibrates with a text.

Brielle: Can you do whatever super sleuthing you can on a Rachelle Turner?

Me: Why?

Brielle: Because I asked you to and you're supposed to be helping, which you're not at this moment.

I grin, imagining her face as she typed that.

Me: Is your laptop broken?

What Brielle doesn't know is that I have remote access to her computer and already know she did a search about an hour ago.

Brielle: No, but I don't even know where to start.

This is totally going to piss her off.

Me: At the beginning.

Brielle: You are such an ass.

Me: This is true. I'll do some digging tonight.

Brielle: Thanks. I had a rough day, so I am going to bed. My head is pounding.

I wish I could go over there and hold her through the night.

Me: Hope you feel better. I'll talk to you tomorrow.

Brielle: Are you home?

Me: No, I'm out.

I don't want to tell her I'm next door or that I'm here most days just to be close in case she needs me. Emmett thinks it's because I want to hang out with him, which I don't.

Brielle: Hot date?

Me: I don't think either of these two are particularly attractive.

Brielle: Two? Wow.

Me: Nor are they my type.

"Are you going to play or text whatever girl you're banging now?" Holden asks.

"I'm not banging anyone."

Emmett laughs. "Yeah right. You're never without a woman in the wings."

Sure, I did everything I could to cultivate that misconception of my personal life. I was always seen with some girl and I never brought the same one around twice. Mostly because I wanted easy and the idea of being in a relationship was exhausting.

Being in superficial relationships was much more satisfying. The girl didn't think we'd be more, and I never gave a shit about what she did.

"Well, I am now."

Holden rubs his chin. "You know, it's been a while since I've seen you with anyone."

Emmett scrunches his face. "He's right. I haven't seen you with anyone since you got back to town."

Not since I saw Brielle after my piece on the war was published.

"I grew up," I say, hoping they'll drop it.

Emmett, who did his own stint in the service and saw just as much as I did, replies, "I think it's something else."

"I'm sure you can understand it, Em."

He nods, and a moment of kinship passes between us.

My team lived through more than eighteen months of absolute hell in the same country that his was. I was granted permission to follow an elite military team with the understanding I was not allowed to report on what they did, only what they uncovered. But still, we experienced a lot of the same things that Emmett did.

The entire reason I requested that assignment was because of Emmett. He had just made it through his special forces training. There was this deep-seated fear, one that kept me up at night, that he wouldn't make it back.

If I could be there.

If I could be close, then maybe I could help.

It was insane, and Isaac was the only person who knew an inkling of the truth.

Instead of him trying to talk me out of it, he encouraged me to go. Emmett is our brother, and there is nothing I wouldn't do to protect someone I love. So, I went through a year of their training, because there would be no lifesaving efforts made for me, and went off to war.

The things I've seen. The sounds and smells are things that will never leave me.

That article earned me a Pulitzer, and since then, I haven't written a single word.

What the hell could I write? Nothing will ever measure up.

I walk back to the table, and Emmett takes the dealer's seat. "You know Holden kicks our ass every hand."

Holden smirks. "It's because you two don't respect my superior intellect."

"You may be smart, but you're a fucking dumbass," Emmett says, dealing the cards.

"And that makes zero sense."

Emmett looks to me. "You know what I mean?"

"Yes, and I agree. He's the smartest dumbass I know."

We all laugh and play a few hands. Holden and I both battle it out, and he wins two of the five hands. The one thing Holden can't do is lose graciously.

"Two more hands," he demands.

Emmett leans back, a shit-eating grin on his face. "Don't do it, Spence. Let him lose."

As I'm about to tell him to kiss my ass, my phone lights up, and I see I have about twenty alerts from Brielle's laptop.

Spencer Cross.

Spencer Cross model.

Spencer Cross dating history.

Who is Spencer Cross dating now?

Spencer Cross Pulitzer article.

Last known girlfriend of Spencer Cross.

The list goes on and on as she attempts to dig into my history, and I can't stop the pang of excitement that she's searching me. It means she's thinking of me. It means she can't sleep, and whatever I said is heavy on her heart. While I don't know what she'll find, it doesn't matter because it means that she cares. She also wants to know if I'm dating someone.

"Spencer? You ready to have me take all your winnings?"

A little bit smug thanks to the alerts, I turn to Holden. "Let's play. I could use a little extra spending cash."

"Good morning," I say, holding a cup of coffee in front of Brielle.

"You look happy."

"I'm always happy when I have a good night."

Her smile falters a little, but she recovers. "Glad you and your two dates enjoyed yourselves."

I laugh. "My dates were Emmett and Holden, and I very much had a good time taking all their money."

Brielle's lashes flutter, and she sucks in a breath. "Why didn't you say that? I . . . I am stupid. I'm sorry."

"Would it have bothered you if it was two girls?" I ask, goading her a bit.

"Of course not. It's none of my business who you date or whatever it is you do."

She speaks quickly, which is a clear sign she's very much bothered by it. Good. I want it to bug her. I want the idea of me and another woman to make her rage because she's the only woman I want.

"What if I told you it's been a long time since . . ."

She raises her hand. "Seriously, it's not my business."

Oh, Brielle, if it weren't a risk to the prosecution's case, I'd tell you everything. I'd fall to my fucking knees, confess everything, and beg you to love me again. I'd cut my heart out of my chest and give it to her if it meant it would give her the memories back.

"All right then," I say, taking a sip of my coffee. "Emmett asked me to take you to that MOTY ceremony in a few days."

She blows out a long breath. "I hate that stupid thing."

"We all do."

"Isaac almost peed himself when he was nominated."

I pause because he was nominated two years ago. "He was?"

She nods. "Yeah, he went on and on about it being an amazing honor and talking about what he was going to do if he won. Because that prime parking spot in front of the town hall is such a great prize." Brie takes a drink and then looks at me. "What?"

I don't want to point out that she just remembered something new because I don't want her to start pushing for more. I want her to stay relaxed and maybe she'll remember more. "Nothing. I have this for you."

She takes the folder that contains the information she asked for on Rachelle Turner and the youth center. Brielle opens it and heads to the couch before thumbing through it. I dredged up some information that she wouldn't find on her simple searches. Things like the financial records and public holdings.

"Wow," she says as she reaches the page showing the profits. "They're doing well."

"They have two major benefactors."

"But they're recent," she notes.

"They are. It looks like the second donor stepped in around a year ago."

"Jenna mentioned when I interviewed that she was a benefactor."

I figured that was her company on the statement here. "Anything with the orange is what I assumed was Jenna's non-profit."

We scour through the papers and make notes in the margins. It feels so fucking good doing this. For the first time in over three years, there's a slight thrill to investigating. I used to love this part. Each detail can lead to something bigger, and I relish in the idea of finding it.

Brielle puts her coffee down and grabs a pen, circling two amounts. "These two are not donations and are almost identical amounts, off by just three pennies."

"Both just under the amount you have to declare to the government as well."

Her eyes find mine. "What do you mean?"

"Any deposit over ten thousand is reported, but these are eight days apart, so they weren't likely flagged. But look at this." I point to another line item on the statement. "There are six withdrawals in a forty-eight-hour period. All of them are small enough not to tip anyone off."

"Is that important?" Brie asks.

"It could be."

"Why would I be looking into the financial records of my job? How would I even have had access to that?"

"I don't know."

"Is there anything in here that explains the withdrawals?"

"No, those kinds of records take a bit longer to get access to, but I'm working on it."

I rifle through another pile and hand it to her. It's an employee list compiled with dates of hire and any terminations. "Where did you get these?"

"I have sources, Brie, and I don't divulge them."

She rolls her eyes. "Okay, Mr. Mysterious. Can I assume these aren't mine, though?"

"Yes, these came from somewhere else."

"What's your theory? That maybe I saw discrepancies and went to Rachelle about it?"

"It's possible, but why wouldn't you have gone to me or Emmett? Why would you have kept all this quiet?" While I understand it's a work thing and coming to others wouldn't be normal, we shared our days.

We talked about everything. She would tell me stories about her coworker who hit on her constantly or the kids when they did something fun. Her not telling me is what I am most concerned about.

She leans back on the couch, pulling her legs under her. "I don't know. I would've told Isaac and he probably would've told you and Emmett. If that was what happened, then you would know all this and then I would've gone to my boss. So, that doesn't really make sense."

Her mind is a beautiful thing.

"I think you're right. If you went to Isaac, he would've mentioned it. So, I have no idea what these deposits and withdrawals mean. We can't jump to conclusions, just follow the facts. So far, we know that there were two deposits that seem off. Let's keep looking through and see if there is anything else odd."

She goes back to the papers, circling different things before handing it to me. Not for nothing, she would make an amazing journalist. She's looking at everything critically and examining things most people would dismiss as inconsequential. It's impressive.

"Look." Brie's gaze finds mine, and she extends the paper. "These deposits and withdrawals are smaller and there are more of them, but it's the same pattern again."

Sure enough, she's right.

"Did you add them?"

She shakes her head. "I'm starting to get a headache."

"Why don't you take a break while I calculate them. I have a feeling this total is going to be larger than the last two."

"It's a lot of money over the course of a month," she agrees.

I start to highlight and do the math. The amount is staggering. "It's over twenty-thousand dollars."

"Why wouldn't someone want to just make a donation of that amount at once? It's a charity, right?"

"It's not a charity, it's funded by the town."

Her eyes widen. "Wait, so it's publicly funded?"

"Yes. About a year ago." I hand her the paperwork detailing the transfer. The town wanted to provide a place where it was for all kids in the area.

"But they're getting large donations of twenty thousand dollars almost monthly. If I was at all aware of something sketchy going on, could there have been more in my office?"

"That's what I wonder, but if you did, there weren't any records of it here."

"And you have no idea what this is?" she asks.

"About this? I know only what you know. I swear." I wish I did because at least then I would have some fucking clue what might have been in the missing paperwork from her office. "What I've learned is that when money is involved with corruption, there's not much someone won't do to silence others."

Even kill.

CHAPTER *Fifteen*

BRIELLE

I don't know that I have ever been this comfortable. Everything around me feels warm, and I could sleep like this forever.

I squirm deeper into the blankets, not remembering anything about how I got here. Spencer and I were in the living room, talking about the fact I may work for a bunch of criminals, then my head started to pound. That's it.

For once, though, I'm not disturbed by the lack of memory. If it's the beginning of a migraine, I really have no desire to recall it. No, I'd much rather stay here in the bliss.

I let out a sigh of contentment and hear a low chuckle, which has my eyes flying open.

When I see the source of the sound, I gasp. "Spencer! Oh my God! What are you doing? Why am I on top of you?"

First fact, I am not in my bed. I'm on the couch . . . with Spencer.

Second fact, the sun is *not* where it should be. The sky is light blue—not dark blue with pinks and oranges of sunset—with the sun sitting low on the horizon.

Third fact, I have been asleep a long time. In his arms.

While I have dreamed of this moment since I was a teenager, I'm not nearly as happy as I pictured myself to be. If I could remember how I got here, maybe I would be.

Ugh.

"You had a headache, so I had you lay down, and you passed out. It's fine."

"Yeah, it's fine. I mean, it's totally fine. Everything is *fine*."

"Why do I have the feeling it's actually not?" he asks.

I rest my head in my hands and groan. "Because you're Spencer!"

"And you're Brielle."

"No, you don't get it . . ."

I should really shut up.

"What?"

I lift my face, hands dropping in frustration. "You're *Spencer Cross*. I had a crush on you my whole freaking life. I'm just a little . . . freaked out."

"Had or have?"

I'm not answering that. "My point is that I'm on top of you."

He laughs. "You know I had a crush on you too?"

My lips part as I take in a sharp breath. He what? He had a crush on me? Liar. "You promised never to lie to me."

"And I'm not."

"You had a crush on me?"

He nods slowly. "I have always thought you were beautiful, smart, kind, and funny, even if you do say the most ridiculous things sometimes."

The heat rises in my cheeks. "I'm not beautiful." I turn away, not wanting to see the way his green eyes fill with anything. Nope. I'd rather just stick my head in the sand, thank you very much.

Spencer's finger moves to my chin, tilting my head to look at him. "You are. You are so beautiful, and more than that, you're beautiful on the inside. I absolutely had a crush on you, and I still think you're incredibly gorgeous. Don't tell me you're not beautiful, Brielle, because I will prove you wrong."

My breathing is shallow, and I swear I could pass out. What is happening? Spencer is looking at me like he wants to kiss me, and God, I want to kiss him.

Even if it's just this once. Even if I could be engaged to someone else, I don't care. I want this right now because I'm pretty sure I'm dreaming anyway.

His gaze moves to my lips, and that's all I need. My hand goes to his cheek, fingertips brushing the scruff on his jaw. "Before I lose my nerve, I need to ask you something."

"Anything." His voice is thick.

"Will you . . ." I clear my throat, working through the nerves. "Will you kiss me? You don't have—"

I don't get the rest of the sentence out before his lips are on mine. His fingers press against my face, holding me where he wants me,

Spencer's touch is both delicate and strong. He pulls back, rubbing his nose on mine. "Relax and kiss me back."

The moment our lips touch again, I'm so completely freaking lost. Forget the lack of memories, this man has erased my entire life in one kiss. I don't care about the past because all I want is the present. I want his mouth and his touch and the heat of his body against mine.

I want to drown in this kiss and never come up for air.

When his tongue strokes mine, I could die. Spencer is all things at once. He's sun and rain, fire and ice, fear and safety, and each second brings another wave of sensations, leaving me breathless.

I moan into his mouth, and then he shifts me so I'm straddling his hips. Even from the bottom, he's in control.

He deepens the kiss, fingers fisting my hair as I hold his lips to mine. It's the most passionate kiss I've ever had.

Our breaths mingle, creating new air that's equally us.

God, if I knew this man kissed like this, I might have mauled him sooner.

He kisses as though he's just as starved for this as I am.

I don't know how long it lasts, but when it ends, it's far too soon. My forehead rests on his as I struggle to breathe and he rubs my back soothingly.

"Brie . . . I . . . I don't know."

I lift my head and press my finger to his lips. "If you ruin that for me and say something about that being a mistake, I will never forgive you."

He smiles and pulls my hand away. "I wouldn't dream of it."

"Well, I have. Not the ruining it part—the kiss. I have dreamed of it for a very long time."

Spencer shifts my weight a little, but he doesn't move me off him. "And did I live up to the dream?"

I shake my head. "Nope."

I almost laugh at the affronted look he gives me, but I hold it in. "No?" he asks.

"You far surpassed it."

"That was mean."

"That was me trying to control the situation a little," I explain.

Spencer's hand moves to my cheek, and his thumb brushes the soft skin right below my eye. "I want to give you control, which is why I want to help you so much. Sure, finding Isaac's killer is part of it, but it isn't all of it. I want you to regain what you lost."

My pulse kicks up a notch as I grapple with that last part. "What if I don't want back what I lost?"

His eyes narrow. "Why wouldn't you?"

I think about that velvet box with the big ass diamond in my drawer. The fact that another man, who probably doesn't kiss like Spencer does, gave it to me. How, even weeks after the incident, I don't remember him. I don't know what he looks like, if I see him daily, or if his absence from my life means he has something to do with what happened. He's just the guy my head doesn't want to recall.

I could be totally crazy, but there's something there.

"What if the new future I could forge is better than the one I don't remember? What if what I had was the wrong thing, and somewhere in my mind, I know it? Don't you think I am forgetting for a reason?"

"It doesn't really work that way, Brie."

I feel ridiculous sitting on him like this, so I shift away, tuck my hair behind my ear, and prepare to look like an idiot as I explain. "I know that. I mean, I do, but I also wonder if my mind is protecting me, not just from the shooting, but where I fucked up."

"You think you did something to deserve this?"

I'm not explaining it right. "No, I think the man I was dating or engaged to wasn't the right one. If he was, he'd be here. Not to mention, Isaac was my best friend. I told him everything. Everything. How could he and Addy not know about an engagement? Or even that a guy existed! It's like I knew it was wrong and hid it."

"How do you know you didn't tell Isaac?"

I blink for a second because I don't know that I didn't. "Maybe I did and asked him not to tell anyone yet. Maybe he was happy for me. Or, just as possible, he and the guy hated each other and that's what caused all this. Not that anyone hated Isaac, but there is this feeling in my gut that is telling me the two things are linked. Maybe I was engaged to someone at work and found out he was stealing from the company. Isaac would've been who I went to with that information. If I did that, which is likely, and my fiancé found out, it would explain all of it. The attack, the office being trashed and why he's disappeared. He could've been looking for the information I had and the ring, because it all links back to him." He sits unmoving, watching me work through my thoughts. I turn to him. "And do you know what else? If I loved this guy so much, I wouldn't be kissing you. Because do you know what I felt just then?"

"No."

I smile. "I felt so happy. So full of hope for what could be. I want to find Isaac's killer. I want to know that who did this is behind bars so the security guys can all go home to their families or their next job. On the other hand, I don't know if I do. What if I can have something new? What if I can find someone else who kisses me and makes my toes curl?" Spencer is quiet, and I worry that I've said too much or made him think I somehow believe one kiss means it should be him. "I don't mean you," I say quickly. "I wasn't trying to insinuate . . ."

He lets out a sigh and stands. "I want to help you remember, not allow you to forget." He walks over and grabs his sweatshirt and notebook.

"Where are you going?" I ask.

He doesn't turn to face me for a long minute, but when he does, he says, "We all have shit in our past we'd rather forget. I know that better than anyone, but hiding from it doesn't erase it. Just because you can't remember, doesn't mean it didn't happen. So, you choose if you want my help to piece together your life or if you'd rather start this new version of it."

"What I want is to have some fun and not have everything be so crushing."

Spencer's green eyes study me. "Maybe that's where we're going wrong with this."

"What?"

"Maybe we need to listen to everyone else and give your mind a chance to breathe and not force it back. Maybe we shouldn't be investigating and we should let you live." Spencer takes a few steps, closing the distance between us. His hand pushes my hair back as his thumb rubs my cheek. "Maybe you need to go on a date."

Oh. Oh God. "With who?"

He grins. "With me."

I am going on a date.

A date with Spencer.

After kissing him. It's fine. I am totally not freaking out.

Lie.

However, I am dressed in shorts and a T-shirt, which is what he instructed me to wear to wherever he plans to take me. For the first time since all of this happened, I feel a pinch of joy. I'm going on a date . . . with Spencer.

He sends me a text, and then I'm standing at the door waiting.

"Hey," he says when he gets to the door.

"Hey."

He hands me a bouquet. "These are for you."

"Flowers? For our fake date?" I bring them to my nose to hide my blush. Henry never brought me flowers, and I adore that Spencer did.

"Who says this is fake?"

"Well, I did. We're not dating."

"We are going on a date. A real one. So, are you ready?" he asks.

"Let me put these in water." I head into the kitchen, fill up the pitcher, and put the flowers in there. I rush back over to him with a smile. "Ready."

"Perfect."

He extends his arm, and I take it.

"Where are we going?"

"It's a surprise."

I pout a little. "I really would love it if you'd tell me."

He grins down at me, his dark hair falling in his eyes for a moment. "I know you're in the dark a lot lately, but I want you to enjoy not knowing what's to come."

"That's very philosophical of you."

Spencer laughs. "I'm a man of many mysteries, Miss Davis."

"Not so much."

He tilts his head. "Is that so?"

"Yes, you're not very mysterious. I know you just as well as I know myself."

"Well, considering you don't know yourself all that well lately, I think I know you better."

"Do you now?"

"I do."

I shake my head with a grin. "You're cocky, I'll give you that much."

"I'm confident. Big difference."

"Okay, how about a wager?" I challenge.

"About what?"

"That I know you better than you know me, but it has to be pre-memory loss stuff. I'm talking about the things that are in our pasts that you think I don't know and vice versa."

"You're on. What's the wager?" he asks as he opens my car door.

I hold on to the top of the door, leaning my head on it as I smile at him. "If I get more than you, then you have to kiss me again."

"That's one way to get me to lose. Besides, this is a date, so aren't I obligated to kiss you at the end anyway?"

I giggle. "Okay, fine. If I win, you have to tell me one thing about my life in the last three years that I don't know."

"Anything?"

"Anything."

I could push my luck and try to get him to tell me something specific, but really, so long as it's more than I already have, I'll be happy.

"And if I win"—Spencer rests his hands on either side of mine—"then you have to go on another date with me."

"Isn't that customary to ask at the end?"

"Maybe I'd like to go in knowing I'm already winning."

God, I am in so much trouble. This is every damn fantasy I've had all coming to fruition. Here he is, flirting with me, talking about kissing me, and planning another date. I want it all. I wish this were my life instead of just a day of fun.

"I don't know if that's all that fair," I say, moving just a smidge closer.

"Why is that?"

"Because what if I want to lose now."

"That's for you to decide. Is winning better than losing?"

I lift one shoulder, biting my lower lip. "Winning is always better."

"All right, then, you go first. What do you know about me that I think is unknown?"

He has no idea how much dirt I have on him. Not only things I've overheard or things Isaac told me in confidence but also things I saw when he thought no one was looking.

"Fine. You like pizza because you say anything made on a base of bread is a win. You love dogs, but you won't get one because your job requires you to travel. Your middle name is Jesus, but you tell everyone it's Jacob. You have six tattoos, one not many have seen, but I walked in on you after a shower and saw it. Your first kiss was with Jenna's older sister but you lie and tell everyone it was Marissa."

"Where did you hear that last one?"

I scoff. "Please. You and Isaac didn't know what inside voices were, and I learned to put a cup to the wall and eavesdrop very early in life."

"Marissa was my first kiss."

"She was not."

Spencer narrows his eyes. "What else did you hear?"

I smile widely. "Wouldn't you like to know?" I sink down in my seat and close the door.

I am so ready for today. It's different from the last few weeks of constant stress. I am tired of appointments and worrying about everything.

Spencer and I will never be an item, but maybe I can pretend for just today that it's real.

He gets into the car, shaking his head with a smile. "All right, that was impressive."

"Do you think you can do better?" I ask, turning toward him.

"You hate any food that is purple. You won't eat eggs because chickens poop them out, therefore it's crap. You lost your virginity at a party in the warehouse, which is where you now live, to Kyler Smith, who had a black eye the day after."

"Which you gave him!" I interject.

"Glady gave him. You puke if you drink so much as a sip of tequila. You tell everyone your favorite music is country, but you know every word to every rap song. Oh, and . . . you believe that ghosts haunt your childhood home."

I roll my eyes and snort. "Please, half of those everyone knows."

"Which half?"

"My virginity was town gossip, so that doesn't count. And . . . purple food is unnatural, which everyone also knows I believe. I'm calling a tie."

"So, then we both get what we want at the end of the date?"

My lips are in a thin line. "A second date, a kiss, and a memory?"

He rests his forearm on the console. "What do you think?"

"I think that we should see how the date goes."

Oh, I want all of it. I want it all and more, but that doesn't mean I should reach out and grab it.

He chuckles and then sits back in his seat. "Are you ready to go on the best date that has ever happened?"

I raise my brow. "The best? That's a pretty lofty boast, my friend."

"I'm confident this is going to deliver."

I lean back in the seat. "Then let's go and see if you know me as well as I know you."

CHAPTER *Sixteen*

SPENCER

I pull up to the park where the event is being held, and I'm really confused. There is supposed to be an adult water balloon fight with rides and all kinds of games. However, based on the number of mini-vans in the parking lot, it looks like a moms' group has taken over the park. Plus, I don't see any rides where they normally are when there's a carnival here.

"We're at a park?" she asks.

"Yes, but there's a huge event here."

"Okay. Is it a soccer tournament for a kid or something?"

I snort. "Not soccer, but it is a tournament of sorts."

"I'm intrigued."

I love the glint of mischief in her eyes, and I grin right back at her. "Come on, let's go register."

We get out of the car, and I take her hand, proving it's a date after all. Brielle looks up at me with a soft smile.

I realize I haven't told her how beautiful she is, which I really should've done. Her long blonde hair is up in a ponytail, and she's wearing a light-green top and shorts. She always looks pretty, but today, she is really stunning.

We get to the front table, and I smile and prepare for her to be blown away. "Hello, we'd like to register for the event," I say to the woman sitting in the plastic folding chair.

"You'd like to register?" she repeats before glancing at the woman to her right.

"Yes. The two of us."

Again, the woman checks with her friend and then looks at me. "Two of who?"

"Us. The two of us. Has the tournament begun?" Maybe I missed it. It said from four to nine. I made sure we'd be here for the start of it so that we could get to dinner by six. After that, we'll go to the beach, watch the sunset, and I hope to enjoy that kiss she teased me about.

"No, sir, but . . . where are your kids?"

"My what?" I ask a little too loudly.

Brielle giggles. Great, now she really does think I have a secret child.

"Ma'am, I'm here for the tournament and the rides. I read on the flyer that it started now."

"Mister, could you hurry up?" says a kid behind me. "I don't want to miss this."

I turn and try not to glare at the group of boys. They are maybe nine years old and have goopy white sunscreen on their noses.

"Relax, I'm just registering and then you'll get your turn."

The one kid laughs. "Great, now the old people are here too."

"Yeah, Mom said it was supposed to be without parents."

"I'm not a parent," I say more to myself.

Brielle laughs again.

The kid groans. "This guy is taking *forever*."

I'm going to take my sweet ass time now.

Brielle cuts in, smiling to the woman. "If you could give us the paperwork so we can fill it out, we'd appreciate it. I know these boys are excited."

The other woman leans down to grab the form. "Okay, if you insist."

I have no idea why she's being so weird about this. "Are we in the right place?" I ask.

"I'm not sure, sir. You said something about a flyer?"

"Yes, I saw it posted in Rose Canyon."

She rummages through her purse and pulls out a paper. "You saw this flyer?"

I swear to God. "Yes, the water balloon tournament and carnival. It said it's from . . ." I lean down and point.

Brielle bursts out laughing.

"What?" I ask.

"Oh, nothing, Best-Date-Planner-in-the-World."

I look at the paper again and dread fills me. That's not the time . . . it's the ages.

You have got to be kidding me.

"This is for kids?" I ask her, not willing to glance at Brielle, who is still laughing.

The older woman leans closer. "Yes, it's a kids' carnival."

"So, no rides for adults?"

She shakes her head. "Nope."

I want to sink into a hole. I had it all planned out. We were supposed to be doing something completely crazy and different. I must salvage this.

"Is there one later? Maybe after hours?"

"Honey, it's this or nothing."

I look to Brie, who is standing there with a shit-eating grin on her beautiful face. "We'll find something else."

"Oh, no we won't. We're here, and you promised me a date to remember."

"Wait, you want to do this?"

She nods. "Why wouldn't I? We're here, and I mean, the flyer says a day of fun, so . . ." The kids behind us are complaining louder about missing out. "Besides, we're holding up the line."

This is going to bite me in the ass. I know it. I turn back to the women at the table. "We'll do the water balloon competition please."

Brielle grabs my arm, resting her head on my shoulder. "And some rides. Also, he'd like to cover the boys behind us since they've been so patient."

They start giving each other high-fives and cheering when they hear her. "Thanks, lady!"

"My pleasure. You know"—Brie releases my arm and turns as I pay a ridiculous amount of money for rides and water balloons—"I could use some help on my team."

"What team?" I ask.

Brielle looks at me and smirks. "You didn't think we'd be together, did you?"

"That's the point of a date."

She slides back a few steps so she's standing behind the four boys. "Well, then you should've planned better, Spence. My new friends here and I are going to kick your butt."

"Yeah we will!" says the kid who called me old. "You're going down, old man."

"You should watch it, or you're going to be my first target."

Brie crouches so she's closer to their height. "Don't worry, boys, I played softball in college."

"You were a bench warmer," I correct.

"And what sport did you play? Oh, that's right, you didn't because you were too busy doing what again?"

I love her. I fucking love her even more right now. She's back to the girl I remember, who's all quick wit and humor.

"I was running the journalism club."

The boys snicker. "You're a nerd."

"He totally is," Brie agrees.

"You know, I did train with the Navy SEALs."

That at least earns me a little respect from the kids. "Whoa, that's cool!"

I nod. "Are you sure you don't want to be on my team?"

Brielle puts her hand on two of the boys' shoulders. "Find your own team, Cross. These boys and I have to go strategize."

The woman from the table smiles and hands each of the boys a white T-shirt. "I don't have adult-sized shirts for you since this was meant to be a youth event." She looks to Brielle. "The youth extra-large should fit you." Then she turns to me, her lips pinched in thought. "We could pin one to your shirt. Helena and I were going to be captains, but you and your girlfriend will definitely be better. I'm Sara, by the way."

"Thank you, Sara. I'm Brielle, and this is Spencer," Brie says, taking her shirt. "We are really excited."

"Oh, so are we."

I bet. It's going to make for a great story no matter what.

Sara hands me a youth extra-large, and it doesn't even go halfway across my chest. The hits keep coming.

Sara pins my shirt on as Brielle does this magic trick where she pulls one shirt on before taking the other off. I have no idea how she does it, but it is most definitely not something the male gender could accomplish.

Then she throws me a cheeky grin. "See you on the flip side, Cross."

"Yeah, the losing side," I toss back.

She winks and then leads her new entourage over to where it seems a few more of the kids' friends were waiting. We walk to where my team is apparently going to be, and . . . well, I'm screwed.

It's apparently boys versus girls, and I am leading the girls. I'm not all that great with kids' ages, but I'm guessing these are the younger siblings of the turds who are with Brie.

"Kids, this is your team captain, Mr. Cross. He's going to help you guys try to win," Sara says.

I wave, and one of the little girls raises her hand. "Yes?"

"Can I hide behind you? I don't want to get hit."

At least I know my weakest link. "That's not really how it works, but we'll figure out a plan."

The girl next to her raises her hand. "My name is Mable, that's

Taylor, and I don't like water. My mommy says I have to take baths because it's the law. I don't like the law."

"Okay. Good to know."

"Where are your kids?" the first girl, Taylor, asks.

"I don't have any," I reply.

One boy, who apparently didn't make it over to the other side, stares at me. He's the oldest and possibly my best player. I think. "You mean you're just here to play?"

"I'm on a date."

Not sure why I relayed that info.

His face scrunches. "My older brother, Theo, says you take girls to the movies."

"Theo would have the right idea, but I was trying something new. What's your name?"

"Matt."

"Well, Matt, welcome to the team. Can you throw?"

He shakes his head. "If I could, I'd be on that team."

Right. "Can you run fast?"

"Yeah."

"Good, then do a lot of that."

I turn to the last girl. "And what's your name?"

She sways back and forth and looks at the ground. "I'm Penny."

"And do you not like to get wet, can't throw, and are afraid to get hit?" I ask, hoping that maybe I have at least one.

"I don't like any of those. I'm ridiculous."

I'm speechless on this one. "Why are you ridiculous?"

She shrugs. "That's what my teacher says."

"Your teacher should be fired," I inform her.

All right, well, this is going to be a bloodbath, and I am never going to live it down. Brielle is going to tell people about this date, and I will never hear the end of it. So, I am going to take my team and form a plan that includes a lot of hiding.

"Is that pretty girl on the other team your girlfriend?" Mable asks.

She's my world. "She is a very good friend who I like very much."

"So, she's your *girlfriend*!" Mable yells this time. "Why aren't you with her? Does she like Timmy? He's my brother, and he said he's going to hit me in the head with the balloon."

I'm in the eighth circle of hell. "We won't let that happen, Mable. You point out Timmy, and we'll make sure he's the first out." I'm really hoping it's the mouthy kid who keeps calling me old.

The two women stride onto the field and stop by the four large drums in the center. The one has a megaphone and calls everyone in.

"Welcome to the second annual *kids'* water balloon tournament. Each team has four drums that are filled with balloons. Two are here, one is on the right side of the park, and one is on the left side of the park. Some balloons are filled with clear water while others are filled with colored water. As long as you're splashed with a clear water balloon, you stay in the game, but if you're hit with a colored water balloon, then you're out. The object of the game is to capture the other team's flag. In the bottom of one of the drums here is the map with where your flag is hidden and two clues as to where the other team's flag is. You want to guard your flag at all costs while also attempting to capture theirs. Do you want to flip a coin?"

Brielle shakes her head. "No need. You should let Spencer pick first."

"No, flip the coin," I say.

"We don't want it. We'll concede the coin toss."

I'm about to toss her over my shoulder and show her what she'll concede. However, Sara cuts in.

"Spencer, do you want to be the green team or the red team?"

Whatever. Sooner I can get this over with, sooner I can redeem myself on this date. I look to Mable. "What do you think?"

"Green!"

"Green it is."

"Brielle, your team will have the red coloring."

"Are you ready?"

Brielle grins. "Oh, we're ready, right boys?"

They all yell their agreement.

Sara looks to me. "Are you ready?"

"We're ready, right girls?"

Silence.

I turn to look at them. "We're ready, right?"

Taylor shrugs. "Can we get cotton candy?"

"After we win," I tell her.

"You're not going to win," says the kid who has been heckling me since we got here.

"Is your name Timmy?" I ask, hedging my bet.

"Yeah, why?"

"Just making sure." I grin. Totally going to be my first target.

Then I remember the kid is like nine or ten and I'm sitting here thinking about taking him out. I'm losing my damn mind.

Brielle saunters up to me. "Want to wager again?"

Hell no, I don't. This is literally me against her entire team, and yet, my stupid mouth says otherwise. "What do you have in mind?"

"I think this one is winner's choice—after the win. No stipulations."

"I'm not agreeing to that." She's crazy if she thinks I would be that dumb. For all I know, she'd make me do some embarrassing shit in town square. No way. I know this woman, and she's savage.

"Scared?"

I almost rise to the bait, but I grin instead. "Nope. I have nothing to be scared of because you're going down, Davis."

She smirks. "I don't think so, Cross. Besides, if you were that confident, you'd take my bet."

I step closer, her head tilts back to look at me. "I am more than confident."

Her hand moves to my chest, resting over my pounding heart. "About what?"

"That you're having the best date ever."

She laughs softly. "Are you saying the date is almost over?"

"Not even close." I lean down, forgetting we're on a field with two teams of kids watching us. "I plan to stretch this out as long as I can."

"I like that idea," she says softly, lifting just a smidge up on her toes.

I could kiss her so easily.

But then, the little brats yell. "Eww, she's going to kiss the old guy!"

Brielle laughs and drops back down, moving back. "May the best man win."

And then, before I can get to my drum, the horn blows and ten water balloons come flying at me.

Game on.

CHAPTER *Seventeen*

BRIELLE

It's been fifteen minutes, and we are still trying to execute the plan to get our map and find their flag. The only goal I had was to take Spencer out. The rest of the kids were collateral damage. All the boys are on board with this plan, but to his credit, Spencer is good.

He ducks and dodges, rolling to seek cover.

We hit him a bunch of times, but the balloons are clear water.

Spencer's team used our error to only focus on him to get their map first. The second they found it, they scattered and are either hiding or making their way to our flag. I turn to Timmy. "We need the map. We have to get their flag first."

"I'm on it!"

"Wait," I say, knowing that running off is not the right move. "We have to do this right."

Darius takes off anyway and is eliminated while he is digging through the drum, but Spencer was like a sniper tossing balloons at him until he finally hit him with a colored one.

Timmy, Brian, Kendrick, Saint, and I are behind a bush as we regroup. "Okay, boys, there's only one way out of this." They all look to me. "We need to take Spencer out and now. We can't let him stay in any longer."

Timmy looks irritated. "We know that. My sister can't throw at all and the other girls are probably pretending their balloons are dolls."

The boys all nod in agreement. Brian speaks next. "We need a better plan."

"Well, who has one?" I ask.

Saint has been the quiet one, and I am hoping he'll speak up. I can see that he knows what we should do, he just needs a chance to be heard.

I look to him. "Any ideas?"

"We could surround him."

I exaggerate my face a little and gasp. "That's brilliant. We should."

Timmy, who is the leader of this pack, thinks on it for a second. "How?"

Once again, I give Saint the opportunity to form our plan. "One of us has to sacrifice for the team."

I want to laugh, but I don't. "I'll do it," I volunteer.

Kendrick looks horrified. "You're the leader."

I smile. "I think you boys have a solid option. Saint will lead you all to victory. I'll make a break for the drum while you guys do what he says."

We huddle together and come up with who is going where. My hope is that Spencer will have a little mercy on me, since he's clearly nine again and wants to win, and he'll focus on them.

With a plan in place, we bump fists, and they yell, all going in different directions. I rise and beeline toward a drum. We need that map and I will go down swinging. Spencer yells for the girls to take cover, and the boys are launching balloons in every direction, hoping to hit someone in the wood line.

Balloons don't come at me for a few seconds. Then I hear Spencer shout, "Get her!"

Well, so much for mercy.

I move faster, zig-zagging in odd patterns to avoid getting hit. I reach the drum and drop down, using it for shelter.

Brian calls to me. "I'll cover you, Brie!"

I nod once and stand, digging as fast and deep as I can for the map. Balloons hit all around me, one splashes on my back, the cold water soaking through. "I'm hit!"

"It's clear!" Brian calls back.

My fingers brush against the edge of the plastic and grope for it. Once I grab ahold of it, I pull back fast and sink behind the drum.

"I got it, boys!" I let them know.

All but Timmy responds. I hope that means he found Spencer's hiding spot.

Brian army crawls his way to me. "Where is the flag?"

I look over the map again, tracing where we are and the park. A balloon hits my elbow. "Watch out," I tell him and he ducks as three balloons fly over our heads in an arch.

Then I see the spot where our flag is. "It's at the swings."

We both turn our heads to where it is, we have to run through the open field.

"What about their flag?" he asks.

I read the clues and grin. "It's in the treehouse behind us. Here's what we're going to do. I'll fill my bag with balloons and run, throwing as many balloons as I can to distract them while you head to the treehouse. That's where Spencer will be. Once you're their target, I'll come back and fill up the other bags. Tell any of the boys if you see them."

Each of us have a small bag that can fit about ten water balloons. If I can get the second one from our fallen teammate, then I have an advantage.

Brian is smiling broadly as we head off. It's like a slow-motion scene from a movie as I guard Brian's mad dash toward the target. Brian is fast and doesn't get hit a single time.

I spot Darius watching from the sidelines, and I whistle to him. When he looks, I whisper-shout. "Toss me your bag!"

Grinning, he runs over to me and hands it over.

"Thanks."

He's retreating when I catch a glimpse of Kendrick hiding behind our other barrel.

"A good teammate never leaves a man behind!" he offers his excuse for hanging back, and I grin.

"Thanks for having my back. We need you to guard our flag, think you're up to it?"

"You can count on me." He goes to run and then turns back. "Where is it?"

"It's on the swings, if you hide on the outer part of the playground, you can guard it without being seen."

"I'll protect it," Kendrick promises.

I gather as many balloons as I can into the bags and then use the bottom of my shirt to hold more.

Satisfied I can't possibly carry any more, I make my way to the treehouse, which seems far too quiet. I crouch, making sure I'm not missing anything.

Where is he?

Brian runs out of the bushes, and he doesn't make it more than a handful of steps before balloons start flying toward him from every direction. A colored one hits him in the back, and someone sounds a buzzer, announcing that he's been eliminated.

Shit.

I need to be patient and hope the other boys do the same.

However, Timmy has zero chill and runs out. Again, there are balloons coming from all around. This is where the girls are too. Spencer is smart. He hid them and told them to throw. He gets closer this time, but he's throwing balloons too and must've hit one of the girls.

"Timmy! You got me out!" she complains.

Then another girl comes down from where she was. "I'm out too. I hate water."

She wasn't hit with a color, but apparently the balloon splatter was enough.

"Taylor! You're not out," Spencer hisses, and I grin because he just gave up his position.

Then the first girl looks at Timmy and laughs. "You're out too! I hit you!"

Timmy looks affronted and then sees the green splatter on his shirt. "Mable!"

The pride on her face is enough to make me grin, even if she took my teammate out. I love how happy she is.

However, now it's only Kendrick, Saint, and me left, but Kendrick isn't here.

I walk around the back way, catching a glimpse of his white shirt. Oh, he's done now.

I put my balloons down in front of me where I can grab them easily and look for the best way to get him. There isn't much room, but I'm going to try. I throw two balloons quickly and duck down.

They hit him because I hear him curse. "Where are you, Davis?"

I grin. I'll never tell. I move a little to the right, make sure I have a clear shot, and then throw two more.

"That was close, sweetheart!" he yells back. "Why don't you show yourself so it's a fair fight?"

I roll my eyes. Yeah right.

I grab two more, ready to go back, and hear him laugh. "I see you, babe!"

Damn it.

It's do or die. I throw my balloons quickly, grab more and load my shirt back up. I'm down to just four balloons. I am going for it now. I run while throwing them at him, and he does the same. As I do that, I hear Spencer let out a long yell. "No!"

I throw another, hitting him in the chest, and it's red. "You're done!" I call out, so much glee in my voice.

Then a balloon hits me, spraying green water everywhere.

"You are too!" He laughs.

Then I turn when Saint breaks in. "We win!"

And there he is, holding the flag above his head with no dye on his shirt.

Spencer is smiling as he walks over to me. "Well done."

Laughing, I jump up into his arms and plant my mouth on his. Yes, this was well done and the most fun I've had in . . . well, since I can remember.

The rest of our date is a blur. After the fight, we went to the carnival and laughed as the kids recounted the most epic balloon fight in all of the world. Timmy and Spencer managed to find common ground when Spencer revealed his deep love of a book series.

The two of them talked about the likelihood of being born of a God and having powers. It was far over my head, but it was nice when Timmy referred to him by his name instead of "The Old Guy."

I have been floating. We've held hands and even rode a ride together. Well, it was bumper cars and Spencer's knees were in his chest, but it was fun and we promised the kids we'd come back next year for a rematch. They assured us the teams will be much bigger because they were going to bring everyone they knew.

We had dinner out of a food truck two towns over, and they were the best empanadas I've ever had.

Now we're pulling up to my apartment and the lightness of the day seems to be setting behind us. I don't want it to end. I want the fun like I had today. Where I'm not worrying about killers or a mystery fiancé who may knock on my door any minute. I want to live every day like what I had today.

I look over at Spencer with his thick beard and dark hair that I want to run my fingers through and sigh.

"What was that for?"

"I had the best day."

"I told you," he says with a smirk.

"You did, and it was amazing to see some of your special op training in real life."

"I feel like a lot of what we did in training is a big game of capture the flag, only we used paintballs that hurt like a bitch when you got hit."

I smile. "Thank you for this."

"You're welcome."

"I'm sad it's over," I admit, glancing over at the car sitting opposite of us. "Just looking at that reminds me that my life isn't a fun game of capture the flag."

He sees the car, lifts two fingers as a wave. "Quinn is a good guy."

"Were they with us all day?" I ask.

"Yes."

"I didn't . . . I didn't even see them."

Spencer shrugs. "That's how it's supposed to be. But they are always close in case you need them, even if you're with me."

I lean back, staring out at the inky sky. "How is this my life? It's not what I ever thought I would be dealing with."

He squeezes my hand. "We'll get to the bottom of it."

I laugh once. "That's what else I was sighing about."

"What?"

"For the first time since all of this happened, I was so happy. I had a chance to go out and just have fun. We didn't talk about memories or the past. We were here, living in the moment. I imagined this date might . . . well, this might be a prelude to something more and I am sad it's over. I'm worried that when my memories fully return, I won't want the life I'd been living."

Spencer shifts so that he can grab my other hand. "The dates and fun don't have to be over. I am . . . I want to go out again. I am asking you, do you want to go out with me again?"

My lips turn up, and I bob my head quickly. "Of course, but aren't you worried about all the other stuff?"

"I'm only worried about this. You and me." Spencer moves his hand to my cheek, cupping it ever so gently. "And now, I want to make good on my promise."

I play coy. "Which one is that?"

"I'm going to kiss you good night."

He moves in, and the kiss is sweet and slow and perfect. It's the kiss that I wished for and dreamed and I will never forget it.

CHAPTER *Eighteen*

BRIELLE

"Yes, Addy, it's totally safe," I reassure her with the same words I said to my mother an hour ago.

"I just . . . worry."

"You're supposed to be worrying less since you left."

"Well, clearly, I'm failing."

I sigh. "How is Elodie?"

"She's good. She's been having fun playing with Devney's family. She has a lot of nieces and nephews. She is trying to crawl!"

"Oh! I wish I could see it."

"I'll take video," Addy promises.

"So, you're comfortable in the guest house?" I ask.

"It's not a guest house." She laughs. "It's a freaking huge house. When I first saw it, I was completely thrown off because it's amazing. I was really worried about fitting in, but her sisters-in-law are all amazing and we're comfortable here. Ellie, Brenna, and Sydney all stop by or make us come over for dinner, and they are just—kind. Brenna's husband died a few years ago, so it's been nice to have someone who understands what it's like to be a widow."

I hate that she even has to utter that word. "I am so glad it's been good for you."

"It has been. I really needed this."

"How long do you think you'll stay?"

She sighs. "I don't know. The Arrowoods told me I could stay as long as I want, and since Sean is in Florida for the start of the season, it's helping Devney not be alone too."

I had this horrible feeling that Addy would stay much longer. "I miss you."

"I miss you too. I really do, but it's been really nice getting away. I will definitely be back by her birthday."

Four months. Great.

"That's not that soon."

"No, but that's the deadline I've given myself. I've been able to go to the store without someone stopping me to cry about Isaac. I can take Elodie for a walk without pity stares. It's just allowed me to grieve a bit on my own."

"I understand. I do."

"It's not that I don't want to be there for you or . . . anything like that. I just don't want to relive everything over and over."

"I really do get it."

I wouldn't want to either. This town is small and intrusive, even though they mean well. Addison wasn't able to have time alone because people just want to help.

"Tell me what's new there."

I debate telling her about my theory on the connection to the youth center. I can't stop thinking that there's a tie-in with it and Isaac's murder. The money trail doesn't add up, someone broke into my office, and I am not sure what exactly I may have known or if I shared my concern with him. If I did, he wouldn't have sat idly by. So, maybe the answer is with her.

Instead of saying any of that, I go a different route. "I made out with Spencer, and we went on a date."

"You *what*?" she screeches.

I wince. "Umm, we kissed—like really kissed."

She laughs. "You're kidding, right? Spencer, like, our Spencer?"

"The one and only."

"That's . . . well, I don't know," she says, but I swear I hear the smile in her voice. "It's a little shocking, but at the same time, he's kind of perfect for you. The two of you have always been close and he cares about you, anyone can see that."

"Yeah, but more like a sister than a . . . girlfriend."

"Well, I don't know about that since you two are making out. And dating!"

"One date, but he did ask me out again. It's weird, though—the kissing—well . . . not weird in a bad way. It's weird because when we kissed, it's like we couldn't stop it. As though there's no other choice but to kiss."

Addison giggles. "You and Spencer. Wow. But what about the ring thing? What about that guy?"

"What about him? No one even knows who he is, and he hasn't tried to get in touch with me. Is there something you know and aren't telling me?"

"No, I really don't know who he is. I promise." Addison's sincerity rings through her words. "I wish I did because if I did, I wouldn't be going over every person I've ever seen you with, trying to figure out who it is. It's annoying not knowing."

"Oh, you're annoyed not having information?" I toss back.

"Sorry."

I sigh. "It's fine. I get it. All for the greater good. I just . . . how could I love someone who loved me back so much that he gave me a huge rock, but I didn't talk about him to anyone? How could I love one man and kiss another without any hesitancy? I keep asking myself this because I don't know how I go forward after kissing Spencer and knowing what a kiss like that can be like."

"So, it was good?"

"Very, *very* good."

"I can see that," Addy says.

"You can?"

"Sure! Spencer is a ladies' man. He's always had swagger. You know, when we were ten, I had a huge crush on him. I thought he was *so* cool. Then a boy picked on me, and Isaac shoved him to the ground, after that . . . I was in love."

I smile. "He was always the protector."

"That's why I think that he died trying to protect you."

"I think he did too."

Addy clears her throat. "Even if he did, it wouldn't be your fault, Brielle. No matter what. Emmett called me yesterday and said they had a lead, so if that pans out, maybe your testimony won't be the crucial part of the case."

"A lead?" I ask, feeling slightly hopeful.

"Don't get too excited. Four other leads have been dead ends."

That's depressing. "No one has said anything to me."

"Would you really want to know? Until your memory fully returns, it's sort of a moot point anyway. You can't ID the person, and now that I've learned what I have about these types of cases, nothing moves quickly and there are more leads that go nowhere than tips that pan out. But let's go back to the lip locking with Spencer."

I roll my eyes. "He'll be here in about ten minutes, so I'd rather not."

"The MOTY awards dinner is the second date?"

"I don't think so. It definitely didn't start that way, anyway. Spencer was stuck driving me since I am still not allowed and everyone is paranoid about me going anywhere alone."

"Rightfully so."

Yeah, yeah. "I have my panic button."

"A what?"

I guess I haven't really talked about it since it's new. "A few days ago, the owner's wife was stuck on my detail. She's amazing, by the way. I think she is a spy or maybe she is a hitman, I'm not sure. Anyway, Charlie and I started talking, and she gave me this panic button that looks more like a key fob. She said if I ever think I'm in danger or could be in danger, all I have to do is press it. They will pull me out and get me to a secure location where I will be locked down for a minimum of twelve hours while the team investigates. It's to make sure I'm safe, especially with my messed-up brain."

"You had that before," Addy jokes.

"Anyway, I'm even better now that I have it, which brings me back to why I don't know if it's a date."

"Let's call it a date anyway."

"Let's not."

"Fine, but it's totally a date. What are you wearing?"

We launch into a discussion about my attire, which she approves of, and then sighs longingly. "You should wear the diamond studs."

"I hate wearing the studs."

They were a gift from my father on my sixteenth birthday. Each time I wear them, I get all teary.

"Fine, then wear the gold choker that drops down the back. Oh, and you're like six inches shorter than Spencer, so make sure you wear the really cute four-inch heels."

That's not a bad idea. My dress is pale green and clings in all the right places. The showstopper part of it is the open back. It drapes down to right above my butt. I love this dress. I got it for a wedding I went to right after graduation.

I do not love those shoes though. However, the height will help.

"My feet are going to kill me after an hour."

"Beauty is pain, sister."

I grab the necklace and slip it on, the cool metal sliding against my back. It's that perfect jewelry piece that is understated but makes a statement at the same time.

I close the drawer and see the ring box sitting there. I haven't looked at it in a few days. For the first few days after I discovered it, I would randomly hold it in my hand, wishing the memory of how I got it would come back. I open the box, seeing the gorgeous diamond safely in its spot.

"Hello! Earth to Brie!"

I close the box and shake my head. "Sorry. I put it on."

"Good. Will you send me a photo?"

"Sure, I'll send one." I laugh.

"Perfect. Thank you for calling. I needed this."

"What?"

"This talk, it felt like . . . old times."

I grin. "Yeah, it did."

"Have fun tonight and don't worry so much. You are amazing and everyone loves you. Also, be sure to make out with Spencer again and make sure it's as good as the time before."

I laugh. "You're such a bad influence."

"Hey, this is what sisters do."

My phone pings with a text from Spencer, letting me know he's on his way up.

"I gotta go, he's here."

"Make bad choices!" she yells and then hangs up.

I sigh. I can do this.

I'm insanely nervous about tonight because everyone from the town will be there. I'll be surrounded by people who will know me and some who I won't remember meeting. More than that, I worry the killer will be there, and I won't be able to tell. It's horrible to look at people's faces and wonder if they're who killed your brother and tried to kill you. Thankfully, the security guys will be shadowing me the whole time, so that makes me feel a bit better. They are actually all cool.

Charlie informed me this morning that she and her husband, Mark, would be attending the dinner but sticking to the background. Apparently, it was easier to blend in if they looked like they were attending instead of acting as my private security while Quinn stays and watches the apartment.

Quinn Miller flew in from Virginia Beach last night, and I got to meet him. He's married and has a son, who he showed me a bunch of photos of. Super adorable kid. He and Charlie are my security detail this week, but next week, they will rotate out with someone else.

I bring them out coffee each morning and before bed, I flick the living room lights so they know I'm going to sleep.

I head to the door, smoothing my dress against my body and checking my hair in the mirror by the entry.

He knocks once, and because I am a nervous wreck, I throw the door open with zero chill.

"Hi," I sputter, more than a little stunned.

Holy. Freaking. Shit. He's wearing a black tuxedo with silk lapels, and it's as though the fabric is conforming to his body. Every inch of him makes my mouth water. His broad shoulders block out the light behind him and I could melt right here. His green eyes look even brighter tonight and his hair looks damp and finger tousled. He looks incredible.

I wait for him to say something, but Spencer doesn't speak. Instead, his eyes do a very slow assessment of the green satin wrapped around my body, neckline that mimics the back with it draping low enough to show the swell of my breasts. I curled my hair into long waves and did my best on my makeup after watching a few tutorials online. It's a little heavy, but I think it's sexy.

"Spencer?" I say, suddenly uncomfortable and shy. "Do I look okay?"

His gaze meets mine, and we hold for a few seconds. I see the moment his restraint snaps, and he moves into the room, kicking the door shut behind him. I stutter back a step, but he's already there, pushing my back against the wall, caging me in. I am so glad I wore the heels. We're almost the same height and I can see the desire swimming in his eyes. My heart stops before doubling in speed. He's going to kiss me, and I am so here for it.

"I shouldn't."

"You should," I say. He shakes his head, rubbing his nose against mine. "I want . . . please tell me you want me to kiss you."

I want that more than anything. I move my right hand from his chest up to his neck, wrapping my hand around it. "I want it."

Like two magnets drawn together, we collide. His mouth claims mine in a searing kiss that's infinitely better than the last one. There's no restraint on either of our parts. No slowness or tenderness. This kiss is desperate need and desire. I melt against him, needing his heat, which is a complete contrast of the cold against my back. I taste the mint on his tongue and inhale his cologne, the musky scent that is all him.

His mouth leaves mine, and his lips and tongue slide down my neck and along my shoulder.

"Spencer." I moan his name when he makes his way back up, nipping my ear playfully.

"You take my breath away." His deep voice rumbles. "You are so beautiful, and I want you so badly."

Head injuries, I've decided, are not all bad. If they make your life-long dream of having the man you lusted after your whole life want you, then I am really okay with this.

"I . . . I don't know what is happening," I say oh so eloquently.

"What do you mean?" He looks deep into my eyes, making it so much harder for me to string words together.

"This. You. Kissing me and . . . whatever this is. I don't care anymore. Does that make me a bad person?"

That's basically the gist of my confusion. Spencer has never once made any kind of advance on me. At least not that I can remember. So, why now? Is it because of Isaac's death? Is there something I don't remember?

Spencer steps back, and the loss of his heat is immediate. I am an idiot. I should've kept my trap shut and just enjoyed the kissing.

"I wanted to kiss you, and I didn't take into account the entire situation. Fuck!" He runs his hand through his thick brown hair. "I'm such an asshole."

"For kissing me?"

"Yes!"

"Please feel free to do it again," I say as I adjust my breasts back to where they should be. "Not to mention, we kissed a few nights ago, and we weren't upset about it then."

Spencer's eyes move from my face to my chest. "What do you mean?"

"I liked it. I want it to happen and keep happening. I understand that we've been through a lot, and this is probably a really fucking bad idea, but I don't have it in me to care."

His lips part and then close. I can see I've confused him as well.

"You want me . . . to keep kissing you?"

"Yes. I mean, if I can't remember the dude I may or may not be engaged to, it's not really cheating, right?"

Spencer sighs. "What if you love him?" His voice is low, but I hear the question as though he screamed it. "What if he's the one you really dream of, Brielle? What if this guy is so in love with you that he's dying inside? What if—"

"What if there's no guy? Hell, if there is a guy, where the fuck is he? It's been weeks and no mystery guy has shown up looking for me. If he loves me so much, why isn't he here? For all we know, he's the one who killed Isaac and tried to kill me and that's why he hasn't shown up. There are a million questions we can go through and still end up right here." I step toward him, placing my hand on his chest. "Right here and right now, there's no other guy. There's you and there's me, and I want you to kiss me. I want to kiss you. I want you to be the guy, Spencer, don't you see that? You are the guy for me, right here, right now. When I'm with you, I'm safe and happy," I breathe the last part.

"You are supposed to be safe with me."

The way he says that, as though feeling and being are different, makes me pause. "Am I not safe with you?"

Spencer's finger moves to my cheek, pushing a stray hair back. "Not right now you're not."

I press my body just a little closer to his, craving his warmth. "I have never felt safer than I do when you're around."

"You really shouldn't."

"Maybe not."

A door slams across the hall, and we jump apart. My heart is pounding in the way it always does when there is a sudden, loud noise.

"Brie." His voice is full of concern.

"I'm fine. I'm fine." And I am. I'm okay, and I am safe. Spencer would never let anything hurt me. I am just a little skittish still. As my heartbeat steadies, I step to him, not wanting to stop the conversation. "I mean it, Spencer."

"I know you do, but you don't know everything that's happening."

Another step. "Then tell me. Please, just tell me so I can know."

He leans his forehead against mine before pressing his lips to the same spot. Spencer lets out a breath through his nose. "I want to, but I can't."

Another door slams, but this time, I don't jump. This time, I feel calm and secure. He's right here, looking down at me, and I search for something to explain why I feel this way with him. A knock comes almost a second later, breaking the moment, but I don't move away from him until the person on the other side knocks again.

Throwing on my best smile, I open the door, and Charlie is there with a man in a tux.

"Good, you're still here," Charlie says, looking like a supermodel. "This is my husband, Mark Dixon."

He extends his hand, and I shake it. "I'm Brielle."

"It's great to meet you," he says and then sees Spencer. "Cross! Who knew that you could look like something other than a bag of ass?"

Spencer laughs and walks to him. They shake hands and do that manly hug where there's a lot of back slapping. "Good to see you, Twilight. It's been a long time."

"Well, when I heard we were out here guarding someone on your request, I figured I should come see what's going on in this . . . small fucking boring town."

They laugh, and Spencer jerks his head toward me. "Brie has managed to find the only trouble that exists in Rose Canyon."

I shrug. "Guilty, I guess."

Charlie smiles. "I think trouble finds beautiful women."

"She would know," Mark says with a smirk. "That one can find trouble where it doesn't even exist. I swear she makes it just to have fun."

"Yes, because you're the poster child for saintly living," she chides.

Mark walks back over, wrapping his arm around her back. "I am divine."

She rolls her eyes and focuses back on me. "Anyway, we're heading over and didn't see you guys exit the apartment, so I wanted to check on things and make sure we are all on the same page for tonight."

"I really don't think anything is going to happen at the MOTY awards."

I understand why I need security, to some extent, but I wish if something were to happen, it would already. It's been over three weeks and not even a peep.

"Sometimes, it's the places we think we're safe that we actually aren't," Mark says.

Spencer and I glance at each other and then I look away. I just said how safe I felt with him. He just warned me I shouldn't.

Charlie steps forward. "Has something happened?"

"No, why?"

She smiles softly. "No reason, but if someone has contacted you and it slipped through our safeguards, you need to tell us."

"I would. I haven't had any strange calls or messages. No one has been following me around or threatening me."

"Good." Mark nods once. "Let's head out and see what this Man of the Year thing is all about."

Charlie looks at me. "Make sure you have your keys."

Right, the button is on my key ring. I grab those, toss them in my clutch, and head for the door. Before I get there, Spencer's fingers wrap around my wrist, halting me. "What?"

"Are we . . . okay?"

God, that one question has so many damn possible answers. "Are we going to have fun tonight?"

"I hope so."

"Do you have water balloons strategically placed anywhere?" I ask with a grin.

He laughs. "I wish I did."

I tilt my head. "Hopefully, you have better evasion skills tonight then."

"So, you have them hidden?" Spencer asks.

I lean in, my lips grazing his ear. "You'll just have to wait to find out."

I kiss his cheek, and he chuckles. "God, I love—like being around you."

He extends his elbow, like the gentleman he's always been, and I take it. We lock up and make our way to where Charlie and Mark are waiting by the main entrance. "We'll follow you in our car," she explains.

Spencer places his hand on my back, guiding me to where he's parked. When we get to the sidewalk, I stop dead in my tracks. I blink back the tears that threaten to form.

In front of me is the red sports car from my memory. The one Isaac bought but Addison made him sell. I turn to look at him. "You have it?"

"He sold it to me and made me promise to keep it safe from your sister-in-law."

My world seems as if it's spinning backward. "Do you own it?"

"I do."

Okay. So he's who bought it. "For how long?"

He shrugs. "Not that long."

"How long?"

"Brielle, I want to answer you, but we both know that these questions lead us down a very dangerous path."

"No lies," I repeat his words.

"Exactly, it's better if we avoid talking about specifics, okay? Besides, does it matter how long I've had it? I could've bought it two days ago and that doesn't change anything."

"Did I ever get to drive it?"

He lets out a soft chuckle. "Isaac never let you, but you might get a different answer if you were to ask me."

"Well? Can I?"

He chuckles. "I promise I'll let you."

"When?"

"When you're medically cleared to drive."

I huff. "Fair enough."

Spencer leans in and kisses my temple. "We have time, sweetheart. Just be patient."

That's easy for someone who has nothing but time. "We both know that time isn't a guarantee. Not for any of us."

"No, it's not, but we both know you're not allowed to drive now and, who knows what will happen as your memories keep resurfacing."

I jerk my head back a little. "What do you mean?"

"Nothing."

He clearly meant something by that. "Did you uncover something?"

"No. I never should've said that." He glances at his watch. "We're going to be late. Come on, let's go drink for free and watch Emmett make a fool of himself."

I place my hand in his and let him lead me to the car, wishing that niggling feeling in my gut wasn't growing and vowing to find out what he's hiding.

CHAPTER *Nineteen*

SPENCER

"One day, it'll be you, Spence," Emmett says as he slaps me on the back. "Who knew that I would be getting this award?"

I wonder how many shots he's had because, a few days ago, it wasn't a big deal, now he's on the brink of crying. "Dude, it's a Rose Canyon award where you were up against the mayor's son, who drove his ATV into a ditch because he tried to drive it with his helmet on backward. It wasn't exactly a pool of winners."

He shakes his head and grabs his drink. "I'm a winner."

"You're something."

"I miss my friend," he says, looking around. "I miss . . . well, all of them."

Emmett was really there for Addison and Elodie before Addison's mother could get there. Watching Addison crumble, knowing he couldn't help, and grieving his own loss, wasn't easy for him.

I understood, to some extent, how Addy felt, but while Emmett was helping her, I focused all of my energy on Brielle. A part of me didn't register that Isaac was dead because I couldn't handle any more than the fact that my entire world was almost taken from me too.

"We all do," I say and then lift my glass. "To Isaac."

"To Isaac, who really was the man of every year."

We clink glasses, and I scan the room, looking for Brielle.

So far, the town has done a great job of following the rules. People who she met within the last three years have stayed on the fringe, not doing anything to make her uncomfortable. She's sitting with Jenna, her smile is easy, even though tonight has been anything but.

"She looks good," Emmett says.

It appears I wasn't doing so great hiding it. "She does."

"You guys getting along okay?"

I turn back to him. "Why wouldn't we?"

"Just curious."

Emmett is never just anything. He's smart and observant. He's been back in town six months and has been focused on his new job, moving, and getting his life straight. It's the only reason I was able to get away with seeing Brie under his nose too.

Isaac was easy to fool.

Which I regret now.

"Yeah, we're fine."

Emmett puts his glass down. "Spence, you're like a brother to me, and I know you pretty well. There's something going on there."

"Let it go," I warn.

"I would, but part of my job is making sure that we keep Isaac's case from being thrown out."

"And you think I don't share in your concern?"

Emmett smiles at someone who walks by and then turns back to me. "I didn't say that, but I live across the hall and I'm briefed every day. I can see the same logs you can and, if you remember, I can see her messages."

I use that training from years ago to mask my emotions, but the panic is building. I force out a laugh and clap him on the shoulder. "You and I know what the truth is."

Emmett doesn't share in my fake laughter. "Yeah, Spence, we do, and I'm telling you that if you fuck this up, she'll never be okay with it. Isaac was her brother, and she loved him."

She loves me too. Whatever Emmett thinks he knows, he doesn't. I have not done anything that would jeopardize this case. "I have never told her anything."

"You also answer questions you shouldn't. Look, I have a pretty strong impression that there's a lot that I'm not aware of. If you and Brie had something going on, which I think you did, then you're in over your head, brother."

I don't want to have this conversation. "We're done talking about this now."

"Yeah, after I say this, if you keep going down the road where you're feeding her things, then you're going to have to make a choice."

My back straightens at the implied threat. "What exactly are you saying, Emmett?"

"You can't give her memories. You can't tell her things."

"I'm not."

"She told me that you are the only person who will answer the questions she asks directly."

No lies.

"I won't lie to her. She's Brielle. She deserves more than this. If she weren't the only witness in her brother's murder, we would've told her everything and shown her the life she had."

I push down my anger, but Emmett knows me too well. He hears the things I'm not saying. "Spencer, either you break contact with her until this is over or you keep lying to her and let this happen the way it needs to. If I'm right and you're the person who gave her that ring—" He sighs deeply and runs his hand down his face. "Which we are going to discuss when we aren't in a room with two hundred people, then you have to do the right thing." He downs his drink, puts the glass down, and rests his hand on my shoulder. "I don't think you want to break contact completely, but if you push me on this, you'll find yourself locked out of the building."

Emmett walks away, leaving me stunned. Walking away isn't an option. I would rather lie than abandon her—abandon us. When she does remember, then what? How do I explain I had to leave because I wasn't strong enough to do what I needed to? I can't. I can't do to her what's been done to me over and over again.

I start to head toward her, and Jax, one of her coworkers, stops me. "Hey, Spencer."

"Jax."

Jax is a fairly new guy in town. He moved here about a year ago, and no one says anything bad about him, but I get a bad vibe from him that I can't explain. One night, Brie and I were having dinner in my apartment, and she brought him up, saying how he was always asking her out. She needed advice on how to turn him down easily.

Apparently, he didn't get the hint because he was still giving her flowers once a week up until the incident.

"How's she doing?" Jax asks.

"She's doing better."

"Still no memories?"

I shake my head. "No, not yet. Did you guys figure out who was in her office?"

He shakes his head. "No, it's so weird. The exterior cameras were disabled too, so there's nothing."

I already knew that, but I was curious as to what he'd say. "Has Brielle talked about anyone at the center?"

"Nope."

"Bummer, I keep wanting to talk to her, you know? We had this connection."

I almost laugh in his face. There was no connection. None.

"Well, you know the rules."

He nods. "Yeah, the rules. She keeps looking over here, and I'm hoping she remembers me. It would be nice to talk to her. Plus, I really want to help her come back to work. Everyone misses her there, especially the kids. Listen, one of the kids at the center is really messed up. Brielle was really close with Dianna, she's about eight. Brielle helped the family a lot, and they were asking if they could see her. I know she loved the kids and maybe it would help?"

Brielle loves those kids more than anything. She wanted to help each one of them and she gave them the support and encouragement they needed to reach their potential. Everything she did was to benefit them, even if it wasn't the best for her. She took a pay cut a few months back so the money could help fund extended hours for an afterschool program.

I can imagine there are a lot more families that miss her.

"I'm not sure that's a good idea."

"Yeah, I told them not yet, but everyone just wants to help. We all miss her and want her back to normal."

"We all have the same goal," I tell him.

I watch Jax straighten a little, and the air around me shifts. Everything changes when she's near. I turn and Brielle is there, holding her glass of water. "Hey there."

"Brie."

She turns to Jax, her eyes narrowing just a bit. "I'm Brielle," she says, extending her hand to him. "I'm sure we know each other, but I don't remember. So, I appreciate that you're pretending for my sake."

Jax nods a few times. "It's nice to meet you," he says smoothly. "I'm Jax."

Brielle's eyes widen, and she steps back. "Jax? We . . . you . . ."

I move closer to her, feeling her anxiety as if it's my own. "Brielle? Are you okay?"

She blinks a few times and nods. "Yes, I'm fine." Her voice shifts, and I can hear the happiness in her tone. "I remember you. You're Jax. We work . . . I think we work together? You . . . had a song? Something? I think?"

Jax looks to me and then to Brie. I step in, making sure this idiot doesn't say anything. "What do you remember?"

Her dark blue eyes are on mine. "Just a song about Jax and the

Beanstalk? Maybe it's not him or anything, but I remember the silliness."

"Jack and the Beanstalk?" I ask.

"No, it was a parody, and I just remember the kids and I laughing."

It doesn't sound like a full memory, but it's something, which is better than nothing.

"Am I right?" she asks.

Jax smiles. "Yes, I wrote it and we would sing to the kids."

Emmett's threat about what would happen if I told her anything she didn't recall on her own screams in my head. "Is that all you remember?"

She nods. "It's a piece, I know, not the whole thing, but . . . it's something."

"It's something."

I turn to Jax. "Please excuse us."

Brielle shifts her gaze to him, waves, and then turns to me. "That was rude."

"Maybe, but I've never liked that guy."

She raises a brow. "Jealous?"

"No." Yes.

"I remembered that song. I remembered, and I was right."

"You were." I stop her on the center of the dance floor, extending my hand to her. "Dance with me?"

She looks around. "It's kind of hard to say no since you brought me here and have your hand out."

"Do you want to say no?" I ask as the music starts to cue up.

"I don't."

"Good." I smile.

The last time we danced was two nights before the shooting. We stood in her apartment, the ring securely on her finger, and we danced. No music was needed. We just swayed as though we knew every step and beat in perfect harmony.

Brielle's fingers play with the hair on the back of my neck. "Your hair is long."

"I haven't had time to get it cut."

"It's weird sometimes," she says absently. "I don't know anything about your life for the past three years. I don't know anything about where you've been or what you've done besides what I've found on the internet."

I smirk. "You googled me?"

"Don't be so smug."

"I'm not smug."

"Yes you are," she chides.

"Fine. A little."

Brielle grins. "I just want all of my memories back."

Me too. Me fucking too.

Brie sighs. "Are you going to tell me why you pulled me away from Jax?"

Because he loves you and can't have you.

The other part is that, when I was talking to him, warning bells were going off. There was something in his posture, the structuring of his questions, that left me uneasy. He has always had a crush on her, but then there's something in my gut that won't ease up. He's still staring at her as though he's waiting for something, and I don't like it.

"What else do you remember about him?"

I turn her so she's out of his line of sight. "Why aren't you answering my question?"

I huff. "Because I'm not allowed to."

Brielle turns her head. "I know, but . . . whatever. I don't remember him so much as the name and the song. I really hoped—" She stops and chews on her lower lip.

"What?"

She looks back to me, eyes filled with sadness. "I thought I'd see someone or something tonight that would break this fog. It's why I agreed to come to this ridiculous dinner."

"I hoped for the same."

"Too bad it didn't work. You know, some days, I wish I didn't remember anything about my past at all."

My eyes widen at that confession. "Why?"

"Then it wouldn't be so painful. I wouldn't know how amazing Isaac was or how happy I was when I got the job I can't work at right now. I wouldn't have remembered Henry or cared at all about who this mystery ring belongs to. I could start over. I could build a life without the past looming over me as though it's ready to drop down at any moment. The flashes are the worst part. It's like someone opening their eyes to the sunlight and having to slam their lids closed when it burns."

"Don't close them next time, just turn your head and look at me. I'll shade you so you can still see."

The sadness that was heavy in her beautiful gaze is gone, but something else is there. Something like wonder, and God, I'd give anything for it to stay there. "Spencer, can we go?"

"Go where?"

"Anywhere. I just want to talk, and you're the only person that makes me feel normal."

From the corner of my eye, I see Emmett watching us, arms crossed over his chest. I don't care about anything but her. She's asking me for something, and I will never deny her. I know that I will tell her a million lies and beg for forgiveness before I can walk away.

"Sure. Let's go."

It's a beautiful night. The clear skies allow the twinkling lights to offer promises of wishes. I wrap my coat around Brie's shoulders and we lean against the deck railing, looking out at the lake.

"Do you remember the night Isaac jumped in the lake in February?" she asks with a laugh.

"He was so mad about losing that bet."

Brielle turns her head with a grin. "Mad is an understatement."

"So is saying that he was cold."

"That too. I couldn't believe you wouldn't let him off the hook."

There was no way I was going to do that. He bet me that I couldn't go three days without saying no. Well, I did, and he had to pay for it. God knows I paid for all the stupid things I had to agree to. "Would you have?"

She shakes her head. "Not a chance. Just like I didn't let you off the hook when you lost the bet with me."

"Which one?"

"Does it matter?" she asks. No, I guess it really doesn't. I'm glad I've lost every last one as of late. "You realize we have issues in this group with gambling."

"It's always in good fun."

Her fingers slide against the gold chain on her neck. "Some of them are. Others are much more . . . personal."

"Like kisses and dates?"

"Like kisses and dates." Brielle sighs, her blonde hair falling back as she looks up at the starry sky. "I did appreciate that you wrote that paper for me in English. That was definitely worth it."

"I forgot about that."

"I got an A," she tells me.

"Of course you did—or, should I say, I did."

Brie grins and stares back at the inky water. "You know, I had my first kiss here. It was so horrible."

"Isaac punched the guy."

Brie's jaw drops. "That's why he stopped talking to me?"

"Most likely. He was talking to a bunch of other kids at the movies about how he stuck his tongue down your throat and you cried. I walked over, grabbed him by the jacket, and threatened him. Before I could punch him, Isaac stole the honors."

I remember being pissed I didn't get to. Those punks all deserved a beating for the shit they were saying about her and her friends.

"I never knew it was you!"

"See, some things I can tell you."

"That doesn't count as the memory you're supposed to give me."

"I know, since it's not one of your memories. It's just a reminder of your bad choices with men."

Brie turns to me. "Do you include yourself in this?"

"Am I now one of your men?"

She shrugs. "You could be."

"And what does one need to do to be considered for the position?"

"First, I'll need an application, a list of references, and maybe an essay on why you should be considered for it."

I lean in. "I have one very good reason that you'll want to hear."

"Oh? Do tell."

Our faces are close, so close that her breath warms my lips. "I am very, very good in bed."

"That is a good one," she concedes. "I'll have to keep that in mind."

I pull away, feeling the cool air push between us. "You do that."

She smiles and inhales, wrapping my jacket around her tighter. Then her eyes widen in shock as her lips tremble.

"What's wrong?"

"The cigar smell . . ."

Fuck. Fuck. I am a goddamn idiot. I smoked a cigar with Emmett when I got here. The one we always smoke on special occasions. The one that she remembers tasting and has the ring of in that box. I should've thought about that. I should've known it would trigger her. Or maybe Emmett is right, and all I want is for this nightmare to be over, so I keep doing things to push her. I'm being selfish because I miss *my* Brielle. I miss her love and touch and everything we have.

She brings the lapels to her nose, sniffing it again. Her eyes find mine, waiting for the answer.

I steady my voice and pretend to have no idea what she's saying. "Emmett and I had one when we arrived. Why?"

"It smells the same." She steps closer. "The same scent and . . ."

I can see the confliction in her eyes, the warring emotions between wanting to ask for more and knowing I can't give it to her.

"The cigar?" I ask.

Brie nods. "Yes, the same one I tasted on my tongue. Why?"

I shrug, as though it's not a big deal when it is. "We got them from the store in town. They only have two brands."

That's another lie. These are from Cuba and definitely not sold in

Oregon. I have a friend who gave me a box when he came back from Havana. The last time they were touched was the night Elodie was born, which was the first night Brielle and I made love.

"Right. That makes sense . . . of course. I just thought that maybe . . ."

"You thought maybe the memory was of me?"

Brielle looks out at the lake, her body tight as she lets out a heavy sigh. The tension is building between us, and I don't know what is going to finally tip us over.

Whatever she was thinking through, she finds her resolve and her blue eyes meet mine, not wavering. "I hoped. I keep hoping and wondering, and I need to ask this . . . could that engagement ring be from you?"

CHAPTER *Twenty*

BRIELLE

I feel so stupid. So absolutely ridiculous, but yes. I want it to be true. I want to believe, for just a minute, that this ugly duckling grew into a swan and got the prince. He has always been the light that I've reached for in the darkness.

I chose my words carefully, making sure that I phrased it in a way that would hopefully get him to answer the question I really needed answered. I can't keep hoping that what I want now is what I had in the past. That the way I feel around him is because my heart is his. It's crazy, and I need to know the truth, which is why I'm so grateful that Spencer won't lie.

Steeling my nerves to whatever the answer is.

He smiles and shakes his head. "No, it's not mine."

I want to cry.

The scent of that cigar was so strong and so similar to the smell from my first memory, and I guess I just wanted it to tie back to him.

Instead of allowing the tears to come, I force a soft laugh. "I didn't think so. It would've been crazy if we were together and no one knew."

"There's not a chance in hell we could've done that."

No, I guess not. Spencer would never have lied to Isaac. Addy would've known, and she was genuinely shocked when I found that ring.

But, oh, how I wish . . .

As crazy as it is, it's also not. Spencer is the one person in this world I have always thought would be my equal in every way. He's who I want to talk to each morning and the man I think of when I drift to sleep. He has always lived in the back of my mind, but this new version of him doesn't make sense.

Like, why does he kiss me like this? How can he make me forget all my pain and smile when we have never had this kind of connection? Why do I feel his gaze on me everywhere? I've fought against myself, tried so hard to brush it off, but I can't stop thinking there's something between us. "Have we been more?"

"Why do you ask that?"

"Because what would've changed in the last month? Why would you suddenly see me differently?"

Spencer leans his back against the railing, staring into the party. "You have always been different to me. It just wasn't the right time."

"And now suddenly is? After Isaac? That doesn't make sense."

"I don't know . . ." he admits.

The wind blows, and I cinch his jacket tighter. Spencer steps to me, rubbing my arms. I look up into his green eyes, wanting to understand. "It's so hard for me to know what's reality and what's a dream."

He stares down at me. "What do you mean?"

I haven't said anything to Spencer, but I did talk to Dr. Girardo yesterday about the vivid dreams. I wake up, so sure that my dream was a memory. Spencer's hands are on my body, I see his smile as we are in the dream. All of my senses are engaged, and I've woken up more than once, panting and longing for him.

Dr. Girardo and I unpacked the one I had yesterday, and he pointed out that the sequence of events in the dreams aren't in order. I'll be kissing Spencer one second and fighting with him the next. He and I think it could be a mix of a memory of someone else and I'm replacing that person with Spencer. He said that, until I have this occur in an awake state, he would agree with my assessment that it's a mash-up of dreams, memories, and events, but it's unclear which is which.

"I dream of you," I tell him. His hands stop moving, but he doesn't let go. "I dream of us together on the beach like we were a few weeks ago. I dream about us eating dinner in my apartment or of you sneaking out in the morning. I wake up, so sure that it's real, but I think it's just me wishing it were." His breathing has gotten a little faster, and I look him in his eyes as I say, "Tell me, is it a memory or a dream?"

"It can be the future," he says, moving his hands up my arms to my neck, cradling my face.

He leans in, and this will be the first time he's kissed me in public. There are hundreds of people right on the other side of the glass. I close my eyes, ready for his lips on mine.

"Brielle! Brie!" Charlie calls, and Spencer pulls away a second before she rounds the corner. "There you are! I have been looking all over for you. Fancy finding you here too, Spencer."

"Charlie," he says and then clears his throat. "We came out here for some air."

Charlie chuckles. "Sure, you did. I'm not an idiot. You do realize there are a lot of windows in this establishment, right?"

"We weren't . . ."

"I don't care what you two do, I just came out here to stop it before everyone *else* saw the two of you lock lips. We both know how some people react to things. So, laugh now at my hilarious joke." Neither of us do. She lifts her brows. "Go on."

Spencer and I smile and then pretend to laugh. "Okay."

"Now, Spencer, you go inside and get Brielle's clutch since Brielle has a headache. It's best you take her home."

He nods once and heads off.

"Is it that bad?" I ask nervously.

"No, we just had to calm Emmett down a little."

I groan. "What does he have to be upset about?"

Charlie arches a brow. "Babe, you don't remember a large gap of your life and everyone is trying to protect your testimony. Emmett has already been told that he's at a major disadvantage because there is no evidence pointing to a suspect. They are pinning all their hopes on you. He doesn't want to give a defense any possible ammunition."

"What does that have to do with Spencer?"

Her smile is soft, but there's a little censure there. "It's just not the best optics. Not when the DA already has issues with Spencer helping you. The regular protocol would be working with Dr. Girardo."

"I asked him to help."

"And you aren't legally bound to do whatever the protocol is. But you have a team of people who want to protect you and also get justice for someone you all loved. Also, Emmett is a guy who has been to war and seen shit. He's watched people he loves die, and that's never easy, but when you get out of that wartime mindset, you don't think you'll see your friend shot at home. I think everyone here is feeling uneasy."

"There's no one who wants to catch my brother's killer more than I do." And just like that, I'm annoyed with myself because I keep pushing people to answer questions that I shouldn't be pushing them to answer.

As if she can read my thoughts as they chase across my expression, Charlie gives me a small smile. "I know. Go back to your apartment, relax, and let the town party. Tomorrow, everything will be fine. Also, always have your keys. If something happened out here, we wouldn't have been alerted until it was too late. The panic button should go everywhere with you."

She's right. "I'm sorry."

"Don't be. The point of it is to protect you. Let us do that. We have no idea if the killer is walking among us, and we want you to always be protected, no matter what."

"Okay."

Spencer comes back outside with my clutch. "Sorry, I had to . . . talk to a friend."

Charlie smirks. "And I assume that friend had a bit of advice?"

"Ever the spy, Charlie."

She turns to me. "Yeah, it definitely took a spy to figure that out."

"Ready?" Spencer asks.

I take his arm, and we walk out to the car without a word.

The ride home is no more than nine minutes, but it feels like a year because there is this awkward silence in the car. My mind races with the right things to say, but nothing sticks. Charlie is right. I am not okay. I have a large gap of time missing, and I need to remember. I can't start a relationship, not even if it's one I have wanted my whole life, while I'm still like this.

Broken.

Damaged.

Scared.

Spencer has had enough of that from women in his life. There is a very real possibility that my memory will return, and I'll remember the man I may have loved. What then? If I remember how happy I was and want that back, Spencer will have another woman walk out on him.

Then I think of the other guy who may exist, what of him? I don't know who he is or why he hasn't tried to find me yet, but for all I know, there's a really good reason for his absence. How fair would it be to him if I pursued whatever this is with Spencer?

It wouldn't be fair at all.

The car parks and neither of us move, almost as though we know tonight turned a corner.

I should say something. I want to, but I can't.

"I don't know where we go from here." Spencer's voice echoes in the quiet.

"I don't either."

"I know what I want. I know what I wish for."

"Wishes and wants don't mean it's the right choice, and that's what matters," I say, but there's something about the words that bothers me. As though I've heard it. As though . . . I knew it.

Spencer's eyes meet mine in the darkness. The only light is the moon behind him. "What?"

"What?" I repeat his question.

"What did you just say?"

God, what if I'm quoting him? I start to wonder if I am because it sounds like something he'd say. "I've heard it before."

"When?" The question exits his lips like a bullet, fast and strong.

"I don't know. I just . . . said it and then had this feeling like I knew it."

He turns back to the road. "I am trying so hard to do the right thing. The thing we both know we need to do. We can't keep doing this dance, Brie. I never should have allowed any of it."

"What dance? Don't you get it? I don't even understand what the steps are."

"That's the point! I never should've let any of it happen. You are . . . and I'm . . . Isaac deserves more. He deserved so much more than what I'm doing now."

"What are you talking about, Spencer?"

"I never should've kissed you. I shouldn't think about you, dream about you, find reasons to be around you. I never should've made you any promises about memories or kissing or dating. Not like this. Not now when you are dealing with all this. Not when I lost my best fucking friend a month ago. Not when I know . . ."

"You know what?"

He doesn't answer me before he exits the car, walks around to my side, and pulls my door open.

I've had enough of this. Of all of it. I refuse to move. I cross my arms and stay in the car, very aware I look like a freaking idiot.

"Get out of the car, Brie."

"Not until we're done talking."

Spencer sighs heavily. "We are done."

"No, you're done. You decided, and I don't agree."

"Get out of the damn car."

The one thing I know is that no matter what, I am safe. He will never hurt me. He may wish he could strangle me right now, but he'd die before harming anyone he loves.

"You're welcome to get back in or"—I reach into my bag and pull out my keys—"you can go inside if you like, wait there until I decide I'm ready."

He laughs once. "You're kidding?"

"I'm not. You're done talking, but I want you to tell me what happened between almost kissing me at the MOTY awards and now."

He reaches into the car, and at first, I think he's going to pull me out, but he snatches the keys and walks toward the house. "Quinn? Can you watch her?"

I hear an owl sound in response.

"Thanks!" Spencer replies, lifting his hand.

Ugh. That man. He is seriously going to leave me in the car—at night—with no keys. Shit! He has my panic button. Now it's me who is going to do the strangling.

I get out of the car, slam the door, hoping it breaks the mirror or something, and then I hear the beep of the lock after I take my first step.

"Spencer!" I yell, knowing the asshole can hear me. "I'm going to kill you!"

I rush into my building and mumble the entire way about all the ways I'm going to seek retribution. I push open the door to my apartment, ready to unleash the holy wrath of hell, but he's in the foyer, waiting, and there's something in his eyes that stops me.

That undeniable pull is pulsing between us, calling to me, and I can't breathe. I need him. I am angry and confused and all the other things, but more than any of it, is desperation for the man standing in front of me.

I throw my clutch to the ground and stride toward him as he moves toward me. We grab for each other and our mouths slam together. It's too much and not enough. I need to feel his skin, taste him, breathe him into me so I'm whole.

He kisses me deeper, sliding his hot tongue against mine. His hands slide down my back before pulling the zipper down as I start to unbutton his shirt. I don't care that none of this makes sense because it doesn't have to. It's Spencer, and it's right.

"Tell me to stop, Brielle," he pleads.

"Never."

I don't give him a chance to ask me for something else, I kiss him harder, shoving both his coat and shirt off his shoulders, loving the width and strength of his body. We think too much, and I am done.

He doesn't remove my dress, just lets it hang open as his fingers are splayed across my bare back, holding me to him.

I pull back, trying to slip my hands between us, so afraid this moment will end.

"Slow down, sweetheart," Spencer says between breaths. "What do you want me to do? What do you want, Brie?"

As I go to answer, there's a sharp pain in my head. I push back, and he releases me instantly. The throbbing is so overwhelming and sharp that I can't hear anything. I close my eyes, battling the agony, and then, it disappears. The mist is lighter. I can see parts of something.

It's warm, the sun isn't fully up in the sky yet, but the heat is constant. Isaac and I are in a parking lot, talking and joking about something. I can hear his voice and see his smile as we exit the car.

"No," I say to myself and possibly aloud. "No, I can't."

"What do you want me to do?" Isaac asks. "Brie?"

"Just let me handle it," I tell him.

Then it's fuzzy again.

I fight to stay here, to see a face or a name, but I can't stop the nausea or the anxiety in my chest. This is important. It's a memory, and I need it.

"Brielle!" Spencer yells, but I tune him out, forcing myself to stay in this memory no matter how painful it is.

I drop down, holding my head in my hands, covering my ears. My brother is rounding the car, trying to reach me. There's a man. He's yelling, but I can't make out anything he's saying. His face is washed out by sunlight, and the harder I try to see him, the brighter it gets. More yelling. More deep voices, and Isaac pleading as a gun is drawn. The sun glinting off the barrel as it's moved from left to right. I step toward the unknown man, but Isaac grabs my wrist as he calls my name. He tries to put himself in front of me. The pain in my head blooms again, but I still struggle to see, to reach for Isaac, but then there's nothing.

My body trembles, and the tears trickle down my cheeks. The pain of seeing Isaac's face in those flickers of moments is too much. I was there, but I couldn't see what I needed most. I don't even know what parking lot we were in.

Slowly, I return to myself, and new words come into focus. "Please, sweetheart, talk to me." Spencer's voice is shaky and almost a whisper. His arms are vises, holding all my broken parts together.

"I saw it! I saw . . . I saw it!" I cry as Spencer rocks me in his arms.

"Tell me what you saw." There's a crack in his voice, and I can feel his fear mingling with my own.

"The gun. I saw the gun. I saw him grab me and call my name."

"Did you see who it was?"

"No." I sob. "I couldn't."

"It's okay, Brielle. It's okay. You're safe, and it's okay."

But it's not. I was so close. I had a memory hit me. The most important one, and I couldn't remember.

I sit in Spencer's arms, and all I see is Isaac's face. The fear and worry as he reached for me. I hear his voice, the resolve that he wouldn't let anything hurt me. I wanted to reach out to him, to tell him to run and save himself and be there for Addy and Elodie. I remember the panic that I wouldn't see the people I love ever again, that we would both die.

A new wave of agony crashes through me. I look up into his eyes, tears making it hard to see. "Help me forget," I beg him.

"Brie . . ."

I shake my head, not wanting to be rejected or feel anything other than safe. I wrap my hand around the back of his neck and pull his lips to mine. "Please, help me forget. Take the pain away."

Or I might drown in it.

CHAPTER Twenty-One

SPENCER

Her mouth is fused to mine, preventing my refusal from escaping.

If I were being honest with myself, I could stop her if I wanted to.

But I don't.

I don't want to stop her or this. I want to get lost in her touch. I love her so fucking much that it's tearing me apart.

Emmett ripped into me before we left, saying we were going to have a conversation and soon. He sees the way I look at her, the things I thought I was hiding, but he has no idea that Brielle is the first thing in years that makes me feel alive and worthy again.

She didn't see me as a man with an award or a paycheck. She sees the cracks and broken bits and loves me more for them.

Now it's her who is broken, and I may not be allowed to help put her back together like she did for me, but I can do this. I can give her what she's asking for, which is what we both need, and then I'm going straight to hell.

Her small hands are on my chest, shoving me to the ground. I fall back, and she's on top of me. "Brie," I say, both asking for more and to stop.

"No talking. Please. Don't . . ."

I push my hand into her hair, gripping the silky, blonde tresses in my fingers. I pull her mouth back to mine, and she moans. I let her lead, giving her the control I know she's searching for.

When I got back from the last assignment, I was the same way. I didn't know who I was anymore or how to process all I saw, and I needed to have something—someone who could give me that. It was her. And now, I'll do the same.

I kiss her deeper and shift her body a little so I can feel her heat. She groans when I lift up, hitting the spot where I know she needs me.

"Spencer." Brielle's voice drifts over my name.

I grip her hips, and her hands move to my chest so she's sitting like a goddamn queen above me. Her eyes are on mine, the sapphire color turning liquid in her desire. I pull her dress up higher, skimming my fingers over her soft skin.

"Anything you want, I'll give it to you," I promise.

"You, I want you."

She never has to ask for that. I am hers, and I will always be. I love her with everything I am. I will never deny her, damn the consequences.

"Then take what you want," I urge her.

She shifts, pulling my undershirt up, and I let go of her hips long enough to remove it. It doesn't matter that we've made love hundreds of times because, right now, it's almost like the first time all over again.

I remember the wonder we both felt. How we both wanted it and were also apprehensive at the same time. It was never supposed to happen, Brielle and me. We were not a foregone conclusion. No, we were friends who became so much more.

I push the blonde hair behind her ear. "Is that all?" I ask.

She shakes her head with her lower lip between her teeth.

"No? What else?"

Brielle gives me a coy smile, and then we're face-to-face and her hair creates a veil around us. Her lips are on mine as her hands move from my shoulders down my arms until she has our fingers entwined.

I'm at her mercy. Just like I've been for a very long time.

Way too soon, she pushes up and rolls off me onto her side. "Take off your pants," she demands.

"And what about you? I'm going to be naked while you're still in that dress."

She rises, and I do the same. I undo my belt, the button, and then slide the zipper down. I don't give her exactly what she asks for yet. I want to see her. I need to see her. I have missed all of this. The playfulness that we have. The trust that we share, being completely unabashed with each other.

"That's not off," Brielle says.

My pants hang on my hips, but I don't move to take them off. "They're not."

"Why?"

"I think," I say low and husky, taking a step toward her. "I think I might need some help."

"Do you?" Brie asks with a grin.

"I think so. Do you think you could . . ." I skim my finger from her throat to the tops of her breasts.

"Could what?"

Her voice is shaking, and I relish in it.

I lean in closer, my lips against her ear. "Help me remove them?"

Her hands are there a moment later, thumb hooking in the band of my boxer briefs. Then there's no more clothing, just cool air.

Brielle steps back, her eyes moving across my skin, slowly going down to my cock. "Do you like what you see?" I ask.

"Very much."

"Now, take off your dress," I request. Her fingers move to the straps, but I change my mind. "Stop."

Her gaze finds mine in a flash.

"I want to do it," I explain. "Let me undress you, strip you down and see every glorious inch of you."

"Spencer."

My name on her lips is like heaven. "I am going to make you forget everything in this world but me, do you understand?"

She nods.

"Good."

Because if this is all we'll ever have again, then I am going to make it worth everything.

CHAPTER *Twenty-Two*

BRIELLE

My limbs are trembling, but I lock my muscles so he doesn't see. Spencer moves toward me like I am his prey. He's strong, sexy, and while I thought I had control, it's clear that's gone now.

It's what I need.

I don't want to think anymore. I want to feel and be lost because he's what anchors me anyway.

His thumbs move against my collarbone, playing with me for a few seconds. "Are you nervous, sweetheart?"

"No." It's a lie, but I don't want this to stop. I'm nervous, but not about being with him. I'm nervous that he'll find me lacking. I'm not the models he's used to. My body is far from perfect. I have lumps and scars. I have stretch marks on my hips from the summer before freshman year in high school when I grew two inches. I am not perfect. I'm flawed.

"No lies," he says, echoing the promise we share.

My heart rate jumps as his one hand slides the strap off my right shoulder. "I'm not . . . nervous, I just want to be good enough. I want you to like what you see."

That causes him to stop. His hands are holding my face tenderly. "You are perfect. Do you hear me? It's me who isn't good enough for you, Brielle. You're Eve, and I came to the garden when I shouldn't have. I'm here, ready to cut the entire tree down, knowing that the temptation isn't the apple, but you. Don't you see, I'm the one who doesn't deserve this moment."

"If I'm Eve, then you should know I don't want the apple anyway. I want you. I want the snake and the sin and the promise of the future."

Spencer's thumb moves against my lips. "I want the apple. And if I can only get this taste tonight, then God help me because I will never be the same."

My hands move to his wrists so I can hold him as he holds me. "Then take what's offered, and we'll worry about the rest later."

His lids close as he presses his forehead against mine. He gives me a soft kiss, and I wrap my arms around his neck as he picks me up and carries me to the bedroom. Spencer places me on my feet in front of my bed.

Wordlessly, he pulls both straps, sliding them down my arms, and then it pools on the floor.

I step out of it, my heels still on.

He tips my chin up. "I don't even have to look to know how stunning you are. I like every part of you. Every freckle, every scar, every imperfection you see, I see beauty."

I think I might have just died a little.

I push myself up and kiss him because there are no words that will compare to that. He kisses me as he walks me back to the bed and unhooks my strapless bra and tosses it away.

"I want you naked, Brielle."

I push my underwear down, shimmying until they are off and his want has been met.

Spencer grabs my thighs, pulling me up into his arms again, and lays me on the bed. He stands tall, his erection jutting out as he looks at me. I fight the urge to cover myself, but I couldn't deny the lust in his eyes if I wanted to. He is starved, and I am what's on the menu.

Thank God.

"Next time, I want you to keep the shoes on. Tonight though—" He removes my one heel and kisses my ankle. "—I want you comfortable." The other one comes off and he runs his thumb up my calf. I could die from the pleasure. My leg drops and he crawls up toward me. "I have thought of this moment for weeks now," he confesses. "I've imagined you naked for me, wanting me to take you, love you, give you so much pleasure you can't do anything but take it. Do you want that, love?"

I nod. "Very much."

"Sit back against the headboard," he commands. Once I do as he bids, he grins. "I want you to watch. I want you to see everything. There's no darkness here, only light."

I want to cry. My heart is pounding so loudly because he's giving me everything. Not only the sex, which I am so fucking ready for, but also the thing that has been haunting me. I only see the black haze around my memories. But in this, there's no haze and no battle to lift it. He's giving me my vision.

He pushes my knees apart, kissing the inside of my calf, then my knee, and then my thigh. He licks the sensitive skin before blowing softly there. Then inches higher, all the while making sure I'm watching him. If I didn't have the support behind me, I would've melted into the bed when his tongue made its first swipe.

I moan his name, my fingers sliding into his hair, holding him there. Spencer licks and circles my clit with varying levels of pressure. I'm unable to do anything but let him take command of my body as he drives me insane with pleasure. My God, watching him is intoxicating. When his green eyes meet mine, I could come right there. The intensity of his stare drives me wild.

He moves his head side to side, licking and sucking, moving his tongue around and around. I can't take much more. The intimacy of it all is too much. It feels too good. "I'm so close," I mutter. "So close."

"Let go, I'll be here to hold you together."

His finger slides into me as he latches his mouth onto my clit, flicking, sucking, and licking harder. I want to let go. I want to fall apart in his arms because this is what I have always wished for. For him to be the one to catch me.

My legs begin to shake, and the climax nears. I can't fight it—I don't *want* to fight it, so I let him push me into a freefall. Wave after wave of pleasure rolls over me, washing away all the sadness and anxiety and leaving me raw and sated.

He pulls my hips so I'm flat on the bed and braces over me. "You are so beautiful when you come."

"You make me feel beautiful."

"Look at me, Brielle." I turn my head back to him. "I want to make love to you, but I need you to tell me it's what you want."

What a silly thought. This is all I want. It's every fantasy I've ever had coming true. "More than anything."

He reaches over to the left drawer, grabs a condom, and rolls it on. When he's settled over me again, he pushes forward just a little. I don't want to wait. I don't want hesitation. I wrap my legs around him and lift my hips.

"Spencer. Now."

He slides in deep in one thrust. The two of us gasp, and I tighten around him. He feels so good. I never could've imagined how perfectly he would fit inside me, as though he were made for me.

"Jesus Christ," he mutters. "Fuck, you . . . you feel . . ."

"Perfect." I finish the sentence.

He takes my mouth in a searing kiss, and there are no more words between us. He sets a pace that leaves no room for any talking. The only sounds are our ragged breaths and skin meeting skin. Sweat breaks out on his forehead, and I can see the strain of him fighting back, wanting this to go on forever.

I push against his chest, wanting control again. I want to be what makes him finally lose it. He flips onto his back, taking me with him so I am on top, sliding down on his cock. I rest my hands on his chest, moving slowly, and the friction on my clit starts to build another climax.

Spencer's fingers dig into my hips as he urges me to ride him a little faster. Once I'm at the pace he wants, he moves his hands to my breasts. His expert fingers touch me in the right way, kneading before he moves to my nipples, pinching and tugging playfully.

"Please," I manage to get out. "Please don't stop."

"You're close. Your tight, hot pussy is clenching around my dick. You want to come again. Your body knows . . ."

"Yes," I moan.

He shifts to wedge his finger between us and starts to rub my clit again. It is both amazing and painful. I'm wrung out and overwhelmed. It's too much. I can't do it again, but Spencer is determined.

"Ride me, Brielle. Take the freedom you want. Take everything because it's yours. Take it, love. Take what you need."

I scream, unable to hold back as another orgasm rockets through me. I collapse forward, but he's there, holding me to him. His hips jerk up, fucking me from beneath until he's groaning my name into my hair as he pulses inside me.

I lie against his chest, unable to move even if I wanted to, which I don't.

That was the most incredible thing I've ever experienced.

He moves my hair to the side and kisses my nose. "You okay?"

"Huh?"

He laughs. "I'll take that as a yes."

"Uh-huh."

Apparently, all I'm capable of is speaking in sounds.

Spencer's fingers trail along my spine. "I have to clean up."

"Ehh."

I don't want to move. I want to stay like this forever.

He chuckles again and then rolls me to the side. I flop over, my limbs not really cooperating. I close my eyes for a second, absorbing all that happened, but I can't really think too long because suddenly, everything is dark and quiet.

The first thing I note is that I'm hot. Really hot. Like I left the air off and windows open in the summer heat.

Then I realize I'm naked.

I'm naked because I had sex. Amazing sex. Really freaking amazing sex with Spencer.

The night before, the dance, the memory, the incredible hours after that were filled with all things Spencer Cross.

I must've passed out right after, but he tucked me in and then tucked himself around me. I didn't dream or wake up ten times last night. I slept, and now I know it was because he was here, keeping the demons away.

"Good morning." His deep voice rasps in my ear.

I smile and turn over to see him. "Good morning."

"Did you sleep?"

"I did, did you?"

"Like a baby," he replies and pushes my hair back. "Are you okay?"

"You mean about last night?"

The corner of his lip turns up. "Yes."

"Which part? The sex or the memory?"

"Both."

I release a low sigh and give a sort of shrug. "I am processing it all. I'm still a bit overwhelmed by the memory, but I'm also so damn determined. As for us, I am equally happy and terrified."

"I don't want you to be scared."

"I'm more afraid that it'll never happen again. That the memories will return and erase what I want right now." I pause and wait for some reassurance because I keep putting my heart out there, but I don't know how he feels. When one doesn't come, I urge, "Please say something."

"I'm not sure what to say."

Not that, I want to tell him.

"Okay."

Spencer shakes his head. "I'm processing it all too. That's all. We need to take all of this one step at a time."

"Right . . . I know what you're saying. You're right."

I am so stupid. I start to shift out of bed, but he reaches for me. "Brie. Stop. I'm saying that I am not going to push you. I am not going to ask you to make promises or concessions until you know what is in your past. Last night was incredible, the sex part."

I release my breath. "Okay. You're right. I want to call Dr. Girardo and see about going in. He said that sometimes, when the brain has these glimpses, it's good to go to him as soon as possible. He may be able to open up more of it."

"Call him, and we'll go right now." He gets out of bed, and I take a second to admire his body.

Dear Lord, thank you for that.

He catches me staring, and I turn away, heat filling my cheeks as I slide from bed. I call Dr. Girardo, and he tells me to meet him at the office in thirty minutes, so Spencer and I take quick showers and get dressed, and I try not to laugh about him having to put his tux back on.

Yeah, this won't be awkward, but we don't have time to go to his house so he can change.

We walk out of the apartment, his hand in mine, and Emmett is walking toward us, also still in his tux from last night.

He stops.

We stop.

He looks at Spencer. "You spent the night?"

"Not that it's any of your business," Spencer replies.

Emmett's nostrils flare, and he shakes his head. "I can't believe you would risk your best friend's case. That you care so fucking little about Isaac, Addy, and Elodie that you couldn't do the right thing. You think this is right? You'd risk everything, for what?"

I gasp. "Emmett, stop. What is wrong with you right now?"

He turns to me. "You are the only eyewitness, Brielle, and Spencer knows that what he's doing could jeopardize your testimony. We have had four leads, and every single one of them has been a dead end. We've worked every angle, every camera, every scrap of evidence, and we haven't found anything. So, if they think for one second that your memory isn't real, that's it."

Spencer releases my hand and steps toward Emmett. "You don't have to add any more pressure to her than she has already. Everyone is aware of what's going on, but Isaac is dead. He loved his sister and would never want her to suffer—not even for him."

Tears fill my eyes as I watch the two of them fight. "Stop it," I yell. "Spencer stayed with me last night because I needed him. I was broken after I had the last memory. I was scared, and he was there for me. What we decide regarding us isn't your choice, Em. It's mine and his. I know it's not ideal for the case, but I am not the case. I'm dealing with my own life, and I can't be in a bubble." I turn to Spencer. "He's your best friend. He's grieving too. We all are. Both of you have to understand that and not act like this."

Emmett rubs his face. "I just want to solve this."

"I know you do. We all do, but you can't be at each other's throats."

"You said you had a memory?" Emmett asks, but he still can't look at Spencer.

Men are so damn stubborn. "Yes, I saw the murder, but I can't remember the person's face. The memory was fuzzy, but . . . I wasn't okay. I'm still not."

It rattled me to my core. I was right there. I saw everything and nothing at the same time. I was so afraid. I could feel my heart in my chest, pounding as that gun was raised. The pain as the butt of it smashed into my skull. The sound of the gunshot.

My hands are shaking as though it's happening now. Spencer steps in front of Emmett. "She's been through enough. She doesn't need either of us acting like assholes."

"I know, you're right." Emmett comes closer. "Brie, I'm so sorry."

"It's fine. I know you mean well. We are going to the doctor now, but I'll talk more when we get back, okay?"

"Of course."

Spencer places his hand on my back, and we walk out to the car. Before he makes any move to start the engine or pull out of the parking spot, he turns to me. "He's right, you know."

"Right about what?"

"I would lose everything for you."

CHAPTER Twenty-Three

BRIELLE

"It's nice to meet you," Dr. Girardo says to Spencer. "Brielle has told me that you have been instrumental in helping her over the last few weeks."

"Me?"

He smiles. "Yes, if you notice, most of her memories are recovered when you're near her."

Spencer looks to me, and I shrug. "He says it's because I feel safe around you, which you already know."

"Yeah, but . . ."

"It's a good thing," Dr. Girardo says as he walks us back to the room. "I wish more of my patients who experience a type of memory loss had something or someone that could trigger recall."

I reach out and take Spencer's hand. "It's a good thing."

"Well, if I can help, we all want the same thing for her."

Dr. Girardo nods. "Yes, and today we'll do things a little differently. I'd like to try a type of hypnosis with meditation. We'll start with a deep meditation, to get you relaxed and focused. Then I'll attempt to hypnotize you. Since the memory is so fresh, it may be a lot easier to resurface it. Of course, this isn't a guarantee, but I've had some success in the past, and I think you'd be a good candidate."

Spencer's grip tightens around my hand. "You don't have to."

No, I don't, but I am tired of this. I want to know who killed my brother. I want to be able to live my damn life. If I can remember this, maybe all the other things could finally be explained.

"I want to do this," I tell him. I turn to Dr. Girardo. "I need answers, and I am tired of these small moments that I can't control."

"We may not be able to control this, Brie."

"No, but it's worth trying."

Dr. Girardo motions me over to the couch. "Spencer, I'm going to ask you to wait over there. It's important that you not speak unless I motion you over. I want to warn you both that this can go badly. You may panic, get a headache, or see a false memory that may feel very real. Dizziness and drowsiness are also possible. Are you sure you want to proceed?"

"What do you mean false memories?"

That's what I really don't want to have happen.

"It's possible that your mind will meld memories and create false ones. So, anything you say under this may not be accurate. We are working to try to get your mind to work with you to lift that fog you describe, and sometimes things can get spliced together."

I sigh. I don't want fake memories. I want the ones that I had. I want the truth. "How will we know?"

His eyes are full of compassion. "We won't until we have more of your memory recovered."

Spencer stands, moving toward me. "And this isn't going to affect what we've all been protecting her for?"

"You mean the case?" he asks.

"Yes."

Dr. Girardo gives me a soft smile. "These are all coming from you. We aren't going to guide you, so this is not going to hurt that. At least that's what I would say if I were called to testify. What we're doing is allowing the brain to move without fear."

As long as there isn't a risk to the case, then I don't see the harm. "Okay. I think we should do it. I want to try."

Spencer takes my hands in his and then kisses my knuckles. "I'll be over there. I won't leave."

"I know." And I do. He won't abandon me. He never has.

He leans in and kisses my forehead before walking away.

"Get comfortable. You can lie down if you'd like."

I do that because it's the most comfortable position for me, and we begin. It doesn't take me too long to settle into the slow cadence of breathing he taught me to use when meditating. Once I'm nice and relaxed, he begins to speak. He verbally walks me through a series of mental images that slowly become my whole focus, until eventually I'm in the passenger seat of a car while the sun lights the horizon with a new day.

"Do you see that?" Dr. Girardo's voice shifts.

I look around. "See what?"

"The parking lot. Do you see where you're located?" I look around and see Isaac. We're laughing as we exit the car.

"He's here," I tell him.

"Where is here?"

I'm standing on the outside of the memory looking at it from the outside. I see my smile, bright and carefree, as my brother speaks. I exit from the car, looking up at the sign on the building. "Rosie's."

"And what are you doing there?"

"We wanted coffee. I wanted to talk to him about something important."

"Good. Who else is there?"

"Just Isaac. It's early, and no one is here."

Dr. Girardo speaks again. "What happens now?"

"We . . . we stop. He's at the door, and I just exited, but there's someone calling my name."

"Focus on his face, Brielle. Focus on pushing the fog away," Dr. Girardo encourages. "You are safe. Tell me what you see."

"Isaac is telling me to stay there," I tell him. I start to move forward, but there's nothing again. "I can't see . . ."

My breathing starts to accelerate, and sweat beads across my hairline. I'm scared. I know this is bad and I can't see his face. He's there and he's going to kill us.

"You can do it, Brie, I'm here." Spencer's voice is low at my ear. "No one can hurt you. No one will get close. I will keep you safe."

Immediately, I relax a little and the fog lifts. Only I'm not in the parking lot with Isaac.

"I can . . . the fog is gone."

"What do you see?" Spencer asks.

"You."

"Where are we?"

I smile, looking at the scene before me. He and I are in my apartment, just like last night. His arms are around me and he's holding me to him. Spencer's hair is a little shorter than it is now. "We're smiling."

Dr. Girardo's voice intrudes. "Are you happy?"

"I am. I feel this flutter in my chest. Spencer is smiling at me as he takes my hand and leads me into the bedroom." It's like last night, but . . . "We aren't in a tux or dress this time."

"What are you wearing?"

"Jeans. We have jeans on." That's strange, why would we be going into my bedroom?

"Good, Brie, can you see anything else?"

The scene shifts again, and I'm reliving last night. "It's different . . . this is last night," I say.

"Paint me the scene."

"Spencer on top of me, reaching for the condom in the drawer."

Again, everything changes, and I'm back at the parking lot. This time we're past the yelling. "He has a gun! Isaac! Please!" I yell, the panic causing my heart to beat so hard it must be bruising my chest. "Don't! No!"

"You're okay, sweetheart, no one is here. Just tell me what you see," Spencer says, his hands on my shoulders. "What do you see?"

"He's pointing the gun at me, but Isaac is trying to get to me from the driver's side. I tell him to stay there. I know I can handle it. I have to handle it." I look harder, wanting to see who it is. I know him. "His voice . . . I've heard it before."

"How does it sound?" Dr. Girardo asks.

"Angry. He's very angry. He's saying I have no right." Then Isaac is trying to move toward me again. "He's yelling at Isaac to stay back."

The man moves the pistol from me to Isaac. He tells Isaac to stay where he is or he'll kill me. He's louder now.

"Can you describe his voice?" Dr. Girardo asks.

"It's low. I know it. I've spoken to him many times."

Dr. Girardo speaks again. "Stay in the scene, Brielle. You're doing great. Take three deep breaths and describe what happens next."

I do as he says, letting my breathing calm me. Only when I try to go back, everything is gone. There's nothing. No sounds. No voices. Just darkness.

Suddenly, I'm being shaken. "Brielle! Wake up! Damn it, not again! Wake up!"

I open my eyes, and Spencer is there, his breathing is rapid and the panic in his eyes is clear. "What happened?"

He lets out a deep breath and clutches me to his chest. "Jesus Christ. I was . . . fuck. You're okay."

I push away from him, feeling embarrassed. "I'm fine. What happened?"

Dr. Girardo clears his throat. "You passed out. You were very difficult to wake."

"Oh." I don't remember anything other than the memories being gone. "It all disappeared," I explain.

He nods. "Your brain is still healing from the trauma of your injury. We may have pushed you a little too far."

"No, I needed this. I know . . . I know his voice, and I heard it not too long ago." I turn to Spencer. "We did."

He glances between me and the doctor. "Who?"

My voice quivers. "Jax."

CHAPTER Twenty-Four

SPENCER

I'm standing in the shower, water streaming down my face as I try to reconcile everything she said.

Jax.

The voice she heard before her brother was killed is Jax.

Dr. Girardo pulled me aside before we left and explained that this doesn't mean he's the killer. That her memory can be splicing, which we already know it has done a few times.

Like when she remembered us making love and together in her apartment mingled with another memory as though she meshed two together.

But still, that doesn't mean I'm not going to look deeper into this.

I tilt my head back one more time, hoping the water will wash away the anger before I go back to Brie. When it doesn't, I give up and head there anyway.

Once dressed, I go out into the living room and find her sitting on the floor with all the papers from our investigation laid out around her.

"What are you looking for?"

Brie jumps at my voice and then smiles. "The answer is in this."

"The bank statements?"

She nods. "I remembered Jax. When we met at the party, for some reason, he felt important. So, I figure that I felt that way for one of two reasons."

"And they would be?" I ask, already able to guess what she's going to say.

"He's the mystery ring guy and the killer."

Well, she's wrong on at least one of those.

"So why the bank statements?" I ask, crouching beside her.

"You said we have to start at the beginning. Maybe the beginning is my job. I only remembered up until I got hired at the youth center. I met Jax there, started dating him, and found out about whatever is illegal. I must've had files of it in my office. He knew the ring was the key, so he looked for it, but I had it at home. It all fits. He's the killer and I am going to find the answers in here. Jax is involved, now I have to prove it."

I want to grab her by the shoulders and tell her how wrong she is, to confess that I'm who she's in love with. Jax doesn't deserve to breathe the same air as her, and God fucking help him if he is who hurt her and killed Isaac. There won't be a rock big enough for that man to hide under.

I clench my jaw and count to five before I can reply. "What did you find in the statements?"

There's nothing there. I know this because I have poured over them. I've searched through it all, tried to trace the money back, and it's all dead ends. Even Mark had one of his tech guys look into the wire transfers, but they didn't find anything suspicious. They're doing a different dig, but whoever is behind this is very good at covering their tracks. We at least know that nothing leads to Jax, but I still sent them everything from today before I jumped in the shower.

Charlie is reaching out to her contacts to see if she can dig anything up, and the guys at Cole Security are doing the same.

"I haven't found anything yet."

"You should rest," I say, gathering the papers. "You had a rough day."

She grabs the folder from me. "I'm fine. I need to do this."

"You don't . . . we have gone over it a dozen times. There's nothing in here."

"What if we missed something?"

"We didn't."

She stands and walks to the other side of the room. "You don't think it's Jax?"

"I don't know what I think."

"Why do you keep dismissing him? Why do you think he's not the guy I was with? I saw how he looked at me. He and I were dating or he likes me. What has you so confused?" Brie asks with frustration coursing through her words.

The sheer volume of things I'm keeping from her is overwhelming. "I can't answer that."

"Can't or won't?"

"Is there a difference?" I toss back.

"Can't is very different."

I step toward her, my own frustration rising. This isn't easy. This is the worst goddamn thing I've been through. I gave my fucking heart to her, and she doesn't remember me. I've had to watch her struggle with thinking she was with Henry, and now she thinks Jax is her fiancé? Jax, the fucking idiot who she wouldn't even give five minutes to?

No. I am so fucking done.

I am desperate for her to just see the truth in front of her. I love her. I love her so much, and I am desperate for her. To have her, touch her, love her and yet, she still can't come back to me.

My heart is pounding and I move closer. "I can't, Brielle. I want to. I want to tell you everything. I want to lay the whole fucking truth out in front of you, but I can't. This isn't easy for any of us. No one is enjoying this. No one wants to keep secrets, but we were told, we literally can't give you the truth. So, here I am, doing my best to keep my promise to you and also make sure I don't fuck everything up. No matter what I said to Emmett, he was right to be pissed! I am going to blow this entire thing up, and then what? What happens when you hate me?"

Her gaze drops. "I am doing my best to understand this. I just . . . God, I know! I know what's in my heart. You and Dr. Girardo said that once I can piece it together, I'll see clearly. Well, I am seeing clearly. The killer is part of this. He's part of my life and I think it has to do with my job. I remember people and things that matter."

"Your heart tells you that you are in love with Jax?"

She shakes her head. "I don't know! I know that he's important. It makes the most sense."

It makes no fucking sense, and I can't hold it in. "Why? Because he looked at you that must mean that you're in love with him and he's the killer? You are so desperate for it to be the man behind the ring that you are trying to find answers where there are none."

"You don't know that!"

"And neither do you! There is literally no proof that Jax is involved in your life in any way! All I want is for you to . . ." I stop myself. I was going to say it, and I can't.

"What?"

Her big blue eyes are staring up at me, and I want to drop to my knees.

"Nothing."

"No, what do you want? What are we even doing?"

I don't say a word because I have nothing left. Explaining this won't make sense to her. The two of us are fighting to win, but we're not on the same field.

"You don't wear jeans," Brielle says quietly.

Is she having another episode?

"What?" I ask.

Her fingers touch her mouth and then drop. "You haven't worn jeans a single time in the last month."

"Okay, I don't know what you're getting at."

Jeans? What is she—fuck.

"I remembered us in my apartment, but we weren't like this. We were wearing jeans, I had my hair in a ponytail, and I was wearing my coat. My winter coat. You took my hand, and we were laughing as you pulled me into the room. I swear it was . . . I don't know. It doesn't make sense because we aren't a couple."

She's remembering when we decided we *were* a couple and not just fooling around. I remember it all, and so, I once again have to make her think it's wrong because she doesn't trust the memory. "The doctor told you that your memory could make a false narrative."

"Have we ever had sex before last night?"

She's asking me, and I hate every fucking second of this. "No."

"Then why do I keep seeing you in my dreams? Why do I want you so much?"

"Because you have always had a crush on me."

She steps back. "Of course. I think you're right," Brie says on a shaky breath.

"About?"

"That this has been a lot for one day. Can you take me home?"

It's the last thing I want to do, but I nod.

"Okay. I just . . . can I use the bathroom?"

"Second door on the right," I say.

She looks at me with tears pooling in her eyes, but she doesn't let me see them drop. She turns and walks away, leaving me feeling worse than I ever have before.

I shoot a text to Emmett and then throw my phone, not giving a shit what his reply will be.

Me: I'm done lying. Whatever you think you know about us, you don't know it all. I can't do this anymore, and I won't. Fuck your case. Find the killer without Brielle. I am telling her everything.

I sink down onto the couch with my head in my hands and try to figure out how to start the process of telling her the truth about us without ruining everything.

CHAPTER Twenty-Five

BRIELLE

I can't stop feeling like Spencer is lying. He said no lies, and I believe him, but the way he has been since we made love has suspicion taking root inside me.

I exit the bathroom silently and walk back into his room, drawn to the space.

My fingers wrap around the knob and a memory flashes.

Spencer is removing my clothes, throwing them around the room with a grin. "I want you naked."

"I bet you do."

"I'm going to fuck you so hard." His hands grip my ass, pulling me against him.

"I look forward to it."

"You should."

I giggle as he tosses me onto the bed, and then I spread my arms wide and smirk. "I'm waiting."

The memory drifts away, and another appears.

"I don't want to tell him." I am naked with the sheet wrapped around me.

"We are going to have to at some point," Spencer says as he climbs back into bed with me. Immediately, I snuggle into his side, resting my head on his chest.

I don't want to tell Isaac or anyone. I am happy just like this. The bubble we have created is perfect, and when it pops, we'll be forced to deal with everyone's opinions. We are happy as we are, and even if we never become anything more than this, I selfishly want to keep these moments untarnished by the outside world.

I sigh, resting my chin on my hand. "No, we don't. We're grown adults, and it's no one's business what we do."

"You can't want this, Brie. You're not some random hookup."

"Aren't I?" I challenge. "Because that's what this is."

Spencer's green eyes stare down at me. "You could never be random."

"But we can never be more."

"Why is that?"

I lay my head back on his chest, loving the way it feels to be like this. "Because I'd fall in love with you, and then you'd break my heart."

He chuckles. "You're right. I would."

I'm thrown back here, staring at the bed, remembering how soft his sheets were against my skin. I've been with him. Many times. I've slept in this bed—with him. Last night was not a first, and he lied.

I step deeper into the room, wanting more memories to appear. I look around, not sure if what I just saw actually happened. I should leave, talk to him, give him a chance to tell me the truth, but I need *proof* that what I just saw was real.

Instead of being sane, I open a drawer and then another and then, just when I start to think I'm a total asshole, I find a frame. There we are. I'm wrapped in his arms, he's smiling down at me, and my hand is pressed against his cheek—with a diamond ring on my finger. The one in my jewelry box. The one he said he never gave me.

The one he told me, point-blank, was not his.

But it was.

As though the fog is no longer in my mind, but in front of me, I walk out into the living room and stop when I find him sitting on his couch.

He gets to his feet. "Brie? Are you okay?"

I shake my head. "You lied."

"What?"

"You lied to me. I remember." He comes toward me, but I lift my hand. "You broke every goddamn promise you made. You told me you would never lie, and every fucking thing has been exactly that—bullshit."

"No, not everything."

I laugh. "No, just the fact that we were together and apparently engaged." I toss the frame at him, and he catches it before it can crash to the floor.

"Brielle, let me explain."

"Explain? Explain that you're a liar? Explain that I asked you—literally asked you if you were who gave me that ring, if we've ever been together, and you said no."

"I had no fucking choice!"

"No, you had a choice. You chose to lie."

My world is imploding. Everything I thought I knew is disappearing before my eyes. What is true anymore? He has been my constant and the one person I thought I could trust to be honest with me, but he chose to withhold our past. Now, I don't have a clue what my reality is.

He huffs. "Yes, I had a choice. I had to choose between letting you remember, knowing the outcome could be this, or telling you, possibly ruining any chance of you being able to testify against the person who killed your brother. I had to sit back and watch you talk about Henry, the fucking piece of shit who couldn't even be there for you at the funeral when he was trying to get back with you. I chose to watch you convince yourself that you were with Jax. I chose to spend every minute I could with you and give you whatever you needed. I listened to you tell me you wanted to forget the man who gave you that ring because he must be what's wrong in your life."

I'm engaged to Spencer.

Spencer who has always been an abstract.

Spencer who I thought I was building a future with.

Spencer who told me he would never lie.

Spencer who gave me truths others didn't.

Spencer who is the biggest liar of all.

So what else is he lying about?

"And how do I know that isn't true now?"

He blinks, his eyes wide. "What?"

"You heard me. How do I know that you aren't what's wrong in my life? How do I even understand any of it?"

"You really think that I am what you're trying to forget?"

"I don't know. How could I have wanted to spend my life with someone who, not even a few hours ago, looked me in the eyes and lied?"

"Because I never planned to. I never wanted to."

"But you did!" I yell, the anger resurfacing. I turn and move away from him. When he's close, I can't think straight. The pit in my stomach grows, making it hard to breathe. "How could you do this?"

"Do what?"

I grab the frame from his hand. "This! How could you love me and do this? How do I know that this is even real?"

Spencer takes two steps toward me, and I back up. He stops, lifting both hands in the air. "You're afraid of me?"

I never thought it would be possible, but right now I'm terrified of everything—including him. I don't have anything real to hold on to. There isn't a single memory I've made in the last three years that's concrete. No truth because I can't trust that anything I'm remembering is real. It feels as though I'm living on a broken mirror that's reflecting distorted and shattered images and cutting me every time I move.

"Were we even together when this all happened?"

"Of course we were."

I shake my head. "You say that as though I should know, but Henry lied about it, so don't act like I'm crazy for asking you."

His voice is soft, and my heart races as he lowers his hands. "We started as just . . . I don't know. We both agreed it was just sex. Just this attraction we gave into. It was supposed to be one night, but there wasn't a chance in hell I could stop there. Not after finding out how incredible we were together."

I don't want to hear this, but I need to. "And then what?"

Spencer stands like a statue, answering my questions. "We fell in love. Neither one of us planned it, which is why we didn't tell anyone."

That makes no sense. "Why? Why would we keep this a secret?"

He pushes his thick hair back. "It changed each time we talked about it. We had every excuse under the sun. In the beginning it was sex, so we had no reason to tell anyone. It was fun and exciting sneaking around."

"That doesn't sound like me, Spencer. I would never keep something like being engaged from Isaac, especially to his best friend. Is that what happened? Did he find out?"

"Isaac never knew. No one else did."

No, that's not the truth. I wouldn't lie to my brother. The one thing that I had in him was honesty. "I don't believe you."

"So, what? You think he knew, and that's why he died?"

My heart is pounding as everything starts to connect. I have always thought his death was tied to me. Something I knew or said set in motion the events that led to him being killed. I have had this horrible feeling that it all came back to the man who gave me that ring. I just didn't know he'd been by my side this whole time.

Spencer is trained to kill. He said it himself that he was in SEAL school and had to protect himself at times.

It's not a far stretch that he could've done it. He could've been angry at Isaac or me.

"I think anything is possible at this point."

He moves closer again and my body starts to tremble. Oh, God, I can't breathe.

"What does that mean?"

"It means that I . . . I can't . . . don't—" I can't talk. My chest is tight, and panic is starting to overtake my thoughts.

"Brielle, relax."

"I won't relax! All I have known from the beginning is that someone killed my brother. Someone tried to kill me. I have said that I thought it was the man in my life. That my office being trashed, the ring, the paper trail, which you gave me, was all tied together. Now I find out that person is you?"

"You think I could fucking kill my best friend? That I would *ever* hurt you? I trashed your office? What possible reason would I have to do any of that? Are you kidding me? I love you! I would die for you! I have been here for you every goddamn day, making sure you felt safe and were safe. Jesus! You can't really believe that!"

Everything he's saying makes complete sense and it is exactly what someone who didn't want to be caught would say. There are no witnesses, save for myself. So, what better way to make sure he knew the second I remembered what happened than to spend every day with me?

The two of us stare at each other, and then his shoulders fall. "Brielle, I need you to hear me. I didn't want to lie. I had two choices, I do what I needed to in order to protect any case they might build or stay away from you. I couldn't do it. I couldn't not . . . I couldn't."

"I can't believe anything that's coming out of your mouth. I d-don't re-me-member everything. I-I have no grasp on what's real."

"Look at the photo," he says. "Look at your smile. You are wearing that ring because, when I asked you to marry me, you said yes, Brielle."

"That isn't our reality now."

"Why? Do you not love me? Did you not crave being around me? Feel safe in my arms and in every way?"

I shake my head. "You don't get it, Spencer! The safety came from knowing that you were the one person I could trust. I could share myself, my fears, and my heart, and it was protected. Now, I have a million questions and I can't ask you because I can't be sure you're giving me honest answers. How can I trust you?"

He sinks down in front of me, taking my hands in his. "I'll tell you everything. I'll spare nothing if that's what you need."

For weeks, I've been asking for this, and here it is. "Fine. How long have we been together?"

"Nine months before the murder."

"And when did we get engaged?"

"Three days before that."

I blink. "We were engaged for three days before I was hit with a gun and my brother was shot?" I pull my hands back, more sure than ever that my thoughts were right.

"Yes. We hadn't even told anyone yet. Not a fucking soul knew that we were dating. Maybe your neighbor caught on about a week before, but that's it. We agreed that we wanted to tell Isaac first."

His name is like a low blow to the chest. Isaac never knew. I lied to him for nine months and apparently, I thought it was fine. I will never forgive myself for this. "No wonder I protected myself."

Spencer flinches. "What does that mean?"

"Why I forgot. I knew it was wrong."

"No, you forgot because some maniac assaulted you." He stands. "You were happy. You and I . . . we were fucking happy. Nothing about what we did was wrong."

"We are liars! We never told my brother. We snuck around behind his back. Addy, my mother, Emmett . . . we kept it from everyone, and for what? If it wasn't wrong, then why?"

"Because we love each other!" He grips my shoulders. "We didn't want anything to take that away."

"Well, it did. It's gone."

I was engaged to the man who tried to kill me.

And then I remember the man who threw water balloons. The one who danced with me, held me, protected me.

Which is the truth?

I am going out of my fucking mind. I am crazy and irrational, but I literally can't tell the truth from a lie. I don't know if what I saw in the other room is another memory spliced together or if I'm going insane. It's like the people in that picture are strangers, living a life that is wholly separate from mine. I have no idea who that girl is, but I know she isn't me.

"Don't say that." Spencer's voice shifts, noting the panic. "Don't say it's gone."

I can't do this.

Tears stream down my face, and all I want is to be alone and feel safe again.

I wish I never remembered anything.

When I pull my sweater tighter around me, the keys in my pocket seem to get heavier. I need to get out of here.

He moves closer, and I'm already backing toward the door. "Stop. Stop please. You're drowning me, and I can't breathe."

The look in his eyes robs me of breath. The pain that lashes across his face tells me that I have wounded him.

I need to go. I need . . . I have to get . . . I can't . . . this is too much. My vision is getting blurry, and I know I am about to lose it and have a full-on panic attack. Either that or I'm dying.

There's only one way out.

I reach into my pocket and press the button, knowing the people hired to ensure my safety will be through that door in a moment.

And exactly as promised, a few seconds later, the door is thrown open and I'm being carried out, away from the man I thought I trusted and fell in love with, even after forgetting.

CHAPTER *Twenty-Six*

SPENCER

"You know the rules, man." Quinn pushes against my chest as I try to get through to Brielle's door.

"Stop. Stop please. You're drowning me, and I can't breathe."

"I need to talk to her!"

"Stop. Stop please. You're drowning me, and I can't breathe."

"You can't."

"Stop. Stop please. You're drowning me, and I can't breathe."

Over and over like a record that keeps scratching and forcing me to start at the same spot.

"Drowning. I'm drowning, Spencer. You are taking away everything I need." Only this last one is my mother's voice. She said it the last time I saw her, right after the piece of shit she was dating walked away because she had a kid. He didn't like kids.

None of them did.

So, she left me.

"Stop. Stop please. You're drowning me, and I can't breathe."

I won't let her go. I am not a scared little boy anymore. I'll fight to make her see that I'm not drowning her, I'll tread water for both of us so we don't go under.

"She's got it all wrong," I say, feeling the frustration growing. She pushed the fucking panic button. She was terrified of me. Me. The man who would do anything for her. I take a deep breath and try again. "Just let me talk to her. You can all be there."

"Spencer, I get it. I have been where you are."

"Really?" I could punch him for even trying to pretend he knows this absolute hell. "You've been here, needing to talk to the woman you love but she has lost her fucking mind and thinks you are the cause of her pain?"

He nods. "Yup. I sure have. My story with Ashton isn't a cakewalk either. We had a lot of shit to work through, and none of it went smoothly. The one thing I will say is that, if a woman uses her panic button, it means she needs space. Let her have that."

"Space is the last thing she needs. She's convinced herself I could be the one who killed Isaac and tried to kill her."

Quinn steps forward, forcing me back. "I'm sorry, brother. I know you want to talk to her and try to work it out, but you aren't getting up there. If Brielle thinks she's in danger, then the only thing she is trusting is her security team, and no matter what, we aren't going to betray that."

"I am who set up her team," I say through gritted teeth.

"All the more reason for you to honor the terms of her protection. Think about what it would do if I let you go up there. It would show her that nothing promised is true, and from what you're saying, she is already questioning it."

This is unreal. The last thing I want to do is give her time to convince herself even more that any of what she just said is true. God, I fucked up so much in this. I should've told her the minute she opened her eyes. I should've given her the answers she needed when she asked for them.

I sink down, resting on my heels. "How do I fix this?" I ask him.

"You can do what I said and let her calm down enough to see that none of what she's telling herself makes sense. Or you can do what I thought you should have been doing from the very start of this."

I look up. "Which is?"

"Find the fucking killer. You're Spencer Cross. You are the man who uncovered the whereabouts of Aaron when the entire world, including our own team, thought he was dead. You found that underground terrorist ring and exposed them. I don't believe for one second that you haven't been able to find a single clue that would lead you to the killer."

If he doesn't think I've tried, then he's a fool. "I have found nothing."

"Then maybe you aren't looking with the right part of yourself."

I shake my head. "I'm not even sure what that means."

"It means you're thinking with your heart. Look, I don't have to be convinced it wasn't you. There's not a chance in hell that you did that to her brother. You're not a stone-cold killer, and anyone can see you love that girl."

"She can't."

"She can, she is just hurting, and when women hurt, they're a little crazy. Trust me, I'm married to a Jersey girl who happens to be a redheaded Italian. She is as crazy as crazy gets. That woman would put Brielle to shame."

My breath comes out hard. "Brielle is not this way. She's rational and doesn't fly off the handle."

"That was before the life she had was taken from her. You're trying to make sense of a situation that literally makes no sense. She doesn't know her own mind. Imagine what that feels like. I've been there. When I was abducted and held, I didn't know time. I couldn't see light or dark. Everything was one day, but at least I knew my life. If that had been taken away, then I'm not sure what the outcome would have been."

He's right. I know that, but I still want to talk to her. "When can I see her?" I ask.

"The protocol says at least twelve hours, but if Charlie doesn't think she's ready, she can withhold any visitors for twenty-four hours."

I can't wait that long. I am going to lose my mind. "That doesn't work."

"That doesn't matter to us. Go home, Spence. Or, better yet, go use the God-given talent you were gifted and investigate this—not as the man who almost lost the woman he loves, but as a reporter who is searching for what the police missed. You have twelve hours to prove something to her, don't waste it."

My house is a wreck. The papers are all over the place, and my front door is splintered and won't close properly.

I don't even care if someone robbed me blind at this point. They can have everything because I lost the only thing that matters.

I start to gather the papers but then get so frustrated I toss them back onto the ground.

Fuck this.

Fuck the person who took her from me and is doing it again.

Then I see the photo on the ground with a crack in the glass, right down the middle. I kept it safe, hidden in that drawer, and only took it out when I was alone and sure she wouldn't see it.

I miss her already.

I miss her voice and smile. I miss the way she says my name or looks at me. I miss being close to her.

All of it is gone. She left.

No, she didn't even leave. She was so scared of being near me that she was taken.

I pick up the frame and chuck it at the wall as hard as I can. It shatters even more, glass flying everywhere and the frame breaking apart at the joints.

Good. That's how I feel inside.

As I look around, I keep hearing Quinn's words in my head. If I could prove to her that I am absolutely not the killer, then maybe we can find a way. Maybe I can show her that the one thing I have never lied about is how much I care about her.

I could give her the past back by showing her the truth. There is no other way that I can see to fix what's been broken between us. Brielle needs to know, beyond a shadow of a doubt, that what we have is real and fucking perfect.

That means that I have very little time to do my job.

I walk into the room I haven't been in for a long time—my office.

I sit at my desk, running my palms over the cool wood that hasn't been touched in months, and then slide open my laptop. "I need help," I say to the room, and then I look at the photo of Isaac, Holden, Emmett, and me from Isaac's wedding. "I need you to help me, Isaac. Help me see and help me make her happy."

With my hands hovering over the keyboard, I do exactly what I told Brielle to do. I go back to the beginning, and I write for the first time in a year.

CHAPTER Twenty-Seven

BRIELLE

I have finally stopped crying. It took me over an hour to calm down enough to tell Charlie what happened. The whole time I was talking, she sat and listened without judgment.

"You did the right thing," she says for the fiftieth time.

"Did I?"

"Were you scared?"

I nod.

"Then, yes. You did exactly what that button is intended for. You were panicked, which we all saw, and our job was to get you to a secure location."

"And he can't come here?" I ask again.

"No. No one can until you're truly ready," Charlie assures me.

How crazy is this? I am afraid of the man I never thought I could be. Nothing in my life is right, but I would still give anything to have it be a nightmare. At least then, it would be over when I woke up.

But this is my life, and there is no over for me until I really have my memory back and know that it's true.

It's as if there's a gaping hole in my chest where my heart should be, and the thought of staying in this town a second longer has me wanting to crawl out of my skin. "I want to go to my mother," I tell her.

"You want to leave?"

"You said a secure location, right?"

"Yes, but . . ."

"Well, my mother is in California, and she absolutely is not the killer.

I can't be here. I'm not safe, and I can't . . . I can't be in the same town as him right now."

She takes my hand in hers. "We are here to protect you, Brie. The team is on high alert, and no one is getting through that door, okay? You *are* safe."

"And what about when that ends? What then? I know this sounds incredibly childish. I get it, but I want my mother. I want to be with someone who I know loves me to my core. I . . . I thought . . . I thought I had that. I need that, okay?"

If Addy were here, it would've been her, but she's gone. My mother is close enough that we can get there in a few hours, and I just need my mother to tell me what the hell is going on in my life.

"Okay. We'll make arrangements now. I can't make the trip with you because I need to head back to Virginia, but Quinn will be with you every step of the way, and I'll pull in Jackson, who is the owner, as well. We'll handle it."

A sob of relief and sadness breaks from my chest when she doesn't tell me I'm crazy. Charlie wraps me in a brief hug before pulling back. "Go get packed so you're ready to leave when we have everything settled. It should only take an hour or two."

I get to my feet, wiping my cheeks. "And will Spencer know?"

Charlie gives me a sad smile. "Not unless you want him to."

A part of me wants to tell her to call him, let him in here so I can talk to him. The other part of me doesn't trust it. I am too raw to deal with him. He'll either convince me that nothing I think is true or I'll convince myself that he's lying. Right now, I'm not sure I would believe the truth if someone played video proof of it. Even though my heart says there's no way he could ever hurt me or Isaac, my head isn't aligning with anything.

"Not until we're on the road."

"All right."

In under two hours, Cole Security is ready to go. Quinn will be with me the whole way, which per Charlie, is more than enough, and Jackson will meet us at my mother's.

She and Mark take my bags, and when we get to the door, my heart sinks. Emmett is there, his eyes full of confusion. Charlie's hands grip my shoulders. "You don't have to . . ."

"It's okay," I say and move toward him. I wrap my arms around his neck, and he crushes me to him. "I'm sorry."

"I know."

"I have to go."

"I know that too," he says, cinching me a little tighter.

When he releases me, the damn tears are back in full force. "Will you go to him?"

He nods. "Will you tell me what happened that has you running?"

"I can't live in a place where nothing makes sense. Until it does, it's better for me to go to the only person left who is a constant."

Emmett's lips form into a tight line. "I'll let you know if we find anything."

"I'll let you know if my memory returns and I can give us answers."

He winks, and I turn to Charlie. They usher me down the hall and to the car. She gives me a big hug and steps back.

"Thank you," I say before getting in the car.

"Take care of yourself, Brielle. Give me a call if you need anything."

Quinn snorts a laugh. "You don't even work for the company, and you do more than your husband, who owns half of it."

She rolls her eyes. "Now I know why Ashton volunteered you for this assignment."

He gets into the car, chuckling. "Ready?"

I look at my apartment, the building that seemed so different fewer than twenty-four hours ago. I was happy, waiting for Spencer in a beautiful dress. There was so much hope for what we could've been and now all I see is darkness.

I turn to him. "Yeah, I'm ready."

With my earbuds in, I close my eyes, unwilling to watch this slip away from me, and drift to sleep to a song about losing the love of your life.

We're about four hours from my mother's house, and Quinn looks over at me for the tenth time.

Since I moved the location, the team had to readjust completely, and Jackson is meeting us outside the city limits. I feel horrible and silly, but I also know this is the only option I can handle. With each mile we travel, my heart and head settle a bit more. I needed this distance. I needed to get out of there.

"You can say it," I tell him, knowing he's been itching to weigh in.

"Say what?"

"Whatever is on your mind."

"I'm not paid to think," he says, focusing on the road.

"You're his friend."

"I am."

"And . . ."

He shrugs. "I learned a very long time ago that it's best for everyone if I try not to make sense of women."

I shake my head, noting the wedding band on his left hand. "And your wife agrees with that?"

Quinn grins. "It's my wife who taught me that lesson."

"I'm not normally like this," I explain. "I'm the level-headed one, but I don't feel like I have control over anything in my life right now."

"Do any of us ever really have control?" he asks.

"I'd like to think you do right now."

Quinn nods slowly. "We'll use that as an example then. I'm driving. I am in control of the car, but I have no control of anything else. I can't control someone if they decide to change lanes or stop an animal if it decides to run into the road. Life is no different. I get planning since it's literally what I have been trained to do, but even in a carefully constructed plan, control is nothing more than having the ability to adapt. If we don't, we die."

I turn my head to the side. "I feel like I'm dying."

"That's because you're trying too hard to control the parts of the situation that can't be controlled."

"So, I'm supposed to just let it all happen, and then what?"

He glances over at me and then back to the road. "What options do you have? You can't force your memory back."

"No, but I can't accept being lied to either. Not when I don't know the truth."

"And he lied . . ."

"Yeah."

Quinn purses his lips and breathes heavily through his nose. "It sucks for all of you. My friends and I have gone through a lot of shit in our time. We've lost people we love, been hurt both emotionally and some of us physically. None of it was within our control. My wife and I . . . well, we went through the figurative version of hell. I didn't think we would come back from it. I needed her to make me want to live, and she was shut away, wishing she could die to alleviate the pain. After I thought we'd turned a corner, she got on a plane and left me to go to California."

I blink, seeing the similarity to my story. "And then what? Did you go after her?"

He shakes his head. "I didn't."

"Why not?"

Quinn pulls into the gas station, parks, and looks at me. "Is that what you want, Brie? You want him to be in a car a few miles behind us?"

My throat tightens, and the panic boils up. I can't speak so I just barely move my head.

"I don't know what he'll do, but if he's like me, he won't. Not because he doesn't want to or because he doesn't love you more than anything in the world. And I promise you this, he would lay down his life if it meant you'd be happy. That is how I know he'll wait for you."

Those stupid tears threaten to come back when he tells me that Spencer loves me. He knows and believes it, even if I can't get my mind around it. "How do you know?"

He leans over with a sly smile. "They pay me to be observant." He then points out the windshield to a car parked facing the pumps. "That's Jackson over there. I'm going to brief him. I want you to stay in here, lock the doors, and only open it if I say strawberry."

"Strawberry?"

"It's what I call my wife in Italian. Red, sweet, and rots if you leave it for too long. Like all women."

I laugh and then lock the door as he instructed.

CHAPTER Twenty-Eight

SPENCER

I haven't slept yet. I can't. My mind is going in circles as I try to work this out.

There's something that isn't adding up.

I know Brielle thought the money was the tie in for this, but so far, it's all checking out to be legal.

I was an idiot for not chasing that down sooner.

I open my document and review the first thing I've written in a year. My mind works when I'm exploring a story, so this is the story—her. Brielle Davis, a beautiful, vibrant girl whose entire life was altered by a single person.

As I type, the story becomes real. Each word adds to the picture of Brielle and Isaac that morning. Based on one of the neighbor's security cameras, he picked her up at 6:06. He was driving her because Brielle's car was in the shop for new brakes. I'd offered to drive her, but she was adamant we keep things as they were until she talked to him about us. We had a plan. In three days, we were going to dinner at Isaac's. He was projected to win the game and there was no better time than that, if he lost, we figured it would maybe soften the blow.

I wish we hadn't waited. Isaac should've known how much I loved his sister, and no matter what happens, I will always regret that.

I keep writing the order of the day. How they drove down First Street and turned left onto Maple Ave. As they drove through the downtown area, there were flyers up for the big game that coming Friday. That team was why Isaac had been so willing to go into school early. He loved to game plan. Coaching was his pride and joy until his daughter was born.

I can see the sun just peeking up over the mountains in the distance, the sky painted in light blue and yellow, chasing away the dark blues.

My fingers fly over the keys, writing at a pace I haven't done in so long, but the more I write, the more real it becomes. They pulled into the coffee shop around nine minutes later, probably laughing about something stupid he said. He was always telling horrible jokes, and Brielle was letting him know how dumb they were. Maybe they were discussing something cute Elodie did that day before he left to get his sister.

As I move back, ready to start going over it again, there's a knock on my office door.

I look over and Emmett is there.

"How did you get in?"

"I have a key," he says, lifting it.

"Right."

We all have keys to each other's homes. That's what family does.

I glance at the laptop and then back to him. "I need to work."

He moves into the room. "You're writing."

"I am."

"What's it about?"

"What do you think?" I counter.

Emmett leans against the wall, arms crossed. "I came to make sure you're all right. I thought maybe you would need a friend—and a drink. Also, I got a call from Holden, and it seems he's coming back."

So much for writing. I close the laptop and sigh. "Why is he coming back?"

"His aunt isn't doing well, so he's moving back at the end of the month to take care of her. However, that's not why I'm here. Not really."

"I didn't think that was the case." Emmett would've sent a text for that. "You heard about Brie?"

Emmett nods. "I did. Are you okay?"

"No, but I know I can fix it. We'll talk in—" I look down at my watch. Jesus Christ. It's eight in the morning. I've been going over every tip, lead, and clue since yesterday morning. "A few hours. I need to finish this and see what I can find."

"What have you found so far?" he asks as his eyes glance around my office.

If I thought this place was a mess yesterday, it's nothing compared to this. The back wall has a timeline with photos, arrows, and different facts I needed to keep in mind. I stared at it for hours, trying to make sense of everything.

Getting up after sitting for God knows how long reminds me I'm not twenty anymore, and I stretch as I make my way over to the wall. Emmett follows, and I walk him through the information.

"What about this guy?" He points to Jax. "He seems totally harmless."

"That's what I can't work out. When Brie . . . when she was at her appointment yesterday, she said she heard his voice as the shooter."

"And no one thought to tell me that?"

"It was sort of a rough day."

Emmett nods. "Right. Carry on."

"The thing is, Dr. Girardo doesn't think the memory is real. He made a point to say it isn't, but he didn't explain what made him think that."

"He doesn't know Jax, right?"

I shake my head. "I doubt it. Not unless he met him sometime in the last few weeks."

Emmett keeps moving along the timeline I laid out. "Is this everyone who came to the hospital?"

"Yes, all the visitors in and out."

He quirks a brow. "And how did you manage to get it?"

"I didn't steal it from you." I huff. "I have a contact at the hospital."

Emmett shakes his head. "I don't even want to know."

No, he definitely doesn't. "Anyway, no one on it seems to have any connection to the attack or her office being trashed."

"That's the one part of this that has been unanswered. Are the two events connected, and if they are, what was the person looking for in her office? I thought the ring was the key."

"So did she."

"But we were wrong there since you're the ring giver."

I sigh. "The paperwork she's missing is the key, but we can't begin to know what paperwork she had."

Emmett nods. "What else are you thinking?"

"I think it would be safe for us to explore the possibility that the events are connected, which means she was the target."

Emmett sits in the chair across from where I'm leaning against the desk. "Why is that?"

"Everything leads back to Brielle, not Isaac. Since his death, nothing of his has been touched. The house is vacant and there has been no activity there. If it was about him, what he knew, or had, we would've had a move."

"Most likely and her office was trashed."

"She could see the murder, but not the face. She can hear a voice, knows it's a man, but then says it's Jax, whose voice sounds more feminine. Much higher than either of us at least."

"You think it could be a woman?"

"That seems doubtful. It's more likely that she was so desperate to hear the voice that her mind inserted Jax's voice in its place. She ran into him at the awards dinner, and she knew him but couldn't remember him. We also believe based on the position of Isaac's body that he went for the shooter. He may have tried to neutralize the assailant and we all assume it was a man."

That was one of the first things that everyone agreed on. The force of the blow and the angle in which she was hit suggests the assailant was a man. Plus, Isaac played defense from the time he was six until he graduated college. If anyone could take someone down forcefully, it was him.

"It's possible, the evidence suggests a male. There also was that image off the camera of someone getting in a vehicle and the build fits a man."

"I agree, but at this point, I'm not ruling anything out."

"Okay, what were your other thoughts?" Emmett asks.

"This is what we need to get to the bottom of."

Emmett leans down, watching the video. "Where did you get this?"

"After hours of going through footage that a source pulled, I found a recording of Brielle arguing with someone outside her office two weeks prior to the incident. It was late and the tape is very fuzzy, but it appeared that she was upset. Her hand was on a boy's shoulder, and she was pulling him behind her as she argued with who I assumed to be one of the child's parents."

"And she mentioned this before the shooting?" he asks.

"No."

We talked about our days, her work, my lack of work, and everything else, but she never brought up an altercation at work. The date shows it happened on a night we didn't see each other, but we always talked.

Every day.

"Well, you've gotten much further than I care to admit we have."

"I have motivation and resources that you don't. Not to mention, I don't give a shit about the law or the prosecution's case."

Emmett nods slowly. "Yeah, but . . . still."

I shrug. "It's the best answer I can come up with. It's at least a thread I can't tie up neatly. It also gives you a possible person of interest. You just need to find out who that guy is."

Emmett raises a brow. "You make it sound so easy."

"I know."

I already spent hours combing over that angle. Identifying the target was the best place to start.

"Okay, but what if Isaac was the target?"

I pinch the bridge of my nose, just wanting to get back to work. "If the lead on Brielle and this video goes cold, then I'll start over again. I'll reexamine it from Isaac being the target, but I'm going off my instincts and what the evidence I have is showing."

He nods slowly. "You're not far off from my theory. I just don't know anyone in this town who would go after either. Jesus, they talked about making a statue of Isaac if he won states. And Brie, well, she's a damn angel. She works with all those kids, giving time and money to make the programs successful. Who the hell could hate her?"

"That's what I need to find out. Whoever she was in that confrontation with is suspect number one. Once I'm allowed to talk to her in a few hours, I can explain all of this to her. We can talk about everything, figure out a plan, and . . ." I can't even finish because it sounds ridiculous. "I'm a fucking idiot. She doesn't care about this."

He looks up at me with confusion in his eyes. "You don't think she cares about catching her brother's killer?"

I look at the ceiling, letting out a loud sigh. "Of course she does, but that's not going to fix us. I can find the killer, have him arrested, and she still will feel like I betrayed her."

"Is that what she was upset about?"

"Yeah, after I sent you that text, she remembered everything. I love her, Emmett. You know that proposing to her, giving her my entire fucking heart when I am the way I am, wasn't easy. I can't lose her. I can't live my life without her, and . . . she knows in her soul that I love her. Once the wait time is up, I'm going to go over there and beg her to let me explain."

"You can't."

"What do you mean, I can't?"

He gets to his feet and lifts his hands before dropping them. "You can't go talk to her."

"I abided by their rules, I waited twenty-four hours."

"That's not what I mean."

I stare at my best friend, feeling a sense of dread. "Explain."

I can only get one word out because I already know what's coming. I don't have to see the facts laid out to understand the outcome here. But then, this stupid fucking part of me, this hopeful sliver in my shredded heart, wants to believe otherwise.

Brielle wouldn't do this.

She wouldn't walk away.

She wouldn't leave me. Not me. Not us.

Not on purpose or by choice.

Brielle is nothing like her. She is not like my mother. She's not selfish and searching for something she'll never have. She's not looking for someone better. Someone who doesn't drown her.

Emmett looks at me with empathy in his eyes and says two words that shatter me. "She left."

CHAPTER Twenty-Nine

BRIELLE

"Brie, honey." Mom knocks on the door again. "Please come out and talk to me."

She lasted far longer than I would've expected. For three hours, she let me have some time alone to sort out my thoughts. She still paced outside the door, but she didn't knock until now.

Then again, I can't blame her. I just showed up on her doorstep with Quinn and Jackson. After she—reluctantly—let them look around, I came inside and have stayed here, numb.

The tears dried up once we crossed into California. The hours of driving in silence drained the fight out of me.

Still, I needed to decompress.

I open the door, and she sighs. "Oh, thank God. I was debating getting one of the boys to come kick the door in."

"It wasn't locked."

"Well, I didn't know that."

I sigh. "I'm assuming you want answers."

"That would be a good start."

"Inside or out?" I ask, and she smiles. Dad would always ask that when he had something important to tell us. We always picked outside. There is something about the fresh air that makes bad news feel a little less—bad.

"Outside." We walk out to her back deck. It's a small space, but she did a great job utilizing the space to make it inviting. We each take a seat, and she reaches out, holding my hand. "Now, talk to me, Brie."

I let it out. I tell her about everything from the beach to the kiss to the awards to having sex with him. I pretty much forget that she's my mother and Spencer is like a son to her, but I came here for the truth and she deserves no less from me.

Mom, who I didn't think knew what silence was, sits there in it.

I continue, telling her about the memories and the lies. I tell her about my theories regarding Isaac's killer and how it links back to me. All of it.

After I finally get to the part about what forced me to get in a car and drive ten hours to her, she stops me.

"This is a lot to unpack, sweet girl."

That's an understatement. I haven't even gotten to the part where I went crazy and pressed my panic button.

"There's more," I tell her.

She sits back again. "Okay. Let's have it all so we can try to make some sense of this."

I fill in the rest. The fight. The fact that I don't believe my own mind or heart. I tell her about Spencer's face when I pushed the button and how broken he was. All of it pours from me, and it's far more cathartic than I thought it would be.

My mother, as crazy as she is, loves me and will not hold back. She'll be the one person who will help me understand.

"Wow," she finally says.

"Yeah."

Her brown eyes are swimming in unshed tears. "You are engaged to Spencer?"

"I was. I guess."

"I'm both happy and sad."

"Why?" I ask.

"Because, for a very long time, your father and I would talk about what we would do when you and Spencer finally saw each other. He knew that boy was made for you. It drove your father crazy, and I remember a time when your father wanted to stop letting Spencer stay at the house because of it."

I never knew that.

She smiles sadly. "We could never have abandoned that boy, though. Not only because his mother did that enough but also because we loved him. Isaac loved him and so did you. He was a part of our family. He would bounce between our house, Emmett's, and Holden's, but we all tried to love him fiercely since he was always experiencing the opposite end of it."

"I figured all of that. I remember the birthday party that we threw him because his mother didn't show up to pick him up. He was so mad that day."

"She did it a lot. However, it didn't stop your father from worrying that, one day, your relationship with him would change."

"I don't get it."

She takes my hand in hers. "Love has to be nurtured. You plant a seed and hope that it sprouts. Then you have to tend to it like you would a plant. You water it, give it sun, talk to it, and tell it how special it is. If you're lucky, the seedling becomes a plant with good roots because of how you treated it in the beginning. You planted that seed when you were just a girl, and I watched Spencer do the same."

That doesn't make sense. Sure, I did. I was a teenager who thought he was the most amazing man in the world. "Spencer never planted a seed."

She laughs. "Yes, he did. It was when you were leaving for college. The two of you spent the night together at the warehouse that you now live in."

I stare at her in astonishment. "You knew?"

"Of course, I knew. I saw him look at you the next day. It was like he was coming up for air after being tossed in the waves. He planted that seed, and the two of you nurtured it in your own ways."

"And now it's dead," I say, feeling that way inside.

"Why?"

"Because he lied. He let it shrivel up and die."

My mother, who is never one to hold her tongue, scoffs. "You're ridiculous. We *all* lied."

"Yes, but I knew you were."

She leans back. "And you assumed he wasn't part of the unanimous all? I imagine that was tough. I can even understand why you felt the panic you did. It's as though everything you believed you were building suddenly had the foundation washed away. But now what? Now you punish him and yourself? You run away and live out your days at my house when we both know you don't really want to be here, considering we usually last two days before bickering."

I smile. "Sometimes three."

"Yes." Mom laughs. "Sometimes three. My point is, from what it sounds like, you fell in love with Spencer Cross all over again. You didn't have the memories of a whirlwind love affair that ended with a ring, and yet, you chose him. Not Henry, who came back when you believed you were still with him. Not some mystery man, who you thought you were engaged to." She lifts her hand to my cheek. "You, my sweet girl, have the kind of love that others dream of. To know the person, even when you don't know yourself. It's up to you if you're going to nurture it back to life or let it die. Which, let's all be honest, you never really thought he killed your brother, you were scared."

I roll over to my phone glowing in the darkness.

My finger hovers over the button to listen to the voice mail Spencer just left. I know that whatever he says is going to break my heart.

Mom is right. I love him. I love him not for the past but for what he means to me now, which is why I am so goddamn upset that I ran away. I just felt I had no options. I didn't know what was real, and I still don't. Other than I love him. I was scared and worried that it wasn't real and I would lose it.

I look at the ceiling, trying to get the courage to listen.

If he was strong enough to leave it, then I can be brave enough to hear what he has to say.

His rich voice fills the room, and I have to fight back tears.

"Brielle, I debated on doing this. I wasn't going to call you. I hear you loud and clear. You don't trust me, and you need space. I won't beg you to come back. I wanted to let you know a few things. First, I paid your security team in full for the next six months, so you don't have to worry about being in danger. I hope they give you peace of mind. Second, I have been working these last two days, trying to give you something else, something I think you need, but I am leaving Rose Canyon . . . well, now. I don't know how long it'll take me to track down the information I need, but I want you to know that I am sorry that I lied to you. I'm sorry I hurt you.

"Most of all, I love you, Brielle. I love you so much that I wanted to die when I thought I lost you. When Emmett called and told me about Isaac, I thought I knew pain. But then he told me that you suffered a head injury and they didn't know if you were going to make it, and I was more afraid than I thought even possible. As I drove to the hospital, desperate to see you, I begged for God to save you. I bartered my own heart and life in exchange for yours.

"I wanted to tell everyone about us then. I just didn't want to do that to you, so I kept quiet. When you woke up and asked for Henry, my heart was ripped from my chest. I got you back, but you didn't know us. You didn't remember our first date or first kiss or when I proposed. I spent my entire life searching for something worth fighting for, and you were in front of me the whole time. You saved me, Brielle, even if you don't remember doing it. You said I was drowning you, and that is the absolute last thing I want. So, this is me giving you air. I just wanted you to know that, even though I'm gone, everything I am doing is for you. I will always love you. Always."

The voice mail ends, and I clutch the phone to my chest, crying harder. He's leaving Rose Canyon, and I have no idea if I'll ever get him back.

I close my eyes, and like lightning, a memory hits me so hard that, if I weren't already lying down, I would be on my back.

"I love you," Spencer says as we eat dinner on the floor of my apartment.

Out of nowhere.

No forewarning. Not even a hint that it was coming.

I nearly choke on my Lo Mein as I say, "What?"

"I love you."

I place the chopsticks down carefully, swallow, and try again. "You love me?"

"I do. A lot, actually. I love you more than I even knew you could love someone."

I wonder if someone can go into shock from a declaration of love. Because, if so, I'm pretty sure that's what's happening.

Not that I don't think he means it. It's been six months and he has been pushing harder for us to become a couple, a real one that goes on real dates and doesn't sneak around as though we are doing something wrong.

Which we aren't.

But I like this. I like the intimacy of it. I like no one knowing or caring what we are doing. I like having Spencer all to myself.

He leans in, tucking my hair behind my ear. "Say something, Brielle."

Right. I need to . . . speak.

"You know I love you."

"I do."

I smile. "Good."

Spencer laughs. "Good."

Something starts to niggle at the back of my mind. A curiousness that isn't mine to have but is there regardless. "How many women have you said that to?" I ask, hoping he will answer just as much as I hope he doesn't.

It isn't my business. I have loved one other man in my life, but what I felt for Henry doesn't hold a candle to my love for Spencer. With him, I have no fear. He knows me, loves me, and accepts me—flaws and all.

"None."

I drop the chopstick again. "None?"

"I have never loved a woman before you. I have never allowed myself to love another because no one was worth that level of trust. But you are. You are worth it all, and I love you, Brielle Davis. I love you, and God help me because you are a handful."

Spencer is thirty-eight years old. He has dated legions of women, and I am absolutely speechless. How could he have never loved anyone else? But the one thing Spencer and I don't do is lie. We built our entire relationship on that foundation, and if he tells me he's never loved anyone else, then it's true.

And I feel bad for every woman who had this man and never found out what it feels like to be loved by him. Because . . . it's magnificent.

I push the food to the side, crawl over to him, and then take his beautiful face in my hands. "I have loved you since before I knew what love was. I have dreamed of you since I knew what dreams were. You are the air I breathe. The beat of my heart. I love you so much that even the idea of losing this is too much for me to think about."

"You won't lose me, Brielle. Even if you walk away, I will always be here. I'm warning you now, I am going to marry you. You are going to be mine in every damn way."

Yes! I want to scream. I want that more than anything, but I think I've always been his anyway. I have just been waiting for him to want to be mine.

Our lips touch in the sweetest, purest kiss that has ever happened. "I think maybe you're right."

"About what?" he asks, brushing my hair back.

"I think it's time we talk about telling everyone. I don't want to love you in the dark anymore."

"Oh, sweetheart, that never happened with us. You are the light; I just held you in the shadow."

I rest my forehead to his. "So, we make a plan to tell Isaac and Addy?"

"Yes, but not now. Right now, I want to make love"—he kisses me—"all. Night. Long."

Tears leak from my eyes as my heart feels all of that moment again. I love him. I have always loved him and he loves me. Enough that he was willing to do anything to help me, even at his own pain.

And now he's gone.

What have I done?

CHAPTER *Thirty*

BRIELLE

After a night full of regrets, I came to the one place that has always been soothing to me—the beach.

It was a hike, but Quinn never complained. Now I'm walking along the shoreline, the water lapping over my toes before retreating back into the sea.

Sometimes I feel as though this is how my memory is. It comes ashore, ready to meet the land, and then runs back.

I called Dr. Girardo this morning and our session was very hard for me. I am grappling with fragments of reality mixing with dreams, and I keep having these flashbacks that feel so real. We discussed how to tell them apart. He helped me realize that when all my senses are engaged, then the memory is that—a memory. When I can only see from the outside or I can't feel anything, then it's most likely a mixture or fragment.

That means that what I remembered last night was real.

What I saw that day I was standing in Spencer's bedroom was real.

I stop, tilt my face toward the sun, and close my eyes. It's so peaceful here, and for a moment, I can believe that everything will work out. The sun will rise, the tides will ebb, and anything that I've broken can be repaired.

As I turn, a loud bang rings out, and I drop to the sand, my hands over my head as I struggle to breathe.

"I guess we're getting coffee?" I ask my brother as he pulls into RosieBeans.

Isaac grins. "I thought you'd never offer."

I didn't offer, but I know my brother well enough not to push it. He did pick me up early to take me to work, so the least I can do is get him coffee. It's so weird how, in the last few days, everything has changed.

I'm engaged.

I'm getting married to the most amazing man, and I haven't told the best man I know.

Tomorrow is the big day. Spencer will pick me up, and we will go to dinner and tell them. Then we'll let the rest of the rejects know. I really hope it goes well. I don't want fists thrown, but I guess we would deserve it at this point.

Isaac is telling me about some new play he wants to run as we head to the front of the car when someone yells at us.

"I'm going to fucking kill you!" Bill Waugh yells as he storms toward us.

Oh, God. He looks pissed off, which means his wife told him about my visit yesterday.

"Get in the car, Isaac." I turn to Isaac and try to get there myself. This man is crazy, and we need to leave.

His eyes go between the man, who is now running toward us, and me. "Brie?"

"Hurry!" I call back to him.

Bill told me he'd kill me if I reported my concerns. As a social worker, it's my job to do that. The law is very clear. If I witness any signs of child abuse, I have to report it. I informed Bill's wife last night that I was going to do so and if she and Myles needed refuge, to come to my office today.

Before I can get to the door, Bill's hands are wrapped around my arms. He's pulling me back. I stare at Isaac, willing myself to stay calm.

"You bitch. You think you can take my family? You think I'd let you get away with it? You think you have the power to do that?" Bill snarls in my ear.

I try to rip my arms free, but he tightens his grip. It's painful enough to make me want to cry, but I hold it together.

"Easy, man," Isaac says as he starts to come around the front of the car. "Just let her go so we can work this out."

"Did you file the paperwork?" Bill asks.

"Yes. This morning," I lie. I want him to think it's already done. Killing me does nothing if he thinks it's too late to stop me.

However, he doesn't see it that way.

He shoves me backward, slamming my head on the frame of the car. I see stars, the world spins, and when I crumble to the ground, my head bounces off pavement. By sheer force of will, I keep my eyes open.

That's when I see it. The sun glints off the metal barrel of the gun he pulls from under his jacket. Bill is going to kill me.

Isaac must've moved because the gun is now pointed at him. No. No. He can't. He can't kill him. Not when this is my fault. Not when I'm who did this.

"Stay the fuck back or I'll kill you both."

I can't let him die. I have to save Isaac. I force myself to sit up, and the gun swings back to me. "You don't want to do this," I tell him, praying my words aren't slurred. "Please, you can get in the car now and drive off. Nothing will change."

"Everything has changed! You're taking them from me! You're taking my family, you stupid bitch! Now, I am going to take yours."

Hot tears fall down my cheeks as I turn to my brother. I push up, needing to get in front of him, to protect him. He has Elodie and Addison. He can tell Spencer what happened. He can make him understand and get him through this. I can't be responsible for my brother's death.

I won't.

"Brie!" Isaac yells at me. The ground is unsteady under my feet, and I have no idea what is up and down.

"I didn't file it," I try to tell him. "In my office."

"You're a fucking liar!" Bill roars and then something slams against the back of my head.

Blackness seeps around me, taking me into oblivion. I float until I hear the crack of a gunshot that's followed by the sound of something falling beside me. In that moment, I know in the depths of my soul, he shot Isaac, and I hope I never wake up.

"Brielle!" Quinn is holding my shoulders, shaking me gently. "Brielle, you're okay! It was a car backfire."

I shake my head. "I saw it. I saw it all." I force the words out between my labored breaths. "I saw who shot my brother. Get me back to Rose Canyon. Now!"

"You're leaving?" Mom asks while I shove stuff into my bag.

"I need to go back."

"To Spencer?"

"To everything. I remember, Mom. I remember it all. I need to get back."

She helps me put more of my things in the bag. "You remember?"

"I saw the whole thing. I remembered the noises, the air, the cold, the sun, and the gun. I know who it was and why he came after me. I . . . I have to go."

"Tell me," she requests.

So, I do. I speak so fast, I trip over my words, but I get it all out. My heart is racing as I explain Isaac's face and the sound of his voice as he tried to get to me. It's all there. Every single thing I could see, hear, feel, smell. It's not my mind playing tricks on me or changing details. It's what happened, and I need to get home.

"What about your safety?" Mom asks.

I look over at the two hulking men in the corner. "They will not let anything happen to me."

I have never been in danger because Spencer wouldn't allow it. He's made sure I have someone here the entire time. My protection was always his priority.

Quinn grunts, and Jackson just grins. "She remembers and trusts us," he says to Quinn.

"It would seem so."

"Do you think we'll get to watch her fix the other part?" Jackson asks.

"Probably not. We always miss the fun stuff."

Jackson snorts. "It's unfair, which is par for the course."

I ignore the two of them as I zip my bag. "Well?" I ask impatiently. "Are you packed?"

Quinn smirks. "Oh, are you ready for another ten-plus hour drive, Sunshine? This will be more fun than the one here since you are eager for another reason. Yes, I am packed. I am always packed when I'm on a mission."

"I used to like you, not anymore."

Quinn shrugs. "I'm used to women disliking me."

Jackson walks over. "You're sure you want to go back? We can handle things from here."

"Positive."

My mother looks at him. "I can't lose her. Now that she remembers who killed him and tried to kill her, she's in danger."

"She is, but we will do everything we can to protect her," he promises.

I don't care about any of this. I want to go home and fix this. I want to make sure Myles is safe from his father, have Bill arrested, and then I want to find the man I love and beg him to forgive me.

I was so stupid to ever think he could hurt me or Isaac. Not him. Not ever.

Mom wraps me in her arms, holding me tight. "I am so sorry you went through this, Brielle. I wish I could take it all for you." She pulls back. "You are strong and courageous. You were trying to help that little boy and save your brother at the same time. None of this is your fault, and I just want you to be happy, okay?"

I nod.

"You only get one life, don't waste it."

I give her another hug, grateful that we were able to have this moment. Then I grab my bag and we head out to the car.

"I've already called Emmett. He is taking the information to the district attorney. In the meantime, they sent a unit to make sure Myles and his mother are safe. If they can, they'll make an arrest before you get into town," Jackson explains.

"What about Spencer?"

"Spencer Cross is not a helpless human, Brielle," Quinn tries to reassure me. "He's been trained by the best, and whether he's used those skills or not lately, that doesn't just go away. I honestly feel bad for whoever is stupid enough to try to go after him."

"He can't stop a bullet. That man killed my brother and would've killed me. He probably thought I was dead, which is why he didn't shoot me. He wanted to take from me, and who better than the man who spent every day of the last month with me?"

I want to wail and scream and fly to him. I never should've left. If anything happens, I will never forgive myself. In my anger and hurt, I pushed him away, accused him of the unthinkable, and walked out just like the women before me.

No wonder he left town.

"We'll find him." Jackson's voice is full of confidence. "Look, when guys are hurt, they need time to lick their wounds. He's probably off in the mountains on a hike without cell service. Or he's drunk in Vegas. One of the two."

I roll my eyes. "Vegas and those boys are a bad idea."

"Vegas is a bad idea for any boy," Quinn says with a laugh.

"Well, at Isaac's bachelor party, the four of them ended up in a shitload of trouble. Spencer was out thousands of dollars. Isaac almost didn't get married once Addison found out about the money he spent. Holden hooked up with some girl in a bathroom. She left him blacked out in the stall, and Emmett spent the night sleeping on the hood of his car because he lost his keys. Trust me, he hates Vegas and vowed never to go back." Plus, it's where Spencer's mother would go whenever she needed to get away from him and find herself.

The only way that Spencer would go there is out of desperation.

"Wherever he is, we'll track him down and make sure he's safe as well. Let us worry, Brielle. You just prepare your apology speech." Jackson squeezes my arm and steps back. "Miller, make sure you're giving me updates."

Quinn nods. "I'll be in touch every two hours."

The car lurches forward, and I prepare myself for the longest car ride in history.

CHAPTER *Thirty-One*

SPENCER

It's been a week of dead ends. I know this is part of the job, but I am at my wits end. I took the video of the altercation to my video guy. He was able to enhance the video, but the man's face was in the shadow too much to make a positive ID.

He is working on digitally recreating it, but that takes at least a day.

All I have now is the boy she was protecting. If I can get information from him, then maybe he can tell me who Brielle was upset with.

I'm driving back toward town when I see the sign for the park we went to a few weeks ago. I can't resist the pull, so I turn in.

There are the swings where her flag was hidden and the grassy area where the barrels of balloons were placed.

I step out of the car and head toward the swings when someone yells my name. "Hey, look, Timmy! It's Spencer!"

Great. I need these heckling kids like I need a hole in my head. I turn, and sure enough, Brielle's teammates are strolling over, and Timmy has a soccer ball tucked under his arm. "Hello, boys."

"Hey, man. You came back for another butt whooping?"

"Not this time."

The one kid, I think his name is Saint, comes closer. "You okay? You don't look okay."

I force a smile. "I'm good."

I'm sure I look like shit. I haven't slept. I can barely eat. I sure as hell haven't used a razor in five days, and I have been living in my car while I searched for any answers.

"Where's Brielle?"

Gone. She's fucking gone, Saint, that's where. "Not sure. She went on a trip."

Brian steps forward. "Did you upset her?"

"Why would you ask that?"

"Because you look like you did," Timmy answers.

I don't even want to ask what that means. "She's fine."

At least I think she is. When I called Quinn five days ago, he informed me that he could not inform me about Brielle, her whereabouts, or anything to do with her situation. However, what he could say was that he was okay, his friend he was with was sad, and he was staying by the coast with a friend's mother. Basically, everything I am not supposed to know. After that, I was done.

I shut everything off and did the only thing I could do, which was to focus on finding the man in the video.

"Well, you don't look fine. You look like you're a mess."

"And I am so glad I came here to get your opinion," I say, irked at these kids.

Timmy nudges Brian. "He totally messed up with her."

"I did not."

Okay, I did, but I'm not telling a bunch of ten-year-old kids that.

Saint nods slowly. "He did. And Brielle is the best."

"She totally is. For a girl," Timmy adds. "What did you do?"

I groan. "I didn't do anything."

"Then why isn't she with you?" Brian asks.

"Because she went on a trip."

"Without you? My mom went on a trip once without my dad and now she lives in Tucson," Brian notes. "Is Brielle in Tucson too?"

Just put me out of my misery. "No, she is not in Tucson."

"She could be in Vegas," Saint informs us all. "I heard my dad say that all girls go to Vegas."

"Your dad is wrong," I let him know.

"My dad says he knows everything," Timmy pipes in.

As if this conversation could get any more ridiculous, Brian calls another kid over. "Hey, Kendrick, come here! Spencer upset Brielle, and now she's in Vegas or Tucson!"

I swear I am going to start yelling at these kids in about two seconds. "She is not in Vegas or Tucson."

"Well, she's not here and you are, so you don't know that." Timmy shrugs.

Kendrick runs over. "Man, we love Brielle."

"I do too."

"Then you should marry her," Brian says. "Girls like that."

"And you know this from all your infinite experience?" I ask.

"I have a girlfriend," he says, pointing toward the swings. "She brought me two sodas to school yesterday."

"The foundation of your love is rock solid, Brian. I'm impressed."

He beams. "She can't resist."

Kendrick, Timmy, and Saint start to laugh and make gagging noises. These kids remind me so much of my group of friends it hurts. Emmett was the first of us to have a crush, ironically it was on Addison. She smiled at him and he fell. She was the girl all of us wanted. She was smart, pretty, and brought cookies to school every day. Really, what more could a bunch of dumb boys want? But she loved Isaac, and Emmett, being the friend he was, decided no girl was worth fighting over. However, when Isaac and Addy started dating, we gave him so much shit for it. Mostly because we were jealous.

I smile and grip Brian's shoulder. "You hold on to that girlfriend of yours. No matter what your friends say. Women make the world a better place."

He grins. "And they sneak you soda."

"And they do that."

Timmy moves in. "Then why did you let Brielle go?"

"I didn't want to," I admit.

"Then get her back," Kendrick offers his advice. "Tell her you're sorry and get her flowers. My dad is always getting flowers for my mom. He said he messes up a lot, but women are difficult and I should learn this early."

"Your dad is right about that," I mutter under my breath before saying, "I'll fix it. I just need time."

A whistle sounds, and the boys turn like prairie dogs after just popping their heads up. "We gotta go! That's coach!"

"Go have fun," I say, waving as they run off.

I'll fix it.

I just need to get home and figure out who is on this tape.

Instead of going straight home, showering, and trying to fix myself, I go to the youth center. Rachelle and Jax tell me that the boy on the tape is Myles Eastwood. His father, Bill Waugh, is a prick. According to his file, he seems a lot like a man my mother would've loved. He's been in and out of jail, can't hold a job, and likes to intimidate.

I call Emmett, but he doesn't answer, so I go to the station instead.

"Sheriff Maxwell is busy," the officer at the front desk explains.

"Tell him Spencer Cross is here to talk to him."

She rolls her eyes but gets up and goes back to find him. My heart is racing. I know who the killer is. I have evidence and a name. No matter what happens with Brie, we can make this right.

Emmett comes out and waves, letting me know I can come back.

The second the door to his office is closed behind me, he asks, "Where the hell have you been?"

"Following my lead," I explain.

Then I place the file in front of him. "This is the information I obtained. I have everything you already saw, plus a few new puzzle pieces."

"I don't need this."

"What the hell do you mean, you don't need this?" I ask.

"Just what I said, but thanks for stopping in. I have to head over to the courthouse."

"I just handed you the biggest lead in the case."

He shrugs. "I already have that lead, but thanks."

"Emmett. I am going to kill you," I warn.

"Spencer, you can try."

I swear, I'm back to being sixteen when I punched Emmett in the face because he didn't listen to me about the girl I liked.

He tries to move, but I stand, blocking his exit. "What is wrong with you? You have spent months working on this. I do your damn job for you, and you're dismissing me?"

"No, I'm not dismissing you. I have to meet someone in two minutes, and I'm already going to be late."

"No. You need to look at the information in that folder." I step closer to him, and he rolls his eyes.

"Go home and wait for me to call. I will have news then."

I narrow my eyes, trying to decipher what he's not saying. "You have to go to the courthouse?"

"Yes."

"And you don't need the information in that file, why?"

"Because I don't. Now, I can't answer any more questions and I need to go. Do you understand?"

He knows something. He found information himself. "Why aren't you telling me anything?"

"Because I am not able to. Now, get out of my way and do as I say for once."

I step back. "I'll head home then."

"And maybe shower and make yourself look human," he suggests before he walks out.

I grab the folder and walk out after him, watching as he gets in his cruiser. I can feel it in my bones that he's going to get a warrant or something from the prosecutor.

The drive to my house feels like it takes twice as long as usual. I pull into the driveway, jump out of my car, and rush toward the front door, but my heart stops in my throat when I get there.

Brielle is sitting on my front step. Her arms are wrapped around her legs, and as soon as she sees me, she pushes to her feet.

We look at each other, both frozen, and when I see her lower lip tremble, I finally speak. "Brielle?"

"Spencer," she says and then rushes into my arms. Her body slams against mine, and I catch her.

She tucks her face into my neck, pulling me closer. Her body shakes as she lets out a soft sob. "I need you."

"You have me. Jesus, you have me." I hold on to her as tight as I ever have. She has no idea what being away from her has done to me. "What's wrong? Why are you here? Why are you crying?"

She pulls back, tears brimming in those blue eyes. "I was so stupid. I am so sorry. I never should've left you like that. I never . . . I remember everything. I remember our kisses and the way you love me. I remember us making love and you asking me to marry you. I remember us talking about telling Isaac, and . . . I remember the end. But I remember us." Her hands go to my scruffy face and she smiles. "I couldn't really forget, and even when I did, I still wanted you. I longed for you, wished it was you, and that's why I was so upset."

It's not her fault. None of this is. She didn't do this, and I wish I made different choices. I can't go back in time, but I can make sure we have everything in our future.

"No, baby. I was wrong. I never should've gone along with the lies. I should've told you from the beginning."

"That's just it, I never would've believed it. I am just so sorry."

"You remember that I love you?" I ask, making sure I heard it all.

"Yes."

Brielle lifts up at the same time that I bend, and our lips meet. She moves her hands up my chest and then her fingers tangle in my hair. This is everything. This is all I wanted but thought I had lost for good. I thought I had hurt her so deeply, broken the trust so irrevocably, that she'd never be mine again.

I kiss her harder, needing her to feel everything I am. The love, the happiness, the desire to give her everything she wants.

All too soon, she drops back down, both of us struggling to catch our breaths. "I remember the shooting and who did it."

"Did you tell Emmett?"

"I did. I have to talk to the DA in an hour. I . . . I just needed to see you. I needed to make this right."

"You being here is right." And I was right too about Emmett. It's why he was heading out there. "Where is Quinn?"

"He's right there." She points to the chair on the porch.

"Don't mind me," Quinn says. "I'm just glad I got to witness this. She's cried so much over the last few days, that it's nice to see her smile."

It's the best thing in the world. "Brie, you're not safe now that your memory has returned."

"You won't let anyone hurt me." The confidence in her voice is too much for me. I've been in agony these last few days. I've missed her so much that it felt as if everything in my life had been upended.

"No, but we still shouldn't take chances. Plus, I want to hear everything." I usher her up the steps, and Quinn stands, jerking his head to indicate he has information to share. "Can you let Quinn tell me whatever he needs?"

"Sure."

As soon as she goes inside, he comes closer. "Listen, I know that you know. If you didn't, you would've asked her who it was the second she told you her memory returned. She told me the name and what happened, but I don't have a good description. Can you . . ."

"I'll grab the file in a second."

"As soon as we had a name, we started digging, but he hasn't been seen in weeks. I do find it strange that no one in town thought that was suspicious. It seems like a place where everyone knows everyone," he notes.

"They moved here a few weeks before the shooting, so I don't think they were here long enough for anyone to notice. Still, the fact that they're gone is alarming. I have no idea where they went. The youth center was so focused on losing Brie and dealing with the town mourning the loss of Isaac, so it was likely the best time for them to disappear."

He scratches the back of his neck. "Do you think he got whatever he was looking for in her office and fled?"

"Wouldn't you if you were him? We'll still find him," I vow. Not only did this man take away my best friend, he almost stole the woman I love.

Like I said before, there is no stone I will leave unturned. I will find him, and he will pay for what he did.

We walk to my car where I grab my file with the information and the thumb drive with the video. "Here is what I have."

Quinn smirks. "See, I knew you'd do some good while you were all sad about losing your girl. I'll get this to my people and see what they can come up with."

I give him a small smile and clap him on the shoulder. "Thanks, man. Now, I am going to need at least three hours with Brielle . . . uninterrupted."

He laughs. "You do your thing. I have some work to do. Lock the door, though."

"I will."

I head inside, and Brie isn't in the living room. So, I walk through the house, checking the rooms, and then I find her in my office.

On the desk is my notepad that I started the story on. She's reading it, oblivious to the fact that I'm watching her.

As she flips to the second page, I interrupt, not wanting her to get any farther. I got a little dark when I started to write about the panic button. "You know it's rude to read someone's story without their permission," I say, slightly joking.

Her head turns quickly. "Oh, God. I'm sorry—" She stops herself. "No, I'm not, actually. You're not just someone, you are—or, were—my fiancé. And . . . it's about me."

"Am," I correct. "I am your fiancé, and you are my whole fucking world." I step into the room, and she nibbles on her lower lip. "How far did you get?"

Brielle's eyes move to the paper and then back to me. "The part where you started actually talking about what you know about the case instead of how much you love me."

I rub my thumb on her lips. "The entire story is a love letter to you."

"Then I should get to read it."

"Maybe, but right now, I'd much rather kiss you."

She grins. "I'd like that too."

So, I do as the lady wants and kiss her again. The fact that I'm doing it is surreal. I wasn't sure I'd ever have this again.

I break the kiss and stare at her. "Why did you come back?"

"For you. For us. Because I needed to make things right all the way around. It wasn't just because of my memories," she assures me. "I was already coming back before that. I think I was coming back the minute I left, I just . . . I needed to go. I was so scared and tired of the constant feeling of being crazy. I'm sorry that I hurt you. I know I left you and said you were drowning me."

She'll never know how those words struck me. The fact that my mother said it constantly, telling me I was the weight on her ankles, drowning her. "She used to tell me that when she dropped me off with whoever was willing to keep me that week."

"She was wrong, and so was I. I was drowning and refused to take the life raft you offered. It wasn't you, Spencer."

"I appreciate you saying it."

"I mean it."

I believe that she does. Brielle isn't spiteful or selfish like my mother was. "So, you remember everything?" I ask.

"I do." She steps back, running her fingers through her blonde hair. "You haven't asked about the shooter."

"Do you want to tell me?"

She shakes her head with a laugh. "You already know it's not Jax. How did you know already?"

"I spent the last few days researching, which is what I should've done from the second it happened. I should've done what I could to help you."

"I think you did exactly what helped me. I needed to remember on my own, but how did you figure it out?"

The only reason any of us kept anything from her was to catch the killer and make sure he pays for what he did. That's why I won't say anything more. "I don't want to keep secrets from you, Brie. I learned that lesson, but I think we should do everything we can to make sure the information we have is admissible. The less you know, it may be better. The information I have is with the authorities, and after you talk to the DA, we can talk. Do you agree?" I have no idea of the rules on this, and I'd rather not make a misstep.

"That's why I went to Emmett first. I gave my statement to him and I'm waiting for the next part."

I figured as much. It's why he didn't need the file and he was meeting with the prosecutor.

"How long do we have?" I ask.

She looks down at her watch. "About an hour. Why?"

"Because I'd very much like to make love to you."

Brielle's blue eyes turn liquid as she grins. "I'd like that too."

CHAPTER *Thirty-Two*

BRIELLE

Having my memories back makes walking toward his bedroom a different experience. The anticipation is there, but now there's more. The feelings I had before, the ones that made me think I was crazy, are amplified. It's like all the love we shared has doubled.

He pulls me down the hall and then stops once we're inside his bedroom. "I love you," Spencer says in a rough voice as he faces me.

"I love you."

"No, Brielle, I love you more than anything. I have wanted to say those words to you so many times since you woke up."

I push back his overgrown locks. "I love you, Spencer Cross. I have loved you my whole life, and I don't ever plan to stop."

"I will give you the world."

I smile at that. "I just want you."

"You already have that, my love."

He leans in, kissing me softly as we let the emotions pass between us. When I left him, a part of me broke, and now I feel whole again. He makes me that way.

What started off slow and sweet, grows faster and hotter. His hands move to my breasts, squeezing gently. "I need you naked," he says against my lips. "I need to touch you, taste you, make you mine."

I have only ever been his. He lifts my shirt off in one motion, and then my bra and pants follow.

I move my hands to his clothes, wanting the same. "Let me see you. Let me memorize this all over again."

Not that I forgot. I just want to experience him all over again.

Spencer and I tumble onto the bed, naked and open to each other. He takes my hand, moving it to his cock. "Stroke me," he commands.

I push my hand up and down, feeling him harden against my palm. "Now what?" I ask.

"Kiss me."

His hand in my hair holds me to him as I continue to stroke him. I tighten my grip, moving faster. I want him so much. I want to taste him, make him crazy, remind him of how amazing we are and can be.

I pull away before pushing him flat on the bed. "I want to do more."

He grins and slides his hands behind his head, putting himself on full display for me. "I'm all yours."

"Is that so?"

"Always."

I bite my lower lip and wink. "Well, since you're mine to do what I want with, I think I'd like to suck your cock first."

"I love your fucking mouth."

"Good." I run my tongue along the tip and then take him deep. The last time we were together, I didn't get to do this. He was much too focused on me. Now it's my turn to be in control and give him the pleasure he deserves.

My head bobs as I move up and down, taking him as deeply as I can. Spencer's breathing accelerates as I try to go faster.

"Jesus, Brielle, I can't." His fingers tighten in my hair. I work him harder, taking longer, deeper pulls, sliding my tongue against his shaft. "Please, love, not yet. Fuck, not yet."

He moves so fast I don't have time to do anything but squeak as he pulls me all the way up his body. His lips tug into a mischievous smirk as he positions me over his face. "Grab the headboard, Brielle."

When he pushes my ass up, I have no choice but to do it.

"Good girl. Hold on and let's see if I can make you beg."

He pulls my hips down, and my head falls back as his tongue swipes against my clit. Spencer moves his face back and forth, getting his tongue in all the right spots. Sweat breaks out against my skin as my orgasm grows. I was already halfway there just from making him crazy, and his mouth is throwing me closer to the edge embarrassingly fast.

My legs begin to quake as his thumbs move inward, brushing against my entrance. He moans as my thighs tighten around his face, and I try so hard to hold on.

He moves his thumb more, pushing up and circling as he continues to move against my clit.

"Spencer. I'm close," I warn him. "I'm so close." He does it again and then moves his thumb back farther, pulling my ass cheeks apart. I gasp when his finger rims around the hole. "Oh God." I moan louder. He breaches, just slightly, and the sensations are too much. I shatter, unable to hold back.

He grabs my ass, keeping me steady as he drains every last ounce of pleasure from my body. I am probably suffocating him, but I am falling to pieces, and he's the only thing keeping me together.

Spencer adjusts my legs, and I flop down on the bed. "That was . . ." I pant.

"Just the beginning." He doesn't pause before settling between my thighs and pushing against my opening just enough to tease me. "I want you this way. I want nothing between us. I want to make love to you without barriers."

"What if we . . . what if I get pregnant?" I ask.

"Would you want that? A baby? A family . . . with me?"

He hesitates on the last part, and my heart breaks. Spencer has always been forgotten by everyone, including me. When he proposed, he said he wanted a life, a family, a future filled with everything I could want. Being a mom, having my own family, is what I long for.

I smile up at him, tears pooling and making him blurry. "I want everything with you. I always have."

"If it happens . . ."

"It happens." I bring his lips to mine. "I love you, Spencer Cross, and I need you now. Nothing between us."

He slides into me, filling every crack that has been left from the past. He makes me complete, and I never want this to end.

Lying here, the sheet wrapped around us and the sun streaming in from the window, feels like that memory I had, only better. This is real and amazing and I feel safe.

Then I remember there's a crazy person on the loose. "Do you think Emmett found him?"

"If he hasn't, Quinn will."

I lift my head at that. "Quinn?"

"Yeah, he's doing his own investigating."

I'm not sure why I'm surprised by this, but I am. "When did you send Quinn out on this mission?"

"When I knew I was going to strip you down and make you scream.

I figured you'd appreciate the privacy. Plus, I wasn't about to let you out of my sight so I could do it."

"I mean . . . that was the right move, but I'm surprised you let me be here without a trained gunman."

He laughs. "Sweetheart, I am a trained gunman. You are equally as safe with me as you are with Quinn."

I shrug and tilt my head to the side. "Are you sure? Quinn never does this."

"He better fucking not."

"I'm just saying, am I all that safe right now?"

"Brielle, I would fight until there was literally no breath left inside of me to keep you safe. No one will get close to you. I have the team around just in case, but right here, in my house, you're safe."

I believe him. I'm just a little wary. "No one has seen Bill or his family?"

Spencer sighs. "No."

"And no one at the center checked on Myles?"

He runs his fingers up and down my spine. "Not that I know of."

I sit up, pulling the sheet with me. "We have to find them! He will hurt them. I don't remember everything that was in those files, but he was beating Sonya. Myles had bruises too. He would tell me about his father and the things he was doing for someone or something . . . I don't know. It was bad and I . . . we can't stay here while that kid is in danger."

"Brie, you're not . . ."

I am already climbing out of the bed. "I am going to help find that boy. He is innocent in all this. I never filed the paperwork, so he's been with him for over a month without anyone knowing the danger he's in!" I have to help that kid.

"Brielle, stop. You're not going to find him."

"I can't just sit here."

"I didn't say to do that," Spencer says with exasperation. "I know you want to help him, we all do. There is a team of trained SEALs and the whole police department looking, and that's not including the citizens who are keeping an eye out for anyone in the family. So, for just one second, can I relish in having my girl back?"

I shake my head, pulling my pants on. "I love you, and I will be yours for a very long time, but you know that I could never let this go."

He flops back against the pillow, groaning as he covers his face. "I'm in love with a madwoman."

I laugh a little and then lean in to kiss him. "Get up. We have paperwork to take care of."

Spencer grabs my wrist, halting me from grabbing my shirt. "I want a different type of paperwork done."

"What?"

"I want us to get married." His green eyes bore into my blue ones. "I want to marry you. I want to be able to do all the things I couldn't when you were in the hospital. I want to put that ring and another one on your finger and marry you in front of our friends and your family."

I get down on my knees so I'm level with him. "I can agree to that."

"I mean it, Brie. I don't want to wait. I don't want to hide anymore."

"I know."

"Okay. Let me get some pants on and let's go file paperwork that I want done." He gets out of bed, and I smile at his perfect ass as he walks by.

"And they say romance is dead."

CHAPTER
Thirty-Three
BRIELLE

"You brought me back to the park?" I ask Spencer with a brow raised.

"I need to show the kids that I fixed it."

"Fixed what?"

"Us."

I laugh. "And how do the boys know you broke us?"

He shrugs. "I may have come here and ran into them. They said I looked like shit and must've messed up."

Well, if that isn't the cutest thing ever. "And now you want to show me off?"

"Exactly. Now, I just hope they're here . . ."

"Hey! It's Brielle!" Kendrick runs over. "You're back."

"I am! Hey, guys!"

"Oh, she's with him," Timmy says when he spots Spencer.

I laugh because it's hilarious how much they really don't like him.

Spencer grumbles under his breath. "Yes, she's with me. I brought her here."

"You owe me twenty bucks," Saint says to Timmy.

"Did you bet I wouldn't be able to fix it?" Spencer asks.

"I did. I thought she'd be smarter."

I snort and try to hide my amusement. "Well, as fun as this has been, we have to get going. I am glad to see you all though."

"See ya," they say and race off.

I hook my arm around his, and we walk down the path. "This is nice."

"What is?"

"Our park," I say as we stroll leisurely. This park may be a bit out of the way, but it's now ours. That date really changed him for me all over again. It wasn't about the past that day, it was about what we had together in the moment.

"This is ours."

"I think so."

"Maybe we should make a donation or do something in Isaac's name."

His suggestion makes me smile, and I look up at him, saying, "I would love that. We could put in a see-saw or something like that."

He laughs. "A see-saw?"

"You don't remember?"

Spencer grins. "I guess I don't."

"When I was, like, six, you guys would take me to the park and would launch me! I would hold on for dear life and my ass would slam on the ground every time one of you jumped off your side and sent me plummeting."

"Plummeting?"

"At six, it sure as hell felt that way."

"I'm not at all surprised we did that. Emmett's brother would do awful shit to us as kids, and we were all too happy to pay that forward to you."

I shake my head before resting it on his shoulder. "Lucky me."

"I think you are."

I sigh heavily, enjoying the warmth and the sun. "Spencer?"

"Yes, love?"

"Can we go to the grave?" I ask. "I would like to tell Isaac about us."

Spencer stops, pulling me into his arms. "Of course."

The mound still looks fresh, and the headstone isn't in yet, but none of that matters. There is a plaque with a flag, and on the ground around his marker are various things that people have left.

There's a letter from the high school football team, a pacifier, which is probably Elodie's, and a lot of flowers and photos. I lean down, lifting the one that had to have been left by Spencer, Emmett, or Holden.

"I brought it here," Spencer says. "I came home after spending the day with you, and I missed him. I wanted to tell him everything, and yet as I stood here, the words wouldn't come."

The guilt I've struggled with regarding my brother's death seems to be never-ending. I didn't come visit his grave. I didn't do enough to keep my sister-in-law here. All these things that Isaac would have done if it had been me who died that day.

"I don't know that I have them either," I tell Spencer.

"Do you think he needs them?"

I shrug, placing down the photo of them and picking up an origami swan. There's something about this swan that draws me to it.

"Did you make that?" Spencer asks.

I look over at him. "Me?"

"Yeah, you love doing all this stuff. I still have the star you folded out of my last report card."

"I forgot . . . I mean, I know I loved origami, even as a kid, but that I still did it." I turn the paper over. "It's not mine, I haven't been here since he was buried."

"Do you know who else would've made that?"

A memory of the kids and I at the youth center when the power went out comes to mind. I wrote a note inside and then folded them. The kids had a lot of fun trying to unfold and then refold them so the word was on the outside. Then we would send notes that way when we wanted to mess with Jax.

I tell Spencer the story and he laughs. "It's your own code."

"It could've been."

"I wish we would've done that with Isaac. Tell him we were together in code so he would have known all along," Spencer notes.

I place it back down and reach for his hand. "I keep thinking he had to know. Isaac was too smart."

"If he did, he never let on."

"I remember being so worried about him right before I was hit on the head."

"Do you want to talk about what happened?"

Sinking onto the cool grass, I touch the dirt and relay my memory. It's harder this time than when I did this with Emmett. To tell Spencer the things that were said and see Isaac's face so clearly again, while knowing he's right here with me, is almost impossible. Tears flow down my cheeks as I express the fear that I had for not only myself but also for Isaac.

"I knew he'd protect me. Even then, as I was begging him not to."

"Of course, he would. Isaac didn't know how to run from anything, and he wouldn't have started by running from the guy threatening his sister."

I meet Spencer's eyes. "And look what that cost him. Was it worth having Elodie grow up without the love of the most amazing father she could've had? What about Addison who lost her husband?"

"And you don't think you were worth it?" Spencer asks. "What would I have done, Brie? Living in a world where I could never touch you again?" His fingers wipe away a tear. "What would any of us have done? Neither of you deserved what the guy did, but your brother could never have lived with himself if he hadn't done something."

Maybe that's the truth, but I don't have a child who will suffer. Elodie is what my heart aches for more than anything.

"I just wish it all went differently," I say, making a pattern in the dirt as I stare at his name. "I would've told you, Isaac. We should never have kept this from you. I am so deeply sorry that I didn't trust you, and that we didn't trust us." Spencer's hand squeezes my shoulder. "I'm going to have this one-sided conversation and hope that, at the end, there's some kind of sign you can send me. Spencer and I are together. We have been for a while—almost a year. We kept it from you and know that you probably feel betrayed by this, and I am so sorry for that. It wasn't our intention to hurt you by keeping this a secret. Honestly, we just needed time for ourselves without being judged or having other people weigh in. Then we fell in love. Deeply in love. The way you look at Addison is how Spencer looks at me."

When I turn my face to him, he leans in, pressing his lips to my temple. My words are coming out broken as my emotions become too much.

Spencer's deep voice takes over. "I would do anything for her, and I want you to know that I will always be good to her. I will protect her. I will be there for her. I will never betray her or do anything you'd kick my ass for. You have always had more faith in me than I did in myself, and that's why I am able to promise this."

I pull myself together. "I love you, Isaac. I hope you can be happy for us and forgive us for not telling you."

"He wouldn't hold it against us"—Spencer looks down at the grave —"for that long, at least."

I smile, imagining that he would've been pissed, but then he would've come around and been okay with it. "I think he would've loved seeing us both happy."

"I agree."

We stand, his arms wrapped around me from behind, and I let a few more tears fall. I tell my brother I miss him again and ask for forgiveness.

Spencer's phone vibrates, and he releases me. "It's Quinn."

"Go ahead. I'll stay here," I inform him.

"Don't move."

"I won't."

I turn back to the makeshift memorial to Isaac, looking at a stuffed football and a copy of a letter from a college, but the swan keeps tugging at my attention. I lean down and pick it up, noting the small folds on the wings that I taught the kids to do. Carefully, I unfold it, and there, in the center of the page, is a note:

Please, help. He will kill us if you don't come alone.

Myles

At the bottom of the paper is an address. It's for a hotel in Portland.

Spencer returns, walking toward me quickly. "His lead went dead. He's heading back here and wants us to stay at your apartment."

I slip the note into my pocket and force a smile. "Sounds good."

Spencer takes my hand and leads me back to the car as I try to figure out a way to slip past my security to save that little boy.

CHAPTER
Thirty-Four
SPENCER

I pull her tighter to my chest, sighing as I feel her bare skin against mine. Last night was incredible. We made love I don't know how many times, and that fucking ring is back on her hand.

Brielle rolls over to face me. "Morning."

"It is."

"Yes, and you have to wake up because Holden and Emmett are coming over. Not to mention, we have a video call with Addison."

After I slipped her engagement ring back on, Brielle was adamant we not keep this from anyone else. Emmett and Addison are fully aware, but I'll go through the charade with her. What she doesn't know is that Addison will be coming home in three days, which is when our engagement party will take place. I sent emails out while she slept, asking everyone to make it happen. I am not kidding when I say I am not waiting.

"We should at least put pants on." Brie smiles. "I am sure Holden and Emmett will appreciate that."

I groan and flop onto my back. "If we must."

She slides out of bed and pulls her robe on. I really liked the view without it, but when I see the clock, I get my ass moving. Emmett is always respectful of time. He is never late, which means I have three minutes before he's knocking on the door.

"Did you get food delivered?" Brie asks from the bathroom.

"I didn't."

"There is probably nothing here then."

"Probably not, but do we really want to feed them? They may never leave."

Brie pops her head out. "Yes, we are going to be nice to them and allow them whatever interrogation is required. Then you need to take me into Portland so I can do some shopping."

That is news to me. "When did I agree to that?"

She grins. "You didn't, but it's necessary."

There is something I selfishly want to do while we're there, so I am not going to buck against this request. "Where do you want to shop?"

"I'm not sure yet, so maybe we can spend the night," she suggests.

"You want to spend the night in Portland?" She fucking hates that city. It's not at all Brielle's style.

"We'll see how late we are. Can you turn the coffee pot on? *Someone* kept me up most of the night."

I throw on my hoodie and head out to the kitchen with a smug smile. Damn right someone did. After hitting the button, I grab my phone and scan my emails. I have one from my editor, asking if I am ever planning to work again, one from Jackson, letting me know they found nothing on Bill's whereabouts, and one from Addison, letting me know her flight details.

I don't know how long she's going to stay, but I know it's not permanent. This is a visit so she's here for the party, and she was pretty clear that she wasn't ready to fully return.

Even though we're all pretty sure Addison and Elodie aren't in any danger since Brielle is who he was after, she was informed of Bill being a suspect. Since we still have no idea where he is, her security team in Sugarloaf was given his photo so they could keep an eye out for him.

Brie exits the bedroom just as someone knocks on the door, and I sigh. "Well, here we go."

I open the door and in walk my two best friends. We do the customary hugs, and they both kiss Brie on the cheek.

"You look much better," Holden notes.

"I feel better," Brie explains.

I walk over, wrap my arm around her waist, and look at them. "We asked you both here to tell you that we're engaged. We were engaged before, in fact. I am the mystery ring giver, and Brielle is my fiancée."

She slaps my chest. "Seriously?"

"I told you, no more waiting. We're not going to shoot the shit when we have stuff to do. So, here it is."

Brie lets out a long sigh and walks to them. "Isaac didn't know, and . . . it's one of many regrets I have about that day, so we want you guys to know."

Emmett looks to Spencer. "I already knew."

"Yes, but now you know in the way we wanted you to." I look at Holden, who hasn't really moved. "Sorry, bro, I forgot you didn't know any of this."

"You guys were together before?" he asks.

"Yes."

"And you didn't tell me?"

"We didn't tell anyone, and I wasn't going to tell you before she remembered. I just . . . I couldn't."

Holden turns his attention to Brie. "And you're sure you like this idiot?"

She smiles. "I love him. I always have."

"Yeah, I guess that's true. I'm happy for you both. Engaged . . . wow."

Emmett snorts. "Seriously, you guys could've clued everyone in a little sooner than before you walk down the aisle."

She moves back to me, wrapping her arms around my middle. "We kept it a secret for all the right reasons, I hope you know that."

Emmett shrugs. "Far be it from me to understand the workings of his mind. He's a mess, and I won't pretend otherwise. I am happy that the mystery ring person isn't a loser—well, not a total one."

I flip him off.

Holden clears his throat. "Why did you put the ring in her kitchen and not take it? I'm assuming you did it when you and Em came here to clean up before she got discharged?"

"I knew where she kept it when she wasn't wearing it, so I moved it."

"But why not take it?" Holden asks.

"I couldn't. I just couldn't fucking take it back. It was like I was giving up and losing her again. So, I put it where I thought she'd never go."

Brie tightens her arms. "You never lost me, Spencer. Not even when I was lost."

I look down at the gorgeous woman I love. "Maybe not, but you were gone in a way. That ring was all the proof I had that you were mine. We didn't tell anyone, and I . . . just hoped that, if you saw it, the ring would trigger something."

She lifts up on her toes. "I always wanted it to be you."

Holden makes a gagging noise. "Seriously. You could ease us all in a little."

Emmett sighs. "As much as I'd absolutely love to sit around and watch you two be disgustingly in love, I have to get to the station."

"Have you found anything?" I ask.

"No, and I wouldn't be able to disclose anything anyway. I'm going to assume you have Cole looking into it and they haven't found anything either."

"I do and they haven't." There's no point in denying it. If they find this guy, and I don't kill him myself, it'll be a miracle. He should pray for Emmett to find him first.

He moves toward us. "Be careful. Please. I know you were trained, but you aren't a police officer, so don't screw up the prosecution's case by bulldozing over evidence, okay? We not only want Brielle safe, but also we want justice for Isaac."

"I'm not going rogue, Maxwell. Just do your job, and I'll let you know if we uncover anything."

He shakes his head. "Right. I'm going to work. Spencer, congratulations on somehow convincing one of the most wonderful women we know that you're worth a damn. Brielle, I wish you so much luck because you're with one stubborn ass."

Brie attempts to smile, but there's a hesitation there. "You okay?" I ask.

"I am." She turns to Emmett, the smile growing and becoming more authentic. "He may be an ass, but I love him regardless."

He shakes Holden's hand, but when he reaches for the doorknob, I stop him. "Hey, Emmett."

"Yeah?"

"You remember the agreement?" I ask.

"No . . ."

Holden chuckles. "Best man . . ."

When we were eighteen, we joked about Isaac getting married. He was already talking about it with Addison. It was crazy, but we made a pact about who would be the best man at each wedding. I was Isaac's best man. Isaac was Holden's. Holden will be Emmett's, and Emmett is mine. The reason Emmett chose me was because he never wanted the honor and figured I'd never get married.

"Fuck!" Emmett says as he turns. "Come on . . ."

"You agreed."

"Have Holden do it! He'll be better."

"Nah, you're it, and I want one hell of a bachelor party."

He groans and then opens the door. "You get that after I make this right."

Our call with Addison was great. She already knew since I had to tell her, but she was beyond happy as she and Brielle cried through it.

Women.

Now we're shopping in Portland, and I'm getting updates from Quinn. It seems he's in the area as well and wants us to be on alert. He said he followed a trail that puts Bill possibly in Portland.

Little to no surprise, I am ready to get the fuck out of here.

I want her safe in her apartment, not walking around the streets where anything can happen.

"I like this store," she says, pointing to a boutique on the corner.

I also don't like that we are about a block away from—

"Brielle?"

Henry.

"Hey, Henry. I . . . how are you?" she asks, moving toward him.

"I'm great. I just came over to get some coffee, and I thought it was you." He turns to me. "Spencer, it's great seeing you."

The feeling is not mutual. "Hi, Henry."

"What are you doing in Portland?" he asks.

"Shopping. Brielle needs a dress for a party we're going to. It's sort of going to be a big announcement for us."

Her eyes widen, but I don't care. I had to watch this prick kiss her.

"Announcement?"

She smiles. "I got my memory back."

"I'm so glad. Truly."

I'm so sure he's not. He hoped she would go back to him, which I can't really blame him for. She's fucking perfect, and I would want the same.

"Thank you. Spencer and I were together before and . . ."

He looks down at her hand. "He's the fiancé?"

She smiles softly. "He is."

"I am."

He looks back and forth between us. "Damn. I am so sorry about all that. I can't imagine it was easy for you when she woke up."

"No, it wasn't."

"Yeah, I . . . I'm really happy for you," Henry says again. "I really do want you to have everything you want."

Her hand rests on his arm. "Thank you. We both appreciate it."

"We do," I say since it seems I am to agree on this point.

"I have to go. I have a meeting in twenty and I need coffee. It was great bumping into you."

"Bye," I say, done with this conversation.

The hairs on the back of my neck keep rising. I want us out of here and out of Portland.

As soon as he's gone, the blue eyes of the woman I love, which are typically soft and sweet, turn hard with anger. "You were an asshole."

"Let's go to the car and you can berate me the entire way back to Rose Canyon."

"Spencer, I'm serious. Henry did nothing wrong, and you were being such a jerk."

I could give two shits about how I treated her piece-of-shit ex, but it seems that this upsets her more than I understand. "What does it matter?"

She shakes her head quickly and grumbles. "He was being perfectly nice."

"He also lied, kissed you, failed to show up at Isaac's funeral, and is a fucking asshole. So, I'm sorry I wasn't nice to him. Next time, when we're not out in the middle of the city, I'll be nicer."

"What does us being in Portland have anything to do with you being nice?" Brielle asks, looking around.

"I just would like us to go."

"And I would like to know what you're keeping from me."

This woman is going to be the death of me. "Quinn is in Portland as well. Okay? He's here, and I think we should go home."

Brielle purses her lips with her arms over her chest. "No."

"No?"

"No," she repeats. "I will not live my life like this. I spent how many weeks feeling unsafe? I do not have a dress for our party, and I am going into that store."

Seriously. I count to five, which does very little for my exasperation, and then start again.

In that time, Brielle decides that she's not going to wait and marches off. I follow like the lovesick puppy I am, and spend the next three minutes trying to figure out what to say to mend this. I am glad she's not scared, but I also hate this entire thing.

"I'm going to try these on," she informs me. Then she kisses my cheek. "I love you."

And there goes all my anger. Just like that. "I love you too."

"Good. Now, wait here, and I'll come out once I'm ready."

I take a seat on a pink tufted couch and wait.

And wait.

And wait.

She didn't look like she had that much—

I'm on my feet and striding toward the fitting rooms, ignoring the woman behind the counter who is yelling at me. I throw open the door of the changing room, fully expecting Brielle to chide me for being ridiculous.

Only she's not inside.

Nothing is here.

The clothes she was going to try on are on the hanger, but there's no girl to try them on.

"Brielle!" I yell, moving toward the back entrance. It's open, and I don't stop until I'm standing in the middle of the alley, searching for any trace of her.

She's fucking gone.

CHAPTER *Thirty-Five*

BRIELLE

My heart is pounding so hard I feel like it'll burst through my chest, but I had no choice. He left me a note, and I needed to come here.

Myles is an innocent child, and I am a grown adult. I just have to hope that Spencer found the clues I left.

I know there wasn't a chance in hell he'd ever allow me to go through with this on my own. He would never put me in harm's way. I love him for that, but I also know that this little boy is afraid, and I promised I would protect him months ago.

I failed him once, and I won't do that again.

I have no idea what name they could be under, so I go to the front desk and ask if there's a Bill or Sonya Waugh staying.

"No, I'm sorry, we don't have anyone here under that last name."

I think hard, trying to remember, and then it hits me. She and Bill weren't married when they had Myles and his last name is Eastwood. If law enforcement is looking for him, it would make sense to use her maiden name.

"What about the last name Eastwood?"

The hotel—or really motel—is the exact place to hide. It's old, the carpets are the 90s style with red and gold that is worn. There is a vending machine over in the corner and I am pretty sure they rent rooms by the hour.

It's the perfect place to go if you don't want to be found. The girl looks in her computer. "No, ma'am, I'm sorry, I don't have anyone by that name here."

"I'm her sister, and . . . she said she was here. She has a little boy named Myles. The man she's with, he has dark brown hair, and he's a —" I pause as urgency claws at my stomach. "He's horrible. I just need to find her and get her away from him."

The girl looks back to the monitor, going through the bookings again. "I don't . . . I'm really not."

I lean in. "I know you're not allowed and that it's probably against policy, but I'm terrified for her. She isn't here willingly, and I got a message from Myles. I just . . . I need to help. Please."

I may not be her sister, but I'm still terrified for Sonya and Myles. I'm hoping that Sonya has been able to keep them both relatively safe, but I already know there is only so much she can do. When he told me what his father was doing to them, I cried. No child should endure the pain that he has, and Sonya is one of the nicest people. Neither of them deserves what Bill has put them through.

I should've filed that paperwork without giving her a warning. I should've never let him leave the center that day at all.

The front desk clerk sighs. "I can help you, but . . . I can't tell you anything. If you happened upon that information . . ."

"Whatever you can do, I appreciate."

She jerks her head to the right, and I follow her into an area marked for employees only. "If you're willing to become staff, there are lists of the names on some of the housekeeping carts."

I reach for her, pulling her in for a hug. "You're an angel."

"I'll lose my job if—"

"No one will ever know what you've done, but I will never forget."

All too often people sit on the sidelines, waiting for someone else to step in and help. I won't do that, and it appears that neither will she. I came here of my own volition to do what was right. To help someone who needs me. I just have to hope Spencer and Quinn are right behind me.

I change into the uniform and grab the cart before searching over the list of names and room numbers. None of them stand out, and I have to assume Bill booked the room under an alias.

One of the housekeepers gives me a look. "You're new."

"Yes, actually, maybe you can help. I was cleaning a room the other day, and there was a little boy and his parents. I think the man's name was Bill, but I promised him I would come back and bring some extra towels, and now I can't remember the room number."

She rolls her eyes. "You write it down next time. Do you know the complaints I get because we can't keep help?" The woman grabs her clipboard off the side of the cart. "They're in 208. Bring them towels, and then you can clean that floor. There was a bachelor party in 222, so you can handle that."

I inwardly cringe, imagining that parties thrown in this establishment probably don't leave the room very tidy.

"Thank you. I'll handle what I can."

I push the cart ahead of me, feeling more nervous than before. This motel is not a nice place. It's clear it is somewhere people go when they don't want to be seen. The drapes on the windows are a yellow color, and the cart is filled with things that probably fell off the back of a truck.

As I get to the second floor, the resolve I had starts to diminish slightly because it isn't until I step out into the hallway that I remember he has a gun. I have no idea what I'm going to encounter, and I really thought Spencer would be here by now.

He had to have found Myles's note that I left in the dressing room. Maybe he's waiting for Quinn or the police.

I pull out my phone, finding ten missed calls and eight text messages.

Oh, I am in so much fucking trouble.

Nine of the missed calls are from Spencer and one is from Quinn.

Then the texts.

Spencer: Where are you?

Spencer: Seriously, Brielle, where the fuck are you?

Spencer: Baby, please don't do this. Please, just call me. Wait for me. I'm coming for you, and I will do this.

Spencer: Brie, I can't . . . I can't do this!

Quinn: I am on my way to you. Do not go to that room alone.

Spencer: I swear to God, if you get yourself killed, I am coming to hell and you will never hear the end of this!

Quinn: Brielle, answer one of us.

Spencer: I am begging you, wait for us. We are on our way, but Jesus Christ, Brielle, just wait. Please.

He's right. I should wait. God, what am I doing? I am risking destroying that man's world when he and Quinn are trained to do this. They can help me.

I tuck back behind the wall, my chest heaving, and I swipe his number.

"Brielle?" His voice is full of panic.

"It's me."

"Are you safe?"

My hand is on my pounding heart, and guilt and regret are souring my stomach. "Yes. I'm so sorry. I thought there was no other way. I had to help him."

"You—I am not going to lecture you right now. I just need to know where you are."

"I'm at the Superior Eights motel. I am on the second floor."

"Stay. Hidden." Spencer sounds as if he's on the fringe of losing his mind. "Please. I am on my way, but—move!" he yells, and I hear a slamming noise. "Quinn is close, and I will be there in five minutes. Just stay there and wait for us."

"Okay," I promise. "I'm sorry." And I am because I know I screwed up and he's worried and I should've trusted him. "I never should've come here alone."

Then I hear a voice, chilling and familiar. "No, you shouldn't have."

I look up and see Bill standing there, holding a bag of food and pointing a gun at me.

CHAPTER *Thirty-Six*

SPENCER

I get to the motel exactly seven minutes after the phone goes dead. I am running on pure adrenaline. Quinn is already situated in the parking lot, keeping an eye on Bill, who keeps peeking out the window every few minutes.

When I meet up with him, my hands are shaking uncontrollably.

Quinn looks at me. "Get a grip right now or I'm doing this alone."

The hell he is. "She's my world."

"And she's my responsibility. So, get yourself under control. This is a mission, and you need to treat it as such."

He's right, but how do I tell my heart that? I close my eyes for a few seconds and calm my heart rate. I use every ounce of training I have to separate myself from Brielle. She is a hostage, and we need to handle it as such.

I force my voice to remain steady. "Did we get the police involved?"

"I informed them of what was going on. Jackson called a few friends on the force, and we will have backup soon."

"And your plan?"

He nods once. "We get her before that."

"Good."

Quinn explains the layout and what his plan is. "The manager says he's been here about a month, he's paranoid, and they are on their last week that they paid in full. The guy knows he's about to go up on first-degree murder charges, which means he's desperate, and desperate people do stupid shit."

"And Brielle just gave him another hostage."

"She did, but we are trained to handle this. There's a small bathroom window. I want to smash it, create the illusion that we're coming in that way, and then we'll blow the door off the hinges. Straightforward and single-minded. We get Brielle, the kid, and the mother."

"And if he hurts them?"

"Don't go there. Let's handle the situation we're dealt," Quinn says and then stands. "The manager is willing to break the glass for us. That will give us the opportunity to go in at the same time." Quinn hands me one of the guns he had stashed. "Try not to shoot him. Remember we also need to preserve the case. No matter your personal feelings, you are no good to Brielle behind bars."

As much as I want to punch him in the face for his reminder, I probably needed it. This man, if I can call him that, has taken more from me than he ever should've been allowed to. Now he has Brielle, and I am beyond angry.

Quinn makes a whistle noise. "That was the signal. She's going to wait two minutes and break the glass. Let's go."

We creep along the exterior of the motel on the first floor. I take the right side and he takes the left. We move like we were trained to do, quietly and quickly. I duck under the first room's windows, and when I pop up, he motions for me to go to the next. We continue that way until we are both in the position to breach the door.

I signal to Quinn that we should move, but he shakes his head.

I can't wait. She's in there with a man who has already tried to kill her once. Sitting here is killing me.

My body is ready to strike, but just as I am about to make the signal to go again, we hear the commotion.

Someone is yelling inside the room, and Quinn is moving to kick the door in.

Before he can, it flies open and Brielle is rushing out with a little boy in her arms.

She sees me. Her eyes widen. "Go to the car! Now!" I order, and then Quinn and I enter the room.

He grabs Sonya, pushing her out and instructing her to follow Brielle.

"Keep a cool head," he warns as we move deeper in the room. The closet is to the right, and I pull the door open and Quinn does a visual check. It's empty, which leaves one other place for him to hole up. The bathroom.

The door is closed, but I can hear movement. "You have nowhere to go," I tell him. "Come out now with your hands up."

Quinn moves to my left. "Don't be stupid, just exit nice and slowly."

"Fuck you! Fuck you all! That's my wife and kid. You think I don't know how this ends?"

"You should've thought of that earlier," I say through gritted teeth. "There's only one way this goes now."

Quinn taps my shoulder and points for me to move to the side. "Listen, Bill, I'm a dad, and if it were my kid, I'd be like you if someone wanted to take my son away. But you killed a man, and . . . well, you held your wife and son here against their will." Quinn turns to me. "Keep him talking, the police are almost here."

The sounds of the sirens are echoing in the distance. "Why did you do it, Bill?" I ask.

"I-I just wanted my boy." His voice cracks over the admission. "I didn't mean to hurt him—any of them. I had no choice. If the cops came around my house, we'd all be dead."

"You love him."

"I do. I just . . . I had to make sure no one came around. I was going to get help."

"It's good that you tried to get help, Bill. But the police are here, so you have to make a choice. Are you going to show Myles the right way to handle things or not?" I ask, knowing my time in this room will end very soon. We won't be a part of this once the police take the scene.

"They'll come for you next. Tell them . . . that I'm sorry."

Quinn moves back, tapping me as he goes, and then I retreat as well. The door to the bathroom flies open and then the shot rings out.

CHAPTER
Thirty-Seven

BRIELLE

That sound. The sound of a gunshot is something that I feel in my bones.

I move away from Myles, who is shaking.

Oh God.

Spencer.

I start to walk, but Sonya grabs my arm. "No, you can't."

I shake her off, running now.

The only thing going through my head is that I need to get to him.

Spencer.

I take the stairs two at a time. My hands are shaking, and I can feel my heart against my ribs.

Please, God, don't take him.

The sirens blare outside, and people are shouting, but I block it all out. Then I get to the top of the steps, and my entire world stops.

"Spencer." I nearly choke on his name as he grabs me to his chest.

"It's over. It's over."

"We need to move," Quinn says from behind him.

Spencer lifts me into his arms, carrying me back down the staircase as I sob. My tears stain his shirt, and he only holds me tighter, as if he needs the contact as much as I do.

"Is she okay?" Quinn asks.

I don't hear what he says, but I'm not okay. I'm insane and upset and angry. I have no idea what happened, but the police are around us, talking to Spencer and Quinn.

I know I'm weak and ridiculous, but this is all too much. Facing the man who killed my brother and tried to kill me, seeing Myles that terrified and Sonya frozen in fear . . . it was all just too much.

He was terrifying, and all the bravery I had before I got here evaporated the second I set eyes on him.

"Brie, you need to answer some questions," Spencer says while rubbing my back.

I slowly release the death grip I have on him as he lowers my feet to the ground, and I wipe my face. For the next hour, I answer every question I can, and then I watch as Quinn, Spencer, Sonya, and Myles go through the same thing. By the time the police tell us we're free to go, the sky is dark and we're all exhausted.

In the end, it worked out, I guess. No charges will be filed against any of us, and my brother's killer no longer walks this earth.

Still, it isn't as satisfying as it should be.

I wanted him to be put away, but I should be content that, at least, there is no chance of him ever hurting anyone ever again.

My emotions level off as the adrenaline subsides, and Myles walks over.

"Hey, bud."

He smiles. "Thank you for saving us."

Spencer crouches in front of him. "You were very brave to leave that note."

"Brielle always told us that if we need help, we should ask. I sent the note to a friend who delivered it."

"That was smart," I tell him.

"Very," Spencer follows up.

Sonya comes over, wrapping her arms around her son. "We are going to head home. I am so sorry, Brielle. I am sorry for what he did to you and your family. I am sorry that I was not strong enough to leave him years ago."

I grip her hand. "It's over, and it's not your fault."

She nods once and then walks off, and it's the first moment Spencer and I have had alone.

"You scared the fucking hell out of me," Spencer says, taking my face in his hands.

"I . . . I have no excuse."

"No, you don't."

I hold on to his wrists as he leans his head against mine. "I was so afraid that he hurt you."

"Whatever fear you had, sweetheart, amplify it by one thousand. That's what I felt when you were gone."

I lean back, staring into his deep green eyes. "I knew you'd come for me."

"After I went crazy running through the alleyway."

"I knew you wouldn't let me be here alone."

He drops his hands. "Damn right I wouldn't have. I would've called the cops and had them do their job. Then Quinn and I wouldn't have had to hope the receptionist could throw a brick through the back window. We went through all that, and you didn't even let me rescue you."

I force myself not to smile. "When he went into the bathroom, I wasn't going to wait around."

"But you knew we were coming."

"I did, but I also thought—"

"Stop doing that," Spencer says, not looking amused.

"Doing what?"

"Thinking. Next time you think yourself into a great idea, run it by a rational person. Blindly running to save a boy from a madman who has a gun is not a good plan."

"No more thinking," I promise.

He sighs deeply and pulls me to his chest. His lips press to my forehead and stay there. "No more thinking."

"We're safe now," I muse.

"We are. There's no more threat to you or anyone else."

"For now," I say, leaning against his strong body.

"Yeah, until you find the next stupid thing to get caught up in."

I laugh at that and melt into him. "I love you, you know?"

"I do."

"I like those words," I tell him.

"Your turn to say them," Spencer demands.

"I do."

"I like them on your lips." He stares down at me, something glimmering in his eyes. "Run away with me."

"What?"

"Let's leave. Now. We don't go back to Rose Canyon, not as just Spencer and Brielle anyway."

My brows scrunch together. "What would we go back as?"

"Mr. and Mrs. Cross."

My lips part and turn up at that idea. "You want to marry me?"

"Yes. Right now."

"We can't . . ."

He takes both my hands in his. "I want to marry you, Brielle. I want to spend every day of whatever life we have left with you as my wife. I want you to know I am always here and that I will love you until the day I die. Let's go."

He's crazy. I shake my head, trying to slow him down. "We can't."

"We can. Let's get in the car right now and drive to Reno."

"Reno? You want to get married in *Reno*?"

"I want to marry you in the next twenty-four hours. So yes, I want to go to Reno. Will you marry me? In Reno . . . today?"

As crazy as it is, there's nothing in this world that would stop me. "I would marry you any day or anywhere, you crazy insane man."

Spencer kisses me as we both grin. "I'm going to make you happy."

"You already do."

And with that, we rush to his car and head to Reno.

Epilogue

BRIELLE

"I swear it's like I don't even know you," Addison says with a laugh.

I move Elodie to my other hip and smile. "I don't know that I knew myself either. Or maybe I'm only myself when I am with him."

She looks over at Spencer, my husband, and shrugs. "He would've liked this."

"You think?" I ask, knowing she's talking about Isaac.

"I do. He loved him like a brother, and he trusted him. Isaac only ever wanted the people he loved to have someone special to love them back."

Elodie grabs my necklace in her tiny fist and proceeds to try to fit them both in her mouth. "And what about you?"

"What about me?"

"Do you think he would want you to be happy?"

She laughs. "I am years away from happiness, but I'm at least starting to come out of the rain."

"That's a start," I say, hopeful that she'll find the sun. "And coming back home?"

Addy looks around. "Soon, I think. Being here this week has been really good. It's not as hard as I thought."

"I miss you, Addison. I really do."

"You have a family now. You are a married woman and will probably have your own kids soon . . ."

Spencer's hand lands on the small of my back just as her words drop off and he makes a choking noise. "Did I miss something?"

I laugh. "I'm not pregnant—at least, not that I know of."

"Okay then. Listen, your mother is giving me a load of shit because I took her only daughter off to Reno. She's mad that she missed it and demands 'her' wedding."

I groan. "I thought we could avoid this."

When everyone came into town yesterday, I was stunned and elated. Spencer went to so much trouble to give me a perfect engagement party, which sort of turned into a wedding reception.

Only, no one thinks our wedding counts.

They all demand a redo so family and friends can be in attendance.

I have spent most of today trying to explain how unnecessary that would be.

"She has a point," Addison says.

"Addy!"

"What? I'm just saying that, if Elodie did that, I would be broken. A mother only gets this once."

"It's a wedding. Why does she need that?"

"Because she needs something happy. We all do."

Spencer and I glance at each other. "I already got the marriage part. The wedding is all you."

I let out a breath through my nose. "Fine"—I turn to Addison—"you're my maid of honor though."

"Me?"

"Yes. You're my best friend and sister, which means you're going to have to come back here to help me plan."

At least I will be able to have that much.

Addison's eyes widen. "I can't do that."

"Then I can't have a wedding."

"You can't do that!" She scoffs. "It's totally unfair of you to blackmail me."

"Maybe so, but I want this little peanut to have Auntie Brie around to corrupt her little mind, and I want you back home. So, if the wedding accomplishes that, then you can call it whatever you want."

Spencer grins. "Savage, love."

"You're nuts."

"You haven't given me an answer. Am I getting a wedding or are you going to break Mom's heart?"

Addison rolls her eyes. "Fine, but it doesn't mean I'm staying."

I kiss Elodie's cheek. "You don't have to stay forever, just for a bit."

She takes Elodie back into her arms. "I'm going to get some food. It looks like Emmett has the mic anyway, and I don't want the fallout in my vicinity."

Oh no. I look over, and sure enough, he does. "Shit," Spencer mutters.

Emmett makes a tapping noise, quieting everyone down. "All right, everyone of Rose Canyon. Welcome. I'm Emmett, Man of the Year, in case you didn't know."

Holden yells. "No one cares about you!"

He flips him off. "You weren't nominated, sit down."

Spencer chuckles. "This is going to be a mess."

No shit.

Emmett turns back to us. "You two, come here."

Spencer and I reluctantly make our way to the front of the room. "We are all here to celebrate the joining of these two people. Spencer has been my best friend since I was twelve. As you all know, he's a complete and total waste of space. I mean, who needs a Pulitzer Prize winner in their town anyway? Not to mention, he's a total stud. Sorry, man, you're hot," he says, and Spencer just shrugs as Emmett turns to me. "And, Brielle, well, I don't know what to say about this headcase. She is the bravest, smartest, and stupidest woman I know. Yeah, I hear the contradiction there, people. I know it. However, that's our Brie. She'll do anything for someone she cares about, even marry them. I wish I knew that before this guy scooped her up," he says.

The entire crowd is putty in his hands. They laugh, shake their heads, and clap for each outrageous comment he makes.

"However," Emmett continues, "there is something I couldn't stop thinking about the other day. We were twenty and Brielle was still in diapers."

I roll my eyes. "I am not that much younger! It's only ten years!"

"He's nearing AARP, darling, trust me, you are."

I rest my head on Spencer's chest, hiding my laughter.

"See how cute she is?" Emmett asks, eliciting more clapping. "I digress. There was this one day when we all went out to the cliffs—not the make out ones, easy, Mama Davis—and were watching the sunset. A lot of times, Isaac, Holden, Spencer, and I would hang out there and talk about life. It was easy where no one could hear you talk about things that scared you. Anyway, on that day, we brought Brielle, and like she always did, she sat next to Spencer. She told us that she was worried her heart would never find the person it was meant to be with. I remember thinking, 'What a weird thing for an infant to worry about.'" More laughter from the crowd. "But Isaac leaned over, looked at his sister, and said, 'Your heart is meant to be with the person next to you.'"

Tears fill my vision as I look up at Spencer. "I remember that day."

He smiles. "Me too."

"Of course, we all laughed, thinking how funny it would be that Brielle and Spencer would ever be together. But it's not that funny. In fact, I think it's incredibly perfect. So, my dear friends," Emmett says, as though Spencer and I aren't having a serious moment, "while Isaac may not be here in body, his heart is here with us. He is watching, knowing his little sister and the man beside her on that rock is who will walk next to her for the rest of her life." He raises his glass and everyone does as well. "To Brielle and Spencer."

"To Brielle and Spencer."

The clinking of the glasses tells us to kiss, and we do, both a little teary-eyed.

I hug Emmett after. "I can't believe you remembered that day."

He smiles. "I remember because we thought it was nuts, but I'm not the only one. About two years after it happened, I asked Isaac if he remembered saying it."

"And?"

"He said he always thought you two would end up together someday. And he thought it would be funny to freak Spencer out."

I laugh because that's such an Isaac comment.

"He said a lot of things to me over the years, especially over the last few months."

"Oh?"

He looks over at Addy. "He asked me to take care of her if anything ever happened to him. To make sure that she was always safe. He loved her more than anything, and I've let him down."

I rest my hand on his arm. "You have never done that."

"No? I didn't catch his killer."

Spencer shakes his head. "Let's not go there. You did everything right and had our psycho GI Barbie over here not tried to test her luck, you would've."

He leans in and kisses my cheek. "Yeah, don't ever do that again."

"I promise I won't." I have zero intentions of ever being that dumb again.

"Good. I'm happy for you both."

Spencer and Emmett clasp hands. "Just think, you'll get to do this again in a few months."

"Do what?"

My husband grins with mischief in his eyes. "The speech. We're having a big wedding."

"Great." He grumbles. Then Emmett goes stiff, staring at a beautiful woman with long brown hair.

"Who is that?" I ask.

Emmett doesn't respond, he just stares at her. "Fuck," he says quietly.

"Umm, Emmett?" Spencer grips his shoulder. "Is that—"

"Yup."

Well, I'm so glad they know who it is. I gently slap Spencer's chest. "Can you clue me in?"

"That's Blakely Bennett. She was in the military with Emmett."

My brows rise. "Oh? Are they friends?" Because it doesn't really seem like it with the way Emmett still isn't moving or responding.

"I guess, she was his captain."

That snaps him out of his daze. "No, we were equal."

"She totally was his boss," Spencer says softly to me.

She makes her way toward us, and I'm struck by her natural beauty. She's a good three inches taller than I am, slender, and has pouty lips, but if that wasn't enough, her hair moves like those hair commercials as she walks.

When she reaches us, her smile is wide as she stares at him. "Hello, Maxwell."

"Bennett," he responds clipped.

She looks to Spencer. "I thought it was you, Cross. You look happy."

He releases my hand and pulls her in for a hug. "It's because I am. It's good to see you, Blake."

"You too, and I hear this is your wedding celebration?"

Spencer nods. "This is my wife, Brielle."

Her warm gaze meets mine and she extends her hand. "It's lovely to meet you. I know your husband from one of the training exercises we did. I wish you both much happiness."

"Thank you." I like her. I don't know why, but I do.

"What are you doing here, Blakely?" Emmett asks.

"I came to see you, darling."

Darling? Spencer and I exchange a quick glance.

"I sent you paperwork months ago."

She waves her hand. "I'm not here for that. I came for something else."

"What paperwork?" Spencer asks. I'm so glad his nosiness is saving me from being rude.

Blakely shrugs. "Divorce papers."

Oh. Oh no. I'm sorry, did she say divorce papers?

Emmett groans, running a hand down his face. "Jesus Christ."

"You're married?" I ask, a little louder than I should.

"Yes, Blakely Bennett is my wife. And if you'll excuse me, I need to speak with her outside."

Before any of us can say another word, he takes her hand and practically drags her out to the deck. She turns to us, keeping pace, and waves. "I'm sure we'll see each other soon."

Both of us stand with our jaws hanging as the scene unfolds. Once the door closes, the murmurs around us begin. Not wanting our friend, who has a lot to explain, to be even more mortified, I wave to the DJ, who immediately starts playing something.

Another few seconds pass, and I look at my husband. "Did you know?"

"Nope." His eyes go back to the deck. "And that motherfucker gave me shit about keeping secrets."

I laugh. "Well, he's married it seems."

"Yeah, it seems so. Come dance with me."

Hand in hand, we walk to the dance floor.

"She's very beautiful," I tell him.

Spencer pulls me to him, and my arms go up around his neck. "You are the most beautiful woman in the world."

"I am the *luckiest* girl in the world," I correct him.

"Oh?"

I nod. "I have you. The boy I fell in love with just became the husband I'm going to grow old with."

He kisses my lips, and I melt into him. "Who knew all you needed was memory loss to see how great I am."

I laugh. "I knew long before that, Mr. Cross."

"And I'll make sure you remember it for the rest of your life, Mrs. Cross."

That's a promise I intend to make him keep because a life without Spencer is one I wouldn't want to remember anyway.

Thank you so much for reading Help Me Remember. I had an incredible time writing this book. It was so fun to get to go a little heavier on the suspense. I can assure you, we're not done yet! Next is Emmett and Blakely and ... how about that ending?

Give Me Love is next and I hope you're ready for another swoony, suspenseful, and beautiful ride that will leave you breathless!

However, I was done done with Brielle and Spencer quite yet!

There is an epic bonus scene on the next page. I hope you enjoy!

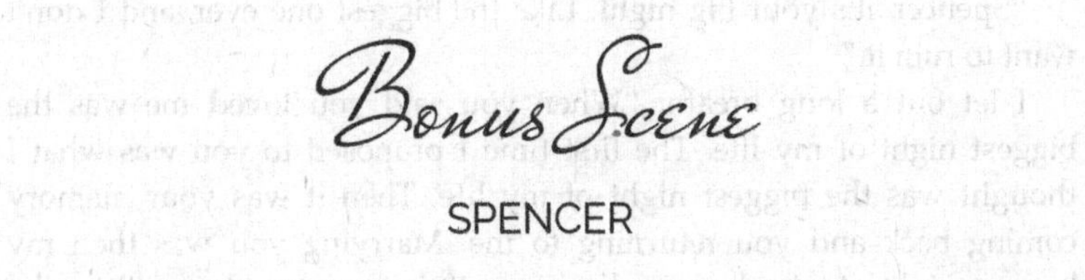

Bonus Scene

SPENCER

"Sweetheart, are you ready?" I call to Brielle, who is now thirty minutes late.

"One second!"

She said that about a million seconds ago, but I can't rush her because she's been an absolute nightmare since we found out she was pregnant.

Not that it's been easy on her. She was insanely sick the first trimester, and despite trying to convince herself that the second trimester would be better, it hasn't been.

She exits the hotel bathroom, her long blonde hair is pulled up in some knot with braids and her long black dress hugs every gorgeous inch of her.

"You look stunning." I can't stop myself from walking to her and pulling her to my chest.

"You are a blind idiot."

"Love is blind, isn't it?"

She smiles. "It is, but not this blind."

"Brie, you are gorgeous. Every man in that place is going to be insanely jealous because you're with me."

"Yes, I'm sure all the sexy movie stars are going to think, 'Hey, see that whale, I wish she washed up on my shore.'"

I lift her chin, waiting for her eyes to meet mine. "They will, and you're not a whale." I kiss her before she can give me any more crap about her size. She's barely gained anything, and if you looked at her from the back, you wouldn't even know she's pregnant.

However, last time I said that, she went off about how I thought she was fat. Therefore, I will keep my mouth shut.

Brielle sighs and then rests her hand on my chest. "Are you sure you don't want to leave me here? I don't mind. No one wants a date who may have to run out to puke."

As if I would ever leave her. "Don't be ridiculous."

"Spencer, it's your big night. Like the biggest one ever, and I don't want to ruin it."

I let out a long breath. "When you said you loved me was the biggest night of my life. The first time I proposed to you was what I thought was the biggest night of my life. Then it was your memory coming back and you returning to me. Marrying you was then my biggest night. And when we have our little monster, that will be the biggest night. This is a drop in the bucket, my love. Everything with you is what matters."

A tear trickles down her cheek, and I catch it with my thumb. "Now I'm going to be all splotchy," Brielle whines.

"You're perfect, but you are going to make us late, so we need to get a move on."

"Okay, let's go then."

We exit the hotel in Beverly Hills and find rows of limos waiting out front. I tell the valet my name, and he goes off to find our driver. The studio went all out since the film is nominated for Best Original Screenplay, which I wrote, Best Picture, plus almost all the major actors are as well.

After everything that went down in the last few years, I promised Brielle that I would put aside my investigative journalism. Not that I didn't love it, but it meant being away for long periods of time in locations that would have her worrying for my safety.

We'd been through enough trauma as it was.

Still, I didn't want to give up writing, so I started recording our story. On a whim, I sent it to a buddy for some critique, and five days later, I was meeting with a producer to make it a screenplay.

Five drafts later, the studio bought the rights to *Help Me Remember* and then it became a major motion picture.

"Are you nervous?" Brie asks as we get into the limousine.

"I'd be lying if I said I wasn't."

She smiles. "I know that you will never accept this, but it is really amazing we're here, on our way to the Academy Awards. It's like you can't do anything without being the best."

"I'm not going to win."

"You might, and no matter what, you won in my eyes."

"Promise me you will be cool when you see Noah Frazier or Jacob Arrowood," I plead.

The lead actor, Noah Frazier, who played me, is nominated for Best Actor, and Brielle is obsessed with him. I have to remind her that he is not, in fact, me. Therefore, she can't kiss or hug him just because he said all the shit I did in real life.

"I am always cool, Spencer Cross. It's you who gets all tongue-tied."

Right.

The ride over is almost nothing and before we know it, the driver is instructing us on the procedure. He will bring us to the beginning of the red carpet where we will walk, pose for photos, and speak to the press.

As if anyone gives a shit about the writer.

Once the driver pulls to a stop, the studio's publicist is there, pulling our door open for us. "Hello, Mr. and Mrs. Cross. Did everything go okay so far?"

I nod. "It's been wonderful, Catherine, thank you."

"Good. You look amazing, Brie," she says, handing her a pamphlet. "I have all the information you'll need about the event here. Where you need to go, who is looking for you, as well as the afterparty information. It's small enough to slip into your clutch. By the way, Jackson says hello. If you see him, just wink as he can't talk to anyone since he's on duty."

"He's here?" Brie asks with obvious affection. Catherine Cole is married to Jackson.

"He's with Noah and Jacob, but there are several Cole Security guys here. I always have extra security when one of my clients is attending an event like this."

"I don't know how you do it," Brie says. "I would be such a mess being around those guys."

I shoot her a look. "I thought you were cool?"

Catherine grins. "My job is to see them as normal people and fix their issues, so it takes that thrill away a bit. You should get going, stick to the schedule."

Brielle grips my arm. "Can you believe this, babe? We are walking the red carpet because you are so damn amazing and talented. I am so proud. So freaking proud."

I love her excitement, but I'm trying not to focus on all this. I never wanted a life in Hollywood. I wanted to follow stories and unearth secrets that people thought should stay buried. In a way, I'm still doing that, it just isn't journalism. Since *Help Me Remember,* I have written three more screenplays that are currently optioned. Whether they ever see the light of day is out of my control. Just like winning tonight.

"Let's follow our schedule and not think about what comes later."

She smiles up at me. "Okay. Let's enjoy all of it and pray I don't puke on your shoes."

God, I love her. I lean down and kiss the top of her head. "I love you, Brielle."

"I love you too."

We walk down the red carpet, no one really caring about us until Noah walks over. Then the entire mood shifts. Cameras click like crazy as he shakes my hand, and Kristin and Brielle introduce themselves.

"Big night," Noah says.

"It is, but . . . you're used to it."

He laughs. "Not these categories."

"Any tips on how to get through it?" I ask.

"Alcohol and pretending you aren't fazed by any of it, which is a lie."

"Thanks."

Catherine scurries toward us. "Hey, you two, off to the interviews. If you see Jacob, tell him I'm going to kill him," she says without her smile faltering.

"That's our cue. I'll see you in there."

We are definitely not seated close to each other, but I nod anyway as though it could happen. Brielle and I make it through the next hour, meeting all kinds of people in the industry and giving the same version of interviews. So many express their enjoyment of the story, which gives me a lot of joy.

Inside it's so much bigger than it appears on television. We are ushered to our seats, which are around the other no-name members of the film, not close to the stage as we aren't A-list celebrities. The lights flicker, and it begins.

Brielle grips my hand and places them on my leg. I look over with a brow raised.

"Your leg was bouncing."

I hadn't even realized, but Best Original Screenplay is next. I'm nervous and excited. I want to win. Not because I really do like trophies but because it's about us. It's the story of loving someone and having to do what's best for them, even when it hurts you. It's finding each other, even when you weren't sure it would happen.

But whether I win or lose, it doesn't matter because Brielle is the prize, and I've already won her. She's everything good in this world.

Her fingers tighten, and I smile over at her as Eli Walsh walks onto the stage. "It is my great honor to present this award tonight. The power of a good script can take a film to another level. One that captures hearts, reminds us that love is all that matters, scare the ever living—

you know—out of us, or take you to another world where you have to fight demons. Here are tonight's nominees."

The music cues up, and the clips roll. The third one that plays is *Help Me Remember* with, "Screenplay written by Spencer Cross," announced at the end.

I turn to my wife. "No matter what . . ."

"You are the most magnificent man, and this changes nothing."

I nod. "I love you."

"I love you."

The final clip ends, and Eli lifts the envelope. "And the Academy Award goes to . . ." I hold my breath, working hard to keep my face impassive so I don't look like one of those assholes on television who is upset. "Spencer Cross for *Help Me Remember*!"

Clapping erupts around me, but I swear I don't hear it. I look to Brielle, who has the brightest smile on her lips and tears in her eyes. I cup her cheeks, pulling her lips to mine. "Go!" she says with a laugh.

Right. Shit. I have to go up there.

I stand and make my way over, the director of the film shakes my hand, and one of the other nominees stands to congratulate me. When I get to the front, Noah is there and he claps me on the back. I climb the steps and meet Eli as he hands me the trophy. "Congrats, man."

"Thanks."

"Good luck on the speech."

I have to speak. Yeah, words. Okay. I let out a deep breath and look to where the cameraman is holding the green card.

"I honestly didn't think I would be standing up here right now. When I wrote *Help Me Remember*, I was coming out of a dark place. My wife, Brielle, had suffered a head injury, and I lost her for a period of time. I needed to work through it, and writing was the logical answer. I have so many people to thank for this, including the director, Thomas Wright. The producer, Michael Williams, and the amazing cast, crew, and everyone who brought the film to life. I'd like to thank my friends back home, Emmett, Holden, and, of course, Isaac, for who this is in memory of." I look to the seats and find her. Our eyes stay connected as I give her my heart. "Most of all, I need to thank my breathtakingly beautiful wife, Brielle. When I was lost, you found me and made me whole. You are the best part of me, and I never knew someone could love another the way I love you. You are my world, and this is all for you. I love you."

Tears fall down those perfect cheeks, and I don't think that any man is as lucky as I am.

Be sure to purchase Give Me Love, the next book in the Rose Canyon series. Emmett and Blakely are another swoony, suspenseful, and beautiful ride that will leave you breathless!

I wrote this before I wrote anything. In the beginning, when I plotted this series, I want to write Addison and Emmett. Then, I realized, I had the stories out of order and couldn't do what I had originally thought and needed Brielle's book first.

The sequence is different than what Brielle remembers, mostly because … well, it just is. I used this scene as a guide, but in the end, things change in edits as well as writing. I wanted to share it since it'll never see a book and Emmett is already married (another thing I never planned) to Blakely. Which is what Give Me Love is all about. One day I might write a book I plan—one day.

In the meantime, here is Isaac's POV! Please note, this is **unedited** and proofread. There will be errors, but I wanted you to read it very raw.

ISAAC

"Addy, I'm heading out!" I call up to my wife who is probably getting Elodie dressed for day care.

"I'll be down in a minute."

I check my watch and sigh. I don't have a minute. Plus, Addison's version of one minute is really ten. I definitely don't have ten. I need to pick up my sister, since her car is in the shop, get her to work and then get to school before the kids arrive. I'm pushing it now.

Instead of waiting for her, I take the stairs two at a time. Sure enough, she's in Elodie's room, trying to get her into a dress.

"Hey."

She smiles. "Hey, I said I'd be down in a minute."

"Yes, but we know time keeping isn't your strong suit."

"She's so not cooperating."

Elodie is crawling around the room in just her diaper as my wife is sitting on her knees with the dress in her hand.

"Elibear!" I squat down, opening my arms.

This is what we do each day when I get home. Maybe I can get her to do it now.

Sure enough, her big green eyes widen and she rushes towards me. Her little arms wrap around my neck and I can't resist squeezing her.

"Ahh!"

In my head, that's "Dad". I smile, not wanting this to ever end. Eight months old and she owns my soul. It seems like just yesterday Addison came out of the bathroom with a test in her hand and tears in her eyes.

We tried for years and went through three miscarriages before we were finally blessed with this angel.

Addison doesn't waste a second, she slips the dress over her head and I adjust my grip to help her get dressed.

"The fancy panties next," Addy instructs.

She grabs them, sliding them on as I hold her tight. Addison smiles and sit back, wiping her forehead.

"Done."

I rain down kisses on Elodie, causing her to giggle. I release her before tapping her nose. "Be good for your Mama," I tell her. "I have to go."

"Ma!" Elodie pouts and then plops down on the floor, pouting a little.

"That's not what Daddy meant," Addy tries to sound stern, but fails.

"Can I have another hug?" Elodie smiles and I scoop her up. After a few seconds I hand her over to Addison. "I'm seriously late."

Addy turns her head with pursed lips. I give her a kiss and then slap her ass. "I'll see *you* tonight. Hopefully naked."

"Do you have practice?"

"You know we do."

Football is my second wife, one that Addison has come to love and accept. We have our season opener on Friday and these boys need all practice they can get.

"Okay. I'll make a plate for you."

"You're the best."

She tilts her head with a smirk. "Don't you forget it."

I kiss her again and another one for Elodie too and then I'm off.

The ride to grab Brielle isn't long, but I hit the three traffic lights this town has on the way. It's like the world is having a laugh at my expense today. As I pass through Main Street, I wave at a few people, being the head coach here makes me a bit of a celebrity. Especially since taking over four years ago and turning us from a pitiful mess into division rivals. It's been hard, but these kids wanted it just as much as I did.

I get to my sister's now nine minutes behind when I needed to be here and honk. She opens the door to the condos a minute later and huffs as she slams the door.

"God, I hate mornings."

"I hate being late," I counter.

"Yes, why were you late this morning?" Brielle asks.

"Elodie."

Her lips turn up. "How is my favorite niece?"

"Good. She is a menace, getting into things. Her favorite word is 'no'."

"It's a good word."

I snort. "Not when you're trying to get her to do something."

Brielle shrugs. "I think more women need to say no to things. We're far too accommodating."

"Right, did you suddenly develop an issue with saying no suddenly?"

My sister is a pain in the ass who never agrees. She's headstrong, smart, funny, but I couldn't stand her as a kid.

"No." Brie smiles.

"She's starting to do attempt the stairs. I think Addy is going to have heart failure."

It was amazing to be a part of. When she started to crawl, Addy and I were screaming and clapping. Being a father is more than I ever imagined. Watching this tiny person grow into her own personality . . . it's miraculous. I cherish each second with her.

Brie clasps her hand in front of her. "Aww, I can't wait to see her. She's seriously the cutest kid in the world. I don't know how she came from you."

"She's all her mother."

"Which makes sense since you totally married above you."

I can't argue with that. Addison is perfect and for some reason, she fell in love with me. "And what about you?" I nudge my sister.

"What about me?"

"When are you going to finally settle down?"

Brielle gives me a look. "I have plans, you know."

"And they are?"

"Someone. I think things are going to make sense soon. I just am ... I don't know ... I have plans though. I have good ones."

I roll my eyes. "Plans?"

"Yes. Plans."

"I know losing Dad was hard and after that, you sort of decided against it. Not all of opening yourself up to someone leads to heartache."

"No, but it normally does. Look at how it went with Henry."

I hope someday, Brielle will let go of the past and embrace a future with someone. I don't think it'll ever happen, but who knows.

Brie turns in her seat. "Oh, did you ever ask Emmett about that family I mentioned?"

Emmett is the new sheriff, and one of my best friends. He returned to Rose Canyon a a few months ago after being in the military for ten years.

"Not yet, after the game we're all going out for drinks."

"You know that hanging out with those guys leads to trouble."

I shake my head. "We're not eighteen anymore. We're all grown."

"Ha!" Brie says loudly. "When you, Spencer, Emmett, and Holden are even in the same vicinity it's like you can't help yourself. You all forget that you're in your late thirties and not nearly as cool as you think you are."

"We are cool."

"For a bunch of old guys."

We make it to her office faster than I thought we would and instead of pulling into her lot, I park across the street. RosieBeans is the best coffee on the Oregon coast and since I made up a few minutes, I'm going to treat myself. Actually, Brielle is going to treat me.

"I guess we're getting coffee?"

"I thought you'd never offer."

As soon as make it to the front of the car, someone I somewhat recognize, but can't place approaches.

"You!" He yells.

"Get in the car, Isaac," Brielle says quickly and moves back that way.

"Brie?"

"Hurry!" There's panic in her voice.

I hit the unlock button, but it's too late. He has his hands wrapped around her arms.

"You bitch. You think you can take my family? You think I'd let you get away with it? You think you have the power to do that?" the man yells and I recognize him.

"Easy, man," I say, moving around the front of the car. "Just let her go so we can work this out."

Not that I have any idea what's going on.

He ignores me. "Did you file the paperwork?" Bill asks.

"Yes, this morning," Brielle replies.

Whatever she filed, sends him into a rage. He roars and I know he's going to kill her. It's seconds before I'm at her side, but it feels like a lifetime. My heart is racing as I try to tear him away from her. Brielle's eyes are wide and she's fighting, but he slams her against the car, her head slamming against the hard metal frame.

I wrap my arm around his neck, yanking him back as she falls to the ground. As we spin, he goes a few feet back, but my eyes take in the shiny object in his grasp.

He has a gun.

He points it at me. "Stay the fuck back or I'll kill you both."

I lift my hands, surrendering the fight and circle, trying to get a better angle and closer to Brielle. I think about is Addison and Elodie.

How just twenty minutes ago everything was so easy and great. Now, I have a gun at me and my sister is lying on the ground, unmoving.

She finally lifts her head, taking in the man with a gun pointed at me. She staggers as she gets to her feet. "You don't want to do this," she says, her voice shaking. "Please, you can get in the car now and drive off. Nothing will change."

His head shakes quickly as though he won't even take in her words. "Everything has changed! You're taking them from me! You're taking my family, you stupid bitch! Now, I am going to take yours."

She gets to her feet, moving toward him. "Brie!"

"I didn't file it," she stutters. "In my office."

His brown eyes are filled with rage as the gun shakes in his hand. I can grab it. If I can get him to relax a little more, I can . . .

I've always heard people say that time moves slowly in a life and death situation. That details become clearer as your senses are heightened. Living it right now, it's a lie.

Nothing about the next few seconds moves slow.

In fact, it's so fast that I don't even know I've taken a full breath before everything happens at once.

"You're a fucking liar!" Bill yells and then he bashes my sister in the head with the butt of the gun, I reach for it, and then the sound—so loud it deafens me—causes me to fall beside Brielle.

But there's so much pain, my chest is burning and I can't speak. I gasp, looking at my sister who isn't moving.

The realization hits me. I'm shot.

In the chest.

And I'm going to die.

I choke, the metallic taste of blood fills my mouth.

Addison. Elodie.

My life.

My . . . gone.

Books by Corinne Michaels

The Salvation Series

Beloved

Beholden

Consolation

Conviction

Defenseless

Evermore: A 1001 Dark Night Novella

Indefinite

Infinite

The Hennington Brothers

Say You'll Stay

Say You Want Me

Say I'm Yours

Say You Won't Let Go: A Return to Me/Masters and Mercenaries Novella

Second Time Around Series

We Own Tonight

One Last Time

Not Until You

If I Only Knew

The Arrowood Brothers

Come Back for Me

Fight for Me

The One for Me

Stay for Me

Willow Creek Valley Series

Return to Us

Could Have Been Us

A Moment for Us

A Chance for Us

Rose Canyon Series

Help Me Remember

Give Me Love (Coming 2022)

Keep This Promise (Coming 2023)

Co-Written with Melanie Harlow

Hold You Close

Imperfect Match

Standalone Novels

All I Ask

You Loved Me Once

About the Author

Corinne Michaels is a *New York Times, USA Today, and Wall Street Journal* bestselling author of romance novels. Her stories are chock full of emotion, humor, and unrelenting love, and she enjoys putting her characters through intense heartbreak before finding a way to heal them through their struggles.

Corinne is a former Navy wife and happily married to the man of her dreams. She began her writing career after spending months away from her husband while he was deployed—reading and writing were her escape from the loneliness. Corinne now lives in Virginia with her husband and is the emotional, witty, sarcastic, and fun-loving mom of two beautiful children.

CPSIA information can be obtained
at www.ICGtesting.com
Printed in the USA
LVHW090318030423
743296LV00004B/407